"THE BIG NOVEL OF THE VIETNAMESE WAR FINALLY GETS WRITTEN."

Buffalo News

"Jonathan Rubin does not try to capture the war in its dreadful magnitudes of size and duration. He ambushes a piece of it from a Montagnard village in the central Vietnamese highlands, just before the machinery of destruction began to dwarf its human masters...Rubin's vision of the Vietnam War may not satisfy rationalists who demand an accounting of the conflict's cause and effect... Successful art, however, satisfies another human need: the desire not to calculate but to know in the heart how things are."

Time

THE
BARKING DEER

JONATHAN RUBIN

AVON
PUBLISHERS OF BARD, CAMELOT, DISCUS AND FLARE BOOKS

AVON BOOKS
A division of
The Hearst Corporation
959 Eighth Avenue
New York, New York 10019

Copyright © 1974 by Jonathan Rubin
Published by arrangement with George Braziller, Inc.
Library of Congress Catalog Card Number: 73-88042
ISBN: 0-380-61135-x

First Avon Printing, November, 1982

AVON TRADEMARK REG. U. S. PAT. OFF. AND IN
OTHER COUNTRIES, MARCA REGISTRADA, HECHO EN
U. S. A.

Printed in the U. S. A.

WFH 10 9 8 7 6 5 4 3 2 1

To Grandmother Pan and Triple Threat
     and
     to Maura

☆ CONTENTS ▲

▲ ▲ ▲   It happened once, in the time of the
Hoang-Bang Dynasty, that Kra the Tiger and Bru the Eagle had
the same idea. Bru the Eagle pounced from the sky, where he had
been lazing around, and Kra pounced from the thick bushes. Bru
swooped down, he screamed like the wind devil with frosty hair
and three grinning heads, and when Bru came to snatch up the
muntjac, he found that Kra was already there, snatching hold too.
They were hungry, Kra and Bru. They both grabbed on. They
fought to carry the muntjac off.

"Why do you want to make off with the muntjac?" asked Bru
with concern, as he tore at Kra with talons and beak.

"To give it a proper home," answered Kra. "A warm snug home."

"But you're a Tiger. Why would a Tiger give a muntjac a
warm snug home? Oh no, Mister Tiger, I know your tricks. You
just want to eat the muntjac all up."

"Why do you?" asked Kra with concern, as he tore at Bru with
his claws and great teeth. "Why do you want to make off with
the muntjac?"

"To give it a proper home," said Bru. "A warm snug home."

"But you're an Eagle. Why would an Eagle give a muntjac a
warm snug home? Oh no, Mister Eagle, I know your tricks. You
just want to eat the muntjac all up."

Kra and Bru ripped at each other, all the time gripping the
muntjac tight. They slashed each other left and right and
the hapless muntjac too.

"It's mine! It's mine!" shouted Bru.

"No, it's mine!" shouted Kra. "I was first!"

"No, me! No, me!"

Kra and Bru made a terrible racket over the muntjac. They

disturbed all the animals of the forest who looked on with wonder, then consternation. Oh, that Bru! Oh, that Kra! They hooked and gnashed and slashed and clawed. They screamed and roared and the muntjac yelped to be let go. That he already had a very satisfactory home. A warm snug home. But Kra and Bru fought on and on—beak and fang, talon and claw—and all the hapless muntjac could do was to close his eyes tight and hope for the best. They argued hard and argued long, till the sky grew dim and the chill set in and the frosty-haired wind devil started to blow. They argued so hard and argued so long that, when they finished arguing, the muntjac had disappeared.

"Where is the muntjac!?" cried Kra the Tiger.

"Where has it gone!?" cried Bru.

There was just a red splotch on the ground where the muntjac had been. A wet blotch. Nothing else. Just a smear. It was all gone.

So Kra and Bru went off too, licking their wounds. Kra slunk back into the bushes. He limped back. He puffed. He dragged his long tail. Bru, he struggled back into the sky. He heaved himself up, flapping half-plucked and heavy-winged. Oh, that Kra! Eeyah! Oh, that Bru! They went their ways more hungry than ever, looking for something else to make snug or to eat, whichever it was.

And, to this day, all the muntjacs who live in the forest, they bark out the story of how bad it was in the time of Hoang-Bang when Kra and Bru had the same idea. They bark out the story for all to hear. For all to be warned. Themselves and the other animals too. They tell the story now and then and especially when mean old Kra or Bru is around. Beware. Take care. Remember. But sometimes muntjacs themselves don't hear and they forget and then they get eaten all up.

Δ OMENS

One-eared Y Blo was squatted down, there atop the Beckoning Virgin. His leathery head was propped in his hands, and his arms on his knees, and the skirt of his breech-cloth dragged in the dirt. Y Blo was looking at the sky, sniffing the air for rain. Then he turned to the ground and ran his hand across the flank of the Beckoning Virgin. How round-hipped she was! But fragile too. How eager she was! How she stirred beneath his hand!

Stringy Y Blo was the wisest *mjao* in all of Dar Lac. His job was to intercede with the spirits, to pacify them. To protect the people from ornery ones—like the spirit of the tree trunk and the spirit of the mole hill. To heal the sick by wheedling the evil spirits from them or bribing them out with sacrifices, by finessing the spirits out; for they couldn't be routed, as he well knew—not with a stick or anything. And to foretell how the future will be.

Y Blo knew more than anyone else about the spirits. That the spirits which hovered and lurked had their own way of doing things. That they went about their business beyond the control of even himself, tho sometimes they might hear an appeal if it were properly presented—with lots of nice sacrifices, of course. The spirits were boss, no doubt about that. But this knowledge didn't discourage Y Blo. For Y Blo also knew that if he kept on the spirits' good side and played all the angles for what they were worth, then the spirits might share their secrets with him.

It wasn't too hard to keep on the good side of the spirits. A basic rapport, a show of respect, that's what it took. But playing the angles was something else. It required a certain caginess. Which is why Y Blo chose to read the signs there atop the Beckoning Virgin. He sought to find out what the summer would bring, how the rains would be—to take the pulse of the coming season. He reckoned that he could best do this in a place of restless stirring.

The Beckoning Virgin stirred beneath Y Blo's scaly paw. She gave promise of fertility, of bountiful crops. The sorcerer grunted his pleasure, his hope. It never entered his cagey mind that the Beckoning Virgin had stirred each May for as long as there had been a Buon Yun, and even before. That, in spite of each coming and passing of summer, of the rains, the Virgin had remained intact, her arm still outstretched, beckoning. Y Blo's horny paw stroked her thigh. He tickled her belly. He probably would have pinched her too, but then she would have crumbled.

Y Blo opened his amulet pouch and, one by one, emptied his amulets out. First came a stone, slippery smooth, polished bright, from the bottom of the chocolate river which slogged along to the south of the village. Next came a handful of earth and of rice from the fields beyond the fence. And a handful of air which you couldn't see but was there anyway. Then the dried stem of an opium poppy. The penis tip of a buffalo. A patch of skin from the breast of a sow. A tiger's incisor. And, finally, an eagle's feather.

Y Blo arranged these contents before him carefully. He laid them on the patch of ground staked out by his feet. In each amulet there reposed a spirit essential to the life of Buon Yun. Y Blo looked down along his nose and between his knees and to the ground staked out by his feet, and appealed to the spirits to show themselves. He called upon them to step out and stand tall and to shout what was going to be: Ah, my dears—pretty dears—come on out. Please come out. Tell what you know. That's it, dears—come tell me please. *Click. Click.* He tried to coax the spirits out by clicking his tongue. His mouth was dry and the clicking came hard, tickling his throat. But Y Blo was a man of discipline and he continued to click away. Ah, my dears, come out, come out. Tell your Y Blo. *Click. Click. Click.*

He wasn't alone—aside from the spirits holed-up inside. A number of women back from the fields and a number of idle Strike Force soldiers watched from the distance. They dared not come close, to get between Y Blo and the spirits. They knew that the spirits needed room to move about, they were touchy that way;

that Y Blo needed room to work. The villagers had the highest regard for their Y Blo. They valued his work and waited patiently for him to finish, for his conclusions. The people stood fixed. They were as snugly bound to the spirits—to the umbilicus of the spirits —as was Y Blo, squatting and clicking, right on the Beckoning Virgin's navel.

Y Blo tugged at his chin, at the gray whiskers there. He was studying hard and pulled a few wiry whiskers away. Once or twice he picked his nose, and blew his nose, and wiped his hand on his breechcloth which was dirty-black indigo blue. He normally would have examined his pickings, for pickings have significance, but now, of course, was not the time. There were spirits to be coaxed, to be wheedled out from inside. Y Blo swayed, he rocked back and forth on the flats of his feet, pondering the situation. Feh! Foo! A tough situation. A sticky one. As tough as when the bunny devils leer thru the trees. As sticky as keeping the planting quiet from the boars. Feh! Foo! An awkward one. Nothing had happened. Nothing so far.

Nothing—there was nothing to show. It was embarrassing for Y Blo. He knew that the others were watching him, that they expected results. He stared at the amulets spread on the ground. He glared at them. Maybe he had placed them wrong. Or maybe the spirits were teasing him. Having their joke. The spirits liked jokes. Or maybe they were just being shy. Whatever it was, Y Blo decided to rearrange the amulets, taking care not to jostle the spirits there inside.

And that's why Y Blo never ran anywhere but always walked. Because the spirits were inside the pouch that hung from his neck, in the amulets. It was a matter of dignity too, but mostly he walked because they were inside. He didn't want to jostle them.

He peered at the stone, at the handful of earth and the handful of rice and the handful of air which was really there, at the stem and the bits of animal. He peered, looking for the slightest sign. But the spirits refused to come out and give Y Blo word of how things would be. Y Blo peered and peered, and blew hot and cold, and grew very vexed. The sky grew gray. The people looked on anxiously.

Once again, Y Blo rearranged the amulets. He took up his watch. He peered at the amulets, mumbled to them, clicked to them, to the spirits inside, then held his breath. The whole world stopped and held its breath. The sky, it stopped its darkening. The wind devil with frosty hair, he stoppered up his three grinning mouths with all his hands and the wind collapsed. The air around got close and dense. The whole wide world was purple-faced and big balloon-cheeked from holding its breath, from waiting to see. Y Blo was sure then that something would happen. Happen! Happen! cried Y Blo. He bleated, he pleaded. But nothing did.

Y Blo was angry, thru with waiting. He gasped for breath, he gurgled for air. He roughly clutched up the polished stone and held it right in front of his eyes. Then he shook it up and down vigorously, almost furiously. Y Blo was no longer afraid of his gods. Feh on the spirits! Foo on the spirits! He was no longer even respectful. Done with appealing, with bleating and pleading. Feh! Foo! Even a gentle prod wouldn't do. Not for Y Blo! Y Blo tried to shake the reluctant spirit out of the stone, heedless of the shameful way he was bearing himself, of conduct unfitting a Rhadé *mjao*.

He shook and shook but didn't see any spirit fall out. So he moved the stone beside his one ear and shook some more. He didn't dare think there was no one inside, that the stone was empty. He shook and shook. He shut his eyes as tight as he could and strained his ears, listening. Eh, what's this!? Ooh, what's this!? Someone was tumbling around inside, he was pretty sure. He put down the stone and picked up the stem. He shook the stem beside his ear. He shook and shook, but this time he wasn't so sure. The sky had thickened. It was black.

And it all began with a calabash seed. With the talent for sucking the seed of a calabash out thru its peel which is said to reveal a gift for healing. A wonderful talent. Even when he was very young, Y Blo could suck out the seed of a calabash thru its peel. So he was chosen for sorcery lessons, apprenticed to a wise old *mjao*. Who brought him along, and drew out his powers, and taught Y Blo all the magic he knew till Y Blo could stand face to face with the spirits. Till Y Blo became the best. But good as he got, his special powers could be used only against lesser evil spirits, because the greater evil spirits were much too great to tangle with. Much too great for even Y Blo. No magic tricks, not with them. Only prayer and sacrifices.

So Y Blo stood face to face and practiced his stuff, and he grew wiser and wiser still and wealthy too. The wealthiest fellow in Buon Yun—tho anyone from other parts would not have been impressed. Y Blo grew wealthy because everything depends on the spirits, and people depend on their *mjao* to intercede with the spirits for them, and Y Blo was constantly interceding, collecting goods for his services to the sick and the injured, to the beset.

And here's where sucking the seed comes in. Why it was a good thing to know, a requirement, for those who would be sorcerers. For, in treating the sick, sorcerers are called upon to suck the sickness out of them. They do this by sucking the patient's body above where he ails, and then producing from their mouths a sliver of wood which is explained to be the arrow that caused the sickness; for spirits shoot arrows into people when they have done wrong. The sorcerer then determines what bad thing the patient has done and prescribes an appropriate sacrifice to the offended spirit. The stronger the sickness, the worse the patient has transgressed, the more expensive the sacrifice. One chicken and five jugs of sour rice wine, the sacrifices begin with that. The absolute bare minimum! Then higher and higher, up and up. A pig and five chickens and ten jugs of wine. Five pigs and ten chickens and rice wine enough to soften the heart of the evilest spirit—usually. Up and up. All the way up to buffaloes.

Which has to do with why Y Blo was conservative. It's like this. If a buffalo sacrifice is prescribed and if the patient doesn't get well, then the buffalo has to be replaced from the sorcerer's stock. So sorcerers are conservative fellows who seldom call for a buffalo when treating the sick. And it may be that more patients died than should have: because some sorcerer failed to prescribe an expensive-enough sacrifice. And sometimes it happens, in seeking a cure, that a tribesman will spend all he has in sorcerer fees and prescribed sacrifices, only to be told at last that the spirits seem to want his body for themselves and that he will therefore never recover. It was tough all around.

Well, anyway, that's how it began. With the calabash seed, with sucking it out. And how it led to Y Blo hunkered there, right atop the Beckoning Virgin, shaking stones and rattling stems and possibly hearing things tumble inside, but nothing to show and the sky turned black.

Y Blo rearranged the amulets for the third time. He was nervous and puzzled and angry. He wondered what the others thought. The others wondered why the reading was taking so long, why Y Blo wasn't done. Never before had their Y Blo squatted so long, there atop the Beckoning Virgin. What could it be? Was something wrong? Had the spirits fled? Deserted them? Ooeee! That wouldn't do.

Y Blo bent closer to the charms, now set out a ways before him. His arms lay crossed upon his knees, his chin rested on his arms. He bent so low he seemed about to topple over. Y Blo glared hard at the amulets. He concentrated on each in turn. His eyes were narrowed and fired red, and he tried to bore right thru to the core of the amulets. To bend the spirits to his will. To drive them out into the open. Oh Y Blo! Beware Y Blo! It was a foolhardy thing to do. It was a dangerous game to play. To stare down the spirits. Oh Y Blo! Mad-blind Y Blo! Y Blo glared and glared. He stared with such concentration and force that his blood bubbled over and his brain hissed and his ear twitched and his eyes became fuzzy. And just when the amulets seemed most blurred, things at last began to happen. The spirits showed! It was like they had stepped right out of a *puff!* They all began to dance but two.

Y Blo was stunned. They were dancing! The spirits were dancing! He had never seen such a thing happen before. He had never even heard of it. No one had. The spirits of water and earth and grain, of livestock and sweet tranquility had all joined hands and were dancing about in a fast spinning circle. Right there! Front and center! Down from his nose! Prancing together in front of Y Blo's wondering eyes. Eeyah! Ooeee! Oho! What a splendid performance, thought Y Blo. What revelry! What great fun it was! How happy they seemed! Y Blo felt privileged, grateful, proud. He, alone, was there to see the spirits making merry.

The spirits whirled around and around, linked together, hands clasped tight, careful not to trip each other. They reeled, they squealed; Y Blo, he heard. And from their unconditional joy, he knew for sure that the coming season would be the most over-whelming ever. Suddenly the whirling grew wild, faster and faster. The whirling grew almost violent. The spirits reeled, the spirits squealed, they whipped about. They flailed each other with their legs as the circle got smaller, tighter and tighter. Had not the spirits been dancing for joy, Y Blo would have sworn they were milling in terror. Faster, faster, faster they whirled. Faster, faster the circle twirled. Y Blo grew fuddled, very dizzy. He swayed. He was headed for the ground.

Then the black rain began to fall. First in a drizzle, then harder and harder. The rain soon doused Y Blo's hot brain. It soaked him thru, it chilled him cold. And, as it did, the spirits stopped dancing and dashed for cover. They threw their arms over their heads. They scurried bent low. They hurried out of the rain one–two–three. Even the water spirit fled. It came down that hard. He must have hopped back into his stone.

The rain drummed down, thumpety-thump, on Buon Yun, on Y Blo. He blinked his eyes, surprised he was wet. He shivered, he tried to shake himself dry. Y Blo was like a dog wet thru and miserable and his ribs sticking out.

The rain beat down, there on the Hump of the Beckoning Virgin. Everywhere. Fat thumping drops. Y Blo was happy. He gathered up his amulets and placed them back inside his pouch. He would never forget what he had seen, what the spirits had shared with him: the merrymaking and the joy.

Y Blo, himself, never showed joy. It wouldn't have done for a man of his calling—for a *mjao*. There was a dignity to maintain, a proper appearance, a dour one. So no leaping up and clicking his heels and letting fly a *whoopee!* Oh, no. None of that. The closest Y Blo ever came to joy was the pinch he gave to the Beckoning Virgin, crumbling her, as he creaked to his feet.

* * *

Matters weren't standing well with Comrade General Ba. He studied the map, trying to glean a hopeful sign, but it was black. The little black flags stuck up all over the Western Highlands

Interzone. They poked up thickest in a line along the frontier. What made matters so unpromising was that more and more of the pesky flags kept poking up every month. Each black flag stood for a Special Forces camp. The snake-eyed, split-tongued Americans were turning the tribes away from Hanoi. And that wasn't all. They were in the way too. The camps sat astride the paths along which supplies and cadres entered the South from Laos and Cambodia. Square astride. General Ba massaged his flank as he studied the map. The camps were like thorns which had to be plucked.

"Choose one. Have it destroyed." General Ba swept his hand over the map. Over the flags, rustling them. "Don't bother me about which one. Any one. They're all the same. Perhaps a fat juicy one. To teach them a lesson. To serve as a warning. To squash it good."

General Ba gave these orders casually. The General never became excited. He went about his making war as if it were some boring task. The world could jerk to a sudden halt, and General Ba would pick himself up and dust himself off and get on with what he was doing. His face had only one expression and that was no expression at all. Had he not been Vietnamese, the General's voice would have sounded quite flat, probably. Maybe it was that his sap had run dry. His office was brown, very plain. Just his desk and the map and President Ho, gazing benignly from the wall behind the desk. The President didn't seem concerned that he was hanging crookedly. It was an overcast day in Hanoi.

"But we set an example one year ago. At Plei Mrong."

"Never mind. We'll set another."

Comrade Colonel Trung had a loose muscle under one eye. It fluttered whenever Trung was excited and Trung was often excited these days. The pace of the struggle was being stepped up and Colonel Trung was stepping smartly along with the pace. He stood before the General's desk and looked at crooked President Ho. The old man made him feel at ease. He had a sweet face—a winning way of looking right back. A lovable face. But when Colonel Trung lowered his head to face General Ba, his bile flowed. These weekly sessions with General Ba were always stirring up something green and bitter-tasting in Colonel Trung. Something intense and belligerent. The nagging muscle under his eye began to flutter.

"They defend the camps very well. It will cost us something. Perhaps many men. Perhaps a big loss," ventured Colonel Trung. He tried not to sound disrespectful. General Ba was on Giap's staff and Colonel Trung, well he wasn't even a General, much less one on Giap's staff. Or a Central Committee member.

Colonel Trung didn't like General Ba. That sucker of rotten turtle eggs! Not at all! He conceded that once, more than ten years before, General Ba had been a true hero in the struggle against the French. But what was before wasn't now, that son of a pop-eyed warty toad! For, in the time since those epic days, General Ba had grown sleek and ambitious. Colonel Trung knew very well that General Ba and most of the others on Giap's staff were more concerned with their careers than with the plight of the Southerners. He knew that General Ba had forgotten how it was to sweat and itch and ache and hear his belly grumble and to bleed. That he had forgotten the blood and guts. He was always talking in figures and symbols and never of people, except in a very general way. Maybe the General no longer cared that much for people.

"The People," said General Ba, "the People are what matter. Their cause, Colonel, it must be won. Whatever it costs. Perhaps many men. Perhaps a big loss. But if we lose many men, then it will have been necessary." General Ba's one expression almost flickered into a second but pulled up short. He was annoyed and not just at the little black flags. "It will cost whatever it costs. One camp. Have it destroyed. Not one American must escape. Especially them. Especially the others too. Especially everybody." General Ba did not understand why Colonel Trung did not understand. Why he was taking so long to say Yes, sir! Anything, sir! and salute and about face and leave him alone.

General Ba flopped back in his chair and squinted at the map to his right. It was there on the wall, catty-cornered from President Ho. General Ba wiped his greasy glasses. He itched to snatch up the little black flags, all of them, and snap them in two. He itched to hear them go CRUNCH! in his paw. But General Ba restrained himself. It wouldn't have been a very professional thing to do, to clutch up the flags and make them go CRUNCH! The General hadn't forgotten how it was to itch. What he had forgotten was Colonel Trung.

"Soldiers are people too," said Trung.

"Eh? What's that?"

"Soldiers are people too, Comrade General. They sweat and itch and ache and their bellies grumble and they bleed. Especially bleed. They do that well."

"What!? What's this!? Especially bleed!?"

"All the men who will make the attack, what about them? They're people too. With all due respect for the General Staff—"

General Ba didn't show his amazement, but he was amazed just the same. Angered too. By Colonel Trung's attitude, by his gall. Colonel Trung was rather amazed himself. His muscle fluttered tickety-tick.

"So soldiers are people, Comrade Colonel? Very good. And people are people. And people are soldiers. So what? You don't sit in a General's chair. You don't command his view of things. You don't see with his clarity." Ba went back to rubbing the grease. "It's very commendable, Colonel Trung, for an officer of the People's Army to show such concern, such loyalty to the men he sends off. But it's far more commendable not to question. To not question is the higher duty. For Comrade Colonels. For any soldier. A higher loyalty, Colonel Trung. An act of faith. Where is yours?"

Colonel Trung looked around the room, possibly to locate his faith but more likely because he was looking for refuge. General Ba looked as bland as ever and hadn't raised his voice, but Colonel Trung knew that General Ba was displeased with him. That he had just made it convincingly clear. Clear that he, Colonel Trung, was fast running out of slack.

Trung had always leaned out of line even when stepping smartly along. He hadn't been unreliable. He hadn't leaned *that* far out; he never would have made Comrade Colonel. No farther out than the tip of his nose. Because he had said some things in the past which he should have left unsaid. But never before had he been so bold. Not with a Comrade General. Not with a General on Giap's staff.

Not with a General who had a map with little black flags. Trung was scared. Proud of himself, pleased with himself, but scared nonetheless. Rubbery-legged, swaying this way and that. Looking to President Ho for help. Scared enough to cut short his stay, and to about face, and to leave General Ba all alone. So finally: "Comrade General Ba. Yes, sir. Anything, sir. I'll make the proper arrangements, sir."

General Ba got to his feet and obscured the face of President Ho. "Comrade Colonel Trung, you're a good officer in all matters but one. Political sense. That's what you lack. A deficiency which should cause you more worry than the men. *Far* more worry, don't you think?"

What Colonel Trung thought was that General Ba had never been so candid with him. He fought to keep his knees from buckling. He swayed farther back and farther forth. Yet, at the same time— don't ask him why—he felt strangely grateful to General Ba. Perhaps it wasn't so bad after all. Perhaps there was time. Perhaps he hadn't run all the way out. Perhaps the Comrade General was just showing him some human concern. A friendly warning to the side. A bit of advice. Perhaps it was that. Brotherliness.

"And why be so concerned for the men. The unit will be a local one. Southerners. Our southern brothers—To the Liberation of the South!" General Ba drew himself tall and waited for the remarkable Colonel to salute first.

"To the Liberation, General Ba." Then Colonel Trung tottered out the door.

* * *

Colonel Quoc was fit to be tied. He gaped at the chart spread out before him and couldn't believe his eyes. According to the worthy chart, which was put out each year by the Astrological Ministry, Hue was not right for Colonel Quoc and he wasn't right for Hue. It was a difficult situation. Quoc didn't want to part with Hue, having grown very fond of her. But he didn't want to defy the chart either, the warning plainly written there. The charts of the Astrological Ministry seldom erred and Quoc had always accepted their wisdom, their advice. It was no easy thing to disregard so wise and trusted and valued a friend. So page-worn a friend.

Colonel Quoc consulted the chart at the onset of each new year to see what the year had in store for him. He consulted the chart to find the best days for tackling tough problems and for making weighty decisions. He turned to the chart whenever Saigon changed its policies or else reshuffled its personnel—for a man had to know how to stay on his feet, how to land on them if things were atumble. He sought out the chart on special occasions such as his birthday, or on the ninth day after the day of the fall of the Hoang-Bang Dynasty, or when he had to choose between filching from this fund or that, or when he chose a new mistress. Which was why Quoc was at the chart now. In a way.

All hunched over. His finger propped upon the chart. Square upon the worrisome spot. He could not understand how he had overlooked these bad tidings when he leased Hue almost six months before. How can this be!? he asked himself. How can it happen to me, Colonel Quoc!? Quoc had reconsulted the chart because his contract with Xuan the whoremonger was up for renewal. The reconsultation had been made simply to satisfy his conscience and not because Quoc really wanted advice, so sure had he been of Hue. He should have known that the Astrological Ministry chart was not a thing to be lightly employed. That had been Quoc's great mistake: to approach the reading breezily. He was paying the price. Oh, why to me!? he asked himself. If only I had left matters alone! If only—if only—but he had not. So Colonel Quoc settled back in his chair and closed his eyes. He had some serious thinking to do. He patted his uniform as he thought. That and his jade-handled revolver which he always wore at his side. He was known as Cowboy Quoc.

Colonel Quoc wore his uniform proudly. He was always patting it here and there, as much to measure how far he had come as to smooth out the wrinkles. He had risen from poor and unglorious ranks and the patting helped. It was a comfort. His father had been a shopkeeper's man and had died from consumption when Quoc was a boy. There hadn't been money to send the sick man to the mountains for a cure, or even to pay for medicine. As soon as the father had been dispatched, Quoc's haggard mother gathered her children, fled the city, and returned to the countryside, to the distant village where she had been born. There in the peaceful countryside, in the time before all the fighting began, she and her sons made charcoal from wood and peddled it in the nearby town. They struggled along, sooty-faced. The rest of them too: hands, feet, everything. Always black-smudged. Barely able to make ends meet. Thankful at least to have ends meet. All except Quoc.

Then one day, after years had passed, while Quoc was peddling his charcoal in town, he met the unappetizing daughter, the shy dumpy daughter, of a local rice merchant. Quoc being handsome in a sly way, uncommonly quick and full of ideas, he courted the merchant's sallow-faced daughter. The merchant did not favor Quoc whom he considered beneath his daughter and somewhat of a rogue as well. Look at that rogue! Look at his face! How sly it is! How sooty it is! The rest of him too! But favor or not, the merchant knew—he painfully knew—that his dumpy daughter, she was no bargain and might never ever be courted again. So, in the end, the merchant consented to their marriage.

And, in a show of good will, the merchant gave Quoc a very generous wedding present. He bought sooty Quoc an army commission, Quoc who loved snappy uniforms so. Quoc left for his unit right after the wedding. He took off so remarkably fast that he forgot to take his bride. His father-in-law's anger was such that he shortly thereafter died from a stroke. His bride was left to tend the shop and quickly wilted, whatever little there was to wilt. Then one year later, in an untypical show of remorse, Quoc returned all of a sudden to share the news of his first promotion, to share it with his dried-up bride. His dried-up bride was overjoyed. Her Quoc had come home! She promptly forgave him everything, and then was struck down in the plague epidemic which chose that glad time to rage thru the province. So fast, so final, so soon in the past. Quoc mourned his sad wife, tho he himself wasn't especially sad. He sold her property for a good price and returned to his unit where he applied himself cunningly and steadily rose up the ranks.

Colonel Quoc never remarried. He spent too much time plotting his rise to bother with raising a family. Besides, he had seen what the wrong kind of wife could do to a career. How some of his brother officers had fallen from favor because their wives were this

way or that or because they weren't. How others could no longer
snap out orders, so accustomed had they become to receiving orders
instead. As for the right kind of wife, Quoc didn't believe that she
existed. At least she was nowhere around. So Quoc remained a
widower and dabbled just the same. Altho he was a trifle skinny,
Quoc was still a vigorous man. He was also the Province Chief
of Dar Lac.

Hue was Colonel Quoc's latest and most durable mistress. Hue
was not an exceptional girl; but she was attractive, undemanding,
and keenly attentive to Colonel Quoc's needs. He had always meant
to congratulate Xuan for leasing him Hue. Sensible, devoted Hue.
Quoc had been so pleased with Hue that he had installed her in a
small but pleasant house on one of the quiet shady streets of Ban
Me Thuot. The house had belonged to a man of letters who, with
all his family, had fled from the North in '54, resettling in Ban Me
Thuot. There they had lived their shiny new life until, in a sudden
belated burst of intuition, Quoc had decided he wasn't so sure
about the lettered man after all, about his allegiance. He had a
mangy look to him. He was always shuffling off to places like the
library where who knew what sorts of strange and subversive
doings went on.

And the rice! Uncle Ben's Converted Rice, that's what they ate!
Perhaps he hadn't really fled. Perhaps his true story remained un-
told. Perhaps he had been converted too! Perhaps he was a Communist! Perhaps—perhaps—. Of course it was all highly unlikely,
but not too unlikely for Colonel Quoc. One had to be sure. The
nation's security was at stake, wasn't it? So Quoc acted fast, Quoc
acted firmly. He had the family packed off to a detention center
where their story could be checked; they were never heard from
again. Well, after a brief but decent wait, Quoc commandeered the
small pleasant house. Hue was comfortable in it.

Hue, sweet Hue! How unselfish she was! In the almost six
months since she had been leased, Hue had asked Quoc for only
one thing—a bicycle. It would give her pleasure, she had said, to
bicycle beneath the trees. To bicycle down the avenue which struck
like a spoke from the center of town to the northwest, toward the
plantation. It had been a small request and so Quoc had bought her

the bicycle. She used it only occasionally yet somehow it always needed repair.

Colonel Quoc opened his eyes and smoothed back his hair. Well, who knows? Perhaps the Astrological Ministry made a mistake. Perhaps this one time. Quoc sat up straight, girding himself. Brave Quoc. Or foolish Quoc. Stuck-on-Hue Quoc. He smacked the chart hard with the flat of his hand. Perhaps just this once. He smacked it again. He chose to ignore the warning it held, Quoc who had always sworn by the charts. Maybe the printers made a mistake. Quoc sighed. He decided on Hue.

* * *

Sniff—sniff—sniff. Sniff—sniff—sniff. The American was sniffing hard. With his hands tightly cupping the little black box and holding it close against his nose and his nose sucking deep. Sniffing right and sniffing left and up and down and all around. Dressed up fine in olive drab, with lots of pips on both his shoulders and lots of medals across his chest. *Sniff—sniff—sniff. Sniff—sniff—sniff.*

The trees were very close together. Sturdy trees tho willowy. And their branches stuck straight out, with lots of little fingery twigs, and everything fluttered in the breeze. The American picked his way thru the forest in a half crouch, sniffing, sucking in deep all the time. It was hard work, wending between all those fluttering trees, but he kept doggedly on his way. Then suddenly the American's eyes, which had been small and very mean, his eyes got very big. *Ooeee!* He was onto something. He was headed on the right track. The American's nose sucked in deeper and deeper. *Sniff—sniff—sniff. Sniff—sniff—sniff.* He was getting closer and closer. To the smell. Slouching along thru the trees toward the smell. Toward where it was strongest. Closer and closer. *Sniff—sniff—sniff. Sniff—snIFF—SNIFF.* Finally! *Yahoo! Yippee!* The American leaped up and down. He clicked his heels. He licked his fat lips (which were rather thin). His face gleamed. He leered happily. He had sniffed out the bad, bad VC. Their body odors. The little black box had found them out.

The American couldn't see far ahead tho he peered and peered and peered thru the trees—the forest, it was very thick—but he had sniffed out the bad, bad VC, he was sure of that. So he put down his little black box and fired his gun—*ratta-tat-tat*—toward the place from where the odors had come. And the artillery went *Boom! Boom! Boom!* toward the place from where the odors had come. And the airplanes whooshed across the place from where the body odors had come and dropped all their bombs—*KVOOM! KVOOM! KVOOM!* And the trees with their branches and fingery twigs fluttered harder and harder than ever from all the exploding.

But on the other side of the trees, in the place from where the odors had come, there was only a lone buffalo. Buffaloes give off body odors just as well as bad, bad VC. The poor buffalo with the sad, sad eyes, he danced all around, he tried to escape. But the bullets and the artillery shells and the bombs, they thwacked into him and the poor buffalo dropped to the ground and shuddered and twitched and thrashed all around and finally died.

When all the ratta-tat-tatting and shelling and bombing was done, the American swaggered to the place from where the body odors had come and there he discovered that it was only a lone buffalo. Oh, too bad. Oh, how sad. It wasn't the bad, bad VC after all. What a shame. He wagged his head, disappointed. How could his box, his dear little box, make such a mistake.

So the American picked up his box and started to sniff all over again. Tightly cupping the little black box and holding it close against his nose and his nose sucking deep. Sniffing right and sniffing left and up and down and all around. Dressed up fine in olive drab, with lots of pips on both his shoulders and lots of medals across his chest. *Sniff—sniff—sniff. Sniff—sniff—sniff.*

He slouched his way thru the sturdy trees which were willowy, with their branches straight out and lots of little fingery twigs and everything fluttering in the breeze. The American picked his way sucking in deep and peering hard and then his eyes, which had been screwed small, they got very big. *Ooeee!* This time for sure he was onto something. This time for sure he was headed right. He jammed the box tight against his nose and he sucked in as deep as he could. *Sniff—sniff—sniff. Sniff—sniff—sniff. Eeyah! Ooeee!* He was getting closer and closer. *Sniff—sniff—sniff. Sniff—snIFF—SNIFF.* Finally! *Yahoo! Yippee!* The American leaped up and down and clicked his heels joyously. He couldn't see very far ahead because the forest was so thick, but he had sniffed out the bad, bad VC. Their body odors. This time for sure. He had lots of faith in his little black box. He was very proud of it.

So the American put down his box and fired his gun—*ratta-tat-tat*—toward the place from where the odors had come. And the artillery went *Boom! Boom! Boom!* toward the place from where the odors had come. And the airplanes whooshed across the place from where the body odors had come and dropped all their bombs—*KVOOM! KVOOM! KVOOM!* And the trees with their branches and fingery twigs fluttered harder than even before from all the exploding.

But on the other side of the trees, in the place from where the odors had come, there were only three farmers from Buon Sop working in a clearing. Farmers give off body odors just as well as bad, bad VC. The three farmers danced about, they tried to escape. They threw their arms up to the sky, appealing to the spirits for help. But the bullets and the artillery shells and the bombs, they thwacked into them and the poor farmers dropped to the ground and shuddered and twitched and thrashed all around and cried out their anguish and finally died.

When all the ratta-tat-tatting and shelling and bombing was done, the American swaggered to the place from where the body odors had come and there he discovered that it was only three poor farmers from Buon Sop. Oh, too bad. Oh, how sad. It wasn't the bad, bad VC after all. What a shame. He wagged his head, disappointed again. How could his box, his dear little box, make such a mistake. Oh well, what the hell, the American picked up his little black box and took off once more thru the trees, looking for the bad, bad VC. He went half-crouched and dogged as ever. *Sniff—sniff—sniff. Sniff—sniff—sniff—*

After the skit about the sniff-sniff, and after the clowns and the acrobats and the jugglers too, the man with three fingers had all the players take a bow. The clowns and the acrobats and the jugglers. Kim who had played the poor buffalo so magnificently. Dan, Van, and Dung who had played the three farmers of Buon Sop. The Fighters of the 825th who had played the trees, standing with their arms stretched wide and their fingers too and everything fluttering in the breeze. Finally, Three Fingers himself, who had played the American, dressed up fine in olive drab with lots of pips on both his shoulders and lots of medals across his chest and a long, long nose stuck on his face—all the better for sniffing.

The people had been well entertained and they gave the players a rousing hand. But they were perplexed because they didn't understand what ammonia was, the stuff which the little black box sniffed out. The people were angry because buffaloes and innocent farmers were precious things—not things to be ratta-tat-tatted and bombed. Eeyah, those Americans! But they were feeling imposed upon because they didn't care for the VC either. Nonetheless the people clapped because the skit had been well done. Then, while the people were loosened up, Three Fingers gathered them more closely round and began his little talk. It was the one he always gave after the sniff-sniff skit. It was his favorite agitprop talk.

"Brave people of Buon Sop. Suffering people. Struggling people. Buffaloes and innocent farmers are not things to be ratta-tat-tatted and shelled and bombed. Buffaloes and innocent farmers are precious things. Precious to you and precious to us. But not precious to the Americans. Oh, no! No! No! Eeyah—those Americans! Nothing is precious to them except their little black boxes."

Three Fingers gave the box a kick. A righteous kick. A vicious kick. He sent it tumbling and clattering.

"Valiant people of Buon Sop. Bad things always happen to those who deal with the Americans. Ooeee—such bad things. Horrible things. Tragic things. Now you know this for yourselves. You have seen."

Three Fingers ordered Dan, Van, and Dung to step forward again and show all the people of Buon Sop where *they* had been ratta-tat-tatted and shelled and bombed and how much it had hurt.

"See the holes! See how it hurts! Such big holes! That's why we have come. To warn you, brothers. That you should stay far away from Americans with all their pips and all their medals and their funny long, long noses. As far away as Buon Sop from Buon Yun. The farther away, the better it will be for you. Much better. Oh, so much better. For you and for us."

Three Fingers leaned into the audience, fixing the audience with his eyes. He looked deep into each single face. He nodded, he winked, he conspired with them, letting all the people know that it would be better.

"Ooeee—those Americans! Much much better to stay away. Oh, much better. So much better. Better for you and better for us," Three Fingers said and made believe to go *ratta-tat-tat* at all the people gathered round.

BUON YUN

Among the villages of the Rhadé, Buon Yun was acclaimed for the wisdom of its sorcerer and for its fortifications. Buon Yun was encircled by an inner and outer fence of sturdy nine-foot wooden stakes. The fences were set twelve feet apart and the stakes were sharp as well as sturdy, each stake having been topped to a point. Between the two fences were rows of lean, fire-hardened bamboo spikes—*punji* spikes—razor-edged, close together, sprouting up viciously like sharks' teeth. And, as if this weren't enough, scores of antipersonnel mines had been planted here and there, who knows where, amidst the *punjis*.

Within this formidable stockade, some thirty-odd longhouses were aligned. They were drawn up in files facing north, toward the Brake of the Rattling Bamboo. Drawn up north-south and not east-west because it invited tragedy for the houses of the living to face the dying sun. There to the west, where the sun died each day, was the Land of the Elephants, less than a half-day's trek away.

The longhouses were communal affairs. Each was shared by the members of one great sprawling family. The houses were thirty to fifty yards long. Each had a floor of wooden beams, smoke blackened walls of woven bamboo and a roof of thick straw thatch. The houses sat on stout wooden piles, five to eight feet off the ground. Underneath, in the rusty-red dirt, was where the pigs foraged and chickens yawped and scabby-headed toddlers crawled.

Aside from its fortifications and from the number of houses within, for it was larger than most villages, Buon Yun was distinguished by an arrangement of swells and hollows which looked like a woman flat on her back with one arm outstretched. These swells and hollows were set off on a table of ground in the northern part of the village. This table of ground was known to the people of Buon Yun as the Hump of the Beckoning Virgin. It had always been called by that name. The people treated their Beckoning Virgin with respect. They always took care to circle around her and never to walk across her top, even when they were in a great hurry. They showered their Virgin with affection. They were very proud of her. There was no other village in Dar Lac, perhaps not even in all the highlands, which could boast of such a thing.

The people were short, hard-bodied and brown. The faces of some were uncommonly handsome and regular, but the faces of most were haggard and warped this way and that, bent all out of shape by a grinding life. Their noses were small. Their eyes were dark and round at the corner, without the extra fold of skin common to the Vietnamese. Their cheekbones were high but not out of sight. Their teeth were rotted. Their grins were shot thru with great halloween gaps. Absurd grins. Grotesque grins. Still it was better than before when they filed their upper front teeth to the gum. Especially for the young girls. Their hair was black, usually straight, and usually matted with dirt. The women wore it pulled back in a bun. Their bodies were hairless but not smooth at all. Their skin was rough and abrasive. Leathered by weather and rasped by the rusty-red powdery grit which covered the village during the dry season months. Their feet were splayed wide, flat as a board and tough as an elephant's hide.

Buon Yun had its share of the sick and the lame, the maimed and deformed. Most of its people passed most of their lives living with one pain or another. They were resigned to this state of things. They couldn't contemplate any other. They shrugged off the small pains as being unworthy of their concern. They endured the big pains as best they could. Maybe matters might have stood better if the people had kept themselves clean. But most of the people went unwashed. Not because they preferred it that way. They liked to be clean like everyone else. But because of the water spirit. He was one of the feistiest spirits of them all. The people feared to linger too long in his domain. They feared to take advantage of him. Oh, it was alright to wash the clothes and to draw water for cooking or drinking. And it was alright to cross the river in order o get from one side to the other. And it was alright for the buffalo boys, only their feet got wet. But as for people splashing around, well that's where the feisty water spirit was apt to draw the line. So when they bathed in the chocolate river which lazily flowed south of the village, the people were very quick about it. The men held their noses and dunked themselves two or three times. The women, who were more coy about bathing, they stood demurely in the river up to their knees, scooped up a handful or two of brown water, and splashed themselves wherever they thought it would do the most good. Still wearing their skirts, of course. They were careful about the splashing.

On dry land too, the people acted sensibly. Nothing rash, or overdone. They moved about in a slow steady gait, doggedly. But with restraint too. They worked when they had to, and then they worked hard. They did whatever had to be done. But they never applied themselves recklessly, needlessly, for there would have been no sense.

The way the people went about had to do with why they didn't chase after the dog. This happened years and years ago when A'de, their Creator, invited the Rhadé to his place to get a language. Other peoples received invitations and they brought pieces of weed upon which to jot down their languages. But not the Rhadé. They played it smug. Hoping to make a good impression on A'de, they brought a buffalo skin instead because it was more sophisticated and expensive than a piece of weed. But on the way home from A'de's place, a dog ran off with the buffalo skin, thereby taking the only copy of their written langauge. The Rhadé could have chased after the dog but they decided, after all, that a written language was not so important. That it wasn't a necessary thing. They had gotten along without one for a long, long time. They got by since.

The people got by because they lived in close agreement with their surroundings. Prescribed agreement. Because they had a policy, a contract, an arrangement. It had to do with the spirits. They acknowledged the spirits in all things. They accepted whatever happened to them, however bad, because to not accept what happened would only have made what happened much worse. When times were bad, when there was much to gripe about, they bore no grudge against the spirits. It was the way of things. When times were good, when the rains came and the crops grew and the animals prospered and not as many children died and there were no catastrophes, then they expressed their gratitude. Unfortunately, it happened that times had been more bad than good.

But to accept the ways of the spirits didn't mean to throw in the sponge. It didn't mean giving up. That there was nothing to be done. It didn't rule out initiative. That was where the arrangement came in. The contract. The insurance policy, so to speak. The people weren't fools. Thru Y Blo—thru the ceremonial sacrifices of chickens and pigs and buffaloes and jugs of rice wine at which the old man officiated—they paid their premiums to the spirits. They maintained their policy. They kept their payments up to date in order to avoid misfortune. To keep the spirits fat and content and kindly disposed.

It was an expensive thing, this policy. Also a time-consuming thing. The spirits required a lot of care and the people were constantly making payments. It was the price of security. And whenever something went wrong—something was always going wrong—the people always blamed themselves and not the spirits. Perhaps they had observed the rituals improperly: said the wrong prayers, or didn't say the prayers often enough, or chanted the prayers out of rhythm, or sacrificed three white cocks and five jugs of wine when a pig was due. Anyway, it was their fault. That's what the people told themselves. That's what they believed.

They had to believe that it was their fault. That the spirits weren't fickle creatures, spiteful creatures, changing their moods and requirements from day to day. The spirits had to be known and fixed, and what they required too. Otherwise, the situation would have been impossible. It would have meant that the spirits could not be systematically approached and brought around, however little, by the proper measures. That was all the people had. Proper measures. Prescribed measures. So much of this and so much of that. Exact measures. To help themselves get by.

The people had gotten along by themselves—they had been left to their peaceful ways, forgotten and uncared about—until the First Indochina War when the French and the Viet Minh had competed for their loyalty, for their services. And the Second, close behind, when it was the Americans and the Viet Cong. The French and then the Americans had competed successfully because the people of the highland hated the lowland Vietnamese, no matter what their politics. Viet Minh—Viet Cong—the Government—it was the same, all the same. Eeyah, those Vietnamese! They were worse than the *k'sok* who lurked in dark hiding places and were full of nasty tricks like all of a sudden popping up in front of the people and causing great shocks and miscarriages and things like that. Ooeee, those Vietnamese! They were worse than the *m'tao* who somehow slipped inside the people and there, with the aid of a magic bellows, blew a cloud of poison powder which condensed into a terrible sickness, or else they shot magic darts which acted faster than the powder. Yet in spite of all the popping up and shocking and blowing poison powder and shooting darts, the people felt a perverse affection for the *k'sok* and the *m'tao*. They were just lesser devils. Little imps. But as for the Vietnamese, they were as bad as the *m'klaks* for whom the people felt no affection whatsoever. Eeyah! Ooeee! The Vietnamese! They were as dreaded as the *m'klaks*. The Vietnamese underweighed the people and overcharged them in the shops of Ban Me Thuot. The Vietnamese took their handsomest women, impressed their young men into the army, expropriated their choicest lands—as if these lands weren't poor enough. Sapped and gritty and yielding hard. The Vietnamese administered them with icy, pipy-voiced contempt and generally held the people to be a subhuman breed of animal. *Moi*, they called them—savages.

There was nothing subhuman about the people of Buon Yun. They were the children of A'de—the Master of the Sky. The *anak A'de*, that's how they referred to themselves. Not only the children of A'de, but his eldest children at that. The oldest human race on earth, that's what they believed. That, of the peoples now on earth, they alone could trace their ancestry back to prehistoric times. Back to before the dog ran off with the buffalo skin. It's all contained in their five epic poems and, indeed, the legend of H'Bia Ngo describes a creature which has been identified as a great woolly mammoth. But the lowland Vietnamese, they didn't know about A'de or woolly mammoths or anything else.

It was said among the Vietnamese that the highland tribes had been cannibals. That they had gone about hunting each other and dining upon the choicest pieces, especially the liver. That they had forsaken their cannibal ways only very recently. That, even today, there were some who still preserved the old ways. But, of course, these were only rumors, for who wants a spirit thrashing around inside his belly? It went like this: if a man killed another, the dead man's spirit would haunt the living man forever. So think how doubly calamitous it would have been to kill a man, then eat him as well, and thus be haunted from inside out by some revengeful spirit.

The people of Buon Yun roughed their lives but certainly they were not savages. In fact, they enjoyed those same civilized things which peoples the world over enjoy. They brewed their own sour rice wine which they drank when they were thirsty, or happy or sad, or simply wanted to relax. They cultivated opium and a mangy local tobacco which they smoked for much the same reasons as they drank their sour rice wine. They respected the ways of the spirits—of the k'sok and m'tao and m'klaks who lurked by the wayside and in the dark places and hovered above—and they never tampered with nature, which is more than can be said for many other civilized peoples. They suffered the same kinds of pain and grief that all peoples do. Their lives were filled with the same demands. They met these demands in the same dogged way. They were very human, these Rhadé—all these highland people.

Early each day, in the gray looming hour just before dawn, the women rose to pound the day's rice and to winnow it. During the day they worked in the small fields outside the village—stooping and scratching and weeding. They cared for their patches of dry upland rice and sweet potatoes and manioc and maize and peanuts and bamboo sprouts and melons and jackfruit and pawpaw and the mangy tobacco. They took special care of that. They rooted and grubbed for delicacies in the forest during the summer rains. For young wild shoots and tubers and fruits and mushrooms and certain flowers. For their soups and stews. They gathered everything edible but especially they prized wild honey. They gathered tinder and hauled crushing loads of firewood. The loads so great upon their backs that their trunks were bent parallel to the ground, while their feet shuffled frantically, hurrying home to get the pain done. They tended the chickens and the pigs, what little tending had to be done, for these animals were usually left to fend for themselves. They swept out the houses, and drew the water for cooking and drinking, and scrubbed the clothes down at the river, and prepared meals for their men. A grunt or two of appreciation was all the women asked in return.

During their leisure the women spun thread and wove blankets and rugs, sometimes of somber gray and black, sometimes of red and yellow and blue. They nursed their babies while they worked if the chore of the moment permitted it. At great round breasts. They nursed them while they leisured too. The women wore black midi-skirts. Or indigo blue with a thin red stripe down the side. During the summer they went bare-chested. During the cold winter months, they wore a blouse as well as the skirt. They liked to chew betel and to smoke pipes of tobacco, especially the grannies. Withered old dames with cracked empty breasts and teeth long gone and puckered lips, gripping the stems of their pipes with their gums and sucking so hard that the hollows of their cheeks almost met. Gingery Grandmother Pan sucking hardest. The women gossiped constantly as women do everywhere.

The men didn't work as hard as the women. They never had. And now they worked even less than before. They weren't lazy men by nature, but they no longer helped out in the fields, and seldom went hunting for snakes and lizards and squirrels and boar. They no longer fished or wove bamboo or conducted business or fashioned working tools for the women. Instead, they strutted about Buon Yun and showed off their uniforms to one another. They lounged in the shade and talked about tactics. They sat on the ledges of the houses and cleaned their new weapons. They spat and rubbed, oiled and buffed. They passed their time waiting—being prepared—like the soldiers they were. They passed their time expectantly. They were much too taken up with their places in the Strike Force to bother about civilian things. The Strike Force, it was something else. It was where the action was.

The Strike Force had been organized not long before by the eight Americans. It included most of the men of Buon Yun who were neither too feeble nor too infirm to take up arms. It included boys in their early teens who were too grown to tend the buffaloes and who would soon be taking wives, exchanging bracelets with some girl. It didn't include grizzled Y Bun, the village chief, who had to tend to his chiefly duties. It didn't include spare, sour-pussed, one-eared Y Blo who also maintained a tight schedule, and had the dignity of his office to uphold and who, besides, much preferred to keep to himself. The Strike Force also didn't include a handful of independent souls like Y Gar the hunter who had little use for the new ways and preferred a breechcloth to fatigues.

But for most of the men of Buon Yun, the Strike Force was the pride of their lives. It was all they could have wished for. The Strike Force was status and it was belonging. The Strike Force was standing tall and straight and holding off the bad, bad VC. The Strike Force was freedom from duties at home—from all the nagging unglamorous chores. The men were supposed to be part-time soldiers but they told their wives they were standing by, that they had to stand by. They made standing-by a full-time affair. The Strike Force was freedom from worrying if there would be enough rice to eat. The Americans supplied them rice in great burlap sacks. More rice than they had ever eaten or seen before. The Strike Force, it was a very great thing.

So the men strutted about and lounged about and cleaned their weapons. They dreamt of the honors they would win on the battlefield. Each man did. A one-sided dream. They never dreamt that they would ever die violently. There were good deaths and there were bad, and a violent death was very bad, for then the soul would have to wander the highlands forever.

They dreamt all day of winning honors. At night, when the evening meal was done, when it was warm and snug inside and full of friendly shadows, when they could relax from standing by, the tribesmen drank their sour rice wine and smoked their pipes and told what they knew. The tribal legends and other stories.

They drank the rice wine in great quantities, which was a shrewd as well as a good-tasting thing to do, because the men became quite happy and thereby believed the spirits were just as happy as they and it made them feel all the more secure. They chanted the legends in verse form so that they wouldn't get twisted around, or added to, or subtracted from, as they were passed down to each generation. Legends about their origin. About how A'de had lived on earth with his wife and son and then had abandoned his earthly home when his son was killed by a centipede. About the time of the terrible flood when the founders of their race floated for days inside a drum and the water rose so high to the heavens that the fish nibbled on the stars. About Kra and Bru and the dog who ran off with the buffalo skin, but not so much about Kra and Bru. The same stories over and over. Night after night. The men beat those stories to death. And they drummed. They huddled in their smoky houses and they drummed late into the night.

As for the children of Buon Yun, they played among the foraging pigs and the scrawny squawking chickens. They peeked and poked, shouted and ran, just like children everywhere. They chased each other, the animals too, trying to latch onto the pigs by their dungy corkscrew tails. They walked on stilts and flew kites and spun tops and they swam in the chocolate river because they didn't have enough sense to be afraid of the water spirit.

The children ran all over the village—drippy-nosed, undisciplined—because the people of Buon Yun were very permissive parents. They treated the children almost as if they were adults with minds of their own. They respected their children's every wish because they believed that their ancestors were reincarnated in the newborn and who could tell a respected ancestor what to do. It wouldn't have been the proper thing.

But mostly the people let their children run about unattended, at least until they were five years old, because to pay them too much attention would attract the evil spirits at a time in the children's lives when they were most vulnerable. In fact, during these first five years, the children weren't called by their real names but by stinky vulgar names to confound the evil spirits. To put them off. To protect the children from them. Names like *eh*—excrement, or *bru*—rotten, or *djie*—death, or *trung*—big stomach. False names to trick the evil spirits who would never take note of children with such unattractive names. Not in a hundred years. The real names are used when the children turn five—when the most critical time has passed. Yet however good this trickery was, however effective, the evil spirits still managed to recognize and to kill four out of five in these early years. They were pretty shrewd themselves, the spirits were.

Well, anyway, in spite of being called excrement and rotten and death and big stomach too, the children of Buon Yun played cheerfully. Except for the few who sat in the dirt, gazing ahead, naked and vacant and powdered red and skinny-limbed and bellies truly swollen from sickness and malnutrition. The children played cheerfully, unaware that their years of play would be few—that the time would soon come for serious things. The time for serious things came soon for the young highland people.

The Viet Cong had always been dead serious. They had entered the villages one by one, putting on very pertinent skits and juggling and doing acrobatics, and then speaking plain and fire-eyed and at length. About how the fat, greasy ones from Saigon had hounded and persecuted the people and tried to bring them under control. To shackle them like a buffalo before the blood-letting ceremony. They spoke of how the Government had stolen the people's choicest lands for the settlement of Vietnamese. They didn't mention that the new settlers had been refugees from the North. They spoke of how the ones in Saigon didn't know about woolly mammoths or A'de or anything else and, what's more, how they couldn't care less. The VC, of course, said how much *they* cared. They urged the tribesmen to establish an autonomous zone in the highlands. Come on, boys. You can do it. How about some help? They failed to note that, once the Liberation succeeded, there would be no autonomous zones. They pressed the tribesmen to support the guerrilla bands which operated in the highlands. To come along and operate, too.

The Viet Cong courted the people tirelessly. Knock! Knock! on the village gates. Guess who? That's right! It's us again. Open up and hear us out. Got a great show for you folks today. Skits and acrobatics and speeches and muted warnings and observing the niceties, but none of it worked. Coming in and promoting themselves and hounding the people with reminders about all the bad things done to them by the Government. But none of it worked. Perhaps they reminded the people too well. After all, the Viet Cong were Vietnamese too. The gap was there. Of mistrust. Of long accumulated hate. Much too wide across to be spanned. A few were recruited here and there, but most of the people could not be persuaded that their hopes lay with the Viet Cong.

The Viet Cong were just as human as anyone else. They were skin and bones and muscle and blood and feelings and little weaknesses and drippy noses and jangled nerves and cherished hopes and hoppity twitches and all the other human things. They grew frustrated like everyone. Their tongues curled up at its bitter taste. They cursed and sighed. Their shoulders slumped. Their patience ran watery thin, then out.

So, in 1962, after years of futile courtship, after years of being spurned, the VC reacted accordingly. They scrapped their tactics of friendly persuasion. They did what frustrated people do. They did it in the name of reason. They lashed out. They resorted to terror. It wasn't a blind slashing thing at all, a mindless thing. That would have been nasty enough. It was a solemnly-reckoned thing, a well-thought-out thing, a soul-searched thing. The VC decided it had to be terror. Then they started in.

They persecuted the highland people. They seized their meager supplies of rice and thousands of highland people starved. They executed hundreds of others. *Ratta-tat-tat. Ratta-tat-tat.* But the Viet Cong miscalculated. Their campaign of terror backfired. The hate it released, the hate it begot, proved more powerful than the fear and further alienated the tribes. It literally drove the tribesmen away. Whole villages of highland people picked up their pots and their straw mats and scruffy children and they vanished overnight.

The Viet Cong failed to win over the tribes, in part, because of the work being done by American Special Forces teams. The tribesmen trusted the rangy good-natured Americans as they could not the Vietnamese. They trusted the smiling open ways and open faces and the promise. The promise which the Americans had secured from Diem that the tribes would be granted autonomy if they allowed the Americans to send them up against the VC. The bad, bad VC. So that's what they did. They let the Americans send them up.

Perhaps you may wonder why they would go up against the VC and risk being haunted. Well, it was one thing to murder a man, but going to war was quite another; it was a noble enterprise and thus incurred no persecution from revengeful spirits.

So up they went. Not because they thought the Viet Cong were more bad than the ones in Saigon. Not because they believed in the Government's cause. They let the Americans send them up because it seemed the only way to guarantee their independence. To be free. To be left alone. That's all the people cared about. That's how their loyalty was secured. Of course, later, in '65, Saigon took back its promise of autonomy. But that came after what happened with Buon Yun and Buon Sop which happened in 1964.

The Americans moved from village to village and organized as they went. They treated the tribesmen paternally, affectionately, generously. They used the tribesmen to gather intelligence on local VC activity; to hunt down VC guerrilla bands; to block the paths along which cadres and supplies entered South Vietnam from Laos and Cambodia.

The VC found themselves backed to the wall by the stiff competition. Thus, when they had resorted to terror, it wasn't only because skits and speeches and juggling and acrobatics had failed. It wasn't only because their patience had run watery thin, then out. It was also to head the Americans off. When the terror backfired, it not only drove the tribes away, but also drove them deeper into American arms. Which made the VC apply more terror. Which drove more and more people away. The same highland people who had vanished overnight to escape the terror, they later turned up in Strike Force units organized by the Americans.

The Viet Cong didn't give up. They plugged away, shuttling between persuasion and terror. Dead sure that their way was right, that there was no other. Trying to make the highland people dead sure too. The Viet Cong yammered and hammered away; but more and more villages, like Buon Yun, were turning to the Americans.

In the case of Buon Yun, it was Special Forces Detachment A-123: eight stout-hearted men who arrived in Saigon in April 1964 and were then flown up north to Ban Me Thuot, capital of Dar Lac Province, the fiefdom of Colonel Quoc. From there it was onto the tree-lined drive which struck like a spoke from the center of town to the northwest, faltering into a dusty dirt road: deep rutted, pot-holed, the rusty-red powder caking the faces of the men and lingering, hanging high in the air after the passage of the jeeps. They passed Buon Yak, then the rubber plantation with its orderly rows of trees. They jolted along thru the wild places and finally to Buon Yun: to a silent, wary audience, stoney-faced and toeing the dirt; to a here and there grinning audience and the hysterical yelping of dogs.

They worked at winning the people over. They gave them guns that went *ratta-tat-tat*. They handed out rice. They treated the sick. And the people liked the guns that fired *ratta-tat-tat* and the rice and the strange medicine which seemed to work more consistently than the sacrifices prescribed by Y Blo.

They planted mines between the fences and organized the Strike Force platoons. They trained them, took them out on patrol. They sent them up against the VC.

The Americans were drawn to the people, touched by the people's trusting smiles, by their affection and gratitude. They felt at home. They felt the red grit work into their skins. They felt they had lived all their lives in Buon Yun. That Buon Yun was where they would live out their days.

There was a double meaning here that wasn't lost on Captain Yancy. It had to do with three events, all unwelcome, that followed one upon the other. Perhaps we should begin with the party at Y Bun's. The party had been to celebrate the good news Y Blo had brought from the spirits; and, less so, because a patrol had made contact with the VC and winged one or two. Outside the long-house of Y Bun, the night spirits rustled about their business. Inside, all was warm and snug: the drummers pounded on their drums, the fire crackled, the lantern hissed, and witching shadows danced on the walls wherever they hadn't been blackened by smoke. The drummers pounded in celebration, but also pounded to hold back the night, to check it from rushing into the house and swallowing up the people inside. A barking deer barked from the forest's edge, but nobody heard for all the drumming. They sat in a circle drinking rice wine from a long reed straw; and Sergeant Moon explained to Y Blo how voodoo worked; and Captain Yancy politely declined Grandmother Pan's invitation to dance; and Plunket's stomach rebelled at the wine; and Fritz was hoping the girls would show so he could have a look up their skirts. It was then, and perversely, that Sergeant Lovelace reached into his mouth and took out his teeth, all thirty-two hinged together, and turned to the elder by his side. He palmed the teeth in his freckled hand, then snapped them in front of the elder's nose, threatening— *Grrrrrh!*—to bite it off. The village elder came undone, and so did the party.

A chorus of oohs! and ahs! filled the room when the others saw Sergeant Lovelace's teeth. Snap! Snap! Ooh! Ah! Some of the people were afraid. They looked at the teeth as evil things with a will of their own. Others, younger and not so uptight, wanted to try on the teeth for themselves or just to snap them. They oohed and ahhed and clamored and begged, but Sergeant Lovelace was not letting go. The people gaped, the people pointed. They clicked their tongues, they wagged their heads. It was a miraculous sight. No one among them had ever seen such teeth before.

Y Blo the sorcerer leaped to his feet, mad as can be. He didn't think Lovelace's teeth were so hot, that they were so miraculous. *Not* like the spirits dancing. In fact, they were a calamity. "Why do you ooh and ah!?" cried Y Blo. "Fools! Monkeys! Centipedes! To lose a tooth while toasting the spirits is a bad sign. To lose all the teeth is many times worse. A calamity! Oh! Woe! Idiots! Something bad will come of this—!" It miffed Y Blo that he had been upstaged by the teeth, but nonetheless their meaning was clear. Lovelace, unaware of the facts, snapped his teeth a few times for good measure before he placed them back in his mouth. "Oh! Woe! Calamity!"

"But, Y Blo, you said the signs were good."

"That was before his teeth came out!"

"But he put them back, all of them."

"The teeth came out, didn't they!?"

The people had to agree with Y Blo.

"Mark my word! Something will happen!"

And wouldn't you know, but right then and there, an explosion ripped thru the stillness outside and the drumming within, and sent them racing for their guns; but it was only a foraging pig that had broken thru the fence and gotten itself blown up.

"It was the teeth!" the people had shouted.

"It's just the beginning!" shouted Y Blo.

"What about my pig!?" cried the fellow whose pig had blown itself up.

"What about his pig!?" cried Y Blo.

"The teeth!" they all shouted. "It was the teeth!"

But it *wasn't* the teeth, it wasn't the warning of Y Blo that unsettled Yancy. He couldn't disregard the warning, the spookish effect it might have on the people. Nor could he ignore the grumbling of the fellow whose pig had blown itself up. But these were problems Yancy could live with. No, it wasn't the teeth at all. It was that he was wanted dead or alive. It was the leaflets.

WANTED DEAD OR LIVELY

. . . . (Photograph) . . . .

10000 Piasters

Captain Vernon Yancy, 29, Renegade, Willing lackey of the Washington-Saigon clique, Fascist mad-dog rapist murderer of the people, With small head washy-blue eyes and hair the yellow of buffalo stalings, Blood-slurping monster, Dog and pig, Mountain and social climber, Spreader of filth and Capitalism, All-together beast, West Point pervert. 10000 Piasters for head or nose or ear or hand of this criminal. If you acquire, hold in safe place. We will be coming to collect.

(SIGNED) *Executive Committee, National Liberation Front,*
Dar Lac Province. . .

The People will be avenged!

The leaflets were all more or less the same, full of sprightly expressions. Some had some and others had others; it didn't seem to make much difference which had which. It was like whoever had written them had taken a lot of pride in his work and hadn't wanted to be repetitious.

They were written in English and Rhadé. Badly written, it seemed to Yancy, but that could have been the translation, of course. They were mimeographed on thin oily paper and some were very hard to read. The men were mostly surprised and amused, tho no one especially cared for his likeness. But only Yancy was truly angry.

They sat in the ops hut exchanging leaflets, reading each other's notices, the ones they had found tacked to the fence the morning after the party. Plunket full of appreciation, Plunket quick with witty remarks. Jasperson mumbling that his mammy would give him what for if she knew her son had washy-blue eyes and hair the yellow of buffalo stalings. Lovelace goddamning about the stinginess of the reward, that he was worth more than 10000 Pees. Goodbody wanting to get one thing straight, that he wasn't a West Point pervert too, and Yancy sneaking him dirty looks. Moon wondering if the writer was a humorist, or if he were truly sickened by them, if it had been a trial for him to write about such desperadoes.

"Let's have a public trial!" said Fritz. "A People's Court."

"Try him!" said Lovelace. "Then shoot him dead!"

"I'll be the magistrate," said Fritz. "And you, sir," he said to Lieutenant Plunket, "you can be Captain Yancy."

Plunket agreed, to Yancy's distress.

"And I'll be the public!" said Sergeant Goodbody, catching the spirit.

"I'll be the public, too!" said Lovelace.

"We'll need a defense," said Sergeant Fritz.

"What for? He's guilty," said Jasperson.

"Guilty or not," replied Sergeant Fritz.

"I'll defend the criminal pig," said Jasperson reluctantly.

The real Captain Yancy winced.

"One more thing," said Sergeant Fritz. "We need a clerk to write things down."

"Triple Threat! How about him?"

"Read the charges," said Fritz to the mute, who went on fixing breakfast. "Never mind, it's plain as day. He's a monster, all right. Just look at him." The public drew closer for a look. "Well, what do you say?" he asked of Plunket, there in the guise of Captain Yancy.

"You've got me wrong."

"Then why have you come upon us?" asked Fritz.

"I was invited," answered 'Yancy.'

"I didn't invite you," said Magistrate Fritz, who then asked the public if one of them had.

"*I* didn't invite him," said Sergeant Goodbody, slanting his eyes.

"Nor *I*," said Lovelace, grinning as dumbly as he could.

"There's nobody here," said the magistrate, "who seems to have invited you."

"Well, somebody did!" insisted 'Yancy.'

"Write that down," said Fritz to the mute. "Write that he's being obstinate."

"*Somebody* did," repeated 'Yancy.' "Otherwise I wouldn't be here."

"And now that you are, why do you slurp our blood, you monster?"

"I haven't slurped anyone's blood. I don't even like the taste," said 'Yancy.'

"He doesn't like the taste," said defense.

"Why have you murdered, and why have you pillaged, and raped our women?"

"What are you talking about!?" said 'Yancy.' "I haven't had any time for women."

"And how *do* you spend your time?"

"I help to keep Vietnam free."

"From whom?" asked Fritz.

"From *you*!" answered 'Yancy.'

"*I'm* Vietnam!" said Magistrate Fritz. "*You're* the one whose skin is pink."

"And whose eyes are washy-blue!"

"And whose hair is the yellow of stalings!"

"*I'm* Vietnam!" repeated Fritz. "And so are they!"

"*We're* Vietnam!" chorused the public.

"Are you helping to free us from ourselves?"

"You don't understand," said 'Yancy' in exasperation.

"Oh, we understand, all right, that you're an all-together beast."

"I'm no beast, not even part."

"It says so right here," said Magistrate Fritz, holding the leaflet for all to see.

"It says so, but—"

"Then you confess?"

"He confesses," said Jasperson.

"Wait!" cried 'Yancy.'

"It's good you've confessed," said Magistrate Fritz.

"I haven't confessed to anything!"

"Would you rather be shot?"

"I confess."

"Very well," said Magistrate Fritz, "but now you must denounce some others."

"Do I have to?"

"Yes, you do."

"Who should I denounce?" asked 'Yancy.'

"Anyone you wish," said Fritz.

'Captain Yancy' hesitated.

"Things will go better."

"Then I denounce Sergeant Lovelace for snapping his teeth."

"Anyone else?"

"And Sergeant Fritz—for coveting the Beckoning Virgin."

"Good," said the magistrate with a blush, "the criminal has confessed and denounced. Now he needs to be straightened out."

"Start with his head!"

"Send him to camp!"

Magistrate Fritz acknowledged the public, then turned to 'Yancy': "I sentence you to thought-reform camp."

"My thoughts don't need reforming!" said 'Yancy.'

"Would you rather be shot?" asked Fritz.

"I'll go," said 'Yancy,' "but what should I bring?"

"Sneakers, of course," replied Sergeant Fritz, "and seven changes of underwear."

It was then that the real Captain Yancy spoke up: "The pig! The leaflets! What next!? What the hell are you laughing about!?"

"Pardon us, sir, we meant no harm," said Jasperson.

"No harm at all," said Sergeant Fritz, thinking that Yancy was upset by being sentenced to thought-reform camp, by being spoofed.

"Sorry, sir," said Lieutenant Plunket, "it wasn't intended personally."

But that was just it, thought Captain Yancy, it *was* intended personally. Since only a few of the people could read, maybe one or two, he figured the leaflets were meant for *them*, the Americans; to frighten them off. He didn't care about thought-reform camp; it was the leaflets and what they implied that bothered him. Perhaps even then, while they were all laughing, the VC were planning something new, dangerous, something not so laughable. They would have to keep on their toes, Yancy's men. He had the sincerest regard for them. He worried over them constantly. It made him squirm to hear them laugh, they should have known better. That something was up. Or if it wasn't, that it would soon be. First the pig. Then the leaflets. Captain Yancy was fidgety, chewing on his dark visions. Pigs. Leaflets. What next? Goddamn Lovelace! Goddamn his teeth!

* * *

"It's close by!" ranted Y Blo. "They have to go!"

"What if they stay, but don't fly the plane?"

"To fly is their way."

"Maybe it's not as close as all that?"

"It's close by, I say. Close enough!"

"But if it's holding all that weight, wouldn't it be too strong?" asked Y Gar. "It couldn't be cut."

"Maybe it could and maybe it couldn't," hedged Y Blo. "Do you want to find out?"

No one answered.

"They have to go."

It was Y Blo who had called them together about the rope. As everyone knew, the earth and sun and moon and other heavenly things were held in place by means of ropes which A'de firmly grasped in his hands. Otherwise, they'd fall from the sky or drift away. What Y Blo didn't know was exactly where the rope came down, where it was secured to the earth. Wherever it was, it couldn't be far; for weren't they A'de's favorite children and wouldn't he want them to scamper up first should he ever summon men to his side? The rope was close by, figured Y Blo, and therein lay the trouble. He feared that some American plane would shear it in two.

It was rare for Y Blo to call a meeting. He normally was quite aloof, for when one communes with the spirits, he surely cannot bother himself with worldly affairs. It's not for sorcerers to wipe their noses and hitch up their breechcloths and get in there with the rest of us, scrabbling for bits of happiness. Sorcerers move on the edge of the circle, stepping in only when something goes wrong with the natural order—to set it right, to undo the damage done by men; or, perhaps, to forestall it.

There was a practical reason, too, for Y Blo's antisocial behavior: much of a sorcerer's power lay in the mystery that enfolded him, much of his effectiveness came from the blackness about him. The less that was seen and known of Y Blo, the more mysterious he seemed, the deeper the black. And so Y Blo skulked here and there, doing secretive things, maintaining his distance.

Being a sorcerer, Y Blo was also crotchety—for leading a life apart from others made him impatient with their ways, and hard to please, and with an air of righteousness. And having one ear he interpreted as another sign of his mission—one less ear to hear the stupid prattle of men, for the spirits are heard from inside out, from the heart, and not from some hole in the side of one's head.

When Y Blo did consent to sit among men, as he sat now, he was fierce in his enthusiasms and bitter at those who failed to share them wholeheartedly. He expected others to feel exactly as he did, and was very miffed if they didn't. But he wasn't without his warmth and even sense of humor, tho his warmth was slow to kindle and fast to expire, and his humor was a quirky thing, intelligible only to him, but woe if you didn't laugh!

It was no laughing matter about the rope. Nothing could be more serious. If the world were cut loose to tumble thru space, what good would the Americans be? It would mean the end for everyone. Were the people so dumb? Why couldn't they see?

"Why can't we see it?" asked Y Gar.

"Huh!? Eh!?" said Y Blo with a start.

"If it's so close, then why can't we see? It should be a pretty thick rope."

"The rope is old," explained Y Blo, "and it's been rained upon many years."

"What of that?"

"So now it's thinner than it was. Now it's weaker."

"Maybe it isn't made of hemp."

"Maybe it's made of something stronger."

"We don't know," cautioned Y Blo.

"I'm old," said Y Gar, "and I've been rained upon many years, but *I'm* not about to fall apart. *I'm* not about to unravel, am I?"

You might have thought that Y Gar would have sided with Y Blo; he was as much the traditionalist. He was one of the few who hadn't been taken with the team, who hadn't been impressed. He was one of the few who had, since their coming, avoided all the excitement. Like Y Blo the sorcerer, Y Gar the hunter kept to himself. But, unlike Y Blo, Y Gar wasn't a crusty old bastard. On the contrary, Y Gar had a smile for everyone. He patted the children on their heads. He joshed with all the handsome young girls. He gossiped soberly with the men at night when the evening meal was done, and the fire crackled and spit, and the shadows gadded about on the walls. Y Gar wasn't stuck up or antisocial. It was just that he liked to tend his own business during the day, in the old way, just as he had always done.

What Y Gar always did was go hunting each morning or whenever his larder was bare. Sometimes Y Gar hunted monkeys and sometimes he hunted wild boar, but mostly Y Gar hunted barking deer. Their meat was sweeter and they were easier to hit. Y Gar was successful almost as often as he was not, which was really pretty successful when you consider what he used: a crossbow carved from suju wood. It wasn't a weapon of the highest caliber.

One of the reasons he was successful half the time was because Y Gar consulted the birds. Before he set out on a hunt, he would enter the forest and call to them, then listen carefully to their replies. A reply from the left was a good omen, but one from the right was very bad, portending harm from falling trees or from *m'klaks* and maybe death. No bird calls at all meant simply an unsuccessful hunt. There had to be two calls from the left: one for approval and one to confirm.

Sometimes it took many days before the bird calls were favorable. When omens were bad, Y Gar would go home, set down his crossbow and smoke his pipe. He would go home and smoke, then return to the forest and call the birds as often as five or six times a day, until they answered him favorably. If the birds remained silent or boded ill, Y Gar would resort to another rite to speed the approval of the spirits. He would stand there at the edge of the forest, plant his feet firmly, cross his arms, throw back his head and then declare: "I absolutely wish to go hunting and have success and not be leveled by falling trees. So hurry and sing. Sing! Sing! And from the left, please. I won't leave until you do!"

Y Gar was a traditionalist, but he wasn't blinded by jealousy as was Y Blo. He knew that the rope would have to be thick, pretty thick, to hold up the world, and therefore couldn't be cut in two.

"You're all pretty thick," sneered Y Blo, "not to see the danger we're in."

"*I'm* not thick," said Grandmother Pan. "Speak for yourself!"

"Maybe if we make them promise," said Y Bong, "to not cut the rope."

"How can you trust them?" said Y Blo. "They promised to honor the Beckoning Virgin."

"Well, haven't they?" asked Grandmother Pan.

"The one they call Fritz, I saw him leer."

"You've given her a pinch yourself."

"What!? Eh!? I've done no such thing!"

"*I* trust them," said Y Bong. "And, anyway, it's their world too."

"It's their world too!" mimicked Y Blo.

"They wouldn't cut it loose," said Y Bong.

"What do they know!?" cried Y Blo. "What do they care!?"

"They care enough," said Grandmother Pan, "to put up with you."

"I'm not so hard to get along with."

"Listen to him!" said Grandmother Pan. "You ruined the party."

"*I* did!? It was the beet-faced one and his teeth."

"*I* trust them," said Y Bong. "We're all together, aren't we?"

Y Bong was a good-natured, trusting fellow, perhaps too much so where his wife was concerned, for she was a cheat. He was an obliging fellow, open to all, and accepted everyone else at their face. He was also one of those ill-beset souls, unlucky in one small thing after another. He was constantly stepping out of his boots, and his hearth always seemed to smoke the most, and whenever a buffalo strayed thru the plantings, it was his field that got trampled. But he wasn't a man to ridicule; he was no oaf. He acknowledged fate, and laughed at himself when the fault was his, and he gave the spirits their due. Let the spirits have their joke! Y Bong would say—so long as *he* had the heart to make light, and iron to work, and a dutiful wife at home.

He had joined the Strike Force out of duty, and because so had everyone else. He was puzzled by the Americans: they were a fidgety lot to him, always hustling from place to place; and they tried to show that they belonged, that Buon Yun was their home, but they were only guests, of course; and they looked you straight in the eye, till sometimes it wasn't polite anymore, yet shied from sizing up themselves, how overly confident they were. Y Bong was puzzled, but he committed himself to them as everyone had —almost everyone. He liked having his picture taken, and he liked playing volleyball, and most of all, he liked being paid for dressing up and tromping thru the woods.

Tho Y Bong liked these things, he no doubt would have been just as happy back at his forge, ironsmithing as usual, airing the coals with a pig-bladder bellows, hammering out sickles and knives from old shock absorbers that he had scavenged in Ban Me Thuot, braving the sparks. Once he even made some jewelry for his wife in the shape of a heart, and a lucky amulet for himself which didn't seem to do much good. But tho Y Bong was the most advanced technologically in all Buon Yun, it didn't mean that he doubted the least about the rope. Yet, being the trusting soul he was, he trusted the Americans and knew they wouldn't cut it in two.

"*I* trust them," repeated Y Bong.

"You trust too many," said Y Blo.

"And what's that supposed to mean?" asked Grandmother Pan.

"Everyone knows," murmured Y Blo.

"What does everyone know?" asked Y Bong.

"That Y Blo's an old sourpuss, is what!"

"Enough!" cried Y Bun, silencing them. "We should weigh the stakes."

"What stakes, Y Bun?"

"Weigh them how?"

"What do you mean?"

"I mean which is worse: that maybe they might cut the rope—or for us to stand naked before the VC?"

"If they cut the rope, it's the end of the world."

"If the VC come, that will be our end too."

"It's the end for us in either case," said one of the elders, but nobody heard.

"Don't you worry about the VC. The spirits will keep us," promised Y Blo. "I'll ask them myself."

"The spirits aren't enough anymore," said Y A'dham.

"Aren't enough!?" thundered Y Blo.

Y A'dham lowered his eyes, but he wasn't afraid.

"Aren't enough, you godless lout!?"

"The stakes!" said Y Bun. "We were weighing the stakes."

"He isn't godless," said Grandmother Pan. "He's a nice young man."

"It's the end in either case," repeated the elder, the one who had almost lost his nose to Lovelace's teeth.

"The end, Y——?"

"Yes, what do you mean?"

"Even if they don't cut the rope, it won't be the same."

"What won't, Y——?"

"Our ways, of course."

"Of course!" said Y Blo. "Already the girls are covering up."

"It's not so bad," said Grandmother Pan. "Maybe I should cover up too."

"You!?" said Y Blo to Grandmother Pan. "What for? They're all dried up."

Her eyes ablaze: "Maybe you like to ogle the girls, maybe that's it, you randy old goat!"

"The stakes!" said Y Bun. "We were weighing them."

"They should stay," said Y A'dham. "The Americans should."

Y A'dham was a sturdy young man with a well-shaped head and glowering eyes and shoulders that swung from side to side as he barged your way. He was smart in a dull sort of way and spare with his words and very brave. He had always been first at whatever he did: at shimmying up the highest trees and making the funniest monkey sounds, or swimming the river when it was coldest, or throwing stones farthest; and when he grew up, at drinking more rice wine than anyone else, or borrowing another man's wife, usually Y Bong's. Yet he wasn't a burly-minded fellow; he didn't throw his weight around or raise his voice when he wanted people to know he was there, and no one could have been any nicer to the mute. And it's not that he was belligerent. But he did have a soldierly way about him, and a penchant for leading others, and a need to be admired. He naturally had a lot of pride.

It had all added up to a thwarted young man, and the trouble was lack of acknowledgment. Y Bun was acknowledged in secular matters, and Y Blo in matters regarding the spirits. Grandmother Pan told the funniest jokes and Y M'dhur told the best stories, outlandish tales from Vietnamese folklore which caused the people to shake their heads and goggle their eyes and choke with laughter. Y Bong was the foremost craftsmen of all and Y Gar the best hunter, relying on patience and wiliness if no longer as fit as Y A'dham.

What was there for Y A'dham? He wanted to be acclaimed for something; he wanted to be acknowledged too. But nothing was left; all the honors were taken. He was proud but he had no feats to boast of, for he was too young to have fought with the French. No glorious past, no prospects ahead. His eyes had taken on that glower; his walk a desperate gait.

So when the Americans came to Buon Yun and organized the Strike Force platoons, it was like a godsend. The Strike Force had to have its leaders and who better qualified than Y A'dham to lead the first platoon. Wasn't he the strongest and fleetest and bravest of all the young men of Buon Yun? And so you might say that Y A'dham had the greatest stake in A-123.

"They've got to stay," said Y A'dham. "The rope will hold."

"How come it doesn't get twisted up?" asked Rhadeo.

What did Little Rhadeo mean, and what was he doing there anyway? He was just a boy.

"Moon told me that the world goes around, that it spins like a top. So how come we don't get dizzy?"

This was foolishness, of course; but then why had Moon said such a thing?

"How come it doesn't get twisted up?" he asked again.

"There *is* no rope," said Y M'dhur. "*That's* why it doesn't."

The silence was total. No one stirred. This was going much too far.

"None at all," said Y M'dhur, who seemed undistressed by his revelation.

They stared at him. They feared for him. *Oh, Y M'dhur, you half 'n half. What can you mean? Have you lost your head?*

Being a half 'n half didn't trouble Y M'dhur, not here in Buon Yun, except when it came to choosing a wife. His skin wasn't brown, but amber-colored, almost sallow, which hadn't pleased the young girls of Buon Yun, for they had their prejudices. But he was a considerate fellow, and hard-working too, and owned the fattest buffaloes, and so he had married well enough. And strange to tell, his color was the thing about him his wife had come to like best. She said it gave him a stricken look and, since she was otherwise childless, she took to constantly mothering him, which irritated him no end.

Aside from that, being a half 'n half in Buon Yun was fine with M'dhur. But there had been a time in Phu Dinh when being half this and being half that was worse than being nothing at all; which was often what he had wanted to be—to hide in some hole, or go up in smoke, or shrivel to the size of a pea. It had been a scandal, he later learned, when his father had brought home a Montagnard bride. "Pig! Monkey! Cannibal!" the people had jeered, taunting his mother as she passed, and making signs behind her back, and knowingly nodding to each other. And as *he* grew up and cringed down the one dirt lane of the village, or trudged along the paddy dikes, it was always Pig! Monkey! and Cannibal! So after his mother had died from the flu, and his father from shame, Y M'dhur found his way to Buon Yun where his mother had family.

Buon Yun was now his: its people, its grit, its way with magic, its hopes, its fears, its legends. But much as he was part of Buon Yun, he knew that we were up there by ourselves, that no one was holding us in place. It came with being half civilized. He knew that there was no rope.

"There's no rope," he said again.

"No *rope*!?" cried Y Blo.

"What do you mean?"

"He has only two hands," replied Y M'dhur.

"So?"

"So what?"

"What about all the stars?" said Y M'dhur. "If he's holding up the world by a rope, then he's using ropes with the stars as well. And since there's thousands of stars all around, and since he only has two hands, it must be some other way."

"Some *other* way!?" snorted Y Blo.

"Some way without a rope," said M'dhur.

"Impossible!" shouted Y Blo. "It's always been ropes!"

"Impossible!" said Y A'dham.

"Impossible, for sure," said Y Gar.

While the others disagreed with Y Blo and welcomed support, they were uneasy with Y M'dhur's news, with his reasoning. It was more than they wanted to hear.

"What about the stars? What about two hands?" said Y M'dhur.

"Oh, he has helpers," said Y Gar.

"There are helpers!" shouted Y Bong.

"Helpers, for sure!" cried Y A'dham.

They smiled at each other with relief. For a moment things had looked bad.

"There's some other way!" insisted M'dhur.

"Feh! Foo!" huffed Y Blo. "That's what comes from living with yellows."

"There's no other way," said Grandmother Pan, "but there's no need to worry either."

Grandmother Pan had an ache in her back and in one of her knees. She had trouble chewing and threading a needle and doubtless would have had a hard time doing the boogaloo. She had a bruise on one of her toes from kicking a pig in the ribs, and a crick in her neck from craning to see who was sneaking off with whom—usually with Mrs. Y Bong. She also had a roguish way of meeting you grin-on and peppery-eyed and poking thru your pockets for treats.

Grandmother Pan was a simple soul. She was happy to husk the rice each day, and bounce her grandsons on her good knee, and play an occasional prank on Y Blo, and share a quiet moment or two with her husband, Y Bun. She was satisfied with these artless things and had no need for politics. But the rope had become a political issue, and one which couldn't be dismissed. She had to take sides. So which was worse, she asked herself: the VC, or that they might cut the rope. She didn't have to think very long, and it had to do with cuteness. She thought that Plunket was kind of cute; and Yancy too, if somewhat shy; and Fritz was always good for a laugh; and she was very attached to Moon. It also had to do with spite. Y Blo had spoken against the team and she was against Y Blo. Not that she didn't respect Y Blo. She agreed that he knew his way with the spirits; and that he had served the village well; and there were times, not many of course, when she felt a perverse affection for him. But he took himself so seriously, which rankled her; and he treated her with disdain, which rankled more.

After all, she was the *polan,* the keeper of the ancestral fields; it was she who divided up the land and decided who farmed what. She was the midwife they called on whenever there was a difficult birth. And she knew all the village secrets, the loves and hates and grievances and how much everything cost. Her opinions counted for something, and not just because she was Y Bun's. Anyway, how could Y Blo be so sure of the rope, that it would be cut. Let him keep to his sticks and stones. Let him worry about the signs and not about flying planes. The planes, they were American business.

"They know their business," said Grandmother Pan.

"They don't know a barking deer from a tiger!" said Y Blo.

"Or how to listen for the birds," admitted Y Gar.

"Or how bad it was for me in Phu Dinh," complained Y M'dhur.

"Or when to keep their teeth to themselves," added the elder.

"They're good boys," said Grandmother Pan. "They wouldn't fly where they shouldn't."

"They weren't supposed to drink all the wine," grumbled Y Blo. "They could have left some."

"They know their business," she insisted.

"Then they should mind it and not mind ours. They almost squashed the mute."

Everyone looked at Triple Threat, hunched in the corner.

"He shouldn't have closed his eyes," said Y Gar.

"He shouldn't have lowered his head," said Y Bong.

"He shouldn't have run out there in the first place," said Y A'dham.

"They almost squashed him dead," said Y Blo. "They'll kill us, *all* of us, with their planes!"

Triple Threat looked back at them, smiling but understanding nothing, wondering if he had done something wrong. No one in Buon Yun knew his real name. The people had found him some years before in a VC camp. The VC camp had been deserted and so had he. They had found him huddling terrified and starving and waiting out his life. Since he was mute, he hadn't been able to tell the people who he was or what he was or what he had been doing there. His chimp-like face—the flattened nose, the bony brows, the wild black inquisitive eyes—had touched the people. His whimpering too, his innocence, his nakedness. So they had brought him back to Buon Yun where he lived ever since, where he had a corner of his own in the house of Y Bun. Some people said that the VC had used the mute to haul water and to chop wood and to go first if there were mines. That the VC had left him behind because he hadn't been worth his keep, because there hadn't been any mines. Others maintained that the VC would never have made him go first, he was so fetching in his way. That he had probably been a pet which the VC had somehow forgotten. In any case, mines or not, he came to be treated like a pet by the people of Buon Yun.

Triple Threat had a woebegone head, a chunky body and spindly legs. When he was angry, he flailed his arms every whichway and jumped up and down and croaked his displeasure. When he was happy or amused, he slapped his chest and jumped up and down and laughed with a wheezing gurgling sound as if he were gasping for breath. He was a master of pantomime. He had a great repertoire. Whenever he had something to say or to describe, whenever he sought to attract attention, or to point out some interesting thing, he would gesture for all he was worth, with great brimming overflowing excitement.

There were some in Buon Yun, among the snappish older women, who were always scolding Triple Threat for this or that, he seldom knew what. There were some, among the young boys, who were always teasing and mocking him, who made him the constant butt of their jokes. It wasn't plain meanness; it was intended harmlessly. But tho he knew it was harmlessly meant—tho Triple Threat knew his place was secure, that he was loved, that all the people of Buon Yun accepted him into their family—his nerves were nonetheless worn by the scolding and teasing and mocking. He was easily alarmed and upset and often frustrated, but there were the chickens.

The scrawny chickens of Buon Yun. He took his frustrations out on them. They were the only things in Buon Yun which he could scold and tease and mock, which he could boss. He had always treated the chickens mean, but he had been treating them meaner still since the cargo plane had buzzed Buon Yun on the day before Easter last.

On that fateful day, the cargo plane had released a bundle over the cleared field north of the village which served as a drop zone and as a helicopter pad. Even before the chute caught air and billowed into red and white, Triple Threat was off and running, straight for the center of the field. He stood there waiting, with his yes closed, and with his sad head tucked into his chest, and everything covered by his arms. He didn't hear the warning shouts. The bundle, a wooden crate, landed hard on its edge and split open close by Triple Threat. He opened his eyes, untucked his head, assessed that he was still alive, and went to investigate the strange thing that had popped from the crate. He pointed and grunted and jumped up and down. He was thunderstruck, unmanageable for the rest of the day. And ever since, whenever a scrawny chicken squawked by, he not only kicked at it more viciously than he had before, but also thumbed his nose at it, something he had learned from Plunket. He lashed out and thumbed his nose at them, for now he knew that, wherever his friend Plunket came from, the chickens grew half a meter long and very cold.

"And not only the mute," grouched Y Blo. "They blew up the pig."

"It broke thru the fence."

"It's dead, isn't it? The same with us, the same with our world."

"A pig's not the world," said Grandmother Pan.

"The pig's just a start," said Y Blo.

"It wouldn't have been a tasty pig."

"Yes, Y Blo, he was old and tough."

"Or a useful one," chuckled Grandmother Pan. "He couldn't do it anymore."

"*You're* old and tough," said Y Blo, "and I doubt that you do it anymore. Does it mean that we should blow you up?"

"I'm not so old!" said Grandmother Pan, "and how do you know if I do it or not?"

Grandmother Pan glared at Y Blo and he glared back and the air was tense.

"Yes, how do you know?" asked Y A'dham. "Y Bun's a pretty useful fellow."

Everyone laughed, including Y Bun. "Never mind the pig," he said. "A pig's not so important."

The remarkable thing about Y Bun was that he could sit back quietly and still command attention. He didn't have to make a show of racking his brain; he didn't have to draw himself up and make coughing sounds. He had a presence, an eminence, that made you

take notice; and when he spoke, everyone listened. His integrity
was known to all, and he never misused his authority as chief of
Buon Yun, not even when Grandmother Pan brought on trouble—
offended Y Blo or pried where she shouldn't, and he had to bail
her out. Grizzled, straight-backed, tall for a tribesman, Y Bun cut
a very imposing figure. He had a clean uncluttered face and half
his teeth, which was a wonder.

What was also a wonder was that Y Bun was still alive. There
was a poison the people used on their arrowheads. It was made
from the resin of the kabang tree, with red pepper added and centipede teeth to give it bite. This mixture was cooked, and stirred
now and then, until it became a shiny black goo. To test it for
strength, the hunters would open a cut on their hand, then place
a drop of the poison about an inch away; if the blood stopped
flowing, the poison was strong enough to kill. Y Bun, being a
daring young man, would place the black poison closer to the cut
on his hand than any man—sometimes so close it seemed to touch,
which would have been fatal; and tho it was a more meaningful test
the farther away, Y Bun's daring was acclaimed.

Not only the poison, but there had been girls pledged to other
young men, and sometimes wives, with whom he had carried on
perilously, until he discovered Grandmother Pan. It was then that
Y Bun found himself as well, and he grew to understand how much
stronger it was to be quiet than loud.

In later years, there was the First Indochina War when he served
with the French as a leader of irregulars, receiving a shiny silver
medal of which he was very proud. For his gallant services, Y Bun
was also supposed to receive a pension from the French Government. Of course, he had no mailing address and therefore never
received any money. But mailing address or no mailing address,
Y Bun was held in great esteem, not only in Buon Yun, but
thruout the Rhadé nation. Even Y Blo deferred to him, if not
without some blustering.

Tho he didn't think the Americans were especially cute, as did
Grandmother Pan, tho, in fact, he thought they were sickly com-
plexioned, Y Bun had warmed to them just the same and felt that
Y Blo was making the rope too much of an issue. But since he

was a responsible fellow, since he deeply cared for his people, he would have preferred to be absolutely sure about them, that they wouldn't cut the rope. Alas! as he had come to learn, there were few things in life you could be absolutely sure of: dying was one—tho he hoped it wouldn't be for awhile—and that the sun would rise each day, and that Grandmother Pan would have something to say, or else be up to some mischief. Very few things, conceded Y Bun. There was always risk. It gave men a certain vitality, but lots of indigestion too. Of course there were those risks he had sought out willingly, even foolishly: like with the poison, or daring the spirits to strike him down for being too familiar with them; risks he had sought out when he was young and conceited enough to believe that a man could have his way. Then there were the other kind that all men faced, like it or not: that your woman might stray, or your son grow up a disappointment, or that the *m'klaks* might waylay you. And as you got older and less daring, it seemed that there were more of these. Yes, thought Y Bun, there were always risks and a man just had to live with them. But all the same, he wished he could be more sure of the rope: that the rope was thick enough, or not so close, or that they would know enough to respect it.

"They know enough to respect the rope," said Y Bun hopefully.

"Of course, they do," said Grandmother Pan.

"They know enough," agreed Y A'dham.

"They don't know a thing!" retorted Y Blo.

"They know as much as anyone."

"Less! They know less!"

"Give it up," said Y Bong to Y Blo. "Better to go along with them."

"I'm not going anywhere! They'll be our ruin!"

"Come on, Y Blo. We'll make them promise."

"Promises don't count," said Y Blo. "Just mark my word."

"Come on, Y Blo," entreated Y Bong.

"I'm not coming!" shouted Y Blo. "I'll do what has to be done!"

* * *

Sergeant Culpepper was the medic of A-123. He had served in Vietnam before, and before that in Laos. These tours had made him both glad and sad that he was a medic. He was glad that he could do his part to help the people, sad that he could not do more. He was sad because, day after day, week after week, he knew the misery of the people in a meaty bare-handed way which none of the others could. His fingers were constantly poking around in the soft rotted spots.

There was nothing rotted about Culpepper. He was cut square and hard, like a block of quarry stone; and ruddy-faced, with the healthy look required for one who would make others healthy too. But tho most of him was cut square and hard, his head drooped low with the weight of his sadness. That's how it seemed, or perhaps it was his large fleshy nose weighting Culpepper forward and down. He was a burdened, sorrowed man who didn't speak much, except with his eyes. They were always at odds with what they saw.

Of all the team, Culpepper had the most regular job, the most predictable. Each morning at eight, regardless of weather, regardless of Y Blo's vengeful eyes—Y Blo whose own practice had steadily dwindled—a score or more of villagers lined up for sick call. Very often the same villagers, tho not always with the same afflictions. They lined up before the dispensary in ragged file. The very routineness, the dailiness of that sad parade was what affected Culpepper most, not the emergencies.

Everyone sought out Sergeant Culpepper except Y Blo. The sorcerer snubbed him whenever Culpepper tried to be friendly. He went stalking by the dispensary whenever he couldn't avoid its path. He went hulking by and wrinkled his nose as if the place were contaminated. He bristled, he bared his toothless gums. Feh! Foo! What did someone not a *mjao* know about the *m'tao* and *k'sok* and how to suck out a calabash seed? What did he know about all the spirits which hovered and lurked, their peculiarities, and how to win their favor? What did he know about sacrifices, whether it should be chickens or pigs? What did he know about the prayers and in which direction and how many times? And how could he suck out the splinter of wood if he could not suck out the calabash seed? Feh! Foo! An American! What did he know about anything? Nothing! Nothing! There was nothing he could know. Y Blo hulked by, wrinkling his nose, glaring at his former patients. Beware!

Beware! he seemed to say, I'm going to sic the spirits on you.

There were times when Y Blo considered burning down the cursed dispensary. There were times he considered convening the spirits, all of them, and arguing for Culpepper's destruction and the other Americans. Which would have been a hard thing to do, for the spirits didn't convene just like that. And, besides, there was the medicine, Culpepper's venomous medicine. Y Blo would need some for evidence.

Sick call: a lineup of mangled and diseased. Waiting bravely for Sergeant Culpepper. Moving up to him one by one:

A man passing blood who asked if Culpepper's medicine was just as good as scorpion's urine, which was what Y Blo always prescribed, but which the man preferred not to drink, it was so bitter.

A granny hand in hand with her grandson, red-eyed, sightless from trachoma—the grandson, that is.

A man who complained of an aching belly; that the *m'tao* had entered his body, shooting him full of magic darts, and would Culpepper please pluck them out.

A child with galloping diarrhea whose mother asked if she should also sacrifice a chicken and five jugs of wine just to be sure.

Abcessed teeth so rotted thru they crumbled to powder when Culpepper gripped them with his forceps and tried to yank them out.

A baby with a wormy scalp who was also malformed. There was nothing Culpepper could do about that, the malformation. It was the work of the evilest of spirits. And even if Culpepper could have done something, the parents probably would have objected because then the spirits responsible would take it out on the next child.

A wasted young girl coughing blood.

A boy who didn't have a nose. It had been bitten off by a sow.

Captain Yancy with a bad head from the night before.

One break.

Two local infections.

Three grinding fevers.

A woman with fingers so gnarled and stiff that she could no longer feed herself or stuff tobacco in her pipe.

And there were more. Moving thru, one by one.

Culpepper worked methodically, with the interpreter by his side. Even so, it wasn't always easy to tell exactly where someone was pained and how. Culpepper worked patiently, telling jokes, trying to put the people at ease. And the people nodded and laughed at his jokes, altho they seldom got the point, even with the interpreting. Culpepper joking, trying to, questioning, tapping, probing with his meaty hands, administering. Culpepper sure-fingered but still bending needles on the leathery butts of the people with disgusting consistency. Culpepper muttering: Sure, sure, just as good as scorpion's piss—Keep him clean—This oughta' pluck those damn darts out—Keep him clean—No, no, no. No chicken, no five jugs. Yeah, well, go ahead, if it'll make you feel any better—Damnit, tell her to keep the kid clean.

It wasn't all grim. There were the pills. Red was the big favorite. But yellow and blue were popular too. The people thought up this and that, some of them, just so they could get the pills. They did a beautiful job of acting, having quickly learned which symptoms went with red or yellow or blue. How they loved the bright-colored pills! Which was strange. Because they couldn't understand how swallowing pills could do much good, they didn't taste awful like Y Blo's potions. When Culpepper saw what was happening, he ordered batches of sugar pills, all in the brightest colors. He knew they didn't swallow the pills, just collected them, maybe strung them as beads, but still sugar pills were cheaper than others. Sergeant Culpepper loved his people and he indulged them. His people, they loved Sergeant Culpepper and the bright-colored pills.

Moving thru, one by one.

Toward the end of the line, almost last, there was a man leaning on a staff, waiting his turn like everyone else. His trousers were torn, his eyes swollen shut; an ear hung loose from the side of his head; his nose was clogged with crusted blood. Just another casualty, that's how the others regarded him. Tho, at first, they had stared at him curiously because the man was not of Buon Yun but of Buon Sop. Worth a stare and nothing more. Just another sufferer. But not to Culpepper. He wasn't as toughened to suffering as the people of Buon Yun. As soon as he saw the man with torn trousers, he had him brought to the front of the line in spite of the grumbling.

The man with torn trousers had shot himself—in a way. He explained how to the interpreter who explained how to Sergeant Culpepper. It was like this: The man with torn trousers had a very old French gun. Many of the tribesmen did. And also very old ammunition, green and moldy. He used his gun when he went hunting and, until the day before, it had worked well enough. But the day before, after he had stalked a barking deer and prepared to bring it down, his old French gun had blown up in his face. The interpreter added that this often happened. Sergeant Culpepper nodded yes, that he had seen those old French guns and so could easily understand how the man with torn trousers had blown up his face. Culpepper nodded but there was something not quite right. Something too sharp about the wound to have been caused by a blown-up gun. Something spooky, Culpepper thought. He treated the man. He sewed back his ear, cleaned out his nose, wrapped his head in bandages. He made the man with the bandaged head go rest in the shade before returning to Buon Sop.

When sick call was done and the people had gone, Sergeant Culpepper slumped down at his desk, and he thought. Culpepper thought about scorpion's piss and how a sacrifice never hurt and magic darts and why they didn't keep the kids clean. He thought about his friend, Y Blo, who wasn't his friend and wouldn't be, and wished that Y Blo didn't take it so hard. He thought about the bright-colored pills and how they would look strung together as beads. He thought about how there were plenty of doctors, Vietnamese doctors, if only they'd come to Vietnam from Paris or wherever they lived. He thought and thought and sprang to his feet just like he had seen a ghost!

That was it! He had seen nothing—or rather he had seen empty spaces. The stacks were wrong; the medical supplies were short. At least so it seemed to Sergeant Culpepper who was a very organized man. A gap peeked here, a gap peeked there, unnoticeable except to him. There were bottles where boxes should have been, and boxes where bottles. Hey, wait! What's all this? Or is it

me? Whoa, Culpepper, just hold on! Sergeant Culpepper closed
the gaps. He reshuffled the bottles and boxes. He was very annoyed
with himself. It wasn't like him to have set things awry. It wasn't
like Sergeant Culpepper at all, but he supposed he had. Too much
thinking, that was it. Too much thinking lately.

Goddamn, he thought, how this country stinks! It stank bad
before the war, and afterwards, whenever that comes, the country
will probably go on stinking. The war, the bloody rinky-dink war,
it only made things harder. A little harder for many people. A
whole lot harder for some people. Terribly harder, tragically
harder, but only harder. This village, Buon Yun, it was like all the
others. Only it was luckier. Because he was there. To fix the poor
bastards who lined up each morning. And only the ones who hurt
real bad, they lined up. Except, of course, for the pill collectors.
But Culpepper knew that all the others were hurting too. That
life in Buon Yun was not picturesque. That it was a shame. That
it was a goddamn catastrophe.

And who gave a damn? Not the Government in Saigon. Hell,
no, not the Government! All the Government cared about was to
remain the Government. Sure, sure, fight the Reds. But for whom?
Not for the people of Buon Yun. Not for the people anywhere.
Only for the Government. So it could remain the Government.
Goddamn right! Yes, sir! He knew. There was only one way to
fight the VC. One proper way. To make things better for the
people of Buon Yun. For the people everywhere. But then the
Government couldn't remain the Government. Not like it had always been. It would have to change a bit. Which is just what it
didn't want to do. All the Government wanted to do was not to
change, to remain the Government just like it had always been
and maybe a little more. And here we are, trying to do the people
good. And how are we trying to do them good? Why, thru the
goddamn Government which doesn't want to do anyone good except itself, that's how. Hell, no, not the Government, it didn't care.
Only guys like himself gave a damn. And maybe, just maybe, the
Viet Cong. Altho the goddamn Viet Cong, they were much too
hungry.

Culpepper was worried that no one cared. He was also worried about the supplies, how they had been shuffled and the gaps. He assumed that he had been the one, but he couldn't swear. Damn, now they were going fast! The sulfa drugs especially. Faster than he had realized. Well, just what the hell could he expect in such a stinking country. Fast, fast, going fast, yes; but something else. Culpepper was leery, uneasy that maybe it *hadn't* been him—what with the blast, and then the leaflets, and the wound which looked too sharp, and now with the gaps and the shuffling around. Culpepper didn't have the willies, it was still too soon for that. But there was a certain spookiness; he felt it haunting Buon Yun.

△ BUON SOP
☆ ──────────────────────────
△ ──────────────────────────
　──────────────────────────

Sergeant Moon sneezed, then he locked tight. He stood as still as a river run dry. He held his breath. He didn't dare move. Not even his ribs. It would have been all over for him. It was gray dark. And the pounding was coming from every direction. Loud, but not too loud, and very steady. Thru the gray dark. And the voices, but not so much them.

Moon didn't dare move, not even his ribs, for as long as it took the spirits to calm. He knew that to sneeze irritated the spirits and that, after sneezing, it was best to keep perfectly still until the spirits got over their anger, Rhadeo had told him so. But, tho he had sneezed, Moon was also in luck, because to sneeze in the early morning just before setting off to work insured good luck for the rest of the day. Rhadeo had told him that too. It was good he was setting off to work and not on a trip for, then, to sneeze would have meant bad luck, maybe even a tragedy, early morning or not.

Moon stood locked tight, he waited until the spirits recovered, then sneezed once more and had to wait all over again. He didn't *really* believe it was true, but he wanted to try it out just the same. He was like that about the spirits. Since he had sneezed harder the second time, he held still longer. He listened to the pounding.

Moon had sneezed because, even in May, there was a chill. The women saw Moon standing locked tight but thought nothing of it. They understood. They had heard his sneeze. Any other American locked tight like that, they would have wondered. But not about Moon. Moon was Moon.

It was the hour just before dawn and the women were out on the ledges pounding. They lifted from the backs of their legs, and from their hips, and from up along their sides. Their strong brown arms swung up, raising the pestles high, then brought them crash-

ing into the mortars. They labored hard. They didn't gossip. No
time for that. Only for pounding. Now and then they did take time
to yell at a child who was doing something he shouldn't or who was
wandering where he shouldn't, but usually they yelled as they
pounded. They yelled if the child were over five.

When the women saw Sergeant Moon unlock, a few of them
called out and beckoned to him from across the way. Tough and
stringy older ones with blackened teeth where they had teeth,
and great fetching grins, black teeth and all, on their withered faces.
They offered Moon their long wooden pestles. They offered to let
him try his skill at pounding the rice. Moon had pounded once
before to their great delight, you should have heard how they had
cackled and clapped their hands and doubled up. He had done it
for Grandmother Pan and all of Buon Yun had soon buzzed with
the story. Sergeant Moon was the only man to have ever pounded
rice in Buon Yun.

The women beckoned. They wanted to see Moon pound again.
But Sergeant Moon grinned and shook his head no, thanks just
the same. He preferred to stand there and watch the young girls,
now that he didn't have to lock tight. The young girls weren't so
stringy and tough, but were soft and round and had white teeth.
He watched the ironsmith's naughty wife too, Rhadeo had pointed
her out. Moon watched them and they watched him, altho they
tried not to let him know. He watched them until to have watched
any longer would have been the wrong thing to do. Even Moon
being Moon.

So Moon watched the buffalo boys instead, as they filed out the
gate. They worked and played in the river all day. And in spite
of this, or because of this, the boys were always covered with filth,
for it was a chocolate river. They sat on the fat black buffaloes,
and shouted and threatened the beasts with their sticks, and hoped
they would soon grow up. The boys wanted to join the Strike Force,
to be among men, with their own guns to clean, and with tactics to
argue about, and even canvas boots to wear. Moon had once
played with the buffalo boys. He had sat on the fat black buffaloes,
and shouted and threatened the beasts with his stick, as they
splashed in the chocolate river.

As a young boy, himself, Sergeant Moon had tinkered with toys, and drawn funny squiggles on steamy windows, and fought with his brothers, and read tales of other, luckier boys who had run off to sea, and dreamt of consorting with peg-legged pirates and having a parrot of his own, or of exploring Africa in spite of strange fevers and how dark it was and all that stuff. Moon growing and wishing and generally meeting the world to a draw. And, as he grew, his visions not changing, but just growing bigger and stronger like Moon. Growing up into a lean, straight young man with dark watching eyes and a mouth forever reshaping itself with his faraway thoughts. Moon the great dreamer. The great one for doing anything once. Fascinated by everyday things, but mostly by new things and also things you did only once. Exploring here, exploring there. Still fascinated, most of all, by the prospect of traveling to far distant places and living a far distant life. Somewhere new.

Whenever he was somewhere new, Sergeant Moon was never bored, for that was where he wanted to be. Yet, at the same time, in some niche of his brain, he was already thinking about somewhere else, some far distant place he hadn't yet been. He was always wanting to be somewhere new, even when he was. He was a forever questing, never quite happy fellow. Thinking his time had begun to run out from the very moment he had been born. All those fine grains sifting down, fast trickling down. It's trickling! It's trickling! he'd cry out inside. It's fast trickling down!

It was because of the trickling down that Moon had upped and joined Special Forces. Just so he could be in Buon Yun or some remote place like Buon Yun. To see what it was all about, how it smelled and tasted and felt. Moon's rapport with the villagers was a wondrous thing. Especially to Captain Yancy who wondered how he could get tight with them too. He could speak Rhadé almost as well as Grandmother Pan and Rhadeo and all the rest. But more than that, Moon had a genius. You could see it in his eyes if you knew how to look. It wasn't music or mathematics, nothing like that. His genius was in knowing what was going on in people's minds but mostly in their hearts. He visited people in their houses, Little Rhadeo took him around, and sometimes without Little

Rhadeo. He liked to go to Grandmother Pan's for her monkey kebabs. She was very generous with her kebabs, and with her possessions, and with other people's too, which had to do with her being a midwife. If a woman was pregnant and she was rich, Grandmother Pan always foresaw a difficult birth and thereby made the family promise a large sacrifice if the birth turned out normal. "It's best to be grateful," she said to Moon; "the spirits appreciate gratitude." And so did Grandmother Pan, who raised her own fee accordingly, adding that not only spirits should profit from the gratitude of the rich.

Moon not only went for her kebabs, but to watch her weave blankets. The blankets were how she passed most of her time, when Grandmother Pan wasn't making kebabs or pounding rice or up to some mischief, for weaving was a peaceful task that even kinky old fingers welcomed. She wove the finest blankets of all and taught Moon how to work the loom. He would sit at her feet and watch her weave, and all the puckish faces she made, and listen to the little jokes, and there was Triple Threat right up close and comical, watching too. Moon knew how they had once filed their teeth and he asked Grandmother Pan if it hurt and how it was done. "You bite on the wood," she had replied; "that keeps the jaws well apart. Then they take a sickle, the kind we use for cutting thatch, and file at the gum until the front four teeth are gone. The upper ones. It pained very much," said Grandmother Pan, "and there was blood; but a boy was a man and a girl a woman when it was done, and prettier too," and she smiled to show him all the better.

So he often went to Grandmother Pan's. But he went to other houses too. He joked with the men and argued tactics and how many fat black buffaloes to pay for a wife if she was pale-skinned and had dark eyes and she was strong. He honored the men. He teased back the old women who teased him first. He snatched looks at the young girls who snatched looks at him. He threatened to swat the buffaloes as good as any buffalo boy.

Moon was the youngest man on the team. He was always questioning Lovelace or Fritz or Jasperson and hearing them out very carefully. They treated Moon just like a kid brother. They told him this, explained that. They shared their funny experiences, their guarded secrets. They, all in all, took him under their wing. But Sergeant Moon was a loner at heart and his best friend remained Sergeant Moon, besides Little Rhadeo, of course.

Moon treated Rhadeo like a kid brother. He taught him to play the harmonica, and that he should never walk under a ladder, and how to wish upon the first star. Rhadeo taught Moon, in turn, that the bark of a barking deer was a bad sign, and that so was a turtle facing east, because Rhadé are buried facing east and the shell resembles their mounded graves. Round-faced Little Rhadeo, being so small and handsome and quick and full of good cheer, would have been hugged and squeezed to death by Moon and the other Americans had he been a girl. So instead they cuffed him whenever they could. Little Rhadeo returned their affection but, of course, most of all, he returned it to Moon.

Moon stood there and thought how much he liked Little Rhadeo, and he wondered what Rhadeo had meant about there being another M'bu and that you didn't have to wait. It had come up during Quoc's inspection, when Rhadeo had turned and said: "So they knew when to use a banana leaf and not to laugh! That's why they strut. But that was a very long time ago."

"Banana leaf?"

"They shouldn't keep reminding us."

"What about the banana leaf?"

"Once men and animals lived together and talked with each other and life was very wonderful. But then the flood came and all the creatures on earth were drowned. All except for a man and woman and two of every animal. They took refuge in a chest—"

"I thought it was a drum," said Moon.

"It was a chest," said Rhadeo, then he went on. "The chest floated on top of the water for seven days and seven nights. Then the man and woman heard a chicken clucking outside. The chicken was sent by the spirits. The chicken told them that they could come out—"

Moon wondered about banana leaves and where they fit in, much less M'bu.

"Soon the man and woman had no more rice and were very hungry, when they heard a tiny sound at their feet; it was an ant with two or three grains of rice in his mouth. The man accepted this gift from the spirits and planted the grains and, the next day, a great crop of rice covered the plain. This man, he was the grandfather of everyone," explained Rhadeo. "So there was rice. And life was almost as good as before. Except that, now, men stopped living with animals and talking to them, and grandfather poked up the sky too high for men to reach."

"Why did he do that?" Moon had asked. "It must have been nice to reach up and grab a star in your hand."

"Oh, it was an accident." And Little Rhadeo explained: "In those days the sky was so close to the earth that trees and bamboo couldn't grow very tall, and the moon was very close and hot—"

And fishes could nibble at the stars when the water rose.

"After the harvest, he took a pole to pound the rice and, while he was moving the pole up and down, he poked up the sky to where it is now. Grandfather was a very tall man."

"What about the banana leaf?"

"Some years later, grandfather learned to make wine from the rice and drank too much wine and fell down drunk. When his older son saw him there on the ground, naked and sleeping from too much wine, he began to mock his father. A younger son scolded his brother and covered his father with a banana leaf."

"Why did the grandfather drink so much wine?"

"It was the first time; he didn't know," said Rhadeo. "Anyway, when he woke up and learned what had happened, he took away his older son's clothes and chased him into the mountains. The older son founded the race of people who live in the mountains and have no clothes."

"And the younger son?"

"He founded the race of Vietnamese. And that's how we came to be different from them and why they strut."

"You should not have laughed."

"We should not have laughed," conceded Little Rhadeo, "but it has been many years with no clothes for just one laugh."

"It must have been cold and very hard."

"It was cold and very hard, but there was M'bu. He speaks to A'de on behalf of us."

"Who is M'bu?"

"A very great hunter."

"A greater hunter than Y Gar?"

"A much greater hunter than Y Gar." Then he explained about M'bu. "One day, while he was out hunting, M'bu killed a peacock which a serpent brought back to life by gathering moss from a magic tree and stuffing the tree moss into the wound. When this happened a second time, M'bu quietly followed the serpent and collected some of the moss. He stuffed it into the mouth of a dead man and, from then on, all dead Rhadé were brought back to life in this way—

"The news spread, distressing the gods, and they summoned M'bu and his magic tree up to the sky. After that, men could die again. But when they die, they seek out M'bu, who speaks about them to A'de and says a good word. A'de then allows them to stay in the sky where life is as it was in the time before the flood and when we laughed."

"But what about dew drops?" Moon had asked. "Isn't that where the ancestors are?"

"The ancestor spirits are in the sky and dew drops too. It's a wonderful place," said Rhadeo, "but you have to wait."

"Wait?" asked Moon.

"No one wants to die, of course."

Moon agreed.

"And sometimes the waiting is very hard—when it's cold and you don't have any clothes." That was when Rhadeo's face had lit up and he had said: "But there is another hunter M'bu and you don't have to wait."

And, as he said it, the trucks had roared off and so had Little Rhadeo, to pick up rocks with the other young men and hurl them after the speeding trucks which, by then, were out of sight.

Moon stood there and wondered about M'bu until it was time. Then he walked to the commo bunker and disappeared into the ground. He placed on his headset, tuned the receiver, flexed his wrist and adjusted the key. Then Sergeant Moon contacted Saigon and received the first message of the day which, when decoded, read out like this: FOUR MAYXX TO ALPHA ONE TWO THREE FROM

BRAVO TWO THREE ZEROXX PERMISSION GRANTED TO CONTACT
NOTABLES BUON SOP AND EFFECT RECRUITMENT BUON SOP INTO
CIDGXXCIDG PROGRAMXX COORDINATE WITH PROVINCE CHIEF AND
REPORT DEVELOPMENTS ASAPXX RE WANTED POSTERSXX FIRST
CASE DAR LAC BUT REPORTED NEIGHBORING PROVINCESXX TAKE
PROPER SECURITYXX ATTENTION LOVELACE PRICE SEEMS HIGH
ALSO LOVELACE HELEN WAITINGXX

* * *

    "What about the sniff-sniff!?" cried Old Wispy.

    "The what!?" cried Yancy.

    "The old man, he say what about sniff-sniff?"

    "What's sniff-sniff? What does he mean?"

    The interpreter shrugged.

    "What about the sniff-sniff!?" cried Old Wispy. *He was angry.*

    "What about the sniff-sniff!?" cried the others. *They were angry
too.*

    Three days after the blast and the leaflets, two days after Quoc's
inspection, one day after word from Helen, they left for Buon Sop.
Captain Yancy strode along forcefully, impressively. He breezed
along. His very fatigues seemed to fill out with purpose like sails
before a wind. Not only was he a purposeful man, but Yancy was
also a West Point man and carried himself rigidly straight. Perhaps
they had taught him at West Point that, if he inclined, his head
would topple off his neck and thunk to the ground. Tho it seemed
improbable, Captain Yancy was taking no chances. The thing
Captain Yancy remembered most fondly about West Point was
all the sports, the competition. He had not made the first team
of anything, or even the second, but still he had been a plucky
one.

    Captain Yancy was very proud, undeniably brave, and moderately intelligent. He was daring in action, except about his head
thunking down, but not in thought. He was properly unimaginative,
and conscientious, and competent, and would likely become a general as his father had been and his before and his and his it seemed
and seemed. He had a dimple on his chin like that of certain
movie stars who were rugged guys, and he took secret pleasure from

having it. His hair was cropped very close to his head and was, indeed, as the leaflet said, the yellow of buffalo stalings. His eyes were a watered shade of blue, sometimes clear, sometimes clouded over. He screwed up his blue eyes whenever he thought. He screwed them up especially tight if he knew that someone was watching. Yancy liked others to know that he thought, but not too much.

Captain Yancy was no martinet, but he expected the best from his men. Whatever his faults, Yancy, himself, always did his best. He had come to Vietnam full of Western notions and hopes about what was right and what was wrong, and how to do right and not do wrong, and not knowing what it was really about but thinking he did. He was big enough to acknowledge that maybe Vietnam had its different ways. Still he figured that if he just did his best, if he made sure that his men did their best, then everything would be okay. What else could a man do but do his best? He figured that, with diligence, things had to work out—unless, of course, there was something basically rotten about the whole shebang. Captain Yancy didn't believe, not for a moment, that there was anything basically rotten about the whole shebang. He couldn't imagine that such a thing was possible—the men who had sent him, they wouldn't have sent him if there were something basically rotten.

Captain Yancy was a well-meaning man. As he breezed along, he thought about his good intentions. He thought ahead to his talk with the notables of Buon Sop and about the benefits he would propose. He thought about what he would say to open the notables' eyes and raise their sights: to possibilities greater than spears and crossbows carved from suju wood. To guns. To automatic guns. The kind that went *ratta-tat-tat*. Yancy acknowledged that crossbows and spears had served Buon Sop adequately. But now he would offer them something better. So they could defend themselves properly. So they could be warm and snug. Surely the people wanted progress. Guns that went *ratta-tat-tat*. Surely they wanted a warm snug home. Yancy was very pleased with himself for bringing good, for insuring the people a warm snug home. Yancy breezing stiffly along.

"What about the clowns and the acrobats and the jugglers too!?" Old Wispy cried. They all cried.

"What!?" cried Yancy. "What do they want!?"

"The people, they talk what about clowns?"

"What about what!? What do they mean!?"

The interpreter shrugged.

"What about the clowns and the acrobats and the jugglers too!?" the people all cried.

Sergeant Jasperson moved along more fluidly, loose and easy. He moved like a winding mountain stream that knows its way but takes its time getting there. Jasperson knew how to pace himself. He flowed along in spite of the fact that he was hefty, solid and smooth like oiled walnut. This solid smoothness about Jasperson extended to his character. He was hard to ruffle and, like the tribesmen, he never did anything recklessly, or anything which didn't need doing. He was diligent but in his own way. Slow and steady, which vexed Captain Yancy, but he always got the job done. He had served in Vietnam before and knew that his kind of coolness was best.

So cool Sergeant Jasperson kept his own head and when he spoke, it was soft and sure. As the ranking enlisted man, he was responsible for the men. After Captain Yancy, of course. He never kicked ass, but instead gently chided, which always seemed to be enough. "Psychology," he explained to Yancy. "You gotta know just when to kick, and when not to kick, but to get them feeling bad all the same." The only one Jasperson ever kicked was Lovelace for kicking someone else.

As he flowed along, Jasporson wondered about Yancy's head, whether it would topple or not. He wondered about Culpepper's gaps, whether they had truly existed. He wondered about the wanted posters, if they were meant as more than a joke. He wondered about the blown-up pig, if Lovelace's teeth had really hexed them. He wondered about Colonel Quoc's warning that there were enemies everywhere, probably right under their nose. Jasperson flowed along in wonder, until the silence was suddenly shattered. The Strike Force soldiers, who had been quiet for most of the hike, began to point and chatter away as Buon Sop came into sight.

Buon Sop was smaller than Buon Yun. It was quieter, drabbier. None of its men wore uniforms, or lounged in the shade discussing tactics, or sat on the ledges cleaning guns. The pigs seemed less sleek. The chickens even scrawnier. The red dirt more brown. The sad impoverished routine more routine and more impoverished and sadder. Otherwise, they looked more or less alike, Buon Sop and Buon Yun.

After a fair amount of confusion, of gaping surprise and fears allayed, of summoning and running about, the meeting was finally organized. Yancy, Jasperson and the interpreter sat down to talk with the notables in the house of Y M'nung, chief of Buon Sop. There was muffled excitement, and tension lurking beneath the floor beams and smoldering in the thatch above.

"Tell them," instructed Captain Yancy, "that we come as friends. That we bring no harm. That we are the friends of all the Rhadé. Of Buon Yun and Buon Sop. Number one friends." Movies flashed thru Yancy's brain. The way they had powwowed with the Apaches and the Sioux. That this was the way. He was thrilled. "Okay? Tell them."

The interpreter told them. The notables waited. They didn't speak. They didn't nod. They didn't acknowledge in any way. They simply sat and waited for more. It was all very nice that Captain Yancy had come as a friend but something more was coming too. As he waited, it struck Y M'nung that Captain Yancy's hair was the yellow of buffalo stalings.

"Tell them," said Yancy unperturbed, "that we want to help."

The interpreter told. The notables put their heads together and buzzed, buzzed, buzzed. They cut in and out of each other's words, trying to drive their own points home. Yancy could only look and wonder. Jasperson too. Then Y M'nung spoke. He spoke to the interpreter.

"He don't understand what means *help*. Help for what? They don't need any kind of help."

Captain Yancy explained. He took his time. He let the people get used to his smell. *Apaches! Sioux! Yahoo! Whoopee!* "Tell them Viet Cong have been seen. Right around here, not far from Buon Sop. Ask if they saw the Viet Cong too. Ask if they're worried. And if they're not worried, ask why not. Okay? Got it? Go ahead."

The interpreter asked.

Heads together. More buzzing. Louder this time. Points pressed harder. Hesitation over something. Disagreement. Some for this and some for that and some not wanting any part. Everyone growing more upset and more excited, especially those wanting no part. The floor beams creaking tho they were thick and solid thru. Buzzing. Buzzing. Buzzing.

"What are they saying?"

"About three fingers."

"What does it mean?"

The interpreter shrugged.

This time, Y M'nung spoke to Yancy.

"Chief, he say what kind of help?"

"Tell him guns. We'll give them guns. That go *ratta-tat-tat*. Make the sound: *ratta-tat-tat!* First we teach how to use the guns. Then we give them the guns. To make them safe." *Guns, yes. But no firewater! Yahoo! Apaches! Sioux!* "Ask him again, ask the chief if they saw Viet Cong."

More conferring. Angry voices being raised. Calmer voices trying to hold down the angry ones. Cases argued for and against. Creaking beams. Then the sharp-tongued old man with the wispy white beard. Angriest. Fearsome. All worked up in a terrible huff. Pointing a bony finger at Yancy. Stammering.

"He say why you kill the buffaloes? Why you do that? Why you not leave alone buffaloes?"

"What buffaloes!? What does he mean!?"

"Buffaloes—"

Captain Yancy extended his hands, palms up. What did he know about buffaloes?

"What about the sniff-sniff!?" cried Old Wispy.

"The what!?" cried Yancy.

"The old man, he say what about sniff-sniff?"

"What's sniff-sniff? What does he mean?"

The interpreter shrugged.

"What about the sniff-sniff!?" cried Old Wispy. He was angry.

"What about the sniff-sniff!?" cried the others. They were angry too.

"What about the clowns and the acrobats and the jugglers too!?" Old Wispy cried. They all cried.

"What!?" cried Yancy. "What do they want!?"

"The people, they talk what about clowns?"

"What about what!? What do they mean!?"

The interpreter shrugged.

"What about the clowns and the acrobats and the jugglers too!?" the people all cried, some of them. "What about the sniff-sniff!?" They were angry about the American with the little black box, what he had done; and angry because there was no skit, at least the VC had put on a show; and some were a little of both. "What about the clowns!? What about the sniff-sniff!?"

Yancy palms up, he didn't know, he was innocent.

Y M'nung spoke.

"Chief, he say them too—they saw Viet Cong. He say Viet Cong not make trouble for Buon Sop if Buon Sop not make welcome for you. For Americans. For any longnose with medal and pip."

"What's pip?"

"Chief, he say—"

Interruption. Stammering.

"Now what!?"

"Old man, he say already they make Viet Cong mad. He say Viet Cong sure to find out about the talking. About you. Lots of pip. He say we should go. Not make trouble for Buon Sop. He say Viet Cong have lots of guns too. They make *ratta-tat-tat*."

"Well, hey, tell the old man—tell them all—that we've got more guns than the Viet Cong. And say that our guns shoot faster and longer. *Ratta-tat-tat! Ratta-tat-tat!* Get the sound right— fast and long. Tell them they'll need our guns when the VC decide to destroy Buon Sop. Tell them how much—" Captain Yancy strung out his words very slowly and very precisely, addressing the notables of Buon Sop as well as the interpreter. He hung out his words so the people could easily latch onto them. It didn't matter that they couldn't grasp a word, Yancy felt that the stringing helped to make things clearer all around. "Faster. Longer. Okay? Go it? *Ratta-tat-tat! Ratta-tat-tat!* Say it two or three times. Make it clear all around. Go ahead, tell them."

Making it clear. More conferring. Old Wispy stammering.

"Old man, he say more guns, less guns all the same. Fast shoot, slow shoot, long shoot, short shoot all the same. No good to him if Viet Cong burn his house or kill his pigs or take 'way his son. No good at all. He say the people must not to let you enter Buon Sop. Not again."

Damn this old geek, this fussy old bastard, thought Captain Yancy. Who does he think he is anyway? Here I am trying to help, I didn't have to hike all this way, and he keeps shooting off his mouth. Damn his old hide, damn his bony finger. Damn his not wanting to be warm and snug. Captain Yancy using his spurs, trying to head off Old Wispy: "Ask if the VC takes their rice. How about that? And their chickens and pigs. If they take them too. Ask them that."

The interpreter asked.

The notables huddled, considering this and considering that. Old Wispy shook, Old Wispy spluttered, he didn't have to consider a thing. Yancy wished he would go off and choke and leave him to persuade the others. The others were siding against Old Wispy, most of them, Yancy thought but he couldn't be sure. Y M'nung spoke.

"Chief say VC take their rice. Not all. Just some. But everyone hungry. They hungry before VC come. Now they more hungry. Belly all the time making noise."

Noise, thought Sergeant Jasperson, a great big noise—

"Tell them about the pigs. How nice and fat they are in Buon Yun and skinny here. The chickens too."

The interpreter did.

Noise, thought Sergeant Jasperson, a great big noise—

"Tell them about the dirt. How nice and red it is in Buon Yun, how brown it is here."

The interpreter did.

Noise, thought Sergeant Jasperson, a great big noise. Something dramatic, something loud. A shove of a big noise to bring them all down, their resistance was tottering. "Cap'n Yancy, sir—their tails are up. They're skittish, sir. Just like deer about to bound off but not knowin' from what. 'Course these guys, they know from what. From Charlie, huh? The old man, he's got a noisy bark but they're not payin' him no mind. Ol' Chiefy, here, he's the one—" Sergeant Jasperson picked up his gun and shoved it hard at Y M'nung who caught the gun in self-defense because, if he hadn't, the gun would have clobbered him on the head. Jasperson wrapped Y M'nung's hands with his own, then he squeezed off a couple of bursts—*ratta-tat-tat—ratta-tat-tat*—which clattered big and loud and dramatic in the closeness of the house. Jasperson, the two of them, had shot a hole thru the roof.

Once the shock wore from his face, Y M'nung looked pleased. With a great slurpy grin. Pleased even tho his dignity had been briefly assaulted. Pleased even tho there was now a hole in his thick thatch roof and it was then into the season of rains. The gun had felt good. It had shot fast. It had shot long. It had throbbed with savagery. Not at all like those rusty French guns. The others, who had been just as shocked, they began to settle down; but Y M'nung the village chief was flying high, up and away.

Captain Yancy quickly pursued. "Tell the chief that we'll give him a gun just like this. And one gun for each man who can fight. One for each man who cares enough to fight for Buon Sop. And also that we'll bring them rice. Enough rice to fill their hunger. Hey, that's good—to fill their hunger. Just like that. Say it like that. Enough rice to stop the noise." Yancy patted the gun as he spoke, the gun Y M'nung still held in his hands. Yancy let him get the feel, the heft of it. He made sure the muzzle was pointed up.

Y M'nung was a very proud man. It wasn't for him to shirk, to lose face. Not after Captain Yancy's words. Especially not in front of the other notables. Y M'nung was wise as well as proud. He had not been elected chief of Buon Sop because he bore himself rigidly straight and was well-intentioned and had a dimple on his chin. He had been elected chief because what he spoke seemed to make sense. But there were some, like Old Wispy, who thought

Y M'nung was not as sensible as he seemed. That he was more proud than he was wise.

But there was more to it than Y M'nung's pride. There was also the law. If a village chief failed to protect his people, if things went badly in his village, then he was guilty of a crime. Y M'nung didn't want to be guilty almost as much as he billowed with pride.

Y M'nung huddled with the notables. Their talk was long and very lively. Much longer than the talks before and even more lively. The floor beams creaked, the time ticked away. For Captain Yancy. For Jasperson. For the notables of Buon Sop—

Finally: "Bring the guns," said Y M'nung. "Teach us first how to use the guns, then give us the guns. The gun had a fine throbbing to it. Bring them and do not mind the old man. The old man was one time the bravest of all. But it is no more. He can no longer hunt and his woman must chew the meat for him. He has forgotten that to fight is the proper way. It always has been. Bring the guns and bring the rice too. Our bellies are all the time making the noises."

All the notables nodded but one, tentatively satisfied. Not quite sure their decision was right, but more sure than less. Only Old Wispy being dead sure—that the decision wasn't. Glaring at Yancy. Giving Yancy the evil eye. Stammering, having his final say. Saying that he would kill his pigs, one by one, and eat the meat before the VC got to them. That he could chew his own damn meat.

"What about the sniff-sniff!?" cried Old Wispy as Yancy and party left for Buon Yun. "What about the clowns and the acrobats and the jugglers too!?"

"Psychology," explained Jasperson on the way to Buon Yun; "psychology," explained Jasperson about shoving the gun and making it go *ratta-tat-tat* and, generally, about Buon Sop; "psychology, Cap'n Yancy, sir, you gotta know when to put the squeeze."

* * *

Mac Dong Dong listened without expression as the man with the bandaged head told of the gun, and how it had gone *ratta-tat-tat,* and the hole in the roof, and how the notables had agreed. The man with the bandaged head spoke in jerky sentences. He was tired and short of breath from having jogged all the way from Buon Sop. He spoke without pause, and now and then he blinked his eyes, as if he were dizzy or feverish. It may have been his somehow too sharp nasty wound acting up. Or the exciting news he bore. Or being nervous about Mac Dong Dong, Mac was a very important man. Or maybe simply the sweat stinging him. When he was done spurting out the news, he received a nod of acknowledgment and a few words of praise and some water to drink. Nothing much, but still enough to make him feel grateful, coming as they did from Mac. Then the man with the bandaged head took off as fast as he could for Buon Sop. The way was long. His feet were hot. He hurried because he had promised his father, an old man with a wisp of a beard, that he would slaughter a pig that day.

Mac Dong Dong sat on a stump, and picked at the grit in the tips of his eyes, and thought about the news which the man with the bandaged head had spurted out. Mac Dong Dong had a very shrewd head, a good head for thinking, and also a very scarred body. He had taken a lot of punishment tho he was little more than twenty. Stretched here. Broken there. Two fingers missing from one of his hands. Mac hadn't been born an ugly fellow but he was so vinegary with hate, so sopping intent on striking back and setting things right, that it had forever soured his face. It was the cowlick that finally saved him from looking diabolical. The cowlick softened his face a fraction, flopping there boyishly down to his brow. There was nothing else boyish about Mac Dong Dong. He was a strong and decisive man and very respected as a leader. Tight with his words. Speaking only when necessary. When there was a plan to be explained, or an order given, or when some subtle political point had to be made perfectly clear.

What was clear to all his men was how much pride Mac took in his work. How much affection he felt for his work, forever soured face or not. For Mac to be doing what he was doing was more important than the wife and sons he loved and whom he rarely got to see and then not for long. It was more important than anything else except succeeding and not having anything left to work for, and then it was more important than that. It had become a way of life.

Mac was a dedicated man. With a dedication that went beyond knowing what was wrong and wanting to go about setting it right and shaking fists and making growly noises. With a dedication that simply went out and got things done, or at least tried. Mac's dedication was so intense that he never wearied of the war. Besides, the war had become his life and who wants to lead a weary life; he might as well be dead.

It hadn't always been that way. Once, his dedication had been to eating enough and having a roof over his head; but what with dunking his younger brother and the water being turned off, Mac had joined the Viet Cong. It happened in the very first year of the Diem regime. With Mac's father having run off somewhere and Mac unable to get any work, nor his older sister—for this was the time between the French and Americans, when maids weren't needed or prostitutes—with things as they were, it fell upon Mac's crippled young brother to support the family. This the boy did cheerfully by begging in the streets of Saigon, tho his legs were so withered that he had to walk on his hands and he would have preferred to stay home and play. So early each morning, Mac would hoist the boy on his back and carry him to the big market place in the center of town. There, by the public fountain, the boy would put out a dirty old hat for passersby to drop in coins or bread or anything they wished. It was a very colorful place and people were nice enough to the boy and also he would amuse himself by looking at all the cars that went by. When business was slow, the boy would move on to another spot around the fountain, pulling himself along on his hands, with Mac following closely behind. The fountain was the best place in town for begging coins and, besides, the boy had to be near water and dunked now and then to keep his legs from getting too stiff. So Mac would pick his brother up and dunk him every now and then. And as he did, as he held him tightly under the arms and lowered him in, he thought about how the French had dunked croissants in their coffee, and how so many Vietnamese had pork and shrimp to dunk in their sauce, and that he should have something to dunk other than his younger brother. In any case, the water felt good after the hot sun, and the boy would splash and laugh.

Things went well enough for a time and Mac's brother usually earned enough to keep the family going. But then one morning, when Mac went to dunk his brother, they found that the fountain had been drained. It seemed that the public servant in charge didn't like people dunked in his fountain and so he had let the water out. The fountain stayed drained, and Mac's brother's legs grew very stiff, and so they had to move to a fountain in another part of town which wasn't so good for begging coins or bread or anything at all.

With that decline in the family's fortune, Mac began to think more and more about there being things to dunk other than a younger brother. He thought and brooded and that was when he joined the VC. He started out as a messenger, and struggled thru Marx, and was assigned to an assassination squad, and studied Ho, and personally killed the province chief of Quang Duc, and studied Harriet Beecher Stowe, and was wounded several times, covering himself with glory, until he became the leader he was.

What Mac Dong Dong led was the 825th Independent Company of the National Liberation Army. The 825th didn't wear snappy uniforms; it had to manage its own supplies and to secure its own replacements; and between operations, its men dispersed and returned home to do their civilian work. But the men were well enough armed and trained and indoctrinated, and their mission had recently grown to include the destruction of strategic hamlets as well as the armed propaganda work. Like the other 'independents,' the 825th was a regional force. It operated in Dar Lac.

Mac sat there, picking the grit, thinking hard about the news. Thinking hard about the 825th. Thinking hard that a stooped back was not enough. Not for a poor old peasant. Not for years of squushing thru mud and bending and stretching and planting rice and harvesting it and the rice half dead from blight. Thinking that stiff fingers were not enough. Not for a poor old fisherman. Not for years of patching his tattered old net and cutting his hands on the wet-sharp cords and then not catching much anyway, then cutting his hands some more on the fish, on their spines. Thinking that a grimy face and grimy hands and just about grimy everything were not enough. Not for a poor old charcoal peddler. Not for years of scrounging for wood and coaling it and lugging the heavy sacks to town and peddling them up and down the streets and coming home black and waking up black and the people turning to kerosene. Not for this. Not for that. Not for anyone.

Mac knew that the favored and well-to-do seldom thought hard about these things, seldom thought any way at all. That when they did, it was only to write off the poor stooped peasant and the stiff-fingered fisherman and the grimy charcoal peddler with a brief lament, or with a shrug. Mac knew that the favored and well-to-do considered such matters to be the proper province of God, or of Fate; and if God abstained, or if Fate seemed to lack sentiment, then what could they do, the well-to-do. The peasant and the fisherman and the charcoal peddler, they also lamented, but they shrugged too. Like the favored and well-to-do, they acknowledged that matters were as they must be.

But matters did not have to be as they were, thought Mac Dong Dong. Matters could be changed for the better. For the unfavored, for the not-so-well-to-do. For all the people. The Liberation would see to that. It would see to everything. It *was* seeing. The Liberation gave men a chance to go about setting wrong things right. It gave them the means. And one of these means was the 825th Independent Company.

Mac considered the means at hand. The loss of Buon Yun. The news from Buon Sop. The entire situation. Then he decided what had to be done about the Americans bringing their guns.

* * *

"It is bad, Captain Yancy. Very bad. You are too much impatient— Slowly, my friend. That is the way things are done. Not too much slowly, but slowly, yes?" Colonel Quoc didn't like Captain Yancy. They weren't friends. "You are first time here. You must learn to be patient. You must learn the ways. To accept the ways as they always have been."

"Colonel Quoc, this is our third meeting. Twice before you promised me that the rice would come. *Twice* before. We need the rice. We need it now. For Buon Sop. It was agreed in Saigon that you would buy the rice for us."

"Yes, it is so. It was agreed." Colonel Quoc patted his uniform and looked somewhat put out and thought that Yancy was a boor. "These things, they will come. I promise again. As soon as we can buy the rice, I send to Buon Yun."

"But, Colonel, you have the money. Remember? We gave it to you. We gave you the money to buy the rice just so it would seem that you and not us were giving the rice to the tribesmen. That's what Saigon wanted. Their gratitude. To win it, to win their allegiance too. To make them think—to make them know how much Saigon cares. We gave you the money to buy the rice and deliver it. So where is the rice?"

Impertinent bastard! thought Colonel Quoc. Wart of a toad! "Yes, the money. Very nice money. You gave it to us. So we will use it to buy the rice. It was agreed, was it not? Very good."

"But when, Colonel Quoc? When will you use it to buy the rice?" Bugger this creep! thought Captain Yancy.

"When? When there is rice available. That is when we will buy the rice and have it delivered to Buon Yun."

"Colonel, the markets are full of rice. Full of kilos of beautiful rice. Thousands and thousands of kilos. The rice merchants, they're doing business left and right. There's no shortage of rice, Colonel Quoc. I passed the shops on my way over here. Bursting, they were just bursting with rice."

"You know this for sure?"

"I'd know it even if I was blind. Because I know we gave rice to Saigon, tons of rice, to sell to the merchants to sell to you to give to the tribesmen so everyone wins."

"Even you."

"Even us."

"Yes," Colonel Quoc agreed, "there is no shortage. It is as you say. There seems to be plenty rice. But do you ever refer to the chart?"

"To the *what?*"

"The worthy chart."

"*What* chart?"

"Of Astrological Ministry."

"Now, look, Colonel Quoc—"

Colonel Quoc shook his head, slowly, sadly. "I believe not. Americans do not refer to the chart." Colonel Quoc looked positively mournful. "You would be wise to read the chart. You would be very wise. It says in the chart that this is not time to buy big bunch of rice."

"Why?" asked Yancy, being patient, just as Colonel Quoc had advised. "Why is it not the time?"

"Hmmm. Yes. I do not understand why myself. But it is so. It says in the chart. And I am not one to do against the word of the chart."

Charts! Reading crazy charts! The man's a nut, an idiot! "Colonel Quoc, you must be joking. You're an educated man. You—"

"And you are not, Captain Yancy. You are not learned about our ways. The chart is the way it is done. The chart tells us everything."

"What about all the others, all the Vietnamese I saw buying rice? What about them? The shops were crowded. *They* read the chart."

"They do not buy big bunch of rice. It is forbidden only to buy a big bunch." Colonel Quoc smoothed back his hair. He was loose. He figured he was still ahead.

"Colonel Quoc, I'll tell you what." Captain Yancy spoke very softly, so that the worthy chart wouldn't hear. Quoc leaned forward and cocked his ear. "What if you went from shop to shop and bought just a little bunch in each? Would that be possible? Could you do that? Just a little bunch in each? The chart wouldn't be offended. Your conscience would be shiny clear—well anyway clear. It would work out all around. What do you say?"

Colonel Quoc considered. "Yes, it would be possible," he whispered to Captain Yancy. Then Colonel Quoc considered some more. He slammed his hand down on the chart. "No, it is not possible."

"Why isn't it possible?"

"We must first let the people of Ban Me Thuot to buy all the rice they need. Then we will buy the rice for Buon Sop."

"For Godsake, Colonel Quoc, all I want is a few thousand kilos. Just a splash. Just a skinny drop in the bucket."

"A few thousand kilo could feed many people in Ban Me Thuot. We do not eat so much as you Americans."

"That's just what I mean. There's plenty of rice to go around."

"No, we must wait a little more."

"And what if all the rice is sold, what happens then? What happens if there's no more rice to be bought? What happens to the money we gave you to buy the rice which we gave you too?"

"I do not understand."

"Me neither."

"It is better to be sure what you say."

"I mean, what will become of the money if there's no rice left to buy? It was agreed—in Saigon—that the money was for the rice."

"There will always be rice."

"But you just said—"

"Oh, yes. In that case—if all the rice has already been sold—if there is no more left to buy—Well, then, Captain Yancy—" Quoc looked Yancy right in the eye. "—In that case, Captain Yancy, there are many uses for the money. More important uses than to buy rice for a village of *Moi*."

"What uses, Colonel Quoc?"

"They should respect me more."

"Respect you more?"

"They shouldn't throw rocks."

"Who threw rocks?"

"There are enemies everywhere."

"Enemies where?"

"They should love the Government."

"What uses?"

"Uses, Captain Yancy."

"Colonel Quoc, I'm surprised at you. I thought you were all sly and sneaky. But this—"

"Watch step, Captain Yancy. Watch step. It is not so good you speak this way. Not so good. I am the Province Chief. You must not forget. And I have very good name in Saigon. I am trusted. Very good name." You hundred and sixty-nine warts of a toad, how sorry you'll be! thought Colonel Quoc.

"Listen, Colonel Quoc—"

"Vietnam *my* country, Captain Yancy. Not your country. If you do not like it, then go. But do not waste your time and mine. Do not like, please go." Quoc was ferocious to behold tho he certainly didn't want Yancy and the Americans to please go.

"Colonel, I apologize. You have different ways. Okay. I understand. Okay. Okay. But—"

"No, Captain, you do not understand. You try to make too much change. It is not possible. Maybe you think I do not like you. I like you very much, Captain Yancy—You will have some tea, yes?"

"Charts!" mumbled Yancy after the tea and on his way out. "Goddamn idiot charts!"

* * *

Lieutenant Plunket needed a haircut. Captain Yancy had told him so. Captain Yancy always worried about Lieutenant Plunket's appearance. "Get a haircut," he said. "Maintain your appearance. Haven't you noticed Grandmother Pan? That she doesn't flirt with you anymore? It's all that damn hair. Get it cut."

"If you'll pardon me, sir, the people don't think you have any soul."

"What's that got to do with your hair!?" barked Captain Yancy, hurt nonetheless.

"They have this belief that, if you cut your hair too short, then the soul will get lost at night."

"Go on, Lieutenant."

"You see, sir, the soul lives inside the head and, at night when you dream, it goes wandering. And when it returns, it can tell the right head to climb back into by the hair. But if you cut off all the hair and throw it away—"

"Who told you all this?"

"Moon did, sir."

"And you believe it?"

"But if you cut off all the hair and throw it away, then the soul searches for it and, finding it thrown away like that, the soul will think that the body is dead. The soul then flees to the world of the spirits."

"Is that all, Lieutenant?"

"Oh no, sir. Without its soul, the body is then obliged to die. That's the worst part."

"Well, I'm alive, wouldn't you say? What do the people think about that?"

"They don't know what to think, sir. It puzzles them."

"And, anyway, their hair's not so long."

"It doesn't have to be long, sir—just longer than yours."

"Yeah, well—well anyway, we're back to you. Do *you* think your soul is gonna get lost and all the rest?"

"Not really, sir, but I'd like them to think that I have a soul."

"Well, *I* know you have a soul, Lieutenant, there in your head or wherever it is, tho sometimes I wonder if you have brains. So get that hair cut! Get it cut! Let's look sharp for the villagers."

Now Lieutenant Plunket knew that the villagers couldn't care less about his appearance. They cared about a gun of their own, about the health of their buffaloes, about a bowlful of rice with each meal. They cared that the call of the m'lang bird should come from the left, which was good luck, and not from the right, which was bad. They didn't care about his hair. Lieutenant Plunket knew these things, for Sergeant Moon had told him so, but still he hadn't pressed it with Yancy who had to see Quoc and was already in a bad mood. So Plunket had come to town with Yancy in order to get a proper haircut.

Plunket entered a barber shop not far from MACV Provincial Headquarters which was commanded by Colonel Nutley. The shop was small and smelled from burnt cooking oil. The smell came from a mysterious back room which was closed off by a bright red curtain. The walls of the shop were covered with pictures of Vietnamese entertainers—songstresses, singers, actresses, actors, clowns, acrobats, jugglers too. It seemed like a cheerful, homey place except for the man with the scowling face.

There were two barbers, a flat-nosed girl and the man with the scowl, who summoned Plunket to his chair. Plunket preferred the flat-nosed girl and hesitated. The man had an ominous look to him; his eyes were bloodless, sinister, and Plunket was leery. He finally settled into the chair and, partly because he was a joker and partly to mask his uneasiness, he made a gruesome face in the mirror. Then a second terrible face. The girl could hardly contain herself. Plunket pointed to his head and cut the air with his fingers. He also wiggled his oversize ears. The flat-faced girl clapped her hand to her mouth. What a funny man, she thought.

Lieutenant Plunket was, indeed, a funny man. He had taken his share of licks and come thru grinning—just like the people of Buon Yun. He had a wisecrack for everything, but not a mean one, a funny one. He was always poking fun at himself. He was as brave as Captain Yancy but not quite so proud. Where Plunket knew how to laugh at himself, Yancy didn't; he only knew how to laugh at Plunket—when he wasn't too angry with him. Lieutenant Plunket knew when to laugh just like Sergeant Jasperson knew when not to kick. He knew when to humor Captain Yancy, how to ease Captain Yancy's concern, whenever he caught Captain Yancy's sidelong disapproving looks. Yancy was always giving Plunket sidelong disapproving looks—he was always expecting the worst—whenever Plunket was given to fancy and talked about one of his strange new ideas. Lieutenant Plunket was full of ideas, like Sergeant Moon; and, also like Moon, he was always willing to try new things; but unlike Moon, he didn't have to try new things when he was already trying them. In spite of the laughing, there were times when Plunket took himself seriously and then he could truly be like a bear, which was what he resembled anyway, but a soft friendly bear, not a mean growly one.

He was like a bear with his long blunt snout, and his big ears set high, and his head wide across like the flat-nosed girl, and the way he flopped out his arms as he shambled like slapping salmon from a stream. It gave a fuzzy cast to his face which was all the more fuzzy because Plunket's eyes were always tenderly blurred with concern for Triple Threat. He was fuzzy-wuzzy Plunket with a heart of gold and lots of fierce, exasperated, well-intentioned energy. His good intentions, *they* moved Plunket, not the other way around. He didn't concoct them, as Yancy did, because good intentions were nice to have. And unlike Yancy who marched four-square, and Jasperson who flowed along, Lieutenant Plunket walked with a jerk as if unsure where to step next. In a way

Plunket walked like Triple Threat. As a matter of fact, he did many things like Triple Threat, or Triple Threat like him.

While you couldn't say they were inseparable, they were nonetheless considered a pair, with Triple Threat following Plunket about and waiting on him and providing gentle fun. It wasn't a friendship in the sense of Moon and Little Rhadeo, but more an alliance fostered by need: Triple Threat needed someone to love him and Plunket needed to love. To Triple Threat, Plunket was a friend, the dearest friend in all the world, but Plunket looked on himself as a ward. He was kind to his mute, and understanding, only once losing patience with him—and that had been in jest. In fact, it was also the only time the Beckoning Virgin had been abused and this is how it happened:

They were all in the mess hall and Y Gar the hunter had just brought them meat so tough it could have been buffalo. Plunket slapped it down on the table where Triple Threat was fixing lunch. Then with the flabby edge of his hand, and with a fierce curl to his lip, and without a moment's warning, Plunket began to chop away, bellowing with each chop.

Triple Threat leaped back in alarm. He feared for himself, and that his friend Plunket had just gone mad. Plunket stopped chopping and motioned Triple Threat forward again, wagging a finger at the mute's nose and ordering him to hold his ground. Then Plunket began to chop again, snarling, bellowing with each chop.

After a few of these fearsome blows, Lieutenant Plunket picked up the meat and pretended to take a bite. Then he pretended to chew the piece he had bitten off, chewing it with the greatest effort. Triple Threat slapped his chest and bounced in place and grunted with pleasure. He laughed his wheezing, gurgling mute's laugh. He was having fun.

Lieutenant Plunket quit his chewing and resumed his attack on the meat. Then he bit off another piece, this one more easily than the first, and chewed it with slightly less vengeance. But easier bit and easier chewed, still the going was pretty tough. He made that plain to Triple Threat who began to wonder why the Lieutenant was eating meat which he wasn't really and which didn't seem to taste good anyway, it was so tough.

The charade went on, one repetition after another, with Triple Threat bouncing in place and grunting, and the men cheering Plunket on. Plunket chopped and chomped and chewed until the mute's face lit up. He understood! He understood! His friend wasn't mad after all!

Triple Threat took Plunket's place. He approached the meat soberly, viciously, and began to chop as hard as he could. Triple Threat grunted, he wheezed and gurgled, with each chop. And then it happened: the bloody slab slid from the table. It squirted from under the mute's last blow and landed in a pail of slop setting on the floor. Triple Threat bounced up and down, pointing to the pail of slop, to the meat on top. He didn't know what to do next.

Plunket knew what to do next. He was hopping mad, or seemed to be, and he chased Triple Threat right out the door. Triple Threat rumbled, he hotfooted it across Buon Yun. Triple Threat ran so out of control, so recklessly, that he ran right across the inviolate Hump of the Beckoning Virgin and stumbled and tumbled and went sprawling headlong over her thighs. He never even pardoned himself.

How alike they were, Plunket and Triple Threat. Altogether, Plunket was a stumbling, bumbling, trusting, optimistic fellow. While others fretted, or pissed and moaned, he looked to a brighter day. Not quite as confidently as Fritz, who was always saying the sun would shine, but very confidently just the same.

His confidence deserted him when he met those bloodless eyes in the mirror and they didn't give. It was then Plunket had a premonition that something was going to happen to him, something nasty, terrible. He all of a sudden knew that the man with the scowling face was his enemy. But Plunket's will deserted him too, and he didn't want to embarrass himself if he were wrong, so he sat there meekly and let out a sigh and awaited the man with the scowling face.

* * *

Fat Anna's whorehouse was set at the end of a narrow dirt street on the outskirts of town, not far from the fruit and vegetable market. During the day, when business was slow, some of Fat Anna's whores could always be seen among the fruit and vegetable stalls, loitering, playfully taunting the men, gossiping with the women. But by five o'clock, all of Fat Anna's whores were back in Fat Anna's dirty gray house, lounging in the big front parlor, waiting for the Americans, for the GIs from MACV Provincial Headquarters. Most of the girls looked forward to the Americans. The Americans could be counted upon to liven the sluggish late afternoon.

The Americans! What funny men! How they could joke! How they could spend! There were many of Fat Anna's whores who singled out one or two or three or more of the Americans for special affection. Fat Anna's whores were a poor scroungy lot but they could be very generous too. Singling out. Sometimes even giving two for the price of one. Of course there were those, just a few, who didn't single out anyone, who didn't look forward to anything. Who went inertly thru the motions and leaped right up when it was done to wash themselves out. Not laughing, not hearing the jokes at all, not even hearing the muted shrieking of their souls. These deaf ones, they weren't popular, so they didn't leave the big front parlor as often as the other girls, which caused Fat Anna much grief. She was always lamenting how Xuan the whoremonger had cheated her, or that he never gave refunds.

Fat Anna, herself, never left the front parlor. She was content to sit back and watch. She was a grimly good-natured lady and sometimes joined in a joke or two. Fat Anna was skinny, her real name was Phuong. She had once been very unhappily married to a miserly Chinaman who sold various curative herbs and restorative powders. He also interpreted omens and dabbled in sorcery. The Chinaman was a moon-faced fellow and had many steady customers, for his predictions were as often right as wrong, and his herbs and powders were acclaimed to be particularly powerful. Whenever the Chinaman planned to market a new remedy, he first tried it out on Anna. He forced the concoction down Fat Anna's throat and meek little Anna, all she could do was to submit with a strangled whimper. The Chinaman drew his conclusions thusly: if the potion did not kill Fat Anna, it wouldn't kill his customers.

For a long time, the Chinaman had only good fortune, and Fat

Anna too. Then one day, after a new experiment which hadn't set well, skinny Fat Anna almost died. She was so frightened by this experience, how unsettling it was, that she stood up. She told her inconsiderate husband to go and swallow some buffalo dung. The Chinaman was so taken back by this turn of events that he promptly had a fit and swallowed his tongue instead. Fat Anna's faith was reconfirmed and she buried her husband the very next day. The Chinaman's friends and customers came to say good-bye; they were sorry to see him go. Only Fat Anna and Chau the pharmacist weren't sorry to see him go. No, not Chau. The China-man, with his herbs and powders, had given the pharmacist stiff competition, cutting into his profits.

After the Chinaman had been seen off, Fat Anna hurried back to the shop and began to search for whatever small fortune he had surely hidden away. She looked into this and looked into that. Over. Under. To either side. In between. She dug one hole after another in the small garden behind the shop where the Chinaman had grown some of his herbs. She looked and dug patiently, tearfully, futilely for a whole week, and just when she was about to give up, Fat Anna discovered the Chinaman's fortune. It had been wrapped in a dirty rag. The rag had been buried deep down in a gourd of dried toad skins. The gourd had been placed in the very most prominent spot of the shop, the one spot Fat Anna had written off. Oh, that clever Chinaman!

With this new lease on life, Fat Anna decided to go into business for herself. First, she purchased a dirty gray house on the out-skirts of town. Then she bought twelve lumpy mattresses from one-eyed Nhu, the opium parlor proprietor. Nhu's clientele, mostly gray-skinned older men with traditional views, had demanded that Nhu get rid of the lumpy mattresses and bring back the straw mats, which were far more comfortable. So having acquired her dirty gray house and the twelve lumpy mattresses, Fat Anna next set about gathering whores. She paid off the debts of a poor family in return for the services of its two daughters. She settled the fine of a fine old pro who had been jailed for stealing a chicken. She made arrangements here and there, but mostly she made arrange-ments thru Xuan the jolly whoremonger. Bargaining for whores could be touchy, difficult work. It required a certain tactfulness, a certain finesse, which Fat Anna lacked. So she dealt mostly thru Xuan the whoremonger. Oh, that Xuan! Ah, the cheat! That son of a monkey! He didn't even give refunds.

Refunds or not, Fat Anna prospered but she stayed skinny. It was the purges, everyone said, the purges for sure. They said that Fat Anna had swallowed so many of the Chinaman's newest concoctions that she would stay forever purged and therefore forever skinny. But tho she was forever purged, Fat Anna had been feeling poorly these many years. It was the purges, everyone said; tho purges are good, they can also be bad, especially if they don't set well. It was the purges for sure, they said, but it was also from worry. From worrying over how much more money Colonel Quoc would ask each time his cut came around. No one knew why, no one could remember when Fat Anna had been named Fat Anna. Neither could Fat Anna.

* * *

Sergeant Goodbody was feeling mighty poorly too. None of the others would have guessed by looking at him, but everyone knew, because Goodbody kept telling them. "I'm feelin' poorly, ever so poorly. My back aches. My shoulder aches. I'm full of gas and I'm losin' weight. Here, take a look at my eyes." Then Sergeant Goodbody would roll his eyes so everyone could take a look and see whatever Goodbody figured they ought to see.

Since Sergeant Goodbody had always been just as skinny as Fat Anna, it was hard for the others to see where he was losing weight. But Goodbody saw, and that was the important thing. Bittersweet chocolate-colored Goodbody, he had been melting since even before Triple Threat had dished out the meat that had fallen into the slops. He had gone to Sergeant Culpepper. He even had Moon bring him to Y Blo. Sergeant Culpepper had urged moderation in all things, and Y Blo had sacrificed three chickens and five gourds of wine, but nothing helped. Nothing could be done for Goodbody, for only Sergeant Goodbody could see anything wrong with Sergeant Goodbody. Yet, the others had to admit that he now picked at his food when before he had been the biggest, the most gigantic eater of them all, skinny tho he was.

Tall and skinny Sergeant Goodbody did have something very infectious and that was his laugh. His laugh was as burly as he was thin. His laugh engaged all parts of him. It boomed into distant corners and cracks, engaging everyone else within hearing and who could not? But sometimes Goodbody got on your nerves by laughing too much or much too long, or yapping too loudly, or making you look deep into his eyes for signs of decomposition.

In spite of Goodbody's boisterous ways, his booming ways—he was the demolitions man—he had his sensitivities. For instance, it hurt him to catch Yancy giving him sidelong disapproving looks. Other sensitivities too. Goodbody had his serious side just as Lieutenant Plunket did. Yet when he tried to be serious, Goodbody was even funnier than when he tried to be funny. That was the kind of turned-around fellow Goodbody was.

So, anyway, he had come to town seeking a cure. He figured that Fat Anna's whores, one of them, might have the answer to his problems. Aches. Gas. Yellow eyes. No appetite. And his laugh, it hadn't been booming as loudly and often as before. I'm feelin' so poorly, ever so poorly. Here, take a look at my eyes!

Fat Anna's whores had the answer, all right, thought Sergeant Fritz, as he and Goodbody strode past the fruit and vegetable stalls toward Fat Anna's dirty gray house. Fritz knew for sure that they had the answer because he was the intelligence man. It was his duty to find out things, to gather intelligence on the VC and then decide what to do with it.

Sergeant Fritz had thick wavy hair and a thick wavering mind. Not empty thick, but cluttered thick with schemes and with conspiracies. Wavering, because Sergeant Fritz could never decide which scheme or conspiracy he liked best. As all his plans turned around in his head, his belly grumbled and his head wobbled about on his neck so that it seemed he was turning cement instead of ideas. He spent so much time turning over his plans that they forever stayed locked in his head and were never put into action. Whenever the Captain asked Fritz what was new, Fritz always answered: "I'm thinking. I'm thinking. Can't you see my head going round? I've got all these plans. It's just a matter of sorting them out. You'll have your information soon, I promise you that, Captain Yancy, sir." Fritz's problem was not that he was overly dumb, but that he was overly smart. He had so many good ideas that he didn't know what to do with them all. He just didn't have the heart to single out one idea over the rest. So he just turned all his ideas around and around and around.

Besides having a lot on the ball, Sergeant Fritz also had more jumps than anyone else on the team including Sergeant Jasperson. Sergeant Fritz loved to jump. He had enlisted years before in order to get up in the air so he could come right back down. He had this thing about coming down. He liked to do it—to fall, then go up and fall some more. Maybe because that was what life was all about—coming down, but getting back up—and Fritz wanted to do it his way, he had his own way of doing things. But probably not. He was an absolute optimist. He didn't recognize comings-down. The sun will always shine for Fritz, Fritz always said.

One more thing about Sergeant Fritz, he collected butterflies. It had to do with his reputation in Saigon where he was known as a butterfly because he flitted from girl to girl, sipping his fill. They teased him about it and played hard to get; but, in the end, they let him sip because he was very personable, and generous too. Fritz had decided that on his next visit he'd give all the girls a butterfly. It would be his little joke and, anyway, a man needed a break from turning things round and round in his head. So Fritz went around catching butterflies and pinning them thru, and the villagers marveled at his collection, wanting to have a butterfly too. Once, Captain Yancy had said to him:

"What kind of man goes around with a net chasing butterflies?"

To which Fritz replied: "A man who shows his gentler side is more of a man, Captain Yancy, sir."

"What's *that* supposed to mean, Sergeant Fritz!?"

"Nothing, sir. Nothing at all— Have you ever grown orchids, Captain, sir?"

"Orchids?" asked Yancy.

"Orchids, sir. It's like playing left tackle and growing orchids, only with me it's butterflies."

"What's this with orchids?" Yancy then asked, watching Fritz work on his butterflies.

But Fritz had simply laid out another and pinned it thru.

So next to sorting out his plans; and going up and coming down; and repairing the sniff-sniff box—it was always out of whack— Fritz spent his time snaring butterflies and convincing himself that he was a ladies' man. As he strode past the fruit and vegetable stalls, Fritz looked forward to Fat Anna's whores, to showing his stuff. He would sweep them right up and bed them down and give them something to warble about. Not one, not two, but three or four. After all, he was Fritz. Absolutely optimistic Sergeant Fritz. The sun will always shine for Fritz, he was always saying.

"Who's he!? Who's he!?" shouted Fritz in the parlor. "He sure looks very suspicious to me—"

No one knew what 'suspicious' meant except Sergeant Fritz and Sergeant Goodbody and, besides, the man didn't look so suspicious. He didn't look suspicious at all. It was just Fritz's grandstanding way, it was his way of making an entrance or maybe it wasn't. He pointed his finger accusingly at a slight, middle-aged Vietnamese who had just emerged from the back.

"Look at that smirk. Look at the jerk. It's for sure he's been up to no good. I can tell. It's my job. Ohhh yeahhh. Whoaaa there. He looks mighty suspicious to me. Well who is he who is he anyway?"

"Him number ten bang-bang. Fast on draw." Bombay Betty, half-Indian and dusky-skinned, said these words as she followed the man out into the parlor.

"Ohhh yeahhh, suspicious for sure. Wha'd you say Betty?"

"Him Hoang Bang. Number ten bang-bang. Fast on draw."

"Yeah, that too, but something else suspicious for sure."

"So fast on draw."

Everyone laughed. The whores. Fat Anna. Fritz. Goodbody. Hoang Bang too. He laughed to hide his embarrassment. He didn't speak English but he understood that he was the butt of Betty's joke. Better to laugh than burn and smoke. Matter of face. So he laughed and bowed to the whores, to Sergeants Fritz

nd Goodbody too. He mumbled something under his breath, then
urried out the door.

As he did, Lieutenant Plunket hurried in, looking pale and
haken. "He tried to kill me!" said Plunket to Fritz, to Sergeant
Goodbody, to Anna and all her whores. "He tried to do me in, I
wear!"

"Easy, Lieutenant," said Sergeant Fritz. "*Who* tried to kill you?"

"Old scowly face, he really did!"

"Easy now, sir," said Sergeant Goodbody. "Get hold of your-
elf."

Fat Anna's whores crowded round Plunket, trying to figure what
t was about.

"I didn't even *ask* for a shave!"

"No, sir, you didn't," agreed Sergeant Fritz.

"So how come I got one? How come a shave?"

"Beats me," answered Sergeant Goodbody, trying to figure it
ut himself.

"Do you think that maybe it's automatic?"

"Maybe, sir," replied Sergeant Fritz.

"And maybe he only wanted to shave me very close, especially
nder the chin?"

"Maybe that too," conceded Goodbody.

Somehow they got him to explain about the haircut and the
shave and how the man with the scowling face had whipped the
azor down on him as if his time had come.

"But how did it end?" asked Sergeant Fritz. "You're still
alive."

"I made him call the flat-nosed girl. I made him give the razor to
er."

"You want a girl?" asked Anna of Plunket.

"Not now, Anna. Thanks just the same. Do you think it means
omething, Sergeant Fritz?"

"I think it means you were imagining things."

"But I didn't *ask* for a shave!"

"Which shop it was?"

Plunket told Fat Anna which. "It's got a red curtain," Plunket
dded, "and all these pictures on the wall."

Fat Anna's whores, who had been buzzing, suddenly hushed. They lowered their eyes. They turned away.

"What is it, Anna?" asked Sergeant Fritz. "Why is everyone acting so funny?"

"Bad barber shop," answered Fat Anna. "Bad barber man."

"What's bad about him? How do you mean?"

"Better that you keep away."

Fritz was about to ask her why when, all of a sudden, Bombay Betty began to cry.

"It's all right, Betty, I'm still alive."

But that didn't stop Betty from crying.

"What's wrong, Betty?" asked Fritz tenderly. "Come on, sweet whore, tell old Fritz."

"I should not make joke at Mister Hoang Bang," bawled Bombay Betty.

"Who's this Hoang Bang?" asked Plunket of Fritz.

"The guy you passed."

"I should not make joke," bawled Bombay Betty. "Him my special customer. All the time ask for Bombay Betty. Bombay Betty do him good. Poor old Mister Bicycle Man."

* * *

Hoang Bang, the bicycle man, dipped his head and examined his fly as he entered the street. They must have been laughing at something else, Hoang Bang decided, for nothing shameful was hanging out. The smirking pigs! The lout-faced whoring American bastards! Jackals! Crows! Cockatoos! Dirt of a hundred thousand behinds! Hoang Bang went on and on and on and gave them what for. Then, satisfied that he was tucked in and that he had given them what for, he strode past the fruit and vegetable stalls toward the north of town.

Hoang Bang's field was bicycles, fixing them. He was very skillful at it. He untwisted them and retwisted them and banged out the dents and other things. He handled the bicycles forcefully yet with respect and even affection. But Hoang Bang never rode one himself. He preferred to walk. He did some of his very best thinking while he walked. To ride a bicycle would have required that part of his mind be occupied with not running down pedestrians, and Hoang Bang needed all of his mind for his thinking. Bicycle fix-it men have to think just like everybody else—just like politicians and generals and literary people. But still it's a fact that Hoang Bang thought more than most bicycle fix-it men. Hoang Bang had lots to think about.

Like the change that had taken place. The change which was written into all the latest directives from the National Central Committee. The directives had the smell of the Northerners rubbed into them, the smell of Hanoi. They might as well have been drafted there. For all Hoang Bang knew, they probably had, many of them.

Hoang Bang was a Southerner. He didn't care to be patronized, which was what the Northerners did. So Hoang Bang resented the Northerners tho he also needed them, the NLF did, for support and advice. He had resented them most of all when the first of the new directives had come. He had been opposed, they were crazy he thought, but of course he hadn't spoken out. To have spoken out, that would have been crazy too. A useless, suicidal thing. Still Hoang Bang had been set against the new emphasis on violence —the spreading terror, the stepped-up military campaign. It had been his hope, his conviction, that the General Uprising could be attained by political action and not military. Hoang Bang had not wanted anyone hurt unless absolutely positively necessary. He had figured that violence would do the Movement more bad than good. He had figured this way, not so much because he was a feeling man, as because he was a political man. Hoang Bang knew how to feel, but he knew even better how to win votes.

But Hoang Bang had come to realize, just as Hanoi had realized before, that the new emphasis on violence was absolutely positively necessary. He had come to see what he had not seen so clearly before—that the Uprising was not in sight. He had come to tell himself that if the Liberation could not be attained in the way he had hoped, then it would have to be attained in the way of Hanoi. It was a measure of Hoang Bang's good judgement and of his flexibility that now he embraced the new strategy as firmly as he had once the old. The Liberation of the people had to be won, it had to be done, whatever the cost in people. Like Hanoi, Hoang

Bang thought in terms of the people and not in terms of each man.

Hoang Bang, the bicycle man, was Chairman of the Dar Lac Province Central Committee of the NLF. He was a very important fellow, tho no one in Fat Anna's house would have guessed, especially not 'suspicious' Fritz, the intelligence man. He was Colonel Quoc's counterpart, more or less, in the political infrastructure established by the NLF to parallel the bureaucracy of South Vietnam. It was no mean position for a bicycle fix-it man. Especially since the provincial committees played the key role in the NLF's struggle against Saigon. They directed the local political struggle and also the military one thru the NLA which they tightly controlled.

As conceived originally, the political struggle was to have taken precedence over the military—and so it had. It was to have been the primary means for winning the Liberation. The early NLF leaders had been staunch nationalists without sticky ties to Hanoi, and had believed that emphasis on political action would bring about a General Uprising of the masses against the Saigon Government. But by the time of Hoang Bang, it had become increasingly clear that there would be no Uprising. Exceedingly clear, tho not a thing to be talked about, not openly. It had also become exceedingly clear that the Movement's growth in the countryside had reached its peak, that new adherents were harder to win. Partly because those most winnable had already been won. Partly because the General Uprising had not come, and the people had begun to tire of the promises and the demands. Partly because of the countering civic action programs of the Americans.

No Uprising. Dead end ahead. What to do? Change the strategy. So when the NLF's political strategy failed to produce the desired result, the NLF resorted to a military strategy—sabotage, terror, combat operations, that kind of thing—tho, of course, the political front remained a hotly contested one. It was a strategy introduced by the Northerners who were coming to dominate the Front, and who soon did. The General Uprising, they scrapped that. Coercion rather than persuasion, that was what they emphasized. *Violence.* Big doses of violence. Buckets full. Not the drops which had gone before. The new violence had begun to spread thru the countryside in the time of Hoang Bang. Later, not very much later, all the PAVN troops would come, but this was after the time of Hoang Bang.

Tho he worked very hard for the people, Hoang Bang had little to do with them. He lived by himself in the small back room of his small fix-it shop. He prepared his own meals, washed his own clothes, he visited Fat Anna's once a month or twice a month or whenever he felt the need. He didn't chat with his customers, and he treated his fellow committee members perfunctorily, he patronized them.

Hoang Bang was a very slight man. He wasn't a bad cook, that wasn't it; and he kept himself fit; and it wasn't because he was naturally thin, which he was. He just never rested. During the day, he tinkered at the worn and twisted bicycles. During the night, he sat up in his small back room and drew up lists of things to do, and reached tough decisions and prepared orders and coordinated plans, and Fridays the five of them gathered to click, but more about the clicking later. His daytime customers easily bargained him down in price. They thought him a fool for not trying to cheat them. But Hoang Bang had no interest in cheating his customers and little in making money. He wanted only enough to make do, enough for his simple sustenance. It would have surprised his customers to learn how masterful Hoang Bang could be in his true enterprise. And it would have surprised Hoang Bang to learn that the good, simple people for whom he was making a revolution, they thought him a fool for not trying to cheat them.

Hoang Bang was incorruptible. He believed in his revolution and wanted only its success. He wanted nothing for himself. Not power, not recognition. Not even that Betty shouldn't make jokes. A conscience well-served, that's all he wanted. Hoang Bang had gotten where he was because everyone knew that he wanted nothing for himself. He had gotten there without any trouble except for the fact that his name was Hoang Bang and there had once been a Hoang-Bang Dynasty, but Hoang Bang had quickly cleared himself of having to do with that.

As Hoang Bang walked across town to his shop, he considered the change in strategy, and also the very latest directive which he had received just the day before. A fitting directive, a slam-bang one. Hoang Bang didn't know if the directive had gone to the other provincial committees. From something about it, he didn't think so. Only Dar Lac, Hoang Bang thought. To set an example. A test of sorts. Oh, what a big stink there will be! What an uproar in Saigon! One whole village! All the Americans! The Americans, they might make things tough. But Mac Dong Dong would see to that. Hoang Bang was sure that Mac Dong Dong would know what to do and how to go about doing it. Mac was good. He did his work well. Mac was the finest commander of Regionals in Dar Lac.

* * *

Fighter Kim raised his hand. "Can't we just kill the Americans?"

"It would not be enough. More would come to take their place."

"To kill so many of the people—it seems a terrible thing. Can't we make any exceptions? At least the one?"

"No exceptions. Not one."

"It doesn't seem right—all of them—to catch them like that. We should not kill all." For once Kim dissented. Fighter Kim who seldom spoke and then it was always to agree. Then it was softly. Now the softness was gone from Kim's voice and in its place was a brittleness, a fear of offending Mac Dong Dong. The men of the 825th, Fighter Dung and Fighter Dan and Fighter Van, every-one, had all turned their heads toward Fighter Kim and wondered at his boldness. "Perhaps three or four would be enough. Then it will be understood for sure."

If Mac was surprised or irritated, he didn't show it. "No, Fighter Kim, you are wrong. Three or four would not be enough. Three or four deaths are worth only a handful of fear. And a handful of fear is not enough. Not to terrify all the others. Not to make their eyes bulge from their heads, to make their hearts crawl into their throats, to make them shiver in the sun and sweat in the shade and whimper in their sleep. To make these things, we must be generous with the killings. *Generous*, Kim. No exceptions. Then the others— in Buon Sop—in Buon Yak—in all the villages of Dar Lac— they'll run fast and hide if the Americans come again with all their pips and long long noses and their lies. Fast, Kim! How they'll hide! Their hearts in their throats and them somewhere else. Then the lies will be useless things, for there will be no one to hear them spoken."

Kim knew that Mac Dong Dong made sense but, at the same time, that he did not. "Our task is to befriend the people and not to kill them. To speak soft words, to make the people promises. To win their trust. You told us this yourself, Leader Mac. Many times. Is it not?"

"Yes, Fighter Kim, it *is* our task to do these things and not kill the people—sometimes it is. But there are other times too, Fighter Kim, when the Americans come with their lies, with softer words, with promises—bigger ones. Then we must lop off those of the people who have been infected. And some who have not. Just to make sure. To contain the infection. And to warn away the others. So that they will run and hide and show their behinds."

"Leader Mac, I don't understand. If our cause is right, then why have the people not shown their behinds? Why not already? To them, to the Americans. Buon Yun—"

"The people are children, just like children," Mac explained patiently. It was better to explain, to show his men concern. Yet as he explained, Mac's eyes grew larger by a fraction. He wondered at Kim's simpleness. Maybe he had been wrong about Kim. "Just like children, Fighter Kim. To soft words, to the promises, they nod their heads whenever we speak, they sympathize with our cause. To soft words, to the promises, they nod their heads whenever the Americans speak, they make a place for them. Yes, Fighter Kim, isn't it so?" Then to the men of the 825th: "Isn't it so?"

All the men, Fighter Dung and Fighter Dan and Fighter Van, everyone, nodded their heads in agreement with Mac.

"Fighter Kim, I tell you this—it is very nice to have the people's sympathy. But it is better, very much better, more important to have their support. So we will go ahead with the plan, with the terror."

"The terror is a terrible thing—for people like children or people who aren't."

"It is a necessary thing. It is a thing to be wisely used— cautiously—sparingly. When and where it will do the most good, and only then and there. Always for a certain purpose, for a good reason, a well-explained reason—so the people shouldn't think that we kill them for nothing. So it will be clear that we kill only those who make a place—who give the Americans a place—and some others too, just to be sure." Mac spoke smoothly, without a waver, pausing only for effect. "The killings will be well used."

"What about the right?"

"What right, Fighter Kim?"

"The right of our cause. Will our cause still be right?" Oh! Oh! This was serious stuff, indeed, and Kim spoke very nervously. Unlike Mac, unlike Hoang Bang the bicycle man, Kim still thought in terms of each man and not in terms of the people. "Won't we become just like the murdering Saigon-American fascist pigs?" Oh, Kim! Watch your step!

"Foooo, Kim!" said Mac.

"Foo, Kim! Ah, Kim! Oh, Kim! Foo on Kim!" Fighter Dung and Fighter Dan and Fighter Van, everyone, all the men of the 825th repudiated Kim.

"Ah, Kim, you were very good as a buffalo. How well you spun around and around and made the noises and twitched and died. Ah, yes but you still have a lot to learn."

"Oh, Kim, you were very good as a buffalo. How well you shuddered and bleated and died. Oh, yes but you still have a lot to learn. Ooh, Kim! Foo on Kim!"

"Kim, do you think that we're cold-blooded men? Do you think that only you have a heart? Foooo, Kim! My heart is just as great as yours. My blood is just as warm. Fighter Dung and Fighter Dan and Fighter Van, everyone, all the men of the 825th are greathearted, warm-blooded men. We use the terror only as a last resort. Only when there is no other way. We kill the people only when it is absolutely positively necessary. So how can you think that we'll ever be just like the murdering Saigon-American fascist pigs?"

Mac turned to all the men of the 825th. "Our cause has always been right, it always will be. But we must be hard so that we will win. We must be hard now. Later, when the struggle is done—when the Liberation is won—then there will be no people to kill, only words and promises. Hard now, not so hard later. The people, they don't understand. A stooped back or stiff fingers, a grimy face, it's not enough. So we must be hard! We will do what is necessary. It's for their own good. For a warm, snug home. The people, they don't look ahead. So we will look ahead for them."

* * *

Sergeant Lovelace cocked his leg and snapped it forward. Again and again. Sergeant Lovelace had little feet, but he drove his point across. Sergeant Lovelace was kicking ass, getting the Strike Force organized, checking their weapons, booting the men into place. The men took Sergeant Lovelace's boot, they took their time, but they fell into place faster than they had fallen before the night of the party at Y Bun's. They all knew about Lovelace's teeth. They didn't want the teeth snapped at them. The sun came on strong like Sergeant Lovelace. The clouds broke ranks and went their way.

Sergeant Lovelace had once broken his head racing stock cars somewhere in the Carolinas. It was a tribute to his thick skull that he had managed to survive. Lovelace had a baby face, a stub of a nose, tiny ears, and a mean little mouth. His skin was hairless and very pink. He often brooded and, when he was intruded upon, he flared up in anger as hot as the burnt-orange hair on his head. Then he reminded Sergeant Moon of a rotten peach. Plunket too.

Sergeant Lovelace was always paring something with his pocket knife, always cutting something away with almost vicious determination. He handled his pocket knife very well, as he handled all weapons. Lovelace was the weapons man and taught the Strike Force how to use their shiny new guns. How to care for them. He taught the Strike Force ponderously, effectively, fiercely when he lost his patience. Then he would kick, sometimes—if Sergeant Jasperson wasn't around or looking his way. What made him kick hardest, what made him maddest, was their eyes. They couldn't keep one eye closed when sighting down the length of their guns; either two eyes opened, which didn't help the sighting much; or two eyes closed, which didn't help the sighting at all. They were used to looking at the world thru both their eyes and didn't see the point in having one eye closed, which Lovelace did, and so he kicked. He was dedicated to his work and took it very seriously.

There were times when Lovelace seemed like the nicest guy in the world. And other times when he seemed like the all-time champion bastard. Then Sergeant Lovelace would spit and snarl, hackles raised, petty, malicious, full of spite, madly suspicious of everyone's motives, ready to bear a grudge to his death, to fight to it too—except with Fritz, for they were tight. But usually Lovelace was his unsurprising, nicely normal self: mild, good-natured, but also insistent that he be left alone.

Sergeant Lovelace knew at all times what he was doing. He did everything with a purpose. So when he kicked the men into place it wasn't because it gave him great glee, but because that was where the men belonged and the sooner the better, and also it gave him great glee.

Captain Yancy and Jasperson emerged from the operations hut and walked toward where Lovelace was kicking the men. It was early morning. Still cool. Yancy sneezed but, unlike Moon, he didn't stand still!—he didn't lock tight!—he didn't know! He just kept on coming, with Jasperson.

"Eeyah!" said Y——.

"Ooeee!" said Y——.

"Look at the Captain, he doesn't lock tight!"

"He doesn't know!"

"How mad they are! How worse they will be!"

"He rattled the spirits. He should stay still till the spirits calm down."

"Eeyah, he keeps coming our way!"

"He should lock tight."

"It's too late now."

"Then the Captain is wrong to leave this morning."

"Jasperson and Lovelace too, they are wrong to leave this morning."

"The Captain must go back to the hut and wait inside till another day."

"We are all wrong to leave this morning."

"Eeyah, not only the sneeze and he didn't lock tight, but also he sets out on a trip!"

"Ooeee, it will be doubly bad!"

"We should not go with him today. For sure he will bring the *m'klaks* down upon us."

But they went along, Y —— and Y ——. So did the others who had seen, all of them. They went along because they knew that Americans had farfetched ideas about many things and would surely not understand. They went along because, if they didn't, they would surely be kicked off the Strike Force, which was worse, far much worse, than being kicked at by Sergeant Lovelace. Maybe worse than the *m'klaks*. So the Strike Force filed out the gate at Yancy's command and was soon into the bush.

The sun rose higher as the Strike Force plodded ahead. The way grew thick, tangled with thorn and with briar, towered over by elephant grass, barred here and there by wildly spreading gingi trees. The men moved very warily, for VC had been seen in these parts. They carried their weapons chest high and cocked. They tried to avoid the steady snapping and scraping of things across their faces. They peered thru the tangle for Viet Cong, for the *m'klaks*.

But no VC showed, no *m'klaks* descended on them; and after a time, they emerged from the bush and entered open country. Tiger weed. Scattered thickets of bamboo. Flaming-red pepper bushes. Happy blue sky. The hiking was much easier, but the men were more uneasy than ever, for word of Captain Yancy's sneeze had long since passed thruout the file. Wherever the *m'klaks* were, the men were getting closer to them—and also closer to Buon Sop.

"Eeyah, he didn't lock tight!"

"He didn't know."

"How rattled they are!"

"How mad they must be!"

"He should lock tight."

"It's much too late."

"He should not have come."

"None of us, *we* should not have come."

"For sure there will be *m'klaks* upon us."

As soon as Buon Sop came into sight, the *m'klaks* fell upon them. The men had only themselves to blame. They should have sensed immediately that the *m'klaks* were about to strike. They should have known when they saw that the buffaloes were untended, which was a very unusual thing, an extraordinary thing. The *m'klaks* struck with stunning force. They slammed the men right between the eyes.

The man at the point dropped to his knees and covered his head, his arms wrapping round. The man behind crashed up against him and toppled over onto the ground. The third man froze, solid thru, too terrified to do anything more. The fourth began to whimper and whine. The fifth to shiver in the sun. The heart of the sixth crawled into his throat. The eyes of the seventh bulged from his head. Some men cowered and emptied their guts. Others stood tall and very angry. No one stepped forward. No one spoke.

There on the front gate of Buon Sop, there on the sturdy stakes of the gate, there snugly fixed on the points of the stakes and arranged neatly in a row, there grinning in the sun and unspeakable in the silence, there were the nine lopped-off heads of the notables of Buon Sop. Basking there, sunning themselves. The blood dry. The stink strong. The heads aligned like some mute, macabre chorus. The faces mad, absurd, gawking, full of the most comic expressions. A goddamn riot, a goddamn joke, a bunch of grinning idiots. But the terror, it was there. You could still see it in the eyes. It was hard to see the eyes for all the swarming feeding flies.

There was Y M'nung, the village chief, propped-up on the left-most stake, drained of his pride as well as his blood, unaccountably smirking. There were the others left to right, simpering, leering, soaking up the bright morning sun on that beautiful day. They all looked so strange up there on the stakes. So down at the mouth, tho the mouths were twisted up into grins. They looked so unhappy, left to right. To the far right, unhappiest, was a feisty old man. His wisp of a beard swayed in the breeze.

* * *

Captain Yancy was fit to be tied. He stared at the chart spread out before him but couldn't find the right provision. It was the chart for Civilian Casualty Compensation. It was a very worthy chart but it didn't seem to contain a provision for lopped-off heads. There were provisions for loss of limbs, provisions for loss of hands and feet, provisions for loss of fingers and toes, for loss of joints of fingers and toes, for loss of any combination of the above. There were provisions for loss of nose, for loss of eyes, for loss of ears, but there was none for the loss of a head, a whole head. For Chrissake, thought Captain Yancy, why didn't somebody think of a head!? How could they miss a head!? There was death from bombing and from shelling, death from shooting and from knifing, death from strangling and from braining, but there was no death from beheading. And there was no plain old death, it had to be from something.

Once again, Captain Yancy ran his finger down the chart for Civilian Casualty Compensation, down the columns. Captain Yancy was trying hard. He was doing all he possibly could for the people of Buon Sop. He wanted to make things up to them. He *needed* to make things up to them. It was because of the program. If he failed to undo the damage done, or at least make amends, then other villages in Dar Lac—not yet part of the Strike Force program—they'd learn how things had gone with Buon Sop and would decide not to be part.

Of course Captain Yancy felt sorry, too, for the people of Buon Sop. He knew that he was as guilty to them as the ones who had piked their notables' heads. What Yancy didn't understand was why the people wouldn't forgive him anyway, for he had meant well. But instead they had huddled back in the houses, terrified, refusing to acknowledge him. And what had made it worst of all was the amusement of the heads: how they had grinned at the Strike Force patrol as it filed by, as it passed in review, and made a ragged showing.

So Captain Yancy ran his finger down the columns. Until his finger came to rest at Section 8, Provision 11: Psychological Injury. Loss of Face. Yeah, maybe. Well, why not? Why hadn't he thought of that before? Yeah, but—aw hell, why not? It would mean stretching the rules a bit, but, after all, the notables *had* lost their faces—in a way. Maybe not psychologically, but they had lost their faces.

Captain Yancy was proud of himself. Maybe now he could wipe out the team's bad image in Buon Sop, regain its credibility, so that the other villages would not decide not to be part of the Strike

Force program. It gave him a very solid feeling. Yet, at the same time that Captain Yancy was feeling solid, he was also feeling haunted. It was his conscience. There were the people and there were the rules. Yancy's conscience was haunting him about the rules.

Captain Yancy had always played by the rules. He had always gone by the book—one, two, three right down the lines. It bothered him to do otherwise. It befuddled his sense of right and wrong. It made him feel very guilty. He had always been a very inelastic fellow. It pained him to make allowances for any reason whatsoever. So when he decided—aw hell!—to stretch the rules, to use Section 8, Provision 11, you had to give him credit.

Captain Yancy was no actuary. He wasn't one for computing rates. He knew nothing about that stuff. Who was he to say how much was too much or too little? But still it seemed that the compensation provided under Section 8, Provision 11 was a very meager one—$1.43 at the official rate of exchange. Very meager, indeed. Then Yancy remembered that it was not an actual face for which Provision 11 provided. Okay, but still—

Captain Yancy sat and thought. He did these things for a very long time. Then Captain Yancy came up with another smashing idea. In his request to Saigon for the authorization, he would also include sub-requests under Section 3, Provisions 4, 5 and 6—Loss of Nose, Eyes and Ears—which came, respectively, to $3.97, 6.16 and 2.82. All together, Yancy's requests worked out to $14.38 for each notable, for his next of kin.

Captain Yancy was proud of himself all over again. $14.38 was more money than any of them had seen at one time. It was more money than most had handled in all their lives. The people would be very pleased, satisfied. Yancy, himself, was doubly pleased. Pleased for coming up with such a handsome sum. Pleased because he didn't have to stretch the rules a second time, to trouble his conscience a second time. They *had* lost their noses and eyes and ears, hadn't they?

Yancy was halfway thru drafting his message when it suddenly dawned on him that the chart made provision only for those civilians who had been killed or injured by American personnel.

Oh, hell! Oh, no! Stretching the rules, that was one thing, but snapping them was quite another. Captain Yancy knew very well that no American personnel had piked the heads of the notables, had lopped them off. That not one single American had raised a hand, or even a pinkie, against the nine. Oh, hell. Oh, well. Yancy's rosiness bled from his face, his cheerfulness. The chart made it plain and clear: by American personnel only.

Captain Yancy thought some more but it was no good. He knew that MACV had this thing for charts. That MACV would reject out of hand whatever hadn't been carefully worked into its charts. That MACV stuck to its charts like a bulldog. Goddamn Sergeant Lovelace's teeth!

So Yancy crumpled up the request. He dropped it into an old coffee can. It dropped lightly, with a plunk. Not KCHUNK! like the heads of the nine when they had been lopped. The heads which Yancy had never ordered taken down.

THE KANDY BEAR

Grandmother Pan was down in the grass on her hands and knees, in the stretch of grass which led to the river and to the forest just beyond. She was inching her way thru the wet grass, slithering from clump to clump, nosing up to each blade. Beautifully ugly Grandmother Pan was the friendliest, dearest, most mischievous hag in all Buon Yun, with darting black eyes and withered cheeks and toothless black gums and wisps of gray hair escaping her bun and straggling onto her face. She was gristly and chewy and horny-skinned and hollow-rumped and hard at searching.

Grandmother Pan shouldered ahead, over the hardness of the ground and thru the wet chill of early morning and into the fog, spun-sugar white, covering the Plateau du Dar Lac. Grandmother Pan searched happily, grandmotherly, peering into each drop of dew, looking for the proper one. The one to be placed on the tip of her newborn grandson's tongue. The one for the naming ceremony. The one which contained the ancestor spirits—from whose names the name would come.

"What is your name, your name is it ———— ?" That's how it went, after the dew drop was placed on the tongue. And the child would smile if he was pleased, if that was his name. Or maybe he would just foolishly grin. But if the child wasn't pleased, if the name wasn't his, then he would kick out or drivel or cry, very vexed, until the right name was struck upon. Sometimes the naming ceremony went very fast—if the child was a smiling one. Sometimes it was a drawn-out affair, a taxing one, if the child was cranky.

Sergeant Fritz was down there too, crawling alongside Grandmother Pan; after all, Fritz was the intel man whose job it was to find out things, presumably dew drops among them. Fritz was happy to be of service, proud that she had asked him along, of her confidence in his expertise. He was happy and proud, but not so inured as Grandmother Pan to the hardness of the ground and the chill and the spun-sugar fog. He wobbled along, bumping his knees, scraping his shins, as patches of wet spread up his thighs and up his arms and blotted along his underbelly. Fritz was happy for Grandmother Pan, and happy because he was always so— because things always worked out for the best. Because they would soon find the proper dew drop, he was dead sure, and then he could get up from all fours and out of the grass and dried in the sun. Ahhh—the sun! Where was the sun? The sun will always shine for Fritz, Fritz always said.

Little Rhadeo was down in the grass alongside Fritz, helping dear old Grandmother Pan because she had always been good to him. He was fifteen or sixteen, he wasn't sure which, with a melon-round face and big brown eyes and gleaming white teeth, and he stood no higher than Sergeant Moon's chest when he was standing and not on all fours; his teeth gleamed because Moon had taught him to brush. Rhadeo burrowed thru the grass, searching for the proper dew drop and also checking to see his harmonica didn't fall out, the one Sergeant Moon had given him, the one Moon was teaching him how to play. Rhadeo was cuddly and eager, taking to Moon like a puppy dog, yelping when his knee struck stone.

Last but not least was Moon, himself, there in the grass because Little Rhadeo was his best friend; and because he was touched by Grandmother Pan's kind toothless mug, and her impish ways, and her happy need; and, besides, he was intrigued. Moon was always being intrigued by stuff like searching for proper dew drops, ones with ancestor spirits inside. So Moon peered into each drop of dew, unsure what they looked like, these ancestor spirits, but still pretty sure he would recognize them if they happened to be there. Maybe they were like tiny people peering back out. Or maybe they were a pale blue light, or a pale green, shimmering within the drop. Or maybe it was just a way of looking at things, of having a feeling. If somehow you *knew*, if all of a sudden you were dead certain that there were ancestor spirits inside, then that was enough—they were inside.

The four of them slithered side by side, getting soaked and dirtied up, and hungry and chilled, but still full of cheer and enthusiasm and the best hopes. They were happy for the newborn child, and for each other, and for themselves, because the dew drop—the naming rites—got one off to a proper start, to a promising start in life. They were four, trying to start a fifth off right. It bound them together; it reflected on them all. And the sun climbed higher and broke thru the fog, just as Fritz had known it would, and shone down bright as a blessing.

Grandmother Pan worked her gums, and now and then swept back a straggle of hair. She got her little nose up to the drops, closer even than Sergeant Moon. And some looked like they might be the one, but weren't the one, and Grandmother Pan would shake her head and forge right on, tough and tender and lovable.

Sergeant Fritz felt his belly get wetter and the ground harder and the way denser, tho the fog was breaking up, but he also felt the sun shining down and took comfort from it. He wobbled on, looked over the drops, and plinked them when they weren't the one.

Little Rhadeo and Sergeant Moon beamed at each other, full of camaraderie, of the truest friendship. They grinned, they winked. Not because they thought it was hocus-pocus. Little Rhadeo certainly didn't, and neither did Moon who had a fine touch for these things. They winked because that was one way they embraced each other, that was one way they shared their delight. They winked at sharing in a great search, a great adventure, for the right dew drop, or it could have been pirates' treasure, tho Rhadeo didn't know about them.

They searched on and on, as the sun climbed higher and shined down brighter, and Grandmother Pan forged ahead of the rest, pulling their formation out of line. The four of them looked for all the world like they were policing up cigarette butts. They crawled on and on; and some dew drops looked like they were the one, but weren't the one; and on and on until Moon cried out: "I've found it! I've found it! It's here! Right here!" So everyone scrambled over to Moon and had a look, and there it was—the proper dew drop! There were no tiny people inside peering back out. There was no shimmering light, blue or green. But they all knew—Grandmother Pan and Fritz and Little Rhadeo knew that it was the one, that ancestor spirits were there inside, because Moon, himself, was so dead sure.

Eeyah! Ooeee! It was a great discovery—Sergeant Moon finding the proper dew drop! Little Rhadeo beamed with great pride at his brilliant friend. Grandmother Pan cackled with joy. She beamed more brightly than Rhadeo tho she didn't have any shiny white teeth. She felt renewed. She felt the depression of the past week lift from her shoulders and flit away.

After all, Buon Yun was Buon Yun and not Buon Sop. True, the people had stumbled about with their heads bent low and their bodies slack and with a scorching in their hearts. And some of them went around blaming the teeth for everything, Lovelace's teeth; Yancy's sneeze too, tho that had come after. But now it was time to steady themselves, to righten their heads and straighten their backs, and as for their hearts being charred on the outside, they were otherwise good as ever. It was time to feel secure again, for things to return to normal.

The Americans had lived among them for almost two months, hadn't they? Buon Yun had become their village too. They had no choice as villagers but to stay and defend Buon Yun. Besides, no one's pigs had been slaughtered, no one's chickens carried off. No one went to bed hungry at night, no one's belly made the noises. No one's head had been lopped off. Maybe in Buon Sop, not in Buon Yun.

The people of Buon Yun felt very sorry for their brothers in Buon Sop. But there was only so much sorrow they could feel about pigs and chickens and notables of a village not their own. About their heads. Didn't their own lives have to be served, thought Grandmother Pan, and couldn't their lives best be served by having things return to normal? It had been a very grim week after the incident at Buon Sop. But now it was time to smile and laugh. It was time to look ahead to the treat that Captain Yancy had promised them.

Finding the dew drop changed everything for Grandmother Pan. She now knew that the worst was over, that everything would go well for Buon Yun. Grandmother Pan beamed because of this omen, because there were better times ahead, and because her grandson would now have a name. Fritz, he pummeled Moon hard on the back, offering congratulations, and also being a little miffed because he was the intelligence man and should have found the dew drop instead.

*   *   *

Mac Dong Dong sat on the stump from which he had heard out the bandaged-head man. From which he had spoken to Fighter Kim and the other men about the propriety of terror. Great-hearted Mac sat on the stump, scratching his crotch joylessly. Not because he itched like a fiend, but because he was thinking hard. The harder Mac thought, the harder he scratched, as if he were rigged up to work that way. He was mauling away, all three fingers. Cowlick flopping. Steeping in his vinegar. Considering the means at hand to set wrongs right, the go-ahead. Mac was very pleased by his thoughts, but he was also worried.

He was pleased about the latest directive, the one Hoang Bang had passed down to him. It was a grand directive: bold, timely, cleverly simple, bound to cause a great stink in Saigon, a great commotion. Mac was proud to have been entrusted with such a directive. It meant that Hoang Bang, or others on the Provincial Committee, thought highly of him. He was eager to execute the directive, to work its boldness, its simple strength into final form. He was eager, too, for the sake of the men. For Fighter Dung and Fighter Dan and Fighter Van and all the rest. Their teeth, their claws needed sharpening; their muscles needed stretching. Most of all, Mac was eager to mete out justice and to instruct. To teach the people of Buon Yun the kind of lesson he had taught to those of Buon Sop. But more strictly. Much more strictly. For, in Buon Yun, there was much more bad learning to undo. He was eager to teach the Americans too, those in Saigon. For there would be none left in Buon Yun.

Mac was worried because the 825th needed more men, and also it needed the party favors, and then there was the plantation.

The 825th was not up to full strength. It had never been, never needed to be. But now the 825th needed to be, if the directive was to be met. New recruits had to be found. They had to be trained and indoctrinated. All in a hurry. But where could new recruits be found, Mac asked himself. Not in Buon Sop. It would be weeks, maybe months, before the people of Buon Sop would be fit for anything. Then where? Not Buon Yun.

The party favors. They were vital. Without them, it would go hard on the men. Mac clucked with concern about the favors, over the men. He clucked like a foreman with a job that had to get done. More like that than a mother hen. Mac clucked like Captain Yancy clucked whenever Plunket lost his head over some crazy idea, or Sergeant Lovelace came down with the sulks, or Sergeant Goodbody pestered him to look into those sick rolling eyes. Mac and Yancy clucked over the men the way they clucked over a rusty gun. They wanted things oiled and smooth and ready so they would function properly. While Mac was clucking, he was counting on Phum and Luu. It had been arranged for them to bring the favors. They were due by the first.

After more men and the party favors, there was the plantation to consider. Hoang Bang the bicycle man had promised to arrange for it, to let Mac know as soon as the 825th could move there. The plantation was right in between. And it was secure. The new recruits could be trained there, the operation could be rehearsed without the Americans sniffing around. Yet, as secure as the plantation was, the men would have to be very sneaky about moving there.

The men—the *men*—thought Mac Dong Dong—they were the most important of all, and the hardest to gauge. Mac had no doubts about their cause and its success, but he knew it wasn't the same with his men. He knew that it was harder for them. Their life in the forest was, at best, uncomfortable; dreadful, at times. Oh, there was always enough rice to eat, more than enough; and dried fish too, tho oftentimes just the heads, which were good only for so much sucking; but never meat, except for a lizard or field-mouse or two which they trapped, not daring to waste any ammunition or to be heard; and vegetables seldom, only what they found in the woods—for the land was poor where they operated and so were the people they taxed. So mostly rice; and rice, he knew, wasn't really enough.

And he knew how little they were paid—80 piasters, what was

at!? It wasn't enough to buy a woman, or even tobacco. Yes,
ought Mac, *of course* it was unrevolutionary to buy a woman, but
ll—but still—his men had their needs. And what did it matter
yway? They never got near a town.

It might have helped, Mac supposed, if this were the home dis-
ct of the men, or even the province; but it wasn't close. He knew
at, however national, however universal their cause, the first
legiance of his men was to their home villages. That was where
eir sympathies lay. They had to be taught to look beyond, to
ke on greater loyalties. The men had been slow to look beyond.

And now, on top of everything, it was during the rainy season,
hen it was so wet and miserable. At the very beginning, too, so
ere would be many months ahead of being wet and miserable.

Not only was all this rough on the men, but rougher still, because
eir dedication wasn't the same as his. He knew, all right, how
me of the men had been recruited and for what unheroic reasons:
ke Dan, for instance, who had seen a propaganda show and had
ought that it would be kind of fun; and Dung, who had heard that
e Viet Cong got all the girls; and some because their friends had
ined, and what could they do but also join.

So their motives were not as refined as his. And he knew how
arsh the discipline must be for them, how unending. Yet what
ere a few months of discipline or a few years, or even more,
mpared to the day that was surely ahead?

And he knew how his lectures day after day bored the men and
ade them drowsy, tho what was so dull about politics? It was a
bject which should have inspired them, should have roused them
learn even more. Self-improvement was a good thing, a righteous
ing. Also a necessary thing for soldiers who would show the way.

No, thought Mac, it wasn't easy—even with history on their side
d being in the right and all. He was no fool. He thought things
ru. He saw the black side as well as the white. No, thought Mac,
wasn't so inevitable; otherwise why did it come so hard, with so
uch gore? He was no ogre. He felt things too. His heart pumped
ood. He choked on gore like any man—tho there were times,
fortunately, when you had to swallow it down.

Well at least, thought Mac, he had tried to be as honest as pos-

sible with the men. He wasn't like some others he knev
like ————, for instance, in Pleiku, who spoke of great victor
even when his men dropped like flies. The men lost too many
their friends; they knew a victory and when it wasn't. They couldn
be lied to about such things. Tho, of course, you couldn't alway
come out and tell the whole truth. Sometimes part of the truth wa
best, or even none; for truth could be a viperous thing, fanged an
coiled there at your feet, which needed to be stepped around.

And what was all this, anyway, about truth and about great vi
tories? There hadn't been great victories, real or fake, or small on
either. That's what made it hardest of all—not having only fis
heads to suck, and not enough money with nowhere to spend i
and the rain, but that there had been no victories. Oh yes, thoug
Mac, a victory would surely help. A smashing great big victor
They would need more men and the party favors and there wa
the plantation to consider. A smashing great victory at Buon Yu

* * *

Sergeant Lovelace and Sergeant Moon caught the milk run fro
Ban Me Thuot. It was thanks to Grandmother Pan. That dear ol
lady had spoken to Yancy about sending Sergeant Moon to Saigo
She wanted to reward him, she said, for finding the dew dro
She told Captain Yancy all about it, as he stood there and blinke
at her. She told how they had searched thru the grass, and peere
at each drop, and that her grandson would have a name. "Sergea
Moon deserves his reward, so let him go," she said. What she didn
tell Yancy was that Moon had put her up to asking. Now, Captai
Yancy had troubles enough. The leaflets continued to darken h
thoughts. And the reparations for Buon Sop. And there had bee
the delegation led by Y Bun: they had made him promise abo
some rope, that it wouldn't be cut. What with all these confoune
ing things, he needed respite. Tho Yancy had doubts about th
dew drop—that Moon had, indeed, seen someone inside, he wante
Grandmother Pan off his back and so had agreed to let Moon g
He let Sergeant Lovelace go as well, so Moon wouldn't get i
trouble.

They arrived in Saigon on a sunshiny promising afternoon. Ou

le the airport gate, they hired a couple of pedicabs pedaled by
o lean Vietnamese with hollow cheeks and flashing gold teeth,
pecially in the sun. Then they went rattling across Saigon to
a Do Street where they took a room at the Catinat, a hotel favored
GIs in the center of where all the bar-girls were. They were
corted to their room by a musty old bellboy who smirked just
e the head of Y M'nung, and who asked if they wanted two
mber-one girls or, perhaps, one fat young boy. Sergeant Lovelace
ased the bellboy all the way down the corridor, trying to land one
cked kick but never quite getting close enough. The Sergeants
owered, napped for awhile, slipped into civvies, left the hotel,
abbed a bowl of noodle soup at Cheap Charlie the Chinaman's,
en set out for Lovelace's favorite haunt. "Hey, wait'll you see
e Happy Bar. It's got the best. There's this one skag, I swear
you, she can do it a hundred and seven ways." "Yeah, is there
e who can climb a palm, and catch me all kinds of fish with a
ear, or maybe little crabs in the sand?" Lovelace looked at
rgeant Moon and asked himself: Whatta my gonna do with this
d? What he needs is a kick in the ass, right up the ol' ass.

From the outside, the Happy Bar looked like all the other un-
ppy joints, the weary joints tho they could seem gay, which lined
a Do Street down towards the river. Inside, it looked like the
hers too. It was early evening and the Happy Bar was jammed
th people and with noise, bouncing with noise, humming with
utual deceit:

I crazy for you please buy me a drink.

Hey, yeah—me too—crazy too—lemme come home.

*Oh I so crazy for you but I live with old mother and ten young
ter.*

Yeah—well—let's go some place.

Anytime. For you anytime. But not tonight.

There were pretty Vietnamese girls, and there were skaggy Viet-
mese girls, and there were girls who fell in between. They were
anding behind the counter which ran the length of the room.
uared off against the Americans who straddled the stools on the
blic side. The girls chatted brightly, or shrilly complained about

something or other, or they just stood silent and bored. The
argued with their customers or played dice with them or held the
hands. Whatever they did, they got the Americans to drink-
steadily, relentlessly—for each drink ordered by the American
meant that much more money to the girls. The girls were dresse
in virgin white. It had been decreed during the reign of Ngo Din
Diem and his sister-in-law, Madame Nhu; and tho Diem and Nh
were gone, the girls still dressed in virgin white.

Sergeant Lovelace and Sergeant Moon had barely gotten thr
the door, when something white came hurtling at them. "Lovel
lace! Lovelylace!" It was Helen. "Lovelylace! Long time I don
see you! Howzabout a kiss for Helen?" Lovelace kissed Hele
and rumpled her butt, but apparently he held something back. "He
Lovelylace, whatsa matter with you!? You don't love Helen an
more? Helen so crazy for Lovelylace. Think about him all th
time. Send message. You get message? Oooh, who your hand
some friend!?"

"Moon, this is Helen, an old snake of mine. Sure, Helen, I lov
you some more. Howzabout two *Ba Mi Ba*s?"

"Howzabout for Helen?"

"Yeah, sure, Snakey-face. Go ahead. Have some tea. Take a
my money."

Helen giggled and began to do just that. She began to drin
tea at a dollar a shot, tea after tea, while the Americans dran
their beer. They had gotten the last two stools.

The pretty girls were all taken. So were the ones who fell i
between. One of the skags, with a hard face and a scraping voic
asked Sergeant Moon to buy her a drink. Sergeant Moon dran
off his beer and bolted out of the Happy Bar.

Moon in the California Bar. Across the street. Having himself
Ba Mi Ba. A young girl with glossy black hair and big almon
eyes sat facing him. Her little nose flared at the wings, just enoug
for a proper exotic touch and not a millimeter more. Her wris
were thin, her fingers long. Her bust was full, it swelled again
her virgin white blouse. She smelled of butterscotch or vanilla

rgeant Moon wasn't sure which. Whichever it was, she was the
m of all the girls he had dreamt about during the long nights at
uon Yun, when he wasn't off at Grandmother Pan's or dreaming
out something else. He was tempted to say "pardon me Miss,"
en gobble her up. The girl spoke softly, musically. Her voice was
veet, like the smell of her skin, but spicy too. More like cinnamon
d cloves than like vanilla or butterscotch.

"Hello. I never see you before."

"I've never been."

"You have sad eyes. Maybe you lose girlfriend, yes?"

"No girlfriend."

"You don't talk much. I should go?"

"No, stay. Hey, can you climb a coconut palm and catch me all
nds of fish with a spear?"

The girl had never heard an American talk like this and she didn't
now what to say.

"What do you say? Come, let's go. We'll go to the river and steal
sampan. Then we'll sail to Cap St Jacques. We'll sleep on the
each and make love in the bushes. I'll crack a coconut on my head
d give you the milk. But you have to catch me fish with a spear—
· drag your fingers thru the sand and catch me little crabs to eat.
'e'll chase each other and wrestle and be very happy together.
kay? Number one? Ready? Let's go!"

The girl who smelled like vanilla or butterscotch, she just
ughed. "I get bad sunburn. My name is Phan."

"I'm Moon."

"Are you funny man, Moon, or are you sad?"

"Sometimes funny, sometimes sad."

"Which more?"

"Whichever one you want me to be."

"I want both."

"Would you like some tea, Phan?"

"No tea. Very expensive. We just talk."

So they did. They talked about a million things which they had
ever talked about, not before, not to anyone. They talked of tiny,
cret fears and of grand, impossible dreams. Phan spoke of being

frightened by the gathering and unfurling shadows as she lay awak
at night and made the shadows with her fingers. The shadows on th
walls of her room. She spoke of very much wanting to see th
sugar-coated Kandy bear at the zoo in Ceylon which a friend ha
told her about. She didn't think she would ever go. Sergeant Moo
he spoke of his fear for the health of his friend, Sergeant Good
body, and of how he was going to help. He spoke of his frien
Little Rhadeo, of the marvelous things Rhadeo had told him. H
also spoke about the Nile, of wanting to discover its source 10
years ago.

It wasn't till twelve, when all the bars on Tu Do closed, tha
Sergeant Moon went home with Phan. She changed into jeans, an
pigtailed her hair, and then cooked dinner for herself and Moon
rice, vegetables, strips of meat. The sunflower oil crackled and spi
A single candle lit the room and Phan's shadow danced on the wal
as she moved about. It was the coziest, glowingest room, the mo
right at home, most perfect room that Sergeant Moon had eve
been in. And Phan was the most fetching vanilla or butterscotch gi
he had ever been in a perfect room with. He was falling madl
in love with Phan. He knew that Phan was falling madly in lov
with him too.

They ate and talked and went to bed quite naturally, as if the
had done it often before but never so excitingly. Never so toppe
with hot fudge and whipped cream and a cherry. In the mornin
they rose late. They took their time getting dressed, ate the last o
the rice and vegetables and strips of meat, then went for a wal
A nice long walk. After the walk, they returned home. They chase
each other around the small room, they wrestled and were happ
together. Phan left for work at four and Moon, he went wanderin
exploring the back streets of Saigon. Moon returned just befo
midnight and waited for Phan. When she came home, Phan thre
her arms tight around Moon and she covered his face with kisse
She changed into jeans, and pigtails too, and cooked them dinn
in the light of a single candle, and her shadow danced on the wall
After they ate, they went to bed. Hot fudge and whipped crea
and a cherry.

Phan told Moon that he stuck out his tongue even in his slee

Moon had this thing about his tongue. He was always sticking it out. Not to razz people, not for that. But to rasp. To taste every sweet and sour bit. To Sergeant Moon, life was a stream which flowed directly before his face. All of life's sweet and sour bits, they bobbed up and down in that stream. So Moon was always closing his eyes, and sticking his tongue smack into the stream, and rasping the sweet and sour bits. If he shut his eyes tightly enough, Moon could really taste them.

When Phan threatened to snip off his tongue, Moon pretended to be alarmed, and buried his head under the pillow, and both of them had a good laugh. As for Phan, Moon told Phan that she twitched her nose just like a bunny when she slept. That she made a small noise like a Dipa bird, especially when he tickled her toes.

That was it. The way it went. Dinner and bed, and walks and bed, and lots of tender playfulness. Lots of fooling around, but earnestness too. Phan making shadows with her fingers every night, then hiding in fright tight against Moon. Phan threatening to snip. Moon making her twitch like a bunny. Hot fudge and whipped cream and a cherry. Sergeant Moon's R & R sped by with this sweet regularity.

On the morning of the last day, as they hugged and kissed good-bye at the door, Phan asked Sergeant Moon for some money. "Maybe you give me some money, yes?" Moon's face exploded. It burst into the hottest, deepest, prickliest red imaginable. His knees buckled. His legs came close to staving in. For an instant, for more than an instant, he had to lean up against the door. He stared at Phan. Why? How come? He was unable to understand. Then he turned and, without a word, he fumbled down the stairs.

While Sergeant Moon's steps could still be heard, the steps which were taking him away, Phan flung herself down on the bed and began to cry. Phan didn't understand. She liked him better than the others. She liked Sergeant Moon a very whole lot. Phan, she had told him so.

Moon and Lovelace met at the Hotel Catinat. They hired a couple of pedicabs pedaled by two lean Vietnamese with hollow cheeks and flashing gold teeth, but not so much now, for the sun was in. Then they rattled across Saigon to the airport. They caught the milk run to Ban Me Thuot. It was then that Moon frightened Lovelace. Moon was sitting there grinding his jaws, and tossing his head from side to side, and walloping the air with his fists, mumbling that he should have known. That she had never answered him about the climbing, or the spearing, or about the little crabs. That she had never said she could.

△ BUON YAK

Casper did not really work for AID, and everyone knew it. His name was there in the book, all right, for all to see: Joe Casper—AID Representative, Dar Lac Province. And Casper even did some of the things, some of the time, that AID men are supposed to do. He filled out forms and submitted reports. He liased with Vietnamese officials. He lent his support to local projects, such as the well at Buon Yak. He did whatever had to be done, so that he could do the other things, the ones which were truly his business.

Joe Casper didn't know that everyone knew he didn't really work for AID. He wouldn't have guessed in a million years that his secret was out. Not in two. Casper was a brilliant man. He was a man who reasoned things thru from beginning to end and back again. He was a man of imagination. A man whose nose could sniff things out. A man who knew his way around, having been in Dar Lac for almost two years. Yet, in spite of his brilliant mind and his nose and his knowing his way around, he had no idea that he, alone, took himself for the man from AID.

The trouble lay in the fact that Casper outdid himself. He was so overwhelmingly inconspicuous doing whatever things he did, when he wasn't doing AID things, that he never failed to call attention to himself. Casper had a folded-up way of sitting in corners and listening to others. Or of stalking the streets and the country paths and gauging everything in sight. He tucked his shoulders and head toward his chest, he sucked in his belly, he bent his knees to shorten his legs. He half shut his eyes and he whistled a silent tune and pretended to be doing absolutely nothing. He made himself as invisible as he possibly could. As small, as innocuous. It was this

inconspicuousness that made him stand out. Whenever something
scraped or creaked, or it rattled for no good reason, whether in
some peasant's hut, or in the back room of some shop in Ban Me
Thuot, or even in a Viet Cong camp, it was said that he was about
because there was no one there.

While Casper didn't care that much about giving aid to anybody,
this doesn't mean that he didn't care for the people of Dar Lac. On
the contrary. He cared that the people of Dar Lac had something
satisfying to do. That they were happily occupied. That they were
amused. So Casper organized games for the people, for some of
them. These games were the other thing that Casper did. He taught
them games like hide and seek. And word games full of nonsense
words. He improvised all sorts of tricks to be played on people
he didn't like by those he did. Casper enjoyed the games thoroughly;
he ate them up. He worked to infect the people with his enthusiasm.
The only game Casper didn't enjoy was when he had to play at
being the AID representative.

Unfortunately, it was that time. It was time for a trip north to
Buon Yak. It was time to see about the new well.

The well had been a troublesome thing, and not so much because
of the digging as because of the rumors. The rumors had reached
not only Buon Yak, but all places where American civic action
programs were in progress. They were terrible, unbelievable rumors,
but nonetheless many people believed them. And many others were
close to believing. And everyone had been affected by them. The
Vietnamese peasants were superstitious, the highland people even
more so. The rumors were spread by the Viet Cong.

They were spread because the Viet Cong were both worried and
vexed about what was happening. The VC were worried because,
here and there, the Americans were winning the gratitude of the
people by handing out rice, by building schools, by teaching the
people how to dig wells. Winning their allegiance too, despite the
bumbling, the coming on heavy, the stumbling headlong over local
traditions when they should have been gracefully skirted. The VC
were vexed, they were hurt, because here and there, the people
appreciated Americans more than VC.

So the VC countered with propaganda. They passed out leaflets.

hey circulated the terrible rumors. The VC claimed that the rice
as hexed and would cause all the people to fall under a black,
lack spell. That the schools would teach only Government lies and
ervert the minds of the children. That the new wells would yield
oisoned water. That whatever the Americans did, they did it for
ome evil purpose. Why should they give away something for
othing? It had never been done before. Certainly not by the local
fficials. It was unknown.

Many people at Buon Yak were cowed by the rumors just as
eople were cowed elsewhere. They were cowed because they were
uperstitious. Because they couldn't imagine receiving something
or nothing. Because they all knew that Casper wasn't really the
man from AID.

So, tho the digging had gone well, there were the rumors. Casper
ad to contend with them.

Casper left town along the tree-lined avenue which struck north-
est and soon turned into a pot-holed dirt road. Casper looked
ery smart. He had told his barber the day before to give him his
ery best haircut ever because he was paying a call on Buon Yak,
nd his scowly-faced barber had obliged. Casper also looked very
leased. He had bought a sturdy wooden bucket for the people of
uon Yak, for their well. He was pleased to be bringing them a
resent.

Casper's jeep sloshed along. He traveled thruout Dar Lac in
at jeep, wherever there were roads to travel and sometimes where
ere weren't. He traveled alone. Yet Casper didn't consider him-
lf a foolhardy fellow. As a civilian, as the man from AID, he felt
e could travel about the countryside as he pleased, without any
ar. After all, he wasn't trying to kill anybody. No, sir. Everyone
new that he was the man from AID, didn't they? And, besides,
ccording to intelligence—his and Fritz's—the area was clear of
C, relatively clear.

Casper carried a gun just in case, but he didn't expect any
ouble. Who would want to play games with him? He didn't know
at he had been spared only because the Viet Cong knew all about
m. Because they preferred to have him around, to tolerate him,

rather than have to contend with someone new and unpredictable. So long as he didn't get out of hand. *That* long. It had nothing to do with affection. So long as he didn't fit into their plans.

Casper left his jeep outside the rear gate of Buon Yak. The well had been dug in the rear of the village, and Casper was anxious to make right for it, anxious to get his inspection done. As he entered Buon Yak, he was greeted by Y —— the notable, and by Y —— and Y ——. Everyone else was off in the fields or working on the longhouse ledges—mending this, tending to that, doing whatever had to be done. There were some children playing nearby but Y —— the notable shooed them away because the inspection of a well was serious business, men's business. They had drawn close to sniff at Casper.

Y —— led the way to the well. All the earth thrown up by the digging still lay in great mounds around the well and hid it from view. Casper made a big to-do of his inspection. He circled the well several times, gauging this and gauging that, making all sorts of gauging noises. Then he noticed the rope was gone.

"Hey, where's the rope? The long, thick rope I left last time."

"It was used to fasten the hammock."

"What hammock?"

"The hammock between the suju trees. The one for the spirits to sleep in during the rainy season. It would not be right for the spirits to sleep on the wet ground."

Y —— and Y —— nodded their heads. Y —— was right. The spirits should not sleep on the wet ground. They nodded tho they didn't speak French or understand.

Casper fetched a rope from his jeep and tied it to the wooden bucket. Then he looked at the three villagers, thinking that they weren't enough. He wanted to present the bucket to all the people of Buon Yak. To do it in some grand, formal way. But there was only Y —— and Y —— and Y ——. Since Casper was in such a hurry, since there was no time to page the others, he made a brief well-wishing speech and handed the bucket, rope and all, to Y—— but Y —— handed the bucket right back.

"Some people say that the water is bad. That it will make everyone sick. That maybe you want to make everyone sick."

"Who says these things? Tell me, who?"

"Some people say them."

"Do you believe?"

"I don't know." Y —— looked lost. "How should I know?"

Then it dawned on Casper. "You mean that no one has drunk om the well!? In all this time!?"

"No one has drunk. Some people said—" Y —— looked down at s feet. "You did not come back."

Casper did the only thing he could do: he lowered away. He wered the bucket, then drew up the water and tasted it. Casper as the very first to drink from the well. The water tasted very od, clear and cool. "Tell everyone that the water is good." He ank again, making a show of swallowing, of gulping down. Casper as proud of his Adam's apple and how it lurched up and back. e was proud to be proving that the water was safe to drink. "Well, hat do you say to that?" Casper drank one more time. "Good ater, eh?"

Y —— nodded. So did Y —— and Y ——. Then they drank om the bucket too. They drank until Casper was satisfied. Then asper finished his inspection.

He leaned over the wooden guard and peered down the shaft the well. The well had been dug as he instructed, deep and raight. The walls were round and very smooth except for the arp prong of a rock jutting out here and there. As Casper was ering down the shaft, Y —— smashed the bucket against his ad, while Y —— and Y —— upended him and shoved him in. asper bounced from wall to wall as he plummeted down. After-ards, they ditched the jeep.

* * *

One week after Casper's inspection, the rumors came true. Buon ak was visited by a plague. A great many people were suddenly ricken by violent, diabolical illness. The children and old ones ffered worst, but all the afflicted suffered badly. Their bellies were utched with terrible pain and their heads soared high with fever. hey felt nauseous, dizzy, weak, dried out. They dragged their odies wearily from place to place when they had to move, but ey preferred not to move at all. Their stools were loose and bloody

and foul. Some of the children went into convulsion. There wasn'
enough scorpion's urine to go around.

Tho no one had died from this visitation, the village, of course
was greatly alarmed. The notables met to talk things over. One or
two were very angry, but most of them were simply confused
Overwhelmed. The sickness had struck so suddenly, for no apparen
reason. There was no epidemic in the district. None of the othe
villages had been visited like Buon Yak. None were clutched an
reeling high and dragging and smelly and getting the shakes
Only Buon Yak. Why them? Why Buon Yak? None of the peopl
had seen a turtle facing east, or had killed a snake in the triba
fields, or had sneezed and not stood still. No one had invited ba
luck, but still the visitation had come.

At first they had thought it might be the teething, for it wa
small children who first took sick and came down with the runs; a
everyone knew, the runs in small children was caused by teething
It was a lot of teething at once. But then the old ones came dow
too. "It can't be the teething! No, not the teething!" everyone said
"All the old ones have it too! It's for sure they've cut their las
teeth!"

The notables yammered about this and that, about anything an
everything, for they knew nothing. The notables spoke of the nee
to appease some spirit or other which the village, all of them, mus
have offended. But which spirit had been offended? Perhaps th
spirit of the tree trunk. Or the spirit of the mole hill. Or the spiri
of morning fog. Or the spirits of the night. Which one? There wer
so many to consider. And would Y ——, their sorcerer, know th
right formula for the appeasement: the right words, and how many
times, and how many jugs and chickens and pigs and even fat blac
buffaloes to sacrifice? And how had they all offended the spiri
anyway? It was a great mystery.

It seemed no great mystery to Y ——. He was the angry one. Th
Americans, they were to blame. They had loosed a great evil upor
Buon Yak and now it was clutching the people's insides. Y ——
pointed out that there had been no sickness at all, none of th
clutching, until they had started to drink from the well. He didn'
point out that it was he who had passed the word that the wate

as good. Y —— claimed that the Americans had poisoned their
ater, that Casper had done this unspeakable thing. You all know
e isn't the man from AID, not really, Y —— said.

Tho all the notables knew of the rumors, tho some had even been
ose to believing, most of the notables weren't ready to accept
—— 's accusation. This Casper he wasn't the man from AID, it
as true, but had he not come to help the people anyway? There
as the well. And the rope for the hammock. And the bucket. The
pe for the bucket. About Casper, no, it could not be. Casper
ould not have done such a thing. No, not Casper. Y —— was
rong. The mystery was still unsolved.

A vote was taken. It was decided to wait and see, to do nothing
bout the well. To see if Y ——, their sorcerer, could get to the
ottom of the matter. Y —— stormed out of the meeting angrier
an ever. He spread his awful accusation thruout the village.

Most of the people hadn't really believed the rumors which
ached Buon Yak. But the rumors had swayed the people enough
wait until Casper had drunk from the well before they drank
emselves. Then they had drunk with confidence, sure that the
mors had been all wrong. Sure that the man with three fingers
as wrong, the man who had warned them what would happen if
ey had to do with Americans. In any way.

Now the people weren't so sure. Perhaps the rumors had been
ue after all. Perhaps the three-fingered man had been right. Per-
aps this Casper had been immune. Some secret potion. Perhaps
is. Perhaps that. There were so many perhapses. But the people
uld not bring themselves to believe, to fully believe, that Casper
ould have done such a thing. There was the well. The ropes. The
ucket. A few accepted Y —— 's accusation. They huffed and puffed
d joined the ranks of those who believed. But most of the people
anted more time to wait and see if their sorcerer could get to the
ottom of the matter. They even continued to drink the water. They
ared not offend the water spirit and refuse to drink from the well,
r it was yet to be proved that the well had been poisoned. One
ffled spirit was bad enough. Two might be catastrophic.

So, for the next few days, the people suffered patiently, not sure of whom or what to blame for the terrible times that had fallen upon them, not daring to foresake their new well. They suffered and waited for Y —— their sorcerer to get to the bottom of the matter. The sorcerer went thru his bag of charms. Thru his store of incantations. Thru all the little tricks he knew. When he had gone thru everything, when he had exhausted all his knowledge and still hadn't gotten to the bottom of the matter, he tried to find some other way. He wheedled the spirits, he flattered the spirits shamelessly. He pleaded with them. He made all sorts of promises. But none of these other ways was better. He couldn't get thru. He couldn't reach the offended spirit, whichever it was.

During these few days of going thru tricks, more and more people were stricken by whatever was striking, until all the people of Buon Yak were doubled with pain and reeling high and dragging and smelly and even worse. The fields and the buffaloes went untended; no one had the will to work. The village stank from excrement. At first it was simply a matter of not being fast enough, of not getting to the fence in time. The people got as far as they could, then splashed their stools all over the ground. First speed, but later it was a matter of strength. Many could not even rouse themselves from where they lay. Could not even drag themselves along. Could not even crawl on their hands and knees out of the houses, much less toward the fence. The youngest children, the village elder began to die off. Life in Buon Yak came to a stop.

Then someone noted, finally, that only the infants had not taken sick. That the infants had suffered on their mothers' thin meager milk, but had not been stricken like all the others. Suddenly there was no more doubt. Suddenly everyone was sure. Suddenly every one agreed that the rumors were true. That the man with three fingers had warned them correctly. That Y —— had been right. That Casper had poisoned their well. Even the sorcerer agreed that it was Casper and not the spirits who lay at the bottom of the matter. All the people huffed and puffed as much as their lack of strength allowed. They shook their fists. They stamped their feet. They swore that they would bury Casper. And in a way they did. They proceeded to fill in the well.

* * *

On the day that the people filled in their well, the man with three fingers returned to Buon Yak. He came alone—with a strange iron box, which had nothing to do with sniffing—and waited by the house of Y —— the notable, for Y —— to round up the men of Buon Yak. Soon a great audience formed around the man with three fingers. A humming one, but silent too. Not all the men came. Some were too sick to move or be moved. And some wanted nothing to do with Three Fingers. They figured he was no better than Casper, that he and Casper were two of a kind. Y —— the chief didn't come. It was not for a chief to be rounded up. And Y —— the sorcerer didn't come either, for sorcerers are reclusive men and can't stand crowds; and, besides, their business is with the spirits. But most of the men of Buon Yak showed up and gathered round and squatted down and listened very carefully. Y —— the notable squatted closest to Three Fingers, squatted proudly. The voice of Three Fingers was scornful and mocking, but it was also commiserating.

"Well, what did we tell you? Hm? What? How things would be, that's what. We said to watch out. We warned you. Because we cared about Buon Yak, what would happen to you. But you wouldn't believe. Not a word. You were all too smart. You all knew better. You just sat and listened and said to yourselves: 'This Three Fingers man, he's fooling us.'" Three Fingers scowled. Meaner than any barber had. He was fed up. He wanted the men of Buon Yak to know. And to know just what he thought of them. "'Oh yes, he's fooling us, this Three Fingers man. He's a sharp one. Better look out.' Well, you've been fooled. You let the American make a fool of all of you. Everyone. I spit on your stinking foolishness." Three Fingers spat emphatically—carefully too—so that he didn't come too close and insult anyone.

"How you stink! How Buon Yak stinks! Like a dung heap. It stinks like a dung heap. With flies all around." Three Fingers pinched his nose tight to make his point perfectly clear. "It stinks because you listened very badly before. So now listen better." Three Fingers tapped the side of his head. "This time much better—The Americans want to kill you all. They're crazy people. Monster people. Not even people. They go around killing wherever they can. They speak of sweet water and poison your well. They bring you presents and, at the same time that you're thanking them, they murder your children and your old ones." Three Fingers looked from face to face. "Am I fooling now? Am I, hm? Am I telling you wrong? Am I, hm? You know it's so. Because you've learned. Ah, you poor stinking fools, you've learned very painfully."

A buzzing erupted among the men. An angry vibration. Angry because they didn't like being taken for fools. Not stinking fools. But angry too, much angrier at the Americans, because it was so.

"I've heard all your whispering. All your brave chatter. Your angry talk. The buzzing now. Well, you poor stinking fools, just how great is your courage? Just how big is your anger? As big as all your fists together? As big as your feet to carry you? As big as the pain that doubles you all? Or little and squeaky? How big? Is it so big that you'll come with us now? Is it the anger of proper men?"

The men were silent. There was no chatter, no whispering. No angry buzzing. Nothing except a sense of edging toward something climactic. They shifted their weight on the flats of their feet. They listened very carefully.

"You, Y——, your son, he was not yet three. And you, Y——, yes, you. Your old father would have lived many more years. So, come! What are you waiting for!? Come with us!" Three Fingers spoke to all the men, not just to Y—— and Y——. "Come with us. And if not—if you can not come—then help us in other ways. We'll show you how. What to do. But do something! Anything! They're crazy people. Monster people. Not even people. How big is it? Or little and squeaky? Put your anger to work."

Three Fingers knew that the men had been listening carefully, tho they made no sound, not even a grunt. He knew they were weighing everything: his words, the pain that doubled them all, the size of their anger. But he also knew they were still uncommitted. That they mistrusted him because he was Vietnamese. That they had all heard about the heads, the executions, Buon Sop.

"Maybe you heard of the executions at Buon Sop? Maybe, yes? Maybe you think these executions—that they were a terrible thing?

aybe, yes? Well, the men who were killed, they were traitors. at's why they're dead. They betrayed the people of Buon Sop. ey betrayed the people to the same Americans who poisoned ur well. For this, they deserved to die." Three Fingers paused. e gave his words time to sink in deep. "You, too, were betrayed. h, yes—you, too."

The men looked around at one another. Who had betrayed them? ow? Why? They were all looking for someone guilty. Someone ith a likely head.

"How? By whom? By yourselves! By the trust you gave to the an named Casper. There! Look at him run for the fence! He can't en run. Betrayed by a foolish trust."

The men of Buon Yak looked at the runner who couldn't run. hey looked at their feet and nodded their heads.

"Learn if you haven't learned by now. Clean out the dirt. You uld grow yams in there, I swear. Listen. Learn. There's no one u can trust. No one at all. Except us. Only us, we can help u."

The men of Buon Yak looked at their hands.

"Maybe you're not convinced? Maybe, hm? No, I can see you're t." He made a great show of hanging his head. "Just what do u think we are? Monsters and spies and murderers too? Do you ink we want to kill you off like the man named Casper tried to ?" Three Fingers spat for the second time. He hit Y ——, the otable, who looked very surprised and unhappy. "Foo! What's the atter with you? Do I have to grab each of you by the shoulders d rattle the foolishness out of your heads? Do I, hm? Do I have to ake out every last fool among you? It will be tiring. Have you st your heads? Have they flown away? Can't you see? Can't you ell? Smell the stink from your bloody stools. It chokes Buon ak. It chokes me, too. Foo, what a horrible stink! You drank the ater and now Buon Yak is fouled with your bloody stools. Smell . Smell it!"

The men looked at one another and nodded their heads. There as no need to smell. There was no way not to smell.

"Listen carefully. Dig out the yams. We're going to help you.

We're going to make everything better—but not for nothin
Three Fingers understood that the men wouldn't understand son
thing for nothing. That they wouldn't trust something for nothi
Not again. Not after Casper. And, besides, there was somethi
"No, not for nothing. First we help you. Then you help us. So,
and prepare your women and chidren."

Prepare? For what? The women? The children? The men we
surprised, very uneasy. What was it all about?

"So you're still not convinced? You still don't trust us? Loc
Look at him run for the fence, he can't even run. Go. Hurry. P
pare everyone. We have medicine to hunt down the poison. To k
the poison that clutches you."

The men of Buon Yak hesitated. They were wary of good dee
They were learning.

"What!? What's this!? Why do you wait? Do you think that we
going to poison you, too?"

No one answered.

"Then you truly are idiots. The medicine, it's for your own good
No one spoke.

"Look! I'll take the medicine first—so you can see." Thr
Fingers reached into his strange iron box, and took out a mu
smaller box, and then a little bottle from that. Then, in front
all the men, he swallowed some of the medicine from Sergea
Culpepper's dispensary. He let each man look into his mouth
make sure that he had swallowed it all. They lined up to look. I
let them all pat his belly to feel where the stuff was hurrying to.

"What do you say? Go and prepare."

"But Casper drank."

"*He* went first."

"Maybe you have some secret potion."

"Did you look into Casper's mouth? Down his throat? Did y
make sure all the water went down?"

"There was no other place to go."

"Did Casper let you pat his belly?"

"No one patted Casper's belly."

"So, there. He fooled you all. That's the difference. Come, p
mine. Pat it again. Make sure."

When all the men were satisfied, they left to prepare their women and children.

Mac Dong Dong remained in Buon Yak for several days, until all the people had recovered, the ones who hadn't already died. Until the men had regained their strength, enough of it. For three days. Then on the fourth night, Mac left Buon Yak accompanied by the new recruits for the 825th Independent Company.

YANCY'S TREAT

It was smoky inside the house of Y Bun. It was pleasant to sit there, in the half-light, among one's friends. It was nice to talk, now that the day was done and a man could relax, sipping the wine and maybe lighting a pipe or two. Nice to say what needed saying, to ask questions and hear some answers, whether they were right or not. Grandmother Pan was also there which, had she been another woman, would have been exceptional. Tho women could be very shrewd and they could speak well, it wasn't the same as being a man. But for Grandmother Pan, there was always a place. She was a puckish irreverent soul, a wise old soul, who lightened their talks whenever things became too heavy. It was quiet outside, and very black, and back in the corner, squatted down and looking on, and for a time, snug in his own silent peace, was Triple Threat.

"You know about Buon Yak."

"Buon Yak is Buon Yak. It's something else."

"What something else!? He came. He did something with the well. People died. What else!?"

"Who knows." Y Bun shrugged. His strong clean face, his grizzled thatch shone in the light. His hands lay loosely on his knees.

"Yes, who knows," said Y Bong. "They're our friends. Culpepper with the big big nose—every morning he tends the sick."

"And the pills." It was Rhadeo.

"The pills, hah! That's just for fun." Y Blo was angry.

"No, it's not! And the jokes."

"Who understands the jokes? Maybe he jokes at you."

"Culpepper with the big big nose," continued Y Bong. "And the Lieutenant, the stumbling one. He's very nice too. He's very good to the mute."

They all looked at Triple Threat, who looked back and grinned. He was happily cleaning between his toes.

"Yes, but what of the red-haired one? Red-faced too. He always kicks."

"Maybe he has some spirit inside. It makes him kick. Maybe you should do something."

"Bah!" said Y Blo. "Whatever he has, he had it when he came."

"And Moon," continued Y Bong.

"Yes, Moon."

"Moon is the best."

"Yes, Moon, but maybe he tries too hard." It was the elder who had almost lost his nose. "He's not really one of us. Maybe it's a game."

"No!" said Grandmother Pan. "He found the drop. He knows how to look."

"No!" said Little Rhadeo. "He knows the sounds. When a buffalo's sad."

"And the long skinny one. The black one. He's not so bad. He taught Y M'dhur the string game."

"What does that prove!? His hands get tangled!"

"The black one, he does make noise." It was the elder.

"Maybe he has a spirit too."

"I looked," said Y Blo. "There was nothing inside." Y Blo waved his fist. "It's not the same anymore. It doesn't even smell the same—"

"It's the same."

"Yes, the same."

"*Almost* the same."

"I sit on the Virgin and look around. I sniff with my nose. I listen to all the rustling sounds. It's not the same—"

"Foo, Y Blo. You're jealous, that's all."

Y Blo glared at Grandmother Pan. Only she would have dared such a thing. Then Y Blo relaxed his face into a look of the most absolute disdain. It wasn't true. He feared for Buon Yun, he told himself—but maybe he also feared a little for Y Blo.

"It's good that they came," said Grandmother Pan. "Not so many children die."

"And now we don't have to work so hard," ventured Y Bong.

Y Blo glared once more. He knew about work and how not enough work could turn a man soft and rotten inside.

"And the VC, they haven't come."

"Now they will come for sure," grumbled Y Blo.

"And the hunting is better, what with the guns."

"Better, hah! No one goes hunting."

"When we do."

"When! When! You can't keep the one eye closed. I saw the red-haired one. How he laughs. It was better before."

Y Gar was nodding all the while. A crossbow was best.

"Fritz, he looks up their skirts. I saw at the party."

"Plunket doesn't like the wine. I saw the funny faces he made."

"They don't respect the spirits."

"Moon locked tight."

"Yes, Moon locked tight."

"So what!? The Captain didn't. Look at Buon Sop."

"That was the VC. It happened before."

"Still, he didn't lock tight."

"The Captain tries."

"So he tries! What good is that!?"

"There's the treat."

"So the treat! What's a treat!?" Y Blo waved his fist again. "No one works. And when they do, they hurry and do it worse than before. They're all so proud, strutting around! Forgetting that young men should know how to hunt and when to plant, and not to strut." The elder nodded as Y Blo went on. "And no one stays home, minding his business, but filing here and filing there instead of filing down their teeth!"

It was quiet.

"They still dream!" shouted Y Blo all of a sudden. "They sleep, so they must dream! Everyone dreams!"

What was this? What was Y Blo talking about?

"And when they dream, no one comes and tells me what. Only the old ones." Y Blo didn't have to explain about dreams, their significance. Everyone knew. "No one says whether they dreamt of red blankets, or broken teeth, or catching a large fish, or eating eggplant."

"*I* had a dream," admitted Y Bong.

"Why didn't you come!?" stammered Y Blo.

"I was going to," said Y Bong. Then he told his dream. "I dreamt that it rained and rained and rained, and yet I woke up thirsty and hot and with a shooting pain in my side."

"See! See! Oh, there'll be a fire! To dream about water means a fire."

"What kind of fire!?"

"Where!?"

"When!?"

"Why should I tell you!?" shouted Y Blo, who was miffed because no one came with their dreams, and also because he didn't know. "And what about strangely shaped trees? Or halos around the moon?"

"What do you mean?"

"Tell us, Y Blo."

"Surely they saw a strangely shaped tree; they went thru the woods!"

"Thru the woods, Y Blo?"

"On their way to Buon Sop! Maybe if they had told me the first time—"

Maybe if they had told Y Blo!

"It's the long-nosed ones, they've taken over. And someday they'll leave—maybe soon. And then what? Who can go back? Who!? *Who!?* The old ways, they'll be forgotten. And the spirits, what about them? Maybe they won't forgive. Who knows. *They* don't forget—" Of course, Y Blo was exaggerating; for hadn't the spirits promised him it would be the most overwhelming year ever? But only exaggerating. "Where will the rice come from then? What good will it have been?"

"We still plant!"

"Yes, we plant—but now we don't whisper so softly."

"I think of the time before they came," said Y Bun. "No one had boots or long trousers and it was cold in the winter months. Now it won't be so cold. And no one had enough to eat."

"There was enough!" shouted Y Blo.

"Just enough. We all could have eaten a little more. And life was not really so simple. There were always lots of worries." Y Bun looked down into his hands, then into the faces of his guests. He was sad, but hoped it would pass. Of course, he minded that some things had changed, that now the girls weren't so pretty with all their teeth, and also that his authority was somewhat less, what with the Strike Force. But it was better for all of them. It had to be.

"It was very nice to file the teeth and other things. But I prefer how it is today. A belly stretched tight and warm dry feet are not so bad. And, anyway, nothing's changed that much." But hadn't it? And he thought to the time when his father had taken him into a sun-dappled glade of the forest, and taught him the names of the trees and the birds alighting in them, and that the rain fell down and not the other way, because A'de lived up in the sky and didn't like to get wet. He thought to the time when there was Grandmother Pan to love, and sons to beget, and telling them of trees and birds and rain. He thought to that happy innocent time, when only the village and the fields and the surrounding forest mattered; when all a man had to care about was eating enough, and staying dry during the rains, and having a little tobacco on hand, and maybe a little rice wine too, and keeping the spirits in good humor. Y Bun sat musing and honored the past, knowing that all the best times had been, and wishing them back.

But wishing never brought anything back, and now another time had come. A very confusing, dangerous time. A time when people lost their heads. And Y Bun thought of Y M'nung there on the stake, how it could have been himself. Was Y M'nung a bodiless head, or a headless body, and had his spirit been severed too, and then how would it make its way to A'de? Y Bun shivered, wondering, for what could be worse than to be in parts, and one's spirit as well, and never to find everlasting peace?

It was a perilous time, all right. A time when forces were about, dark and strange and powerful—like a spread of wings blacking the sun, and the chill setting in, and a rustling in the bushes. Y Bun sat there fretting and wished the specters would go away, that all would be like that glade in the forest, peaceful and green and the sun shining thru.

Y Bun sat there, trying to shake his gloom. It was for a chief to set an example, to inspire confidence; and maybe things hadn't changed that much; and if they had, then maybe he really did prefer how they were today. Y Bun sat there inwardly troubled but looking calm. He eyed his guests, and smiled at them, and picked up where he had left off. "Nothing's changed that much," he said.

"It's changed enough!" shouted Y Blo.

"A belly stretched tight and warm dry feet and others to do the worrying. After all, we're not fools."

"We're fools, all right!" stammered Y Blo. "Burning a village to dry our feet!"

"What kind of burning!? Boots, not burning!"

"Y Bong's dream. It's foretold."

"What kind of village!? What does it mean!?" asked Y Bong.

"Why should I tell you, you didn't come!"

Y Bun went on unperturbed. "Before, we knew only our ways, and things that happened only to us, and also in the forest around; it wasn't enough."

"What is enough!?" angrily asked Y Blo.

"Better for men to play a part."

"To play games, you mean, like Y M'dhur!?"

The half 'n half lowered his head and muttered.

"Better for men to play a part; to learn and grow."

"To learn bad things!? To grow twisted!?"

"Ah, Y Blo. Strangely shaped trees. Growing twisted. It's you who's all twisted up."

Y Bun waved off Grandmother Pan.

"Since before the dog," said Y Blo, "we have followed a certain path. That way we knew where to step."

"Yes," said Y Bun, "and now we must follow the new turnings."

"New turnings!? What kind of turnings!? It's always been straight!"

"A people are like a man. They go for a time and then they have turnings."

"Straight! Straight!" insisted Y Blo. "It's always been straight!"

"Straight! Straight!" screeched Grandmother Pan, in imitation of Y Blo.

"A people must find its way."

"We found it long ago!"

"A people must find its way," repeated Y Bun.

"We'll only *lose* our way!"

"A people must bend as their road bends."

"But then it won't be us anymore!"

"A people must bend," repeated Y Bun, "or they will rot and stink."

"Yes, just like Buon Yak! What about them!?"

"So it's back to that?"

"Back! Forth! What about them!?"

"Maybe they offended."

"Yes, yes, they offended! As we offend right now!"

"Feh! Foo!" said Grandmother Pan. "Burnings here! Turnings there! That's enough." Grandmother Pan rose and hovered over the men. She patted Triple Threat on the head, comforting him. He had been frightened by all the contention. "Tomorrow there'll be a treat. The Captain said."

"The Captain doesn't have a soul," said Y Blo. "He cuts his hair much too short. He can say anything."

"The Captain has a soul, all right," said Y Bun. "Maybe with Americans it resides somewhere else."

"There'll be a treat," said Grandmother Pan, rubbing her hands and trembling with anticipation. "What will it be, eh, Y Bun?" Grandmother Pan prodded Y Bun affectionately. "What do you think, eh, Y Blo? Maybe you can ask the charms." Y Blo gave her a blistering look. "Maybe you know," said Grandmother Pan to Triple Threat. "Maybe your Lieutenant said." Triple Threat hunkered lower. He feared that she was jesting with him. "Just think," said Grandmother Pan to everyone: to Y Gar the hunter and Y M'dhur, to Y Bong the ironsmith and to the elder, "maybe they'll put on a show."

"What do you know about shows!?" asked Y Blo.

"Buon Sop had a show!"

"And look what happened to Buon Sop!"

"That was the VC," said Y Bun.

"VC! Americans! A show's a show! It's a dangerous thing to watch! Someone gets hurt!"

"Maybe it won't be a show," said Grandmother Pan. "Maybe it's a prize instead. Yes, a prize! Something shiny, or maybe something tasty to eat."

"Or some game to play!"

"Or some magic trick!"

"Or maybe a butterfly stuck on a pin!"

* * *

"Sergeant Fritz, wait a minute!"

Fritz was strolling between the houses, hoping one of the women would show, so he could have a look up her skirt. But it was dark, and not likely she would show, and if she did, then not likely he would see anything. Yet Fritz strolled on, being the ever hopeful one.

"Sergeant Fritz, hey, wait!"

Fritz was thinking about his wife, how she was making out. They had parted long ago because he was always looking up skirts, and reaching too.

"Sergeant Fritz, hold on!" Lieutenant Plunket caught up with him and fell into step. "They're talking again."

Fritz shrugged.

"Maybe they're still upset."

"Buon Sop?"

Plunket nodded.

One of the voices, the strident one, hounded them thru the dark.

"Do you think, just maybe, they don't want us now?"

"Naw!" said Sergeant Fritz. "It can't happen here. Don't you fret, Lieutenant, sir."

"I wouldn't blame them," said the Lieutenant.

"Nothing's to blame. Things happen. They buck you and toss you and whip you around. It's how you ride them out," said Fritz. He was from Texas.

They strolled for a time, with Plunket silent and Fritz's eyes scouring the ledges. The moon was just beginning to rise.

"Well, Sergeant Fritz, what's the latest?" asked Plunket who really wanted to ask about something else.

"The latest is—what's happened to Casper?"

"How do you mean?"

"He was supposed to get in touch. Compare notes or something."

"What about it?"

"That was a week ago." Fritz shook his head. "He probably fell in a hole or something. You know how he goes sneaking around."

Plunket laughed. He knew.

"In the dark, too. I tell you, sir—"

Plunket laughed, but his laugh was touched with craziness, or maybe fear.

"Maybe he's been with the planter's daughter," said Sergeant Fritz. "I don't trust that bastard at all."

"Who? Casper?"

"Naw, the planter. You *know* he's gotta be paying them off."

Plunket sighed. They strolled on.

"Maybe he didn't," Lieutenant Plunket finally said.

"Didn't what?"

"Fall in a hole." There was a pause. "Joking aside, maybe he was shoved or something."

"Now, sir. Take it easy."

"Yeah, sure, Sergeant Fritz. But still maybe he was shoved."

Fritz played along. "How do you mean?"

"I don't know. Maybe he finally met up with Charlie. Got himself shot or blown up or something."

"Aw, sir, don't you worry. Casper, he's a shifty one."

Plunket worried. It had to do with what was gnawing away at his mind.

"Listen, Sergeant Fritz, you're the intelligence man."

"You bet, Lieutenant."

"Well, let me ask you something. Okay? It's not as funny as it sounds. And now what with Casper and all the rest, and how quiet it's been, tho it really hasn't."

"Really hasn't?"

"Oh, there's been no contact, except that one time. And no

funny stuff, except for the leaflets. But there've been sounds. I'm very good at hearing sounds."

"Sounds, sir?"

"Well, *almost* sounds."

"Like what, sir?"

"Like the sound a cat makes sneaking up thru the grass."

"So?" asked Fritz.

"So what I've had on my mind is this: is it automatic or not?"

"Is what, sir?"

"A shave, of course. When you get a haircut."

Not again, thought Sergeant Fritz.

"Is it automatic or not?"

"Well, sir, it depends."

"On what, Sergeant Fritz?"

"On whether you needed one or not. Did you, sir? They like to oblige."

Lieutenant Plunket couldn't remember, not for sure, but he didn't think he'd needed one. After all, he had gone to town with Captain Yancy, so he would have had to shave in advance.

Fritz wondered about the Lieutenant. Maybe Lovelace was right, after all, about the Lieutenant being loony. "Listen, Lieutenant," he said at last, "it's nothing to worry about."

"Yeah, Sergeant Fritz, maybe so, but still all these things are happening. What with the leaflets and how did they get there—"

"They sure got the Captain right, didn't they, sir?" Fritz laughed.

"What with the leaflets and with Buon Sop and now with the shave. I'm pretty sure I didn't need one." Plunket flung out his arms in despair. "And with the gaps."

"Gaps, sir?"

"Have you thought what it means?"

Someone stepped out of a nearby longhouse onto the ledge. Fritz turned to see. But it was only a rheumy old man come to pass water.

Plunket went on: "There's something not right, Sergeant Fritz. I mean, how did those leaflets get there and who made the gaps and everything?"

"What gaps, sir?"

"And Buon Sop. The poor lousy bastards. Why at least didn't
hey leave them whole!?"

"Gaps, sir?"

"Yes, gaps. Sergeant Culpepper's."

"Aah, he's always seeing gaps. He's punchy, sir. Gaps in his
head, that's what he's got!" Just like you.

"Now the shave."

"Sir, if you'll pardon me, it's just your imagination."

"Okay, it sounds weird. Sure, sure. But something's kindling,
Sergeant Fritz. I swear I can smell the smoke."

The moon was now well along, casting down its cold white
light. There were no voices, no splashing of water, only the
light breeze laughing gently.

"I've been thinking," Plunket said. "You're the intelligence man.
So what do you think about a scarecrow?"

"Scarecrow?"

"Well, not *really* a scarecrow. But pretty close." And Plunket
explained how sometimes the people made grotesque figures of
straw and bamboo, and armed these figures with bow and arrow,
and set them before the village entrance to guard against hostile
spirits.

"The Captain wouldn't like it, sir. You know that."

"Maybe so, Sergeant Fritz—"

"It's just a lot of superstition."

"Maybe so, Sergeant Fritz, but what do you think anyway?"

"Well, sir—" Now Fritz being the intel man, he should have
been naturally suspicious; but he liked to arrive at his own sus-
picions and thus disregarded Plunket's—and Plunket's scheme—
for he had several of his own turning in his head. "And what's the
reason, anyway? You're not afraid of spirits, sir—*are* you, sir?
What do they have to do with us?"

"Hostile spirits are hostile spirits. It all depends on how you
interpret. They could be scaly things with wings and a long pointed
tail, or Viet Cong, or anything. There's all sorts of dangers lurking, Sergeant."

"Aw, come on, Lieutenant Plunket."

"Well, at least there's Viet Cong. You can't deny that."

"So what good is straw and bamboo and stuff?"

"It's good for my peace of mind, that's what. That's a prett important thing."

"Aw, sir."

"I know. I know. But still I'd feel better."

"And who's going to make it, sir?"

"Let's ask Sergeant Lovelace. He's the weapons man."

"Better not, Lieutenant Plunket."

"Why not? Sergeant Lovelace would be glad."

"Not Lovelace, sir. I know better. Lovelace wouldn't."

Plunket shrugged. "Well, it was just an idea."

The breeze gusted. The moon sidled behind a cloud.

"Look, sir," said Sergeant Fritz, "there's the dark side, an then there's the light. You gotta choose. Me, I always choose th light. And that's the way it always turns out—usually." Fritz wen on. "You see, sir, there's no other way. I mean, there is, but wh wants it? It's just a lot of grief, that's what. So better not t worry, sir."

"Sergeant Fritz, isn't it strange for an intel man not to be su picious?"

"Listen, sir, we intel men are suspicious, all right. We're n one's fool. But only up to a point, of course. If you get too su picious, sir, then you start hearing things in the dark, or seein things where there's not, or putting up fences or scarecrows or wha not to keep out those scaly things with tails."

"Don't get smart!" Plunket said sharply.

"Sorry, sir."

"Look, Sergeant Fritz," Plunket said, after a spell, "I don't kno why. I just feel gloomy."

"Aw, sir, don't get like Culpepper. One's enough. I though you looked at the bright side, sir."

"I do, Sergeant Fritz. It's just that all these little things— Sur they mean nothing by themselves. But put them together, they ad up."

"Sir, if you add nothing to nothing, that's all you're bound to ge Any first-grade kid knows that. *Nothing*, Sir."

"Well—if you really think so."

"Sure, I do. It's all right, sir," said Fritz with assurance. "The sun, Lieutenant, it's gotta shine."

"Let's hope it shines tomorrow. I'm all set to go."

"The Captain came thru, didn't he, sir?"

"Captain Yancy has his ways. Now if only the sun shines."

"It will, sir. It always does. Sooner or later."

PINS AND NEEDLES

Gung Ho Dung strained mightily for the Liberation. He strained for the 825th. He strained for his friends, all three of them, who were expecting big things from him. Dung's face was red, his hands were clenched tight, and he strained for all he was worth. But nothing came of the straining.

"Hurry, Dung. There isn't much time."

"Come on, Dung. Be done with it."

Dan and Van squatted nearby, at the side of a pile of bamboo. Dan hacked the bamboo into two-foot lengths, and Van split the lengths into thirds. Dan had a slightly lopsided face, and was missing the lobe of an ear, which had been bitten off in a fight. Van's hair hung down over his eyes, but somehow did not interfere with his aim. His nose dripped steadily onto his lip, which he kept swiping at with his hand.

"Foo, Dung, what's taking so long? Hurry up."

Kim got the fire going. Then, wielding his knife, he began to slice each split length to a point. As each stake was done, he placed the point in the fire to harden. Kim was wearing brand new sandals, made from the tires of Casper's jeep. So were Dan and Van and Dung.

"Hey, Dung—"

"Yeah, Dung—"

"Hurry up, Dung."

Hard-pressed Dung strained even harder, hair flopping down, ashamed of his unproductiveness. How could he explain to the others? They expected so much from him. How could he tell them that he was very regular? That the time was early for him?

Meanwhile, Dan, Van, and Kim worked productively, hacking,

splitting, slicing sharp. When Dan was done hacking, he helped
Van split. When Dan and Van were done with the splitting, they
helped Kim slice. As the bamboo stakes hardened, Kim pulled
them from the fire and put others in their place. The three men
hurried with their work. They were all really boys, except for
Kim. They hurried, anxious to get it done. It was dark and there
was no one else about, but they were close, daringly close.

Kim beseeched Dung: "Come on, Dung, it's almost morning."

Dan and Van, they beseeched too: "Yeah, Dung, we can't wait
much more."

"Yeah, Dung, not much more."

Poor Dung. His face was purple, his body was stiff from all the
straining. He was dizzy, flagging tho stiff. Most of all, he was
fearful. It was bad enough that he was always on the move, and
ate cold rice, and had to hear the same old lectures, and people
shooting, and all of it not changing things much, not setting them
right. And now the straining on top of that! Fearful he wasn't up to
it. But what could he say to the three of them? That his need wasn't
urgent? It wouldn't do. It was his duty to produce. That they
should have used the recruits from Buon Yak, one or two? But
they weren't trained. And, besides, he had been especially chosen.
It was because of his reputation. Dung cursed his reputation of
which he had always been rather proud. He cursed the fact that,
among the men of the 825th, he was acclaimed for his potency.
Dung grunted and heaved. His body, slender as the bamboo, rattled
with the effort. Dung clenched, he wrenched. He gave it everything
he had. One resounding clap came out. Nothing more.

The other three had turned to look, sure that Dung would at
last have success. But they soon returned to their work, disappointed, puzzled at Dung's lack of success. Wasn't Fighter Dung
the most potent, the most reliable one of them all?

"Agh," said Kim, "it's enough to confound a mandarin."

"Or a political officer," said Fighter Dan.

"Or even Leader Mac Dong Dong," said Fighter Van.

"But Leader Mac is the officer too."

"Well, even him."

"It's enough to confound anyone," concluded Kim.

Soon all the stakes were sliced and hardened and ready to go except for Dung. It was drawing close to dawn and Dan, Van, and Kim became alarmed. They decided that Dung needed help.

Dan, Van, and Kim formed a half-circle around Fighter Dung. They whooped, they beat their hands on their thighs, they smacked them as loudly as they dared. They cheered Dung on. Dan and Van even turned a few cartwheels, altho they hadn't been the clowns and jugglers and the acrobats, but only the peasants from Buon Sop. They cartwheeled for Dung, for the 825th, for the Liberation. They praised Dung, suffered with him, shouted him encouragement. They said all the magic rhymes they knew, repeated them, and then they made up some of their own. But nothing worked—not the cheering, not the cartwheels, not the rhymes— and things began to look very grim. They made funny faces. They got Dung to laugh and to relax. And when that failed, they cursed him and teased him and poked him too. They did all they could to make him angry. Maybe that would give him the strength. As Dan, Van, and Kim kept jabbing him, Dung's anger grew and grew and grew until, at last, he exploded.

When Dung was thru, they all held their breath and smeared the hardened point of each stake. They dipped them good, they worked them round. For it was known among the men of the 825th that nothing could infect a wound better than Dung's excrement.

When the men were done smearing, they set out the stakes. They hurried, for dawn was about to break. The four men barely finished in time, and then they left as they had come, with poor sore-assed Dung bringing up the rear.

* * *

The point went in sharp and clean, burning a line of white-hot pain, and Goodbody screamed. It was a terrible, full-throated scream, a long drawn-out scream—*Aghhhhhhhh!* Sergeant Goodbody twitched on the ground, straining his body against the pain, gasping for air, then he slumped deeper into the dirt. For a moment Goodbody felt strangely relaxed, until the pain jiggled around, and he screamed and twitched once more. Then Sergeant Goodbody settled still deeper into the dirt. He lay there unmoving.

"Hot Dawg, that burned!" There was a squeak to Goodbody's voice. "Why do I gotta lie in the dirt?"

"Cause it's better that way."

"Yeah? Oh yeah? Well it sure is a whole lot dirtier too." Goodbody stirred, Goodbody squirmed. Rebellion began to roll thru him.

"Lay still, Goodbody. Dammit, lay still. This is the way it's always done. So there must be something to it, right?"

"Well, okay," Goodbody squeaked, "but don' you be so drastic, hear?" Goodbody started to talk to the Lord. "Oh, Lawd, what you don' know!" Then he returned to Sergeant Moon. "Hey, what point you lookin' for now?"

Moon was looking for point 4 ST.

The meridian of the stomach ran from Goodbody's face, down his chest and belly, then along the outer side of his leg to the tip of his second toe. Moon scrutinized Goodbody from his face to the tip of his second toe. Moon wasn't sure where, along the meridian, 4 ST was located. Nor was he sure if the meridian ran along the left leg or right, or if it really mattered which.

When Moon decided where 4 ST was, where it had to be, he pinched the point with his fingers. Then he used a short needle, a number two, and piqued one fen deep. (Had Sergeant Goodbody been fat and not the beanpole he was, Sergeant Moon would have had to pique deeper accordingly.) He piqued as Sergeant Goodbody exhaled and toward the direction of energy flow. As Moon piqued, Goodbody bellowed. He made less of a fuss this time. Moon scratched the head of the needle to help summon the energy. Moon piqued the needle one fen deep at 4 ST because he was trying to supply energy to Goodbody's stomach, to restore it to equilibrium, to restore Goodbody's appetite. That's why he piqued for Pu effect and not for Hsieh.

Sergeant Moon knew that Goodbody's stomach was in disequilibrium because it fluttered constantly; Goodbody had told him so. Because point 12 VC had responded painfully to light pressure. Because point 35 ST had been cool to the touch. Because of the yellow in Goodbody's eyes and the fact that he was always humming.

Sergeant Goodbody lay stripped to his drawers and flat on his back, well settled into the dirt. Sergeant Moon kneeled by his side. When Moon was satisfied with his pique at 4 ST, he began to look for 9 SP where he planned another pique. The meridian of the spleen ran from Goodbody's chest, down his belly, then along the inner side of his leg to the tip of his great toe.

"I still don' get it."

"Listen, Goodie, leave it to me. Have some faith."

"Try again."

"There's Yin and Yang. Yin's dark and minus and doesn't move much. Yang's light and plus and jumps all around. They're the two basic elements. They act together to make all the energy needed for life. In the whole world, the universe, in everyone. When they act together like they should, then they make just the right amount. Not too little, not too much. But when they don't act like they should, they make too little or too much. And that's where all the trouble is. Disequilibrium. They call it perverted energy. From the tiniest ache to yellow eyes to packing it in, it's all because of the energy. Maybe too little. Maybe too much. It's all because they don't act together normally. Yin and Yang. You've got to stay in harmony."

"You mean I'm close to packin' it in!? Oh my! Oh Lawd! Hot Dawg! Do it deeper!"

"Dammit, Goodie. Lay still. You've got a ways."

"Well what happens? If it's too little or too much? The energy. Them organs, you said."

"Whatever organ is affected, it doesn't work right. Too fast if there's too much energy. Too slow if too little. The ones deep inside. And then all the systems of the body, they get all affected too and don't work right."

"You mean all my systems is workin' bad?"

"It's not that bad. Not yet. Just lay still."

"But how do you fix it? All this disequilibrium stuff?"

"By supplying more energy where it's lacking. They call it hypoactivity. It's got to be stimulated, perked up. By reducing the energy where there's too much. They call it hyperactivity. It's got to be calmed."

"Yeah? You sure? Well how do you fix 'em, them bad workin' organs?"

"Thru the meridians. These pathways, see— They're strung out just beneath the surface."

"My surface!?"

"Everyone's. Lay still. All the energy you've got, it flows along these meridians. Circulates, just like blood. These meridians, they're connected up with all the organs deep inside. That's where the points are, along the meridians. 354 of them. You restore equilibrium thru them. Your bad working organs, they get all better."

"How they get?"

"First thing, you find the right point. Like this 9 SP I'm looking for now. Then either you stimulate or calm the energy in the meridian, which stimulates or calms the energy in the organ which goes with it. Follow me?"

"Yeah, sure. Not too far. But how do you know which organs is bad, so as you can make 'em better?"

"Well, by a study of the pulses. That's the best way. Supposed to be."

"Hey, you dint study no pulses!"

"Well, I'm not sure I know how. It's complicated."

"I'm leavin' now. Lemme up!"

"Dammit, Goodbody, lay still. By applying pressure to certain points—"

"Like those 354?"

"Yeah, those. If light pressure causes pain, then the organ's got too little juice. If heavy pressure causes pain, then the organ's got too much. If no kind of pressure causes pain, then the organ is normal, see? Or by feeling some other points—"

"Like those 354?"

"Yeah, those—if they're cool or warm. Which means too little or too much. Hypo. Hyper. Understand? Or just by looking at the patient for certain signs."

"Like what?"

"Like funny colors or funny smells or how he gets all excited."

"Hey, I got some yellow in my eyes! Do I have the smells too!?"

"Just lay still."

"So what happens once you know? About the bad organs. Which ones and how."

"Then comes the therapy."

"What you're doin'?"

"Yeah, that."

"You gotta do it down here in the dirt?"

"It's the way. Anyway, this therapy—it's based upon the Great Law of Pu-Hsieh as written in the *Yellow Emperor's Canon of Internal Medicine*."

"You don' say? Who's Pu-Hsieh?"

"It's not who. It's an effect. Cures anything. Works all the time. From the tiniest ache to yellow eyes to packing it in. The Pu effect supplies energy. The Hsieh effect takes some away. Depends on how you work the needles. Pu and Hsieh, they neutralize bad energy and get back the equilibrium and make the body healthy again. Follow me?"

It was then Moon decided on point 9 SP (Goodbody's being so long hadn't helped). When he decided where it was, Moon pinched the point with his fingers. He used a short needle like before, a number two, and piqued one fen deep. He piqued as Sergeant Goodbody exhaled and toward the direction of energy flow. He scratched the head of the needle to help summon the energy. He piqued for Pu at 9 SP because he was trying to supply energy to Goodbody's spleen, to restore it to equilibrium, to cure Goodbody of flatulence.

Sergeant Moon knew that Goodbody's spleen lacked energy because Goodbody's eleventh rib had responded painfully to light pressure. Because point 9 SP had been cool to the touch. Because of the yellow in Goodbody's eyes and the fact that he was always humming. Because Goodbody's flatulence was hard to miss.

"Come on, Moon, gimme it straight. Tell me what's wrong."

"Like I said. What's wrong is you've got too much energy here and much too little over there. Understand?"

"Energy?"

"Jesus Christ! Didn't you follow?"

"Not too far."

"Well, forget it."

"Where? Over where?"

"Just forget it. Lay still."

"Listen, Moon, how did it happen?"

"It happened because you were perverted."

"Hey, man—watch it, huh?"

"Because your energy was perverted. Because you're not in harmony."

"Yeah? Who says?"

Moon didn't answer. He was looking for point 4 CO.

"Listen, Moon, whadda we do—'bout this here energy?"

"Well, according to the Great Law of Pu-Hsieh— Lay still, dammit! Get back down. It's no joke."

Sergeant Goodbody settled back down, with three needles piqued into him, knowing that Moon wouldn't joke about such things. "Okay," said Goodbody, "but tell me again."

"About Pu-Hsieh?"

"About the old man."

So Sergeant Moon told him again, just like he had seen it. He told him while he tried to locate point 4 CO. "There they were, right on the sidewalk, down from Cheap Charlie's. Three squatting Chinamen playing mah-jongg. Four bam, three crack, two dot, got me a dragon. And this one old guy—the fourth hand, see?— flat on his back and stripped to his drawers, just like you—not having a care in the world except to win that mah-Jongg game —and, of course, to get his energy fixed."

"Yeah, of course."

"Four bam, got me a dragon, you know. No one stopped except Lovelace and me. And Lovelace, he stopped only because he couldn't remember about Cheap Charlie's noodle soup. Whether he still liked it or not."

"Great! Go on."

"Well, as the old guy was playing his hand, another old guy squatted beside him and stuck these needles into him. Into his shoulders and chest and legs." Moon still hadn't found point 4 CO. "I asked Cheap Charlie about it later. Acupuncture, Charlie said, it puts your energy right. It picks you up when you're feeling down and sets you down—not enough to hurt—when you're acting up. The old guy didn't wince. He didn't jerk around like you. Just played his game. Feeling better all the time. Not smiling, of course, but feeling better just the same."

"How you so sure he was feelin' better?"

"Well, he won the game, didn't he?" Sergeant Moon was getting close. "It takes a loose head to win at that game. A steady head. Lots of good equilibrium." Sergeant Moon was almost there. "Hey, Goodbody, hold still. Give me a chance. Whoa. Whoaaa. There!"

"*Aghhhhhh!*"

In spite of all the noise he made, Sergeant Goodbody took the pique better than he had before. So either he was feeling better, or he was getting used to the pain.

"So, how come *I* ain't feelin' no better? And maybe even a whole lot worse?"

Goodbody's faith in Sergeant Moon was fast disappearing. He was sorely wanting to get right up, but instead he lay still as Moon worked out at 4 CO. He didn't want to hurt Moon's feelings.

Moon had taken a long time to locate point 4 CO because the meridian of the colon was a very tricky one. It ran from the tip of the index finger, along the outer side of the arm, then over the shoulder and up the neck to somewhere about the nose. Unlike before, Moon didn't pique for Pu but for Hsieh. He used a long needle, a number five, and piqued one pouce deep. He piqued as Sergeant Goodbody inhaled and against the direction of energy flow. He didn't pinch the point with his fingers before he piqued. He didn't scratch the head of the needle after he piqued to help summon the energy. He piqued for Hsieh at 4 CO because he was trying to reduce the energy in Goodbody's colon, to restore it to equilibrium, to relieve the pain in Goodbody's shoulders.

Sergeant Moon knew that Goodbody's colon had an excess of energy, because point 25 ST had responded painfully to heavy pressure. Because point 11 CO had been warm to the touch. Because, just like Goodbody had said, he had this pain in his shoulders.

Goodbody let Moon work out on him because his visit to Anna's hadn't been the answer. He had returned just as food-picky, as flatulent, as pained in the shoulders, as yellow-eyed, just as ex-

citable as before. Sergeant Goodbody had been at wit's end. Nothing
had worked. Not Sergeant Culpepper. Not Y Blo. Not Fat Anna's.
So he had figured what the hell, why not give Sergeant Moon his
chance. Besides, Goodbody hadn't known how not to give Sergeant
Moon his chance; for Moon had been after him all the time, pestering him, claiming he had this great new way. Finally, he had let
Sergeant Moon work out on him because he wanted to help
Sergeant Moon, to get him over those mumbling blues which he
had picked up in Saigon.

Sergeant Moon made one last pique, at point 3 LI. He piqued
for Hsieh, as he had piqued at 4 CO. He piqued for Hsieh at 3 LI
because he was trying to reduce the energy in Goodbody's liver,
to restore it to equilibrium, to calm his excitability. Moon had
known that Goodbody's liver was hyperactive, because of Goodbody's rancid odor.

"Hey, Moon, you think it'll really work?"

"It's got to work."

"Why it's got?"

"Because I have sincere intentions."

"Yeah? So what?"

"Listen, Goodie, it says in the *Yellow Emperor's Canon* that,
if the intentions of the physician are sincere, then it's got to work.
I mean, if he uses the needles right."

If Moon had no doubts about the sincerity of his intentions, he
did have some about the dosage: how long he should leave the
needles stuck in. He knew that it was very important—crucial,
in fact—not to leave them in too long. Not a moment too long.
Especially those which supplied energy. He knew how very important it was to withdraw the needles as soon as equilibrium had
been restored. The trouble was that Moon didn't know how to
tell exactly when equilibrium had been restored. This could be
told only thru a repeated study of the pulses. When the meridians
and their related organs returned to normal, so did the pulses. But
Moon didn't know how to study the pulses. So, instead, he just
kneeled beside Goodbody and waited until he figured that the
needles had restored his friend. Then Moon withdrew the needles.

He slowly withdrew the needles at points 4 ST, 34 ST and 9

SP—the ones with which he had piqued for Pu (Moon had piqued twice in the meridian of the stomach because he had figured that Goodbody's lack of appetite was the most serious problem of all and needed more intensive treatment, Goodbody being such a beanpole). He withdrew the three as Goodbody inhaled. He closed the points by rubbing them. Then he rapidly withdrew the needles at points 4 CO and 3 LI—the ones with which he had piqued for Hsieh. He withdrew them as Goodbody exhaled. He left the points open after he did.

Before Moon let Goodbody get up, he told him not to bathe for awhile tho Goodbody still smelled rancid. He also warned him about overeating—to eat no more than a third of his normal diet for the next few days. To insure the cure. That's what the *Yellow Emperor's Canon of Internal Medicine* advised.

"No more than a third."

"Don' have no choice. It's all I been eatin'. Can't eat no more."

"Yeah, maybe so, but now you're all better. So just take it easy for three or four days."

"Yeah maybe so yourself! I don' feel betta. Not a bit betta. Fact, I feel worse."

Sergeant Goodbody got to his feet, stiffly he did. He brushed the dirt from his back. He examined the points where the piques had been made. He put an arm around Sergeant Moon and thanked Moon profusely, just the same, for doing his best, for having tried: "It's all right, Moon, you done what you could. I neva did like that mah-jongg game. Neva even heard of it. You done jus' fine. Thanks a lot. Gotta get ready. See you soon." Then Goodbody walked away, still stripped to his drawers. He felt real sorry for his friend Moon who had looked so surprised, so hurt when he said he wasn't feeling any better and, in fact, was feeling worse. Goodbody, himself, had not been surprised. Pu-Hsieh! Energy! What kinda jazz is that!? So there he was, stalking away, tall and skinny, stripped to his drawers, dark as bittersweet chocolate, humming, chanting to himself: *One-two—Hsieh-Pu—Up the Yellow Emerperor's gazoo! One-two—*

Sergeant Moon felt bluer than ever as Sergeant Goodbody stalked away, feeling no better and, in fact, worse. He had expected the needles to work. He swore he had done like the Chinaman, that he had piqued exactly like him. Moon was the bluest he'd ever been. He thought about Phan, how things hadn't worked. He thought about the sharp steel needles, how the needles hadn't worked either. He kept Phan tight in his mind, flung the needles to the ground, and stalked off after Goodbody. "Hey, Goodie," Moon called out, "did I ever tell you about the Nile?"

* * *

Goodbody wasn't the only one to be piqued that day. Luu piqued Phum behind the ear and drew more blood. The pique irritated Phum more than it hurt. It hurt, of course, but not nearly as much as a pique to the nose. Phum was a big lumbering fellow, a slow-thinking fellow—certainly not as bright as Luu—and usually did whatever Luu told him to do. But there were times, like the present, when Phum required a pique or two.

Phum was very devoted to Luu in spite of the occasional piques. He understood that Luu piqued him only when his will grew slack, or when he acted perversely, or when his brain wasn't quick enough to accommodate Luu. In a way, thought Phum, the piques did him good. But, of course, he wasn't about to admit this fact to Luu. So, whenever he was piqued by Luu, Phum raised his nose, wrinkled his brow, and trumpeted his displeasure instead.

Phum had worked with Luu for many years and the two of them got along famously. In fact, they were quite inseparable—"friends to the end," Luu always said, and Phum agreed. Whenever Luu went off by himself, which he seldom did, Phum missed him terribly. He would brood, become surly, menacing, almost impossible to approach, until Luu returned. Then he would greet Luu with great squealing joy.

Tho Phum was getting on in years and somewhat wrinkled, he was still a stout worker and could pack a heavy load—if he paced himself properly, and if Luu looked after him. But now Phum was hot and thirsty and tired, ill-tempered too. He had gone without sleep the night before, which had made him nervous—more irritable than all the piques had—and not at all like his usual self. He wished they would reach the watering soon. He could drink a thousand gallons—well, maybe not so much. He was as hungry as he was thirsty. His belly rumbled constantly. They hadn't stopped to eat a thing since the day before. It was Luu's fault. Why was he in such a great hurry? It was Phum who packed the load. Luu, he didn't pack a thing. It wasn't fair. Phum felt weakened by his hunger and his thirst and lack of sleep. The load he packed got heavier each hour that he ambled along.

Phum wasn't overly bright, but he had a very good memory. So in order to keep his mind off his hunger and his thirst, he tried to recall all the grand times he and Luu had shared. Like the grand time two years before at Tonle Sap, during the rains, when he and Luu had taken part in an elephant hunt. The great lake had overflowed onto the land, and he and Luu had helped to drive the wild elephants into the water, where they had been chased down from the boats, and lassoed, and tied to half-submerged trees, then left to keep their great bodies afloat until they were half-drowned and easily managed. Phum recalled the gongs and the tom-toms, the fire crackers, the flaring of the resin torches in the deep gray overcast, their piney smell mingling with elephant smell. Phum tried to recall all the work he and Luu had done together: like clearing the forest and hauling logs, and helping to build the pile houses around the edge of Tonle Sap, the houses of the fishermen, and the smuggling. Phum liked smuggling best of all, crossing the border with contraband, which in a way, was what he and Luu were doing then.

Luu piqued Phum once again to snap Phum out of his daydreaming ways, to make him move faster, for Luu was truly in a great hurry. He was already late with the party favors and feared that Mac would be angry with him. Luu was so fearful that Mac would be angry that he, in turn, became angry with Phum for not responding quickly enough, and piqued Phum two or three times more. The track was thick with thorn bushes and other prickly clutching things. Much of the track was little more than the width of a man, and sometimes not, but with a pique every now and then, Phum rumbled ahead. The tall prickly clutching things tore at Luu's legs, which were now bleeding even more than Phum's ears. Luu had known about the thorns, the clutching things, but had taken this way because it was fastest. He estimated that they were one or two kilometers from the border, that they were still in Cambodia.

Luu was not as smitten with Phum as Phum with him, not with the same wildly enthusiastic unequivocal love. His affection for Phum was stern and comradely. "Now Comrade Phum this—" and "Comrade Phum that—" Luu was always saying to Phum, making sure that Phum understood why things were the way they were and what was expected of him. "Now Comrade Phum, this is no time to daydream. We're late enough as it is and, if we're much later, then Comrade Mac will have my hide, so that's why I'm piqueing yours."

Tho Luu made sure that Phum always knew just who was boss, that Phum showed him absolute respect, Luu respected Phum as well. He respected Phum for his great size. For Phum's gentle ways, his forbearance, which his great size made possible. For Phum's unshakable loyalty. Luu had been with Phum for so long, that people said he would come to his end right atop Phum's back, where he was sitting then, just behind Phum's head.

Luu guided his Comrade Phum by touching his feet in various ways to Phum's head. The soles of his feet were just as cracked and almost as tough as Phum's hide. Luu wore a dirty rag on his head, torn from some worn-out piece of clothing. Luu had once seen an Indian movie in Kompong Cham, full of drivers like himself, wearing rags around their heads. After the movie, he decided to wear a rag too, that he owed it to Phum.

The track grew even thicker and the bushes into trees. Sharper too, clutchier. Luu bent low. He pressed himself close toward the top of Phum's head to protect his own. They were soon in a tangle of thorn so dense that the track disappeared temporarily. As the branches came swiping faster, as they came raking over his body, Luu closed his eyes and covered his head. Then he screamed.

It was hornets, hundreds of them, thousands, millions, even more. A nest of brown hornets had lodged in his lap, tight in the Vee of his sharply bent body. The angry hornets attacked Luu's face, his arms, his legs. They stung his bare skin. They stung him thru his calico shirt. They stung him for riding off with their home. Hundreds, thousands, millions of them. Luu slammed the hornets' nest out of his lap. But that seemed to only make the hornets angrier. They came at Luu from all sides at once, and he beat at them hysterically, flailing his arms to drive them off. But there were so many and each one scored many times. They stung, retracted their barbless stingers, stung again.

Poor Phum didn't know what to do, until the hornets went for his eyes. Then Phum went rampaging thru the thicket, load and all, infuriated by the stings, mindless of Luu perched on his back. Phum squealed and slapped at his eyes with his trunk as he tried to outrun the hornets. Thirsty, hungry, tired Phum, bloody-eared Phum was no longer forbearing. His giant size was no defense against the tiny raging things.

The hornets finally peeled away, but Phum went on crashing thru the thicket. Luu's face was swollen and lumpy. He could barely see out of his eyes. His head whirled from all the stings. He swayed unsteadily on Phum's back. He leaned forward over Phum's head and reached for Phum's eyes; which was a precarious thing to do, even for an elephant driver who wasn't reeling from hornet stings. Luu was reaching to cover Phum's eyes, to bring him to a stop.

It went that way for a time. Luu swayed and leaned and reached for Phum's eyes as Phum lurched ahead, out of control. He reached until he was knocked from Phum's back by a stout overhanging branch. Luu crashed to the ground just short of the border, where he quickly lost consciousness.

When Phum finally came to a stop, he all of a sudden wondered what had happened to Luu. He trumpeted. He charged about in unfinished circles. He was grieved, he was shattered by his loss. Where was Luu? Where was his friend? Why had he deserted Phum? Phum wanted to search for Luu, but he had lost his orientation and he didn't know where to begin. He banged his head in great despair. He beat his head against a great tree until, in his greater despair, he sent the tree crashing to the ground. Bang! Crash! He had to find Luu! But he didn't know how. Nor what he was going to do with the favors.

* * *

"Eeyah, look at Y M'dhur!"
"Ooeee, just like a woman!"

"Look at Y M'dhur carry the wood!"

"He carries it well."

"Well or not, it's work for a woman."

"Look, everyone, look at M'dhur!"

Everyone turned to Y M'dhur, to the amber-skinned half 'n half from Phu Dinh who said there wasn't any rope. The people of Buon Yun looked on amazed, or amused, or horrified, at Y M'dhur's breech of etiquette. Some hooted and jeered. Some rolled on the ground and clutched their bellies. Some asked him what it was all about. Y M'dhur was bent low, weighed down by the huge stack of wood on his back which he was carrying into the village, just like the women did. The half 'n half labored for breath and swore. He told everyone to mind their own business, that he was doing his woman a turn.

"Eeyah, M'dhur is doing his woman a turn!"

"Ooeee, M'dhur is turning into a woman!"

It was good that M'dhur had chosen this time to carry his wood, for the chopper was late and the people were restless. The half 'n half entertained the people as they waited to be entertained by Captain Yancy and his men. The people waited outside the fence, along the south edge of the clearing. They had gathered there for the treat Captain Yancy had promised them—the one intended to boost their morale after the incident at Buon Sop. And one which was doubly welcomed then, for word of the ironsmith's dream had spread and what it meant. Everyone had gathered there except the infirm and Y M'dhur, who was busy doing his woman a turn.

There was friendly, mischievous Grandmother Pan. There was grizzled Y Bun standing very straight. There was Y Gar with his crossbow in hand. There was Y Bong with his naughty wife. There were groups here and there of serious men, of horse-playing men, of cackling women who nursed their babies and weren't quite sure what was going to happen. There was Triple Threat bounding from group to group, sharing his excitement with anyone who would share it back with him. There was Little Rhadeo smiling brightly, clutching his harmonica, chatting with his friend, Sergeant Moon. There was even grumpy solitary one-eared Y Blo, but he, of course, stood off by himself. There was everyone, just about.

After Y M'dhur had gone, the people waited as before, until at last, the chopper appeared, there to the south, from the direction of Ban Me Thuot. It appeared as a piece of grit in the sky, and grew steadily larger and larger. When it grew to the size of a Dipa bird's eye, its drone could be heard as it beat north against the wind. The people pointed toward the chopper, exclaimed at the strange shape of the thing, and led it along with their fingers.

"I'm keeping my promise, Jasperson."

"Maybe so, Captain sir, but that's a mighty nifty wind."

"Not so nifty, Jasperson, not for a bunch of hard-assed men."

"Nifty, sir. Real quick and full of surprises."

"Nifty or not, whatever I promise, I deliver."

"Maybe so, sir. No offense, sir. But it's just not fair to the men."

"Has someone complained? Has anyone? I'll bet it's that damn Sergeant Goodbody."

"No one's complained. Never, sir. It's a mighty nifty wind."

"See those people, Jasperson, all those people waiting there? They expect us to act like hard-assed men. So that's what we're going to do." Captain Yancy thrust his face into Sergeant Jasperson's face. "Look at my face, Jasperson, what do you see?"

"A face, Captain, sir."

"Yeah. Well listen, Jasperson, I aim to hang right onto it. Get what I mean?"

"Yes, sir, you aim to hang onto your face."

"None of that dollar forty-three."

"None of it, sir. I understand."

"No, Jasperson, I don't think you do." Yancy was sure that Jasperson didn't. "It's not that I promised, not that so much. Promises don't always have to be kept. It's because the people should never doubt—not for a minute—that we're a bunch of hard-assed men. That's why I aim to hang onto my face." Yancy had let his voice get hard, so he softened it. Sergeant Jasperson was a good man. "Listen, Jas', everybody has a face. Me, you, everyone. It's the way we go around." Captain Yancy looked around at everyone else. "Everyone, Jas'. *Everyone* cares about his face."

"I don't, sir."

"Then start caring, Jasperson. Cause soon as we let our faces slip—soon as the people start to doubt that we're a bunch of hard-assed men—then we've lost them, Jasperson—our faces and the people too."

"Seems to me, sir, that if everybody slipped their faces about the same time—then no one would have to worry, sir. About being hard-assed or not. They wouldn't have to care, sir. Not you, not me, not anyone."

Yancy considered, then he said: "Maybe so, Jasperson—maybe so— But who's gonna let his face slip first? Who wants a measly one forty-three?"

"What's this one forty-three, Captain, sir?"

"Nothing much, that's what."

"A *real* hard-assed man, Captain Yancy, sir."

"What d'ya mean?"

"A man with hard-assed character. A man with soul."

"Has Plunket been saying things to you?"

"What kind of things?"

"Things like my hair being much too short and how my soul can't find its way."

"No, sir, he hasn't," said Jasperson.

"Yeah, well, he better not!"

"With soul, Captain Yancy," continued Sergeant Jasperson. "A man with hard-assed character."

"Okay, Jasperson—just fine—now what in hell are you talking about?"

"About who's gonna slip his face first."

"What!? For a dollar forty-three!?"

"About the wind, sir—"

"To hell with the wind! We're gonna jump."

The Americans were all chuted up. They rechecked their gear, they tugged at their cinches for the last time as the chopper drew near. They shifted their weight from foot to foot, they silently contained their excitement, all the mushing around inside. If they were worried about the wind, no one was admitting it. The wind was blowing in nifty gusts of up to twenty knots or more.

The chopper soon clattered overhead. Captain Yancy instructed Y Bun to keep the villagers off the clearing. The chopper hovered, then dropped softly to the ground. The rush of its blades filled the air with chaff, with insects too, everything swirling fast and round. The eight Americans slit their eyes against the chaff and all the bugs and clambered aboard. The chopper rose and made a circle to the east. It was decided to fly two passes, four men to a pass. The clearing was only 200 yards long.

It was drafty and noisy inside the machine, and very business-like at first. Each of the men was assigned to a stick, the first or second, and took his position accordingly, as the chopper circled the clearing. Then the chopper made its turn, and began its ap-proach from the east, over the north edge of the clearing to com-pensate for the drift of the wind. The men of the first stick hooked up to the cable which ran the floor. They looked ahead. At the jumpmaster's signal, at Captain Yancy's, they each scrambled for-ward, sat down in the door, pushed off into space. Out went zany, good-humored Plunket. Steady, unruffled Jasperson. Surly Love-lace. Gloomy Culpepper. Out—out—out into space. Down—swiftly down into space.

Five seconds. Six seconds. Then the canopies billowed with air. The wind blew, drove the chutes south. Plunket, Jasperson, Love-lace, Culpepper worked like mad to slow down their drift. They tugged on their risers. They hauled, they strained to lower the gores on the windward side, to tack their canopies into the wind. But the wind was as strong as Captain Yancy's vanity, as nifty as Jasperson had said, and the men were borne along on the drafts. They worked, they jerked, they fought for control. They were lucky to catch the south edge of the clearing, and landed hard, one by one, almost amid the gawking crowd. Then they scrambled to turn their chutes from the wind, to close them to air, so that the chutes with them saddled in wouldn't be dragged over the ground. Plunket —Jasperson—surly Lovelace. All but Culpepper who was still up. He had been last man out the door.

And was now fast closing in on the fence—on the pointed stakes of the outer fence—on the bed of golden bamboo spikes between the outer and inner fence. The villagers loved their Sergeant Culpepper. He gave them powders to fight the powders of the *m'tao*. He made the jokes that no one knew. He gave them pills, bright red and blue and yellow, too. Their Sergeant Culpepper, he was in danger. They waved their arms to shoo him away. They shouted all sorts of the best advice. They tried to hold back the wind with their hands.

Sergeant Culpepper closed very fast. There was no time to haul, to lower his gores on the leeward side, to catch more wind and hope to be borne into Buon Yun, itself. There was no time because he was but twenty feet over the ground, and about to clear the outer fence, about to drop onto the bamboo spikes.

So Sergeant Culpepper emptied his chute. He yanked on the risers with all his might, and spilled the air from his canopy. He collapsed his chute and dropped almost straight down, slamming against the fence as he did. Then he bounced off the fence and crashed to the ground. The people of Buon Yun came running up, fearful for their Sergeant Culpepper. But Sergeant Culpepper waved them off, as he stumbled to his feet.

Yancy admitted to himself that Sergeant Jasperson had been right about the niftiness of the wind. So as the chopper clackety-clacked, as it flew west for the second pass, it flew in a line farther north than before, north of the clearing. It flew right over the forest itself. It flew farther north to make sure this time, to compensate for the drift of the wind.

The men went out over the forest. Sergeant Moon with his far-away thoughts. Punctured, woebegone Sergeant Goodbody. Forever scheming Sergeant Fritz. Proud, dimple-chinned Captain Yancy. They worked, they jerked. They tugged on their risers. They fought the wind which bore them south, right toward the center of the clearing. The men came down without any drama. They all landed hard, got to their feet, and struggled to gather in their chutes. One by one—Moon—Goodbody—Captain Yancy. All but Fritz, the sunshine man. Sergeant Fritz lay fixed to the ground, his ass run thru by a poisoned punji, Fighter Dung's of the 825th.

* * *

Sergeant Goodbody prepared to set fire to the hut and to all the rice inside. He cupped one hand around the flame, for there was a breeze. He reached toward the hut, and all the men gathered close to watch. Then Sergeant Goodbody suddenly stopped and let the breeze blow out the flame. "It don' seem right, no sir. It don' make sense." Now there were times when Sergeant Goodbody seemed not to make much sense himself, times when he waxed hysterical, irrational. But Sergeant Goodbody was really a man who needed good reasons for doing things. "It jus' don' make sense, no sir. Here we be burnin' our very own rice."

"Come on, Goodbody, get it done. There's too much here to pack to Buon Yun." Lieutenant Plunket was disappointed and wanted to get the burning done. They had come all this way, toward the Brake of the Rattling Bamboo, trying to find the Viet Cong who had caused Sergeant Fritz to be fixed to the ground. But they had found only the cache instead. It was set off the ground in a small bamboo hut, which was just enough to protect the rice from rain and mice and other kinds of scurrying things.

Goodbody lit a second match. He cupped the flame, reached forward again, stopped like before, considered a bit, made up his mind, then let the breeze blow out the flame. "No, sir, I'm not gonna do it. I jus' can't do it."

"Whaddaya mean you're not gonna do it?"

"I'm not gonna burn all this here rice."

"For Godsake, Goodbody, burn that rice! That's an order!"

"Well now, sir—"

"An order, Goodbody! Burn that rice!"

"Well now—"

"You better burn it. I'm gonna get you."

"Well, sir—"

"Arhhhh! Grrrrrr!"

"Up the Yellow Emperor's gazoo, Lieutenant Plunket, *sir!*"

Plunket was stunned. So was Goodbody. He backtracked as fast as he could. "Now, sir, it was nothin'. Jus' a ditty. Okay, sir? Jus' a ditty."

"Yeah—well—okay, Goodbody."

"Lieutenant, sir, you're a nice guy. An' I don' mean to be all huffy with you. But you jus' gotta understan' about the rice, the way things are."

"It's okay, Goodbody, I understand. Things have been tough all around—what with you in a bad way, and with Moon making it worse, and what with Fritz being fixed tight—" Plunket's great heart went out to Goodbody, sincerely it did. His soft brown eyes blurred with concern. His fuzzy head wagged in sympathy. He knew what it was to have things tough. "—real tough—yeah, I know— But now let's get the show on the road. Light it up!"

"Sir, I'm not gonna. I jus' can't burn my very own rice."

"*Whose* damn rice!?"

"*Our* damn rice, pardon me, sir. Our very own." Sergeant Goodbody was very intense, more excitable than ever, supercharged with energy. His tall, skinny body practically shuddered with each word. "Sir, you saw all them mouldy sacks. All them empty burlap sacks. You saw 'em, huh? You saw what was writ: 'Gift of the goddamn USA'!"

"Okay, I saw. Now take it easy. Quit shaking like that." But Plunket was getting excited too. He was feeling the heat of Goodbody's cause, whatever it was. "I saw what was written. But so what, Goodbody? What's your point?"

"Lieutenant, sir, this here be the very same rice what was handed out in the villages. Rice what bad ol' Charlie took an' carried off. All them tax collector guys. It be our very own damn rice an' I'm not gonna burn it."

"Okay. Okay. The very same rice. Our rice. So what about it? We've always burned VC rice before, no matter where they got it."

"Yeah, maybe so, Lieutenant, sir—but maybe we been doin' it wrong." They were bright yellow, Goodbody's eyes, as he rushed to explain. "Look, sir, if we burn this rice, then Charlie, he jus' goes from village to village, an' taxes them folks all over again. Then we gotta give them folks more rice jus' to make up what was took. Then we gotta go an' patrol some more, an' be lookin' hard for Charlie's new rice—which really be our very own rice—an' burnin' the rice when we find it, if. An' then it starts all over again—"

Plunket waited. This Goodbody, he was no fool.

"So maybe we jus' betta leave the rice. We save fuss an' save money, an' we be betta off all around. Huh, Lieutenant? Whaddaya think?"

Lieutenant Plunket thought it over. By God, this Sergeant Goodbody made sense. But Plunket knew that just to make sense was not enough. That it wasn't done. "Listen, Goodbody, it just isn't done. We just can't leave the rice like that. We're supposed to destroy everything. Those are the orders. You know that." Plunket felt rotten. He realized that Goodbody meant well. He was sorry that things could not be worked out. He was sorry for Sergeant Goodbody, and sorry for himself as well, that he hadn't thought of it first. "I'd like to help you, honest, Goodbody. I wish we could work it out somehow. But there's no way out of burning the rice. No way, no how. Just to do it. Those are the orders."

"It won't make no difference, Lieutenant, sir. Whether we do or whether we don'. Either way Charlie gets his rice."

"Okay, Charlie gets his rice. But let's burn the rice anyway. Cause this way he's got to work harder for it. Huh, Goodbody, whaddaya say?"

"Charlie, he don' mind hard work. He's a plugger, Charlie is." Sergeant Goodbody knew he made sense and that the others didn't. But, like Plunket, he also knew that just to make sense was not quite enough. So Sergeant Goodbody started to give, but grudgingly. "Lawd, I sure hate to burn that good rice. That cost green, Lieutenant, sir."

"There's lots more green. There's always more green. That's what they keep telling us. 'Don't sweat the green,' they always say. Hey, y'know what?"

"What, sir?"

"They shouldn't oughta keep telling us that."

Sergeant Goodbody thought for awhile, head down, poking the dirt with the toe of his boot. He sure hated to burn all that rice.

"Listen, Goodbody, I want you to know that I like you, see? You're a pretty nice fellow most of the time—when you're not being hysterical, or pestering me to look into your eyes for yellow spots. So it's nothing personal, understand?" Plunket was poking in the dirt too. "But if we leave this rice behind—if we leave it for Charlie to stuff himself with—then the Captain, he'll have your ass and mine. Mostly mine."

Sergeant Goodbody thought some more, head down, rubbing his bony behind. "That's it, sir!" he shouted all of a sudden.

"What's it, Goodbody!?" shouted Plunket.

"It! That's it!" clamored Goodbody.

"For Crissake, what is it!?" clamored Plunket.

"Let's eat," said Goodbody, dead seriously.

"What the hell—!?" said Plunket shattered. "Of all the things to bring up now! Goddammit, Goodbody!"

"Let's stuff ourselves, sir."

"Dammit, Goodbody."

"Damn it, sir—pardon me, sir—but ain't you got no principles? You do got principles, don' you, sir?"

"What the—!"

"It's the principle of the thing. See what I mean?"

Plunket didn't.

"Let's eat as much of the rice as we can. Right now, sir. See what I mean?"

Plunket began to.

"Look at all them scrawny Yards. They know good rice. So let's have a feast. Then we'll burn what's left, I promise you. Huh, Lieutenant? Whaddaya say? If we gotta do it—if we gotta burn it— then let's eat it up a bit."

Plunket laughed. He slapped Goodbody on the back, he pumped his hand. He congratulated Sergeant Goodbody, but he had his doubts. "Listen, Goodbody, we won't even make a dent in that pile. Not you and me and the platoon. Not the tiniest dent."

"Yes, sir. I know that, sir. But still I'll feel a whole lot betta. Oh yes, sir, 'bout everything."

"Listen, Goodbody—"

"Oh yes, sir, you do got principles, don' you, sir?"

At first, Goodbody really felt a whole lot better. The principle, sure, that played a part; but even more, Goodbody had his appetite back! "Oh, Glory be!" Goodbody said. "Oh, Sergeant Moon, it

eally worked! Oh I got my energy back! Oh Lawd! Hot dawg!
take it all back, Yellow Emperor, sir. No more one-two you know
what. Yessir, Moon, you really done it!" Sergeant Goodbody, the
eal Goodbody, with the gargantuan appetite, undid his belt, un-
buttoned his trousers, and ate like he never ate before. Goodbody
ate out of principle. He ate out of joy. He ate because he was
driven to eat by the energy that surged thru his body.

Sergeant Goodbody gorged joyfully, until he began to feel less
and less better, and in fact, even worse than before. Then he just
gorged out of principle, and because he was driven to gorge. And
then the principle of the thing, it didn't count for much.

Plunket and the Strike Force platoon gave Sergeant Goodbody a
chase at first. They molded the rice into little balls and threw
them into the air to cool—once, twice—then gulped them down.
They wolfed down the rice balls and, after every two or three, they
cracked a piece of uncrushed salt between their teeth for flavoring.
They chased Goodbody, but it was no contest. Plunket claimed that
Sergeant Goodbody was all hyped up, that he should be dis-
qualified, that it wasn't fair. "Dammit, Sergeant Goodbody," he
said, "that Moon has sure given you a boost."

"Only jus' back to my natural form, that's all, sir. Jus' back to
my unperverted self."

But Lieutenant Plunket disagreed. "The hell, Goodbody, you're
more perverted than ever before. Who ever heard of eating like
that?"

"Hey you jus' watch it, you jus' betta watch it, pardon me, sir."

As Sergeant Goodbody went on and on, Plunket and the Strike
Force platoon dropped out one by one.

No one moved except Sergeant Goodbody, and then it was only
to nudge poor Plunket. "Come on, sir—for the principle. You do
got principles, don' you, sir?" Sergeant Goodbody had slowed to
a crawl, to a snail's pace, but still he went on. The others lay
stuffed, stupefied. They watched the hut, and all the left-over rice
inside, go up in flames. Their eyes were glassy, their bellies
swollen. They were altogether numb. Y —— had never eaten so
much in all his life. Nor Y ——, or Y ——, or anyone. None of

the men had a care in the world. The fire made a pretty sight.

Sergeant Goodbody nudged Plunket again. "Come on, sir—jus' one more time." Then Sergeant Goodbody closed his eyes, tilted back his head a ways, and opened his mouth as wide as he could. Lieutenant Plunket wearily grabbed a fistful of rice and jammed it down Goodbody's throat. Goodbody didn't have the will.

The blaze was hot, and the men drowsed. Sergeant Goodbody burped mightily, letting out gas. Goodbody burped a second time, letting out more. *Burp!* went Goodbody. *Burp! Burp!* The third burp completely deflated Goodbody. He practically hissed as he collapsed. Viet Cong guns burped from everywhere and deflated the drowsing men.

BAN ME THUOT

The meeting had been suddenly called and everyone came excitedly, full of the highest expectations; but just a little anxious too, in case the news was ominous. What could it be? Some nice surprise? What was all the fuss about? Who was going to get it this time? Everyone gathered in a hush, thinking these thoughts, content at first to question themselves. Then, as they waited for things to begin, they started to buzz, to ask their neighbors left and right: "What could it be?" "Some nice surprise?" "What was all the fuss about?" "Who was going to get it this time?"

The buzzing hadn't gotten a chance, when it was cut off by a scream. The scream took wind and lengthened into a great tirade, an abusive one. Everyone sat glued in place, too stunned to stir or to twitter. All except for Bombay Betty, who laughed as Fat Anna screamed at her.

Bombay Betty was the scruffiest, dirtiest whore in all of Fat Anna's dirty gray house, but Betty had this talent for loving, which was why customers asked for her, why they put up with her. Bombay Betty was skinnier even than Fat Anna, but she was full of brawling vigor. She always gave as good as she got, when she caught flak from her customers, or from the other girls. Betty had started out in Saigon as the bastard daughter of an Indian silk merchant and a Vietnamese rice-cake girl. In an uncommon turn of events, Betty had never known her mother, who had drifted off somewhere, and was raised by her swarthy, hawk-nosed father. The Indian thrived from his sale of silk cloth and later, during Betty's teens, by changing dollars into piasters for all the GIs who slipped into his shop. The Indian fiercely loved his daughter, and Betty grew up a happy girl. Also a somewhat ugly girl who looked remarkably like her father.

One day the Viet Cong came to their shop, and demanded a small contribution, but Betty's father chased them away. The Viet Cong came a second time, and again Betty's father refused to pay. They heard no more from the Viet Cong. Then, one morning, she found her father behind the counter of his shop, on the floor, strangled with a swath of silk, his finest blue. Betty grieved and buried her father. She left the silk on, as it looked so pretty. The shop was claimed by legitimate kin, and Betty set out to seek her fortune.

Bombay Betty had no education. It hadn't been the Indian's way to send her to school. But Betty understood practical things: like not grieving overly long about these sudden twists of fate; like grieving less about whatever wasn't important, or not at all. So happy-go-lucky Bombay Betty laughed when Fat Anna screamed.

"Look at her! Look at her!" screamed Fat Anna. "Look at her, dears, the dirty whore!" Fat Anna looked at Bombay Betty and then eyed each of her girls in turn. "Now listen, girls—listen dears—we know that I try to run a clean place. Isn't that right? A clean place, Betty! Ya—ya—ya—! Now listen, dears, we all know a clean place is good for business. Which means for us. Isn't it so—?" Fat Anna seldom lost her temper, but when she did she was formidable. She lost it enough to be formidable, but not enough not to choose her words well. Anna understood the effectiveness of a lost temper. She had understood since that time, years before, when she lost hers for the very first time, when she told the Chinaman just what to do with the buffalo dung. "Oh yes, dears, it's certainly so. But there's one among us who doesn't care. Not two dong. Does she, Betty!? Ya—ya—ya—! Oh girls, oh my pets, your Anna hasn't been upset like this in years. Listen, dears, you see Bombay Betty? Look at her, dears, the dirty whore! Well don't become like Bombay Betty. Never ever become like that whore."

When the girls understood that Fat Anna's wrath was not on them but only on Betty, they started to twitter, to click their tongues, to wag their heads at Bombay Betty. Who clicked her tongue right back at them, who wagged her head. "Ooh, look at Betty." "The dirty whore!" "What has that Bombay Betty done ow?" "Look at that whore, how filthy she is!" "Look how dark! Look at her nose!"

"That's enough, dears. Now listen to Anna. We all know she ries to run a clean place. Don't we, girls? Because a clean place s good for business. And we know how bad it is for business when ne of Anna's girls is sick."

"Is Betty sick?" "Not again!?" "Is Betty caught with it again?"

"Betty's caught. Oh, how she's caught! Isn't she, Betty!? Ya— a—ya—!" Fat Anna joined her girls and, all together, they licked their tongues and wagged their heads at Bombay Betty. Think of my poor customers. Think of them, dears. Look at her, lears. Look at her laugh. Just like it was nothing at all. Oh, my lears, don't get like her. Oh, think what will come of this!"

* * *

On Friday evenings, without fail, and sometimes on other ccasions too, the Southeast Asia Domino Club gathered to match ominoes. The five regulars of the Club, of the chapter in Ban Me Thuot, gathered in the small back room of Hoang Bang's bicycle hop. It was located in a section of town where anyone, even omino players, might have business, but not in the thick of town, nd it was set slightly apart from the other shops on its street. The icycle shop could be reached from the back thru a maze of ittered alleyways, or from the street, by slipping decisively thru he front door. The regulars always slipped decisively thru the ront door, for the Southeast Asia Domino Club was a respectable rganization, and because it wouldn't do to be seen slinking thru lleyways.

The members of the Domino Club were very clannish fellows. They refused out of hand to admit new members, or to let others vatch as they played. They took their game seriously, having o time for dilettantes or kibitzers, and this Friday evening was o exception. They were playing overtime, snug against the black- ess outside, hidden by the square of cardboard in the window. A urricane lamp lit half the room, and half the faces of the men, who ooked gouged out and quietly mad. The dominoes went *click— lick—click*, sharply when the talking faltered, while outside in he alleyway, hungry rats rummaged thru the litter. The five men

of the Domino Club, of the standing committee of the Dar La
Central Committee, had grown accustomed to the sound, as the
did each Friday night. They no longer bothered to look up alertl
and swivel their ears toward the scuffling sounds. They no longe
flinched. They just click, click, clicked.

Hoang Bang, the bicycle man, played his hand very carefully
gauging how the others set down their dominoes or held them back
He listened very carefully too, weighing what the others said, an
what they didn't. He wished that Buc had more to say. He knew
that of all the others, Buc had the clearest head; that Buc coul
set his mind on one problem at a time and get to the bottom o
the matter.

Buc the barber sat at Hoang's right, cross-legged on the floor
scowl intact, thinking about his flat-faced niece and wishing sh
weren't, and thinking about the other girl, the one they were dis
cussing tonight. Thinking it right down to the bottom.

Deep-thinking Buc was, indeed, a taciturn fellow, a tall gaun
fellow. He had this haunting skeletal look, and Plunket had bee
rightly afraid. He was mean in a low, steady burning way, and no
flashing on and off mean like Lovelace. Yet Buc had his moment
of tenderness too, especially toward his flat-faced niece, tho h
wished she would give a closer shave. The most prominent thin
of all about Buc was not his leanness or his meanness, but that h
was missing his two front teeth. Buc refused to wear gold teeth lik
pedicab drivers or like other Vietnamese. He claimed his incisor
were enough. It may be that Buc cultivated his meanness becaus
of his two missing front teeth. He would have looked very silly, in
deed, if he hadn't looked so mean—if he had tried to smile instead

Buc was a man of authority, but it hadn't always been that way
One day, some years before, as Buc was cutting Hoang Bang's hair
the bicycle man had asked Buc what he thought of the latest Saigo
plan.

"What plan is that?" Buc had inquired.

"The plan to have all good Vietnamese men grow their hair ver
long. This long."

"*That* long!?"

"So when they come—"

"When who comes?"

"So when they come, they shouldn't kill off the good people too, because they would then be able to tell the good from the bad by the length of their hair."

"Who, Hoang, when *who* comes?"

"The Americans. They can't tell without the hair."

That was the first Buc had heard of the plan, but he had seen immediately how the plan would affect his barbering, how disastrously. Buc was no fool. He had also seen that the bad Vietnamese, the Viet Cong, would grow their hair just as long as the good; which would be doubly bad for business. So, from that day on, Buc went to work for Hoang Bang against the planners in Saigon. And tho nothing ever came of the plan, Buc continued to do his share, having been well-indoctrinated. But, actually, the indoctrination counted for little beside the fear, the one in Buc's head, that whoever could once make up such a plan, they could make it up again. Scowly Buc was taking no chances. He worked very diligently, until like Hoang Bang, he too became a member of the Dar Lac Province Central Committee.

Xuan the whoremonger sat next to Buc. Xuan was a solid fellow, with meaty hands and a pleasant face. He was easy-going, fond of a joke, and generally very cheerful. In fact, he was quite a jolly one. But in such mournful company, he tried his best to look mournful too. Xuan the whoremonger sat at Buc's side because he had once been married and, perhaps, still technically was.

Xuan had been married, and perhaps was, to a sharp-tongued bitch whom he had surprised one fateful day, laying with a Government man. Xuan threatened to kill the man. He ranted and raved, made a terrible scene; not from grief or even from anger—for he had long since grown cold of the bitch, but to make a presentable showing. The Government man was unashamed and patronizing, but he was nonetheless alarmed. He offered to satisfy Xuan's honor, to pay Xuan a sum of money, if only Xuan would lower his voice; for he also had a bitch of a wife and feared for her wrath should she find out, which, of course, she was sure to do if Xuan continued to holler like that. But Xuan was shrewd, and he raised his voice instead. He doubled its pitch and thus the

Government man's alarm. When the Government man doubled hi
offer, Xuan howled some more, out of spite, before he accepted
then sold the official all rights to his wife for a further doubling o
the sum. Having made such a handsome transaction, Xuan realize
where his destiny lay. He gathered his money, packed his bag
then took off for the countryside, bent upon whoremongering.

Years later, when Xuan was renowned and his pockets were fu
and his mattress too, when everything should have been settin
well, Xuan felt restless, unfulfilled. Tho dealing in whores wa
gratifying, especially when he tested the product, he was soulfu
enough to want more out of life. So Xuan applied to the NLI
because he wanted something more, and because of his cuckoldr
years before, at the hands of a Government man. He felt that h
could be of use, tho he knew that the NLF recruiters didn't usuall
sign up his kind. But the NLF accepted Xuan. They signed him s
fast they made his head spin. They grabbed him up because h
traveled in all the worst circles and also in some of the best. Becaus
he knew which families were most impoverished, which peasant
most bitter, which men and women most willing to work for th
NLF. Because he could place dependable girls where informatio
was most wanted. Bureaucrats, ARVN officers, influential citizen
all numbered among Xuan's clientele, and ladies like Fat Anna
So he was signed up, welcomed aboard. And ever since that happ
day, Xuan worked for the NLF. He rose swiftly to the top, righ
to the side of Buc.

Unlike Xuan, next to whom he sat, Mau the school teacher ha
risen slowly to the top. Mau was tall for a Viet and drawn ver
thin, something like Buc. His cheekbones poked out from his dar
narrow face and his clothes sagged on his spindly frame. Ma
smoked one cigarette after another when he played dominoes, o
when he did just about anything else, sucking greedily down to th
ends. His teeth were green and his nails were green, dirty, an
long. He coughed constantly, but never succeeded in bringing up
phlegm. Mau was the most mournful of them and didn't care a
all for Xuan, whose cheerfulness offended him, whose very pres
ence seemed to aggravate his cough. Mau was easily aroused an
always ready to recite the latest Party line. He had risen slowly

he was ready to recite, because of the black mark against his name: because his father had been a policeman, and not just any policeman at that, but an internal security man.

When Mau first applied to the NLF, the credentials committee laughed at him. Now why would a policeman's son want to join the NLF? Who could trust a policeman's son? And not just any policeman at that, but an internal security man. So they laughed and sent him away. But Mau was a man with a cause, a man of deep-down bedrock convictions, of stout character, of perseverence. So Mau bid once more. He tailored his bid upon the fact of his dad's missing teeth, that the policeman bolted his food without giving it a single chew. He tailored it in order to prove where his loyalty lay, to prove the deep-down bedrock depth of his commitment. He used bamboo. He spiked his dad's supper with tiny slivers. The policeman died slowly, very badly, while loyal, deeply committed Mau's bid was accepted by the Front.

Since his acceptance, Mau had worked hard to clear the black mark against his name. For, while killing his dad showed a certain flair, it hadn't pierced thru the bedrock suspicion against a policeman's son. Mau was proud of how hard he had worked. Proud of this labor and of that. Most of all, proud of the writing he had put into the leaflets, proud of the fine language therein. Mau had trod a narrow line, so narrow he had to turn his knees in, and step with his toes, and balance himself with a shaft of bamboo, practically. He wrote fine and trod fine and always quoted the latest directives, between his fits of coughing that is, and deferred to Hoang in all matters. But the others were nonetheless aware of Mau's latent arrogance, of his intellectual's smugness. The four of them didn't care for Mau as much as he didn't care for Xuan.

Completing the circle of domino players and directly to Hoang's left, sat Chau the pharmacist. He had risen neither slowly nor fast, but in the steady middle way he did all things. He sat with his arms crossed and resting upon his bony knees, not looking alert or stupid either, but simply looking in his steady middle way. His face was deceptively young, but his hands were splotched on their backs and swollen at the knuckles. His hair was untamed and stuck out from his head like the bristles of some stiff old brush.

Chau listened more than he spoke, but not much more, for in his steady middle way, he wasn't as silent as Buc the barber. He looked down at his feet as he listened, and thought. Like Buc the barber, like everyone else, Chau was thinking about the girl. He steadily spat thru a crack in the floor onto the littered dirt below —as steadily as the school teacher coughed. Each time he spat a rat scurried up to investigate. The pharmacist's pockets were almost as full as the whoremonger's. His mattress too. His own fortune had increased since the death of the herbalist, at which time only he and Fat Anna had gleefully seen old Moonface off. But not too gleefully, of course.

"What about the girl?" asked Xuan. "She's a fine girl, a smart girl, a succulent girl—oh yes, Comrade Hoang, about that I can certainly vouch—but as I proposed—"

"It won't do," said Hoang emphatically. But Hoang wasn't really so sure that it wouldn't. "It won't do at all to drop the girl." Hoang looked at the other three, he waited to hear who would disagree. He had not set his mind one way or the other. Xuan's proposal had its good points and its bad.

"You're right, Comrade Chairman," said Mau the school teacher, "it won't do at all. Much better not to drop the girl."

Chau the pharmacist also agreed, but only halfway. "It may not do to drop the girl, that's so, Comrade Hoang, but there is the directive. The wishes of the General Staff. There is that."

"Yes," said Hoang, "there is the directive—there are the wishes of the Staff. Maybe we should drop the girl after all."

"You're right, Comrade Chairman," said Mau the school teacher, "it's imperative that—*Cough!*—that—*Cough!*—it's imperative that the operation be an unqualified success. The General Staff would take it badly—they would be very hurt indeed—General Ba would blow like three dragons if the arrangements aren't made. As loyal —*Cough!*—as loyal—*Cough!*—as loyal comrades, all of us are called to account—to show where we stand—to show our faith. General Ba, he'll blow like three dragons. So, as you said, Comrade Chairman, we should drop the girl."

"I didn't say we should drop the girl, Comrade Mau. I only said that *maybe* we should." Which caused the school teacher to break out in a fit of coughing.

"I don't think we should." It was Buc. "Let the Staff take it badly. Let the generals sulk in a corner. Let them piss all over their feet. Let this Ba blow like three dragons. Let him snort fire as much as he likes. Who cares!? Why should we care so much for them!? Think of the cost if we drop the girl! Think of the waste!" Buc looked from Xuan to Mau to Chau, wondering how they could be so witless. "We have the rice. We don't need the girl."

"But the rice is nothing, Comrade Buc." It was Xuan. "They all do it, everyone. Even to us. It means nothing, all the rice. Ah, but the girl—now that's something else."

"We have all the soldiers who aren't soldiers or anything. The phantom soldiers. We don't need the girl."

"But the phantom soldiers are nothing, Buc." It was Chau. "They all do it, everyone. It means nothing, all the money. Everyone understands about that. But when there are so many girls to choose from, why her? They won't understand about that. Somehow it's different."

"Think of the waste. Think of how little we'll get in return. And for what? So the General Staff shouldn't be hurt, so they shouldn't feel bad? So General Ba shouldn't blow like three dragons? Let them be hurt! Let him blow! The girl's value lies in not being dropped."

Mau seized the floor. He didn't have to defer to Buc. "Comrade members—Comrade Chairman—it's always been our very first task to support without question, without hesitation, the national priorities, no matter how unclear they seem, how incomprehensible at the time. And one of those priorities is to further the military objective, the local one. As we all know, Comrade members, the military objective is—"

"Foo on the military objective!" It was Buc again and he was angry. His anger hissed thru the gap in his teeth. He sent all the dominoes flying with a sweep of his hand. "Only fools would drop the girl for a thing like this. And we'd be fools, too, if we did the same. It's not necessary, not at all. You say not the rice? Then not the rice. You say not the soldiers who aren't soldiers or anything? Then, all right, not the phantom soldiers. But other ways. There are other ways, cheaper ways to stick a pig. It's crazy, it's senseless to drop the girl." Buc glared at Mau. "And even if it was necessary, still I would vote against dropping the girl. There are much more important objectives—subtler objectives—long term objectives—for which the girl must be saved."

Mau glared back, as much as he dared. "Comrade Buc—Comrade members—Comrade Chairman Hoang—it's not for us to decide which objective is important and which is not, or which one objective is more important than another. It's only for us to—*Cough!*—to—*Cough!*—" Whatever Mau wanted to say, he was too busy clutching his belly and hacking.

"But Comrade Buc," said the pharmacist, in his steady middle way, "altho you are right that there are more important objectives than local military objectives, still it's true that a victory here and there, a military victory, would go a long way toward winning the greater political struggle." Then Chau spat thru the hole in the floor. He watched a rat scurry up. "Isn't it strange, Comrade Buc—about you objecting to local objectives?"

"To *military*, Comrade Chau. Not to political."

"Just the same, Comrade Buc—"

"Yes," said the usually jolly whoremonger, "just the same, Comrade Chau has a point. Perhaps if we were to drop the girl now, she would be more useful to us than if we hold her back. After all, Comrade members, tho she may be succulent now—oh yes, I can certainly vouch for that—who knows how long she'll stay that way? Hm, Comrade Buc? This succulence, it passes fast. So maybe better to drop her now while things are looking good for her."

"Yes," said the teacher, "much better to drop her now—when things are looking good for us—when the end is in sight—when total victory is so close. For hasn't the National Central Committee assured us that victory is within reach? That all it will take is a nudge here and there? I say let's drop the girl."

"It's not so close," said Buc with a hiss, "so don't delude your-selves. And dropping the girl won't make it closer. I say we shouldn't drop."

"It's close!" shouted Mau, "the Committee said—"

"Close enough!" cried Xuan, cheerfully.

"Perhaps not close, but closer than ever," said Chau in his steady middle way.

"Comrade members—Comrade members—remember we're playing dominoes!" It was the bicycle man, at last, calling the meeting to order. The comrade members gathered themselves, then gathered the dominoes scattered by Buc, and prepared to play again. "Comrade members," asked Hoang once more, when everyone had settled down, "what should we do about the girl? Drop her or not?"

* * *

Hoang Bang, the bicycle man, woke early the morning after the playing with a hot and sticky crotch. It was dark and he felt around in his crotch, exploring the thick wetness there. Hoang's fingers came away tacky. He brought his fingers to his nose and he sniffed them anxiously. They smelled sweet and sour at the same time. They smelled like fermented fish sauce gone bad, altho to anyone not accustomed, fermented fish sauce always smells bad. Hoang made a wry face, a very vexed face, then wiped his rancid tacky fingers on an unsoiled part of his trousers. His trousers were stiff where he had run during the night.

Hoang got to his feet, pulled the cardboard from the window, and bent to examine himself in the light. Hoang's crotch was smeared with some poison, yellow and gleety, smooth here, lumpy there. This comes as a bad surprise, thought Hoang. He opened the door to relieve himself in the alleyway. It burned as he passed the poison out, and Hoang grimaced from the pain. Then Hoang clutched on with both his hands, and by gently but firmly applying his thumbs, he squeezed out the last few stubborn clots. The squeezing done, he closed the door, drew a basin of water, and washed himself off. Hoang winced, he sucked in his breath, for the water was cold. He changed his pants, brushed his teeth with his finger, broke apart a rice cake or two, and prepared his morning tea.

Next to *chao tom* and *banh cuon,* Hoang loved rice cakes best. They were simple fare, not at all exciting; but just the same, they brought him pleasure. Hoang sat on a worn straw mat, with his legs crossed and his feet bare, and munched on his cakes. He sat there in the small back room of his bicycle shop, chewing with care, and tho he seemed to stare vacantly, his mind was alert. It was focused on the problem directly between his legs. Then he drank his tea too quickly and scalded the roof of his mouth. Feh, thought Hoang, not that kind of day!? First the poison, now the tea!

The day was starting out very badly, and he considered lying down and getting up all over again. Perhaps then things would start out better, and he could have more rice cakes too. Hoang considered seriously, but he didn't move from the mat. He was very vexed and angry. Vexed with himself for having been so all hung up on Bombay Betty, for having lain on one of gray-skinned, one-eyed Nhu's old mattresses with such a scruffy whore. But more than being vexed with himself, he was angry at the venomous bitch for having contaminated his loins.

Hoang reluctantly ate the last of his cakes, sipped his tea warily, and brooded over his misfortune. It shamed him to think how highly he had valued Betty, how blindly, how single-mindedly. He bowed his head low, guiltily, for only the Movement deserved to be valued as highly as that, as blindly as that. Only the Movement was worthy of such single-minded concern. Jackals! Crows! Cockatoos! Dirt of a hundred thousand behinds! Why didn't they use it on Betty too!? The blue silk cloth! Then drop her into an old trash can? Hoang sat and brooded, and chastened himself for being misled, for being a fool, and his tea grew cold. He took time out from his chastening to relight his stove, then turned to other vexing thoughts as the tea reheated.

It wasn't good—not good at all—that the meeting had gotten so heated. The angry words, the glaring looks, the dominoes flying—not good at all. And it was worse that so much heat had failed to brew a solution. Hoang still didn't know what to do: to drop the girl or not. It had been three to one for dropping—or maybe only two and a half, he could never tell about Chau—but Buc had been the one opposed and Buc had the clearest head of the four. Buc had made sense about the fact that it was pointless to drop the girl, that her value lay in not being dropped. He had never heard Buc speak so strongly before. As for Xuan with his silly succulence, and Mau who recited so ponderously, and Chau with his middle straddling way—all together they weren't worth Buc. Their opinions together weren't worth his. But there was the directive, the General Staff, General Ba. Hoang could almost feel the fire.

He chewed on his thoughts, on his agony, on his indecisiveness. He chewed as carefully, lengthily, as he had chewed on his bits of cake. He chewed and chewed, at times almost sure, then not so sure, until he jerked, as if something electric had shot thru him. "Curses!" cried Hoang. A thousand curses on that whore! A thousand of the blackest kind! On all the whores of Vietnam! Punch their peeholes! Use them up! Drop them into an old trash can! Hoang flung curses left and right. He heaved them from under. He dropped them from high. He dropped his pants for a second look, and to give his problem more air. It was then he decided to drop the girl too.

* * *

Colonel Quoc was inside, relaxing in a large straw chair, when Hoang Bang arrived at the small pleasant house on the quiet shady street. Hoang was returning Hue's bicycle. It had needed fixing again. His customers normally came to his shop to pick up their bikes but, this time, Hoang brought the bicycle. Hue opened the door, let Hoang in, picked up a small bag, and departed.

Hoang entered the room where Quoc was relaxing. The bicycle man looked as meek as ever and out of place. He was covered with grime and grease. The Colonel was very surprised, unhappily so, by Hoang's entrance. What the—!? What was this!? What was a tradesman doing here!? A grimy one! A greasy one! Here inside his pleasant house!? Quoc demanded an explanation, didn't wait to hear Hoang out, and called for Hue. But there was no Hue. Only silence.

"The girl is gone. She won't be back."

"What!? WHAT!? She won't be back!? What do you mean!? Who are you!?" Colonel Quoc got to his feet. He was close to rage. He was very big on etiquette. "Who are you!? Answer, you mongrel! What are you doing here!?" The Colonel advanced toward the bicycle man and was very surprised to see Hoang hold his ground. What the—!? What was this!? Grimy! Greasy! And holding his ground!?

When Hoang spoke again, he spoke with a self-possession which astonished Quoc, which temporarily checked his anger. "Colonel Quoc, you must please sit down. It would be better. Please sit down, sir." But Colonel Quoc wouldn't, so Hoang went on anyway. "I've come to speak of a matter which concerns us both. A matter important to you and me. So please listen well. And don't look for her. Forget about her. She won't be back."

Colonel Quoc had no choice but to listen. He was too speechless to do much else. Too spellbound to move or say a word. The tradesman was mad, he was out of his mind!

"Colonel Quoc, it's simply this. In ten days—on the fifteenth of June—all the men must stay on post. There must be no call-up. No orders given. No soldiers sent out for any reason. Not even for the most desperate kind. No matter what happens, Colonel Quoc, there must be no response. Not from you. Not from your men. On the fifteenth."

This was too much for Colonel Quoc, who was now more enraged than he was spellbound. He leaped at Hoang and grabbed Hoang's throat and started to squeeze. As Colonel Quoc tried to choke him to death, Hoang shouted hoarsely: "The checklist! Nhu's checklist—!" This wasn't gray-skinned, one-eyed Nhu who had sold Fat Anna his mattresses, but Ngo Dinh Nhu, Chief of Secret Police in the government of Ngo Dinh Diem, his brother-in-law, and the late President of South Vietnam. This other Nhu had kept a ledger in which he had, from time to time, evaluated the trustworthiness of the province chiefs, district chiefs, and other such fellows. The ledger had been known as *Nhu's Checklist,* and still was, tho it was a new government which now used it. "Nhu's checklist! Nhu's checklist!" shouted Hoang.

Colonel Quoc stopped choking Hoang. He loosened his hands

reluctantly. What did this tradesman know of Nhu's checklist? How could he possibly know about that? Colonel Quoc slapped Hoang's face twice, once out of anger, once for spite. Then he returned to his large straw chair, sat down and prepared to listen. Listening didn't come easy for Quoc, and he fidgeted in his chair. He fidgeted, too, because of the signs. Things looked the slightest bit ominous, and Quoc was the slightest bit fearful.

Hoang rubbed his neck. Then he walked to the large straw chair and spat twice in Colonel Quoc's face, once out of anger, once for spite. Before the Colonel could leap again, Hoang sang out the magic words: "The checklist, Colonel! Nhu's checklist!" Colonel Quoc settled back in his chair. One more time, thought Colonel Quoc, and to hell with Nhu's checklist!

Hoang began: "You've been very fortunate, Colonel Quoc. So far, very fortunate. Never—never before—has your loyalty been in doubt." Colonel Quoc's unease increased. *Was* his loyalty in doubt? "Eight hundred fifty thousand piasters. Right, Colonel Quoc? That's what you paid. So they made you a province chief. After all, the worst you had done as an officer was to steal from your men, and to shoot one or two now and then. Not so bad. It probably helped. Eight hundred fifty. Right, Colonel Quoc?"

"It's the way. So what? Is *that* all!?"

"Then you did nothing worse than steal it all back from somewhere else. Eight hundred fifty. To make it up."

"So what?"

"The rice money, Colonel."

"Hah! You fool! It's expected. They all do it. Everyone." Colonel Quoc started to rise. "Is *that* all!?"

"And the soldiers who aren't soldiers or anything. The phantom units. You wrote them down, you get money to pay them from Saigon. But there aren't any. Just names on a list."

"Hah-hah! They all do it. Everyone. Is *that* all!?"

"Not all. It's nothing. It's the way. In fact they would have been suspicious, any other. So you got it back. The eight hundred fifty thousand and more. Very much more. They kept you on. You were loyal. That's all that matters to them. That, and you shared some of the loot. Even after fat pig Diem was shot, you were kept on. Province chiefs, district chiefs, everyone went, but not Colonel Quoc. They trusted you, the new ones did. It cost you a few more piasters, of course, but that was nothing to worry about. There were ways to make it up. You've been a very loyal fellow, Colonel Quoc. Loyal to Diem and Minh and Khanh. To everyone. You were loyal—till six months ago."

Hoang drew up a second chair and sat down knee to knee with Quoc. Colonel Quoc didn't speak. He didn't pat his uniform or smooth back his sleek black hair. He didn't even fidget. The Colonel didn't do anything except glare with hatred at Hoang. He knew, of course, that he had continued to be loyal. Not only until six months ago, but to this day. To this very minute. Yet this mongrel, this grimy tradesman, this greasy one, this nothing at all who had soiled his face—twice!—twice!—he spoke with surprising authority, with unmistakable conviction. What could he have done? Ehhh, it was all a hoax! What could he have possibly done? There had been nothing—nothing he knew of. Then perhaps something innocent. Something misinterpreted. They were very suspicious, the ones in Saigon. Perhaps that was it. Who could keep track of everything? What could it be? Feh, it was all a hoax—wasn't it? Colonel Quoc was very confused. He waited patiently for the mongrel, for the grimy, greasy tradesman, for the nothing at all to continue.

"The girl, Colonel, she's one of us."

Colonel Quoc flinched. He blanched, then he reddened, that's how confounded he was. He clamped down hard on the arms of his chair. I'll smash in your face, you puny bastard! You lying bastard! I'll snap your long, skinny neck. I'll throttle it first. It can't be so! It's not so at all! She worshiped me.

"Do you think that she worshiped you? Do you think that she served you—stayed with you—because of your heroic cock, because of this house? Then you're a fool, Colonel Quoc. Then you've been a fool. She belongs to us. We lent her to you. We gave her to you for a time. And now you must give something to us."

Colonel Quoc reached for his pistol. He had forgotten about it till then.

"Don't make a fool of yourself again."

"What's so foolish about shooting you? You broke into my house, didn't you?"

"I was let in."

"What's your word to mine? Eh, you mongrel? Besides you'll be dead. You'll have no word."

"So will you, Quoc. You'll be dead too, soon enough, if anything should happen to me."

Colonel Quoc's hand rested on his holster. It didn't move one way or the other.

"You kept a Communist, Colonel Quoc. In your house. Maybe you're a Communist, too. No? Absurd? The ones in Saigon may not think so. They *won't* think so. They're very suspicious, the ones in Saigon. Very untrusting. You didn't know what the girl really was? Well, that's too bad. They have no sympathy in Saigon. They don't understand. Perhaps the girl stole some secrets. Many secrets. Perhaps you've been indiscreet. No, you say? Then prove it to the ones in Saigon! They're very suspicious in Saigon. They're always assuming the worst, you know. They're very untrusting of people who have been indiscreet. Who *maybe* have been indiscreet. Besides, you *have* been indiscreet. You do talk too much, Colonel Quoc." Hoang shook his head. "Oh, Colonel Quoc, the things she's told us! The things you've said!"

"I haven't said anything!" Colonel Quoc shouted. "Not a thing!" He was very upset, very frightened. "Who would believe you, anyway!? You're just trying to frighten me. Exaggerating, that's what you're doing. That's it! Exaggerating!"

"That's what Colonel ———— said too."

Colonel ———— had been the chief of neighboring Quang Duc Province. Things had ended badly for him as Quoc well knew.

"So what? What's it to me? I'm Quoc, not ————. They trust me in Saigon. They've always trusted me in Saigon. Always—always," Quoc insisted, tho his hand had dropped from his holster and hung loose at his side.

"Just like they trusted————."

Colonel Quoc had come a long, long way from having been a charcoal peddler and he wanted to stay. The old days were fine to muse about. There had been something different about them, something special, he wasn't sure what. Perhaps a certain gritty charm. But there was no doubt in Colonel Quoc's mind that he much preferred to be comfortable, than to have something he wasn't sure what.

"What do you want?" he finally asked. He sounded very weary.

Someone other than Hoang Bang might have allowed himself a smile, but Hoang did not. There was nothing personal in it for him, not in the wearisome little man's fall. He cared only that the operation should be a success, that it should advance the Liberation, however little. It was the most he could expect after this whole tedious business: the heated meeting—dropping the girl—the wearisome little Colonel's fall.

Hoang shrugged his shoulders and he sighed, much too lightly for Quoc to have noticed. Buc probably had been right. Buc was always right. Had he known how unsatisfying a chore it was going to be, he never would have dropped the girl. Never. Never. Well, yes, he would have. It had to be done. Hoang felt as weary as Colonel Quoc. Just as sad, just as grieved, just as depressed. Not because he felt sorry for Quoc. He didn't feel sorry at all, why should he? But because he, himself, longed for something different, something more, something other than playing these games, something the Liberation would bring, he wasn't sure what. He wasn't sure what!? Him, an old pro!? A provincial chairman!? Not sure what!? He'd better be sure! Of course he was sure! But he wasn't.

"Just as I told you," Hoang finally said. "That none of the men will be dispatched on the fifteenth. That they will all stay on post."

Colonel Quoc nodded. He waved his hand limply, the hand with which he had reached for the gun.

"Also the phantom units."

"But they're not units. There's no need to worry."

"Still we want them grounded too."

Colonel Quoc nodded again. "What of myself? What about me?"

"You? What about you?"

"Colonel ———."

"Don't worry so much. Quoc isn't ———. You said so yourself."

"And the ones in Saigon?"

"They trust you in Saigon. You said so yourself. Everyone does."

"And now? Will they still?"

"The fifteenth, Colonel. No mistake."

"But will they still?"

"Don't forget the phantom units."

"You haven't said. Will they still?"

Hoang rose, walked out of the room, and left Colonel Quoc all alone in the house.

Colonel Quoc sat for a time. It was a very pleasant house and the large straw chair was comfortable. Quoc sat and brooded and chastened himself for having disregarded the chart, the worthy chart, the Astrological Ministry chart. The one time! It was always like that! Quoc vowed that he would never ever disregard the chart again. There had been no choice, he told himself, as he thought on. The tradesman's grime had reminded him of his own grimy days. And there was the case of Colonel ————. What could he have done but to agree? To not have agreed would have been his own end. Of course, he had money salted away. A very wise thing, to salt away money. It was all very vague—so shadowy —exaggerated. That's what! Exaggerated! But not to the ones in Saigon, it wouldn't be. They were very suspicious, the ones in Saigon. Very untrusting just like he had said. The ones in Saigon gave no second chances. The ones in Saigon might even believe that he *was* a Communist!

It had been a strange request. Did they plan a demonstration? To attack Ban Me Thuot? No, it couldn't be that. If it was that, then he would have to defend the town. There would be no way out of that. Colonel Quoc tried to think of some way, just in case, but he couldn't. Then what else? To attack some outpost in his province? To harass some village? Then why all the fuss? Why such precautions? It didn't make sense. No sense at all. If it was an attack somewhere in Dar Lac, why didn't they plan to attack at night? He wouldn't move the troops at night, not in any event. Not on the roads. It was much too dangerous. And why the others? The phantom units? They weren't units. They didn't matter. Maybe it was just their way. How many people would be killed? Many, perhaps. But perhaps not. Yes, perhaps not. Well, what could he do? There was the grime, he remembered it all. And Colonel ————. Just what could he do? What, eh? To do otherwise would mean his neck. To not have agreed.

That dirty whore Hue! A thousand curses on that whore! A thousand of the blackest kind! It shamed Quoc to think how highly he had valued the girl, how blindly, how single-mindedly. He bowed his head low, guiltily, for only his standing, his career, deserved to be valued as highly as that, as blindly as that. Only his standing, his career, was worthy of such single-minded concern. What's to stop him from coming again, from asking for something more? I'll kill him. I'll kill the puny bastard! I'll smash in his face! I'll wring his neck! There's a limit. Oh yes, there's a limit. I'll go so far. That's it, only so far. But then Quoc remembered how far he had come and that he didn't want to go back. That he wanted to stay. It was a mess. A terrible mess. Because of the chart. All because of the chart. Damn the chart! A thousand curses on the chart! The chart! The chart! Perhaps the answer was in the chart! The worthy chart!

Colonel Quoc rose from his chair, patted his uniform, smoothed back his hair, and hastened from the pleasant house. In his anxiousness to get to the chart—in his haste, in his great single-minded concern to find out why things had gone wrong and how to make them right again—he stumbled right into the bicycle and nearly broke his neck.

△ DRAWING THE LINE
☆
△

Moon was inconsolable. Lieutenant Plunket explained the facts: that it had been the principle, not the energy. Jasperson, Lovelace, Culpepper tried, everyone tried, but no one got anywhere with Moon. He held himself accountable, to blame for Sergeant Goodbody's death.

"It *had* to be the energy," he told Lieutenant Plunket. "It had to be an overdose and it's all my fault. I left the needle in too long, the one for the stomach. Both of them."

"It's all right, Moon. It wasn't your fault."

"But it's not, goddammit, it's not all right. He's dead, isn't he?"

"Sure he's dead and I'm sorry he's dead. We're all of us sorry. But it was because of the principle and not because of some energy." Plunket paused, to see if he was getting across, and saw that he wasn't. "How many times? How many times do I have to tell you how much that principle meant to him? It meant every-thing—*everything*, Moon. I'm telling you straight, believe me I am. So let yourself go."

But Moon wouldn't let himself go. Even if Plunket was telling him straight—even if this principle had played a part, the energy had been lurking there, deep down inside Goodbody's stomach. The energy had worked from within, subverting Goodbody's faculties. It had been behind the principle, behind Goodbody's noble thoughts. It had been there all the time. That's why Moon wouldn't let himself go. He was sure that the energy had come first, then the principle, and not the other way around. "That's how it was. Not the other way around. That's what energy can do."

"How's that again?"

"The principle—it didn't come first. The energy was in back of it all. It made him think he was being noble, when all he was being was being too hungry. See what I mean?"

"Not yet, I don't."

"Look, Lieutenant, it's like this. I used a number two stainless steel needle—no other number, I'm sure of that—right at 34 ST and at 4 ST too. And I piqued the needles one fen deep—only one fen, I'm sure of that too. So I must've left them in too long and made everything much worse than before, only in the other way. I did the worst thing I could've done. I gave him too much. *Now* do you see?"

"I see, Moon—"

"Or maybe I should've only used one. Do you see what I mean?"

"I see what you mean, some of it. But there's something I don't. I can see where there could've been energy. But I can't see this overdose. That was the way Goodbody was. He had this fantastic appetite, always did. You just gave it back."

"Not like that."

"Sure like that. Just like that."

"No, Lieutenant. Not uncontainable like that."

"Listen, Moon, maybe he did have too much energy. Suppose he did. You did what you could. Right? Huh? How could you know?"

"Come off it, Lieutenant. Leave me alone. Goodbody's dead and it's my fault."

"Actually you won't believe this, but try me, huh?"

"I'm trying, Lieutenant."

"It was my idea, not Goodbody's. It was all my idea to eat the rice, goddammit, it was. I—me—I was the one. Not Goodbody."

"Listen, sir, you're a real nice guy. I appreciate what you're trying to do. But I know that it was Goodbody's idea. Everyone knows—Captain Yancy, everybody—that no Lieutenant in his right mind would've ordered the rice to be eaten like that. Or would've gone along with Goodbody unless he had been uncontrollable. Not on a crazy thing like that. Not even you, sir, pardon me, sir."

They sat there in silence, thinking about the crazy thing. Moon thought awhile, and so did Plunket, and then Moon started to laugh.

"You know, Lieutenant, it wasn't so crazy after all. It was really a pretty great idea."

"Yeah, it was. It sure was, Moon. I thought so too."

Then Moon and Plunket laughed together for awhile.

"Jeez, I wish I could've been there."

"I wish you could too. I wish you could've seen it."

They laughed until they both realized that there was nothing to laugh about. Goodbody was dead. Moon felt twice as terrible— for being to blame and for having laughed.

That's how it went with Lieutenant Plunket, with everyone. Moon was inconsolable, mad with grief, blaming himself for Goodbody's death and for the deaths of his other friends. So when the patrol was formed the next day—the day after Plunket and the platoon had stumbled back, the day after eight Strike Force men and Sergeant Goodbody had been killed—Moon was the most raring to go, mad to go. But Yancy wouldn't let him go. He told Moon to walk around Buon Yun, to do that instead, to cool his heels. Yancy didn't want any madmen going along—for their own sake and for the patrol's—which made Moon even more inconsolable than before.

The patrol consisted of Captain Yancy, Sergeant Lovelace, and two platoons of Strike Force. Moon stayed behind to cool his heels. Culpepper stayed to tend the sick and the wounded. Lieutenant Plunket stayed because he had been roughed up the day before. Jasperson stayed because Captain Yancy wanted him to look after things. Yancy had never thought that much of Plunket, and after the incident with the rice, he thought even less. Fritz was gone, Goodbody dead.

The patrol headed north, past the spot where the rice had been found, right toward the Brake of the Rattling Bamboo. The patrol headed north seeking revenge for Sergeant Goodbody, who had gone north two days before, seeking revenge for Sergeant Fritz. It was the second week of June.

* * *

It was after the leaflets, after Buon Sop, after the *punjis,* after the crazy thing with the rice. It was after events at Buon Yak following Casper's plunge down the well. It was after the girl had been dropped and Quoc co-opted. It was long, long after Luu and Phum should have arrived with the party favors.

It was cool inside and very damp. Dan and Van sat hunched in the dirt and slowly ate the last of their rice. They shaped the rice into little balls, then plopped the balls into their mouths. The rice was cold and gritty with dirt—just like they were, down inside. Kim squatted nearby, thinking about the rice he had eaten, wishing that he had more to eat and worrying if he ever would, now that the rice hut had gone up in flames. He was worrying about rickets, too.

There was no light, except for what filtered down from above. And that was only enough to take the edge off the blackness. Just enough for each of the men to make out his own shape and those of the others. There was little room, but they didn't feel cramped, for they were used to sharing close quarters. It was the dampness that was bad, and the fact they were at the last of their rice. Most of all, it was the waiting. There was nothing to do about that, and nothing to do about the rice, and a fire would have dried the dampness, but also would have taken their air.

No one spoke. Kim wondered about the rice and about rickets. Dan and Van plopped the balls of rice into their mouths and wondered how their friend Dung would fare on his special assignment, his latest one. Fighters Dan and Van and Kim were silent with their wondering, because Leader Mac was deep in thought.

Mac who scratched harder the harder he thought, had scratched himself raw. That's how hard he'd been thinking these days, that's how tough his problem was. Mac who believed not in Fate, but in his command of the 825th, thru which he intended to set things right. Mac who felt strongly for the people and ordered their heads to roll at Buon Sop. Mac who clucked over his men and prepared to lose many of them at Buon Yun.

Mac was scratched raw because his problem was not only tough, but seemingly insurmountable. Mac's problem wasn't men. The 825th was then up to strength for the very first time, tho he would have preferred men more seasoned than the new recruits from Buon Yak. Mac's problem wasn't a staging place. The plantation had been secured, and all the men had left for it except the three inside with him. The last had left just two days before, after the crazy thing with the rice. Rice wasn't the problem either, not right away, even if the burning of the hut had compromised their last supplies and more rice would be needed soon. No, it wasn't men, or a staging place, or rice that was the problem. The problem was where were Phum and Luu? That's why the four were waiting behind: for the party favors, to lead Phum and Luu to the staging place.

Mac picked at his calluses because he couldn't scratch anymore, raw from worry over the favors. He feared that the plan would fail without them. He looked into his hands for guidance, for knowledge of Luu and Phum and the favors. He brought his hands close to his face, and squinted thru the deep brown light. He looked but saw only calluses, and angry they didn't tell him a thing, he tore into them with his teeth.

While Mac was futilely looking for guidance, Dan and Van plopped the last of their rice balls into their mouths, then yawned and curled up in the dirt, for there was not much else to do. Kim squatted nearby, worried of rickets. He wished that Luu and Phum would come, so they could all leave and join the others. He didn't like being down inside, but he knew it was best, for there would be a patrol from Buon Yun after the crazy thing with the rice. Kim didn't like it because he had seen too many others come down with rickets from spending too many months down inside. And tho the four had been down inside for only two days, it was enough to bother Kim's peace.

When Mac was done with his calluses, he decided the favors weren't coming. They had been waiting down inside for two whole days, and for two weeks before. The party favors weren't coming, and there was no way to do without them. So he also decided then and there to postpone the attack. There would be no second chance if they failed once—to take Buon Yun by surprise and to catch all the Americans. And if they were not to fail the first time, they would need the party favors, he was almost certain of that.

Mac called to Kim. He still trusted Kim to do things right, in spite of the fact that Kim had contended that three or four heads would have been enough. "Kim, listen well. Leave right away. Tell ——— to stop with the plan—"

What was this!? Hey, what was this!? thought Kim who left off with his rickets. What was this!? Hey, what was this!? thought Dan and Van who uncurled from the dirt.

"Tell him it's no good without the favors. We must have the favors. Understand, Kim?"

Kim nodded. Hey what was this!? Dan and Van nodded too.

"Tell him to withdraw the men. When we get some favors, then we'll go back. Now off, Kim. Make it fast."

So Kim scrambled up toward the opening. He couldn't wait to crawl outside and have a good stretch. He could hear the Rattling Bamboo. It made a constant clacking sound. He couldn't wait to get some sun. Kim had scrambled halfway up, when Y Bong the ironsmith dropped in on him.

* * *

It had gone like this: when the patrol reached the bamboo, the men fanned out at Yancy's order. Then they all walked abreast, squirming their way thru the bamboo, laboring up one side of the brake, then down the other, looking for Charlie, seeking revenge for Fritz and Goodbody. They crossed to the far side of the bamboo, tuckered and winded and despaired of finding Charlie.

Captain Yancy called for five, and all the men flopped to the ground, except for a few who went off on their business. Y Bong went off deeper than the others, back inside the edge of the brake, for he was modest. Back in the brake, Y Bong dropped his pants, flexed his knees, kicked with his heel at a clump of grass to smooth it down, took a slight shuffle back, and dropped in on Kim.

Y Bong screamed as he dropped in on Kim, then scrambled as fast as he could to get out, screaming the while. But his pants were down around his shins, which made it hard, and Kim had his ankle, which made it harder. Y Bong scrambled and he screamed, and Kim tugged hard, trying to pull the ironsmith deeper, but neither seemed to get anywhere. Happily for the ironsmith, his screaming drew his friends from Buon Yun, who quickly enough surrounded the hole. They gripped Y Bong by his bony wrists, and they tugged. Kim tugged back and they tugged forth, with Y Bong half in and Y Bong half out and very distraught. Back and forth. Back and forth. They finally wrenched their friend free of Kim and altogether out of the tunnel.

"Eeyah!" said Y——.

"Ooeee!" said Y——.

"Look at Y Bong! Look at his pants!"

"Down to his shins!"

"A fine place to go."

"Nice and deep."

"Eeyah, Culpepper will be proud."

"Ooeee, proud of Y Bong. That he chose to go in such a deep hole."

"Very proud."

"Proud, yes, but who's down inside?"

When A-123 first came to Buon Yun, Sergeant Culpepper had made the people dig trenches in the south of the village where they could go at night. "Deeper, deeper," he had kept at them, as he supervised the work. Deeper was better, and so was south, for that's how the night breeze always blew. Before the trenches, the people had simply gone by the fence. As for whoever was down inside, well they weren't coming up to tell. So Captain Yancy, with Lovelace's help, pushed the men back from the mouth of the tunnel, then dropped a smoke grenade down inside.

It was a beautiful deep purple smoke, and the men oohed and ahhed as it came curling out from down inside. They oohed and ahhed too, and hissed and booed, at the three Viet Cong who came up as well, scrambling and coughing and runny-eyed and gasping for breath. The three Viet Cong were grabbed, pummeled, thrown to the ground, kneed in the groin, kicked in the head, trussed up, and then abused again.

Captain Yancy doubted that anyone could have stayed down inside with all that beautiful purple smoke, but just to be sure, he dropped in a second smoke grenade. Again the men oohed and ahhed at the beautiful purple smoke as it came curling out, but this time no one came up as well.

Sure that there were no more VC, Yancy was keen to inspect the tunnel for weapons, for ammo, for anything. So when he figured that the air had cleared reasonably, he ordered one of the Strike Force leaders down inside to inspect the tunnel. Yancy's man dropped down inside and began to crawl forward. The air hadn't cleared reasonably, but before Yancy's man could even complain, the reverberations began. The crack of the shot ricocheted from wall to wall. It resounded in deafening swell after swell. It spun around the walls a few times, then out of the tunnel and into the open.

Captain Yancy reached into the tunnel and dragged his man out by the heels, his man who had been shot thru the face. To hell with all this! Goddamn to hell! To hell with purple smoke grenades! Yancy was thru fooling around. He dropped a fragmentation grenade down the tunnel. There was a boom this time, not a crack—a duller sound, but a louder one. The boom ricocheted from wall to wall. It resounded in deafening swell after swell. It spun around the walls a few times, then out of the tunnel and into the open.

Captain Yancy was just as sure that no one could have lived thru that blast, as he had been sure that no one could have stayed down inside with all that beautiful purple smoke. So he ordered a second Strike Force leader down inside to inspect the tunnel. Yancy's man dropped down inside and began to crawl forward. He vanished into the throat of the tunnel.

"Eeyah, look at Y——! He isn't there!"

"Ooeee, he's been swallowed up!"

"It's deep down inside."

"Nice and deep."

"A fine place to crawl."

"A scary place."

"The Captain should be proud of Y——."

"Very proud."

"But where's Y——? What's happened to him?"

"He's down inside."

"What's he doing down there so long?"

Just then, Y—— reappeared, dragging a fourth Viet Cong whose legs had been shattered, but who was still very much alive and otherwise fit.

Yancy radioed Moon at Buon Yun to radio BMT for a chopper. The chopper was for Y A'dham, the one who had argued for the team, the one who had been shot thru the face. He radioed while the fourth VC was being trussed up.

Mac had made a big mistake, one of his few, when he ordered his men to dig the tunnel. He had told them to dig only one entranceway, which meant only one exit way too, which meant there had been no way to escape into the bamboo brake. Mac had been confident that the tunnel would never be found, not in so remote a place and with such a cleverly camouflaged entrance. The chances were a million to one, he had maintained. And he had been right. The chances *had* been a million to one. If only Y Bong had not been so modest—if only he had squatted a few feet to either side—if he hadn't been so finicky—if he hadn't tried to smooth down the grass. By all reckoning, it should never have happened. But Mac hadn't reckoned on Fate. Mac didn't believe in Fate.

It shouldn't have happened, but it did. What also happened was that the message didn't get thru, the one to call off the attack on Buon Yun.

* * *

"Names and unit," shouted Yancy, "ask for their names and unit."

The interpreter asked. No one answered. Dan blinked.

"The others," shouted Captain Yancy, "ask them how many others there are and where they are."

The interpreter asked. No one answered. Van blinked.

"The orders," shouted Captain Yancy, "ask them what their orders are."

The interpreter asked. No one answered. Kim blinked.

"The tunnel," shouted Captain Yancy, "ask him how he stayed down inside with all that beautiful purple smoke."

The interpreter asked. Mac didn't answer. He didn't even blink.

Dan and Van and Kim were scared, and so was Mac. They had never flown in a chopper before, in anything at all before, but that wasn't why. They were scared because who wouldn't be scared if he's been caught by his enemy, even someone like Mac. They were scared, but they looked sullen instead, trying not to show their fear, as they sat huddled on the floor, trussed up tight. The chopper clattered toward Buon Yun where Yancy, Lovelace, the interpreter, and the four VC were getting off. Y A'dham was going on to Ban Me Thuot, to the hospital.

"No!" he had cried. "Not to Ban Me Thuot!"

"Eeyah, not to Ban Me Thuot!"

"Ooeee, not there!"

"No! Not to the hospital!"

"The Captain is wrong to send Y A'dham."

"It will be tragic for both of them."

"No! Only to Buon Yun!"

"What are they saying!? What's he saying!?"

"Better to die in very own village," said the interpreter.

"Why to die!? He's not gonna die!"

"No! Not to Ban Me Thuot!"

"Eeyah, the Captain will be in big trouble."

"Ooeee, Y A'dham's family."

"Just better," said the interpreter. "The spirits, they cannot protect people away from home. Need protection for after die. Very long trip."

"Hey, listen, I told you. He's not gonna die."

"No! No! Only to Buon Yun!"

"It will be tragic for Y A'dham."

"And tragic for the Captain, too."

"What are they saying? What else?" asked Yancy.

"The men, they say if Y A'dham die away from the spirits, you to blame. His family be very angry."

"Listen, I told you, he's not gonna die. Tell Y A'dham. Tell them all."

"Y A'dham to die."

"Whaddaya mean?"

"The hospital very bad for the people. Good only for Vietnamee."

Down on the ground, the Strike Force prepared for its long

trip back. They had searched for more tunnels, but hadn't found any, and there was no point in hanging around. But they took their time preparing, for if there was no point in hanging around, there was no hurry either.

Yancy, himself, was in a big hurry to get the prisoners back to Buon Yun where they could be interrogated. He was so keen on asking his questions that he had begun right there in the chopper. Sergeant Lovelace was very keen too, on pounding and stomping it out of them. He was keen on fixing the prisoners good, if they weren't keen on answering Yancy. He was keen on revenge as well. He could have taken or left Goodbody, but Sergeant Fritz had been his good friend.

"Names and unit," shouted Yancy, "ask for their names and unit."

The interpreter asked. No one answered.

"The leaflets," shouted Yancy, "ask them where they got the leaflets, who wrote them up."

The interpreter asked. No one answered.

"Buon Sop," shouted Yancy, "ask them who lopped off the heads."

The interpreter asked. No one answered.

"The tunnel," shouted Yancy, "ask him if it wasn't damp."

The interpreter asked. Mac didn't answer. He blinked his eyes.

At times, Sergeant Lovelace could be the nicest guy in the world, and at others, the all-time champion bastard, and that's what he was, there in the chopper. Baby-faced, snub-nosed, pink-skinned Lovelace was angry and churning up even more anger, because the Viet Cong wouldn't answer. Lovelace's anger got hotter and hotter, until it flared as hot as the burnt-orange hair on his head. In his burnt-orange anger, he started to kick the four Viet Cong. He started but didn't get far, because Captain Yancy called him off, so he set to cracking his knuckles instead. Those slopeheaded bastards, he roared to himself, those goddamn gooks, they got Fritz! Goodbody, too—tho I coulda taken or left Good-body—but Fritz, they got Fritz! Besides, Goodbody was no gook.

Who do these bastards think they are!? Don't they know their goddamn place!? I ain't gonna take this crap much more!

"Names and unit," shouted Yancy, "ask for their names and unit."

The interpreter asked. No one answered. Dan blinked.

"Fritz," shouted Yancy, "ask them who set the *punjis* that got Sergeant Fritz."

The interpreter asked. No one answered. Van blinked.

"Sergeant Goodbody," shouted Yancy, "ask them who deflated Goodbody."

The interpreter asked. No one answered. Kim blinked.

"The tunnel," shouted Yancy, "ask him if it didn't get cramped."

The interpreter asked. Mac didn't answer. He didn't even blink.

Lovelace's feelings about *goddamn gooks* had nothing to do with having once broken his head racing cars. His broken head hadn't changed things at all. He had always had strong one-sided feelings about who was who and where they belonged. Maybe not about gooks, but at least about others just like gooks; because everybody was gooky to Lovelace who wasn't like Lovelace and his own kind. So it had been nothing to start in kicking. Even if the gooks on the floor had been any old gooks and not Viet Cong, he would have been sorely disposed to kick. That's how it was. Gooks were gooks, weren't they? So imagine how strongly he was possessed—imagine what went on in Lovelace's head—if he felt that way about any old gooks, and these gooks here had done in Fritz.

"Names and unit," shouted Yancy, "ask for their names and unit."

The interpreter asked. No one answered.

"The waiting," shouted Yancy, "ask them why they were waiting."

The interpreter asked. No one answered.

"Their leader," shouted Yancy, "ask them who their leader is."

The interpreter asked. No one answered.

"The tunnel," shouted Yancy, "ask him if he knows about rickets."

The interpreter asked. Mac didn't answer. Kim blinked his eyes.

Captain Yancy didn't have time to imagine what went on in Lovelace's head. He was busy growing more vexed himself. He was vexed because, tho he hadn't expected instant success, they at least could have grunted or snarled or something. But there hadn't even been a sigh. They just sat there on the floor of the chopper, and once in awhile blinked their eyes. He had asked them the same simple questions over and over, shouting his questions thru the clatter. But no one had shouted answers back, or grunted or snarled or anything, which irked him no end. For he had captured them, hadn't he? He had showed them who was who. The least they owed him was a sound. But all they did was stare ahead —and big friggin' deal they blinked their eyes!

"Names and unit," shouted Yancy, "ask for their names and unit."

The interpreter asked. No one answered. Dan blinked.

"The others," shouted Yancy, "ask them how many others there are and where they are."

The interpreter asked. No one answered. Van blinked.

"The orders," shouted Yancy, "ask them what their orders are."

The interpreter asked. No one answered. Kim blinked.

"The tunnel," shouted Yancy, "ask him how he stayed down inside with all that beautiful purple smoke."

The interpreter asked. Mac didn't answer. He didn't even blink.

"Purple smoke hell!" Sergeant Lovelace suddenly rose. "Names, unit, orders hell! Who in hell do they think they are!?" Lovelace reached for the nearest VC. He raised the VC by his hair and yanked him to the open door. "Just who in hell!?" He held him there, by his hair, with the VC's feet just brushing the floor. "Ask this bastard one more time. Tell him 'no talk, out the door.' You know what bastard means, Y——? Tell the other bastards, too, that he's just the first. One atta time. No talk, out the door. Tell 'em," he growled.

Captain Yancy shifted forward in his seat, not saying a word. He wasn't sure if Lovelace was bluffing, but pretty sure that Lovelace was. Yancy was waiting to see what would be.

The VC whose feet were brushing the floor, his face remained blank except for a widening of his eyes, and the pain of being stood up by his hair. The eyes of the other three widened too, but not quite as much, since it wasn't they being stood by the door.

"Names and unit, you bastards," shouted Y——, "what are your names and unit—?"

"The others, you bastards," shouted Y——, "where are the others and how many are there—?"

"The orders, you bastards," shouted Y——, "what are your orders—?"

"Listen, you bastards, if you don't talk that man will throw you out the door, one at a time. So better to talk. I know this man. He's a very mean man. So better to answer. One at a time out the door if you don't. I know this man. He doesn't joke. So talk, you bastards, hurry and talk."

Well, that was that, thought Captain Yancy, it didn't work. They'd have to try something else.

Well, that was that, thought Sergeant Lovelace, it didn't work. So Lovelace scooped up the prisoner and threw him out the door.

Perhaps things would have gone differently had Mac been able to hear the questions and the threat. But Mac hadn't heard what the questions were or the threat, tho he might have guessed what the questions were and that Sergeant Lovelace was up to no good. He hadn't heard because the gunshot, the boom of the fragmentation grenade, had deafened him. If Mac had heard, then perhaps he would have saved himself, it was one of those things. Then again, because he was a stubborn fellow, perhaps things would have gone just the same. In any case, the point is moot, for Mac splattered to a stop somewhere on the Plateau du Dar Lac, between the Brake of the Rattling Bamboo and the village of Buon Yun.

Captain Yancy sat forward in his seat, very disturbed. What disturbed him so much was what the chopper crew might say, what they might think. Yancy didn't want anybody saying or thinking bad things about him or about his men. What also disturbed Captain Yancy was what Sergeant Lovelace had done. It was no small thing to scoop up a man and throw him to his death. It was no small thing even if the man was a Viet Cong, even if he had shot Yancy's man thru the face, even if Fritz was gone and Goodbody dead.

Yancy felt a little bit guilty about what Sergeant Lovelace had done. He felt somehow accountable. He should have imagined, should have known, what was going on in Lovelace's head. He shouldn't have been so sure he was bluffing. Maybe he hadn't been so sure, Yancy wondered guiltily. Maybe somewhere down inside he had been willing, only too willing, to see what would be—the plot acted out. It was to Captain Yancy's credit that he wondered about his part.

If Yancy felt a little bit guilty about what Sergeant Lovelace had done, he also felt guilty about feeling guilty. It was no small thing, okay, but it wasn't as if the prisoner had been some innocent civilian. It wasn't as if he hadn't known what war was about and his part in it. It wasn't as if he hadn't heard Lovelace's threat and what to expect. It wasn't as if a lot of things, reconsidered Captain Yancy. Not only that, but he had shot Y A'dham thru the face. Probably, had the roles been reversed—had it been him or Lovelace instead, raised by the hair, stood up by the door, and not answering—then the prisoner would have done just the same as Lovelace did. Sure he would. And what about Fritz? What about Goodbody? What about them? What about the nine notables of Buon Sop? And, anyway, concluded Yancy, the prisoner's legs had been shattered far beyond repair. So it was better, much better for him, that he had been thrown. Sure, it was. So why be upset, why be disturbed?

While Yancy sat there, mulling his guilt, Lovelace reached for a second VC, raised the VC by the hair, and yanked him to the open door.

"Now ask this bastard. Ask him once. You know what bastard

means, Y——? Tell him 'no talk, out the door.' Tell the others he's just number two. Tell 'em," he growled.

It was Dan with the lopsided face, with the bit-off lobe. Y—— told the bastard Dan, but Dan didn't say a word. It wasn't that he was exceptionally brave or exceptionally belligerent. Dan wasn't either of them. It was a matter of preference. If Dan had been first instead of Mac, perhaps he would have answered. But Mac had gone first, and Dan figured people who did that to Mac would probably kill them all, anyway, once their questions were answered. Either way, it was the end, that's how Dan felt. So feeling that way, and out of spite, he preferred to take the answers with him. Dan regretted only one thing. He regretted that he would never find out how Dung fared on his special assignment.

Seeing that Dan preferred to take the answers with him, Sergeant Lovelace scooped both up and threw them out the door.

Yancy was sitting just as far forward as he could. He sat and imagined and understood how Lovelace felt—what with Fritz and Goodbody and everything. The enemy was a brutal one, a ruthless one, a bloody one who stopped at nothing. Who did a lot of noisy professing about the people, about how the people always came first, but who always put the people second after their own ambitions. Yancy understood very well. Yancy also understood that the enemy's standards had to be shared, or the enemy would have the advantage. It wouldn't be fair to us, thought Yancy. Fair is fair, isn't it?

But tho Captain Yancy understood the brutality of war, tho he understood that the enemy's standards had to be shared, he also understood that a line had to be drawn. If not, if they didn't draw a line, then they were no better—isn't that so?—no better than the enemy. If not, if they didn't draw a line, then what the hell was it all about!? They would both be the same, it would all be the same, if they didn't draw a line.

So Captain Yancy drew a line when Lovelace reached for a third VC.

"That's it, Sergeant."

"What's it, sir?"

"That's enough, Sergeant. Let go of his hair."

"But why, Captain, why? You saw what these bastards did to Fritz. To Goodbody too. They're gooks, Captain, goddamn gooks. They're not like us. They don't understand civilized things. What they understand is a boot in the ass. Do I hafta let go?"

"You have to let go."

"But why, Captain, why? They're just two gooks."

"That's why, Sergeant. Because there's just two. Because we're running out of gooks. Who am I gonna interrogate?"

"Just one more, sir. I'll save you one, no matter what. That's a promise."

"No more, Lovelace."

"Why, Captain, why?"

"Because it's bad business. Because it doesn't work, that's why."

"Come on, sir, just one more, now that they know we're serious. Maybe it'll work this time."

"That's it, Sergeant."

"Why, Captain, why?"

"Because we have to draw a line."

"What kinda' line?"

"A fine line."

"What does that mean?"

"A line between necessary bad and unnecessary."

"There's no such line, sir. I know that myself."

"Sure there is, Lovelace, and we're gonna draw it."

Lovelace shrugged. He knew he was right and Yancy was wrong. "Anyway, sir, why draw it now?"

"Because it's time."

"But why draw it here? Who's to say? We've come this far, haven't we, sir? So why not just a little farther?"

"Because it's time to draw the line. It just is."

"How do you know, sir?"

"I just know it, that's how I know. Leave me alone. Quit bugging me. Damn it, Sergeant, let go of his hair!"

"Why, Captain, why?"

"Because I'm worried, doubly worried, about the talk."

"What talk, Captain?" shouted Lovelace thru the clatter. "Whose talk?"

"The crew, Sergeant," hissed Yancy, fearful that the crew might hear. "Damn it, Sergeant, not so loud. What will they think? What will they say?"

"What about, sir? There's nothing wrong. We haven't done anything bad. Don't sweat the crew, sir. They're just like us, them flyer boys. And gooks is gooks. Know what I mean?"

But Yancy insisted on drawing a line, and so he did. He drew the line at number two.

* * *

Y Gar the hunter dashed forward and punched plucky Kim in the head. Y M'dhur the half 'n half dashed forward and punched plucky Kim in the head. So did several of the others, rowdy young men. They all dashed forward and punched Kim, because he had spit at them—at everyone gathered to either side. Van was afraid they would punch him, too. He wished Kim wouldn't be so plucky.

Some, instead of dashing forward, only jeered louder than before, thumbing their noses, sticking their tongues out, making bad signs and razzing sounds—which had caused Kim to spit at them in the first place. So Kim spat again, only farther this time, and again Y Gar and Y M'dhur and several of the rowdy young men dashed forward to punch him, but Captain Yancy drove them away.

The men had gathered to either side. They pointed and jeered, or simply watched. The women looked on from the distance. Like the men, they pointed and jeered, or simply watched, and one threw a rotten pomegranate. Children peeked out from behind the piles, or else they ran to fetch their friends. Chickens ran squawking out of the way, inconvenienced by all the fuss. All this happened along the procession—from chopper, thru front gate, across Buon Yun, and toward the operations hut.

Triple Threat led the procession. He bounded, and flung his arms all around, and wagged his poor chimp-like head. He flung out his arms to the men on each side, to the women looking on from afar, to the children, to the squawking chickens. He was making his feelings plain, grunting his excitement to all.

Triple Threat didn't lead the procession because he wanted to taunt the VC. He didn't want to taunt anyone, knowing what it was like, himself. Well perhaps, he did want to taunt them a little, for hadn't they once deserted him, but taunting the VC was incidental. And, anyway, tho the VC were bad and his new friends were good, Triple Threat wasn't all that impressed by the difference between them. He didn't judge things in terms of good and bad, or one side and the other. He judged that the difference between the VC and his new friends was nothing compared to the difference between himself and them all. They had a voice and he was voiceless. That was the one difference he could really appreciate. There was him and everyone else—and there was Lieutenant Plunket.

Triple Threat led because there was a procession to lead, and because it was his joy to be leading. For all he cared, it could have been two elephants, or two buffaloes, or two *m'klaks* trussed up tight and led by a noose around their necks—never mind if no one had seen a *m'klak*, trussed up tight or otherwise. It could have been two of anything, instead of the two Viet Cong trussed up and led by a noose round their necks. As Triple Threat bounced and flung out his arms, he looked to the crowd on either side for Lieutenant Plunket, proudly he did. He wanted to show Lieutenant Plunket that he was in the lead.

Aside from the punching and the jeering and the rotten pomegranate, most of the people simply watched. They were angry and they were excited, but also subdued. They had lost eight young men two days before, and nine altogether, since the Americans had arrived to save them from the Viet Cong. Besides their own loss, there had been Buon Sop and the awful rumors about Buon Yak. The people were sorrowfully subdued because, if things had been bad before—what with the VC taxing their rice, and pressing them to join the cause, and taking a few young men now and then—they had lost far more since the team had come. Of course, the Americans weren't to blame. After all, they had come to help, and things had been bad before, and, as the Americans said, it was a man's place to stand up and fight. But somehow the helping, all the standing up and fighting, had seemed only to make matters worse. It was a problem, a very sore problem, for the people of Buon Yun. They were sore and sorrowful. How do you fight and make matters better, without first making matters worse? And who cares what comes after that, what with everybody dead, what with matters matterless? How? How!? That was the problem.

While most of the people simply watched and wondered what matters were coming to, no one wondered more than Y Bun. He'd had his doubts about the rope, tho Yancy had later assured him on that. He'd had his doubts about their commitment to the team; he didn't want to end up in parts. He'd had his doubts about the changes, generally. Was it truly better, as he had said, for a people to exchange its ways for rice and boots and guns that fired *ratta-tat-tat*? Or had he been deceiving himself; had he been hoping where there was none? It was no easy thing to be a chief, to be entrusted with so many lives. It was hard enough to keep trust with oneself.

A'de only knew that his life wasn't quite what he had hoped, that he wasn't the man he had set out to be. It wasn't easy, no indeed, and the specters only made it worse, the ones he couldn't shake from his head. And what made it most perplexing of all, was that they reminded him of a tale he'd known as a boy, a tale which, for the life of him, he couldn't recall. It was as if the fates were at work, hiding the simple truth from him. He wished he could turn to A'de for advice. But the closest thing he had to A'de was Y Blo, the intermediary, and they seldom saw eye to eye these days, which troubled Y Bun, for between them, they held Buon Yun in trust. So there he was with one-eared Y Blo, disapproving the spectacle, asking Y Blo about the spirits—if things were still looking good for Buon Yun.

While the two old friends conferred, Sergeant Moon was giving Little Rhadeo some additional pointers on the harmonica. Which caused Triple Threat to bound up and down, and fling out his arms, even more sprightly than before, tho, of course, he couldn't hear a note.

So a procession. With Triple Threat leading. Then Lovelace holding fast to the ropes. Then Kim and Van at the other end, with their necks in a noose. Finally, Yancy making sure that no one else got in a lick at Kim. Yancy took time out from making sure, to order that a cage of bamboo be built for the two. He also took time out to shout at Moon.

"Sergeant Moon," shouted Captain Yancy, "knock off with that harmonica!"

* * *

Van was scared and he was hungry. He thought about death and about food, there on the floor of the bamboo cage. He was so filled thru with his hunger and fear, that he had no room for anything else—not even for wondering how Dung would fare on his special assignment. Van didn't mind the hard floor of the cage or even his hunger all that much, for he had lived a very hard life, but he terribly minded the prospect of death.

Van came from a village to the southeast of Ban Me Thuot, where he had lived with his father and mother and three younger sisters and baby brother in peaceful poverty. The family had an adequate hut and enough rice to eat, but barely enough, and for that Van toiled long hours each day, and in spite of that gladly looked to the next. Then three years ago the soldiers came and took Van's father. Van's father hadn't wanted to go, nobody had, but the soldiers had lined up the men of the village and taken every third man for the army. It was Van's strongest memory: how they had dragged his father away, and the other men, and how his mother and sisters had cried. Van had been thirteen at the time.

For Van and his family, times became even harder than they had been before. Where before they had barely enough rice to eat, afterwards they had less than that. They grew desperate for rice, for money to buy it. They couldn't raise enough rice for themselves, not without Van's father. As for the money, their only hope was Van's father too. But Van's father was a lowly private and didn't earn much, and often didn't receive even that, because his Lieutenant often kept the pay for himself. Sometimes, for months at a stretch, Van's father didn't send any money.

Things got so desperate that, finally, the oldest of Van's three younger sisters had to be sold to Xuan the whoremonger who traveled thruout the countryside looking for the prettiest girls. Van took the sale of his sister badly, for she had been his favorite one.

Soon after that, Van's baby brother died from the cholera. What with the sale of his sister and the death of his baby brother, the family again had enough to eat, but just barely enough.

For a long time, more than the usual three or four months, nothing was heard from Van's father. They wondered how things were going with him. Then their old neighbor, who had been one of the number three men and who had run away from his unit, returned to the village. He told them how things had gone with Van's father, and Van hung on to every word. Briefly, this is how things had gone—on the day the platoon was inspected by Major Quoc, the battalion commander.

The Major was known as Cowboy Quoc because of the jade-handled revolver he wore at his side. He was a stickler for spit and polish. He expected all his men to shine, especially if there were generals present. Well, he was inspecting the platoon and was angry because the men were ragged. Major Quoc was especially angry because General ———— was present. He screamed at the men and slapped some hard across their faces. Their uniforms were in disrepair and their weapons were dirty. The farther along Major Quoc went, the more disrepaired and dirty things seemed. Then he stopped in front of Van's father. Van's father was disrepaired too. His uniform was missing two buttons. There hadn't been money to keep up repairs. The Lieutenant hadn't paid them for months.

Major Quoc stood in front of Van's father, and decided he'd had enough. So, for those buttons, he drew his revolver and shot Van's father between the eyes. Van's father, of course, fell dead to the ground, and as he fell, Quoc turned on his heel and strode off in disgust. That was it. That's what the neighbor had to tell. As for Quoc, he was soon promoted to Colonel because of the zeal he had demonstrated in trying to shape up his command.

When Van heard the story, he decided at once to join the VC. That same night he said good-bye to his mother and his two sisters, and they all cried. Then Van slipped out of the village. It had been a very hard village, but once, in spite of everything, he had looked gladly to each new day. He knew where to go. Because of two missing buttons, Van slipped out and joined the VC.

Because of two missing buttons and the ironsmith's modesty, ˙an found himself by the bars of the cage, considering his hunger ˙d fear, mostly his fear. While Kim lay slumped in the cage with ˙m considering the fifteenth of June, Van considered his hunger ˙d fear, mostly his fear, until he leaped back frightened out of his ˙its.

But it was only Grandmother Pan.
Because of the melon.

Grandmother Pan was angry with her daughter-in-law, furious, ˙cause the girl had eaten a melon. Oh, what a girl! Foolish girl! ˙hy did her son have to choose such a girl!? A pregnant girl ˙ust not eat a melon, or any other kind of fruit, because to eat ˙uit would make the baby fall out of her womb just as fruit falls ˙om a tree. Oh, that girl! Idiot girl! "But it was a melon," the ˙rl had argued. "They don't matter. Melons have no place to ˙ll, growing on the ground as they do." Foolish girl! Idiot girl! ˙hat difference a melon or a pawpaw, a fruit is a fruit! Oh, how ˙at Grandmother Pan was mad! She was so mad she had to do ˙mething, else she would burst. Oh, what a girl!

And Grandmother Pan recalled her own girlish days, how it was ˙ith Y Bun in the beginning. They played games like hide-and-seek ˙ the woods, and when they found the other out they would ˙ssle and laugh and roll on the ground and have each other; ˙at was after the bracelets, of course. And sometimes there had ˙en parties at night when they would drink too much wine. And ˙ice she had tried to get Y Blo to suck out the seed from a seed-˙ss gourd. And there were other foolish things; but she was never ˙ foolish as to eat a pawpaw, or even a melon, when she was ˙regnant.

Her family hadn't approached Y Bun's and arranged the mar-˙age, as was the custom. Instead, Y Bun had courted her. He had ˙elped her fetch water and gather mushrooms. And sometimes, ˙hen she could get him to do it, he had sung her courting songs ˙—when no one else was close to hear. And once he had even ˙rought her some flowers from deep in the forest where wild things ˙alk; how brave he was! And there were those times when he

had lain in wait for her and pulled her skirt, then run away;
else pulled her down and gave her a kiss under normal trees
strangely shaped ones, so fired was Y Bun for her. They carri
on until, at last, he gave her a bracelet and she gave him one
return. This meant that Y Bun had entered into a compact wi
Pan to marry her if she became pregnant, which Grandmother Pa
soon enough did. This bracelet exchange was also a custom, but
wasn't the usual way, and certainly not all their carryings on. Ar
back in those innocent times, Pan and Y Bun were considere
quite the frolicsome ones.

Grandmother Pan recalled all about the ceremony, how sl
and Y Bun had squatted before a gourd of rice wine and crosse
their straws while prayers were chanted. How they had shy
drunk the wine, but proudly too, with their feet on a hatchet. Th
marked the permanence of their union; hatchets were surely us
for splitting, but the split wood went to warm a hearth.

Then the sacrifice of a fine white cock to the ancestor spirits f
their blessing and to proclaim that, from that day, there was a ne
hearth in the longhouse. Oh, how splendid Y Blo had been, di
patching the cock and saying the words and generally officiatin
It had been his first performance as a *mjao*.

After this, the guests had been served a square of raw me
and a piece of tripe. It had been very tasty meat and the tripe ha
been properly rubbery.

Then all the guests had filed by and had offered small gift
for which they were given one worth twice as much in return-
gifts such as a basket of bamboo tubes filled with bamboo sho
preserves, or maybe a hen. This giving back twice as dear a g
was supposed to assure Y Bun and her of a rich and prospero
future. Rich and prosperous!? That was a laugh! It had taken a
they had to offer twice as much in return. Oh yes, chuckled Gran
mother Pan, for sure they had started out poor enough; and po
they had stayed.

Grandmother Pan recalled all this and how, thru the interveni
years, they never had to pay a fine to the other, which was th
price for adultery. Never! boasted Grandmother Pan; tho the
were some, she very well knew, who paid each other many a fin

Oh, it had been something special, all right, for her and Y Bun.

What honest years they had been, you couldn't exactly call them happy—what with the poorness of the land, and the years when the spirits had turned a deaf ear, and then the big war, the one with the French and the Viet Minh. She had lost her eldest son in that war, and many a night she had lain awake wondering if Y Bun would also be lost. And what was it for? Well, she hadn't known. And what did it bring them? More grief, that's all, and one less son. And some kind of pension, whatever that meant, which they never received anyway.

Oh, how they had dried and they had stiffened, and now lived for telling the same old stories and spoiling their grandsons and not for chasing thru the woods. No, not for that, thought Grandmother Pan, laughing gently to herself, tho she was no decrepit old thing!

So Grandmother Pan had come to the cage not only because she was mad at the girl and had to do something, else she would burst; but also because of her eldest son, whom Y Bun had taken with him and hadn't brought back.

Grandmother Pan pressed her face up against the bars—shoved her nose between two of them—and peered inside for a better look at Kim and Van. She was small and as light as the dust in the air, and walked just as softly. That's how she happened to be pressed up tight and peering in, before Kim or Van had noticed her. Because she walked as softly as dust, and because it was night and hard to see. It was just a small bamboo cage, but Grandmother Pan had to shove in close to get a good look.

They looked at one another from either side of the bamboo bars. Kim and Van wondered what to make of Grandmother Pan. Perhaps she was only curious or else had come to taunt them. Van liked her wily yet kindly old face, but Kim tensed himself to spring at her and bite off her nose if she should taunt them. Likewise with Grandmother Pan; she wondered what to make of them. They looked just like everyone else—well at least like other Vietnamese. They didn't look so dangerous. Yet she was prepared to jump back fast if one of them should spring at her.

Grandmother Pan pressed her wily but kindly old face tighter up against the bars. She shoved her nose tighter between them. She sniffed at the two men as much as she peered. Van could almost hear the creak of her old knees as she leaned forward. Grandmother Pan smiled toothlessly, winsomely, and spoke a few soft guttural words. "What does she want? What does this mean?" Van asked Kim. Grandmother Pan didn't speak Vietnamese. Kim and Van didn't speak Rhadé.

She spoke again. "What does she want?" Van asked again. But Kim only shrugged his shoulders: how should he know? Then he crawled up close to Grandmother Pan, almost nose to nose, and began to fling his arms around—rather like Triple Threat had done—trying to shoo the old woman away. Kim didn't like people staring at him, especially then, when he was so edgy thinking about what was going to be. He didn't want to be bothered by the likes of her. But Grandmother Pan didn't budge; she only pressed closer, grinning and chuckling over Kim. The more Kim flailed his arms around trying to shoo the old woman away, the more she chuckled, crinkling her marvelous shrunken face.

Grandmother Pan was enjoying Kim, but she hadn't come to be entertained. She was no senile old fool; she knew he was trying to shoo her away. So before things got rough—before the one with the flailing arms sprang to bite off her nose—she did what she had come to do. She produced a small mat of monkey kebabs, a specialty of which she was proud. She raised the mat and grunted softly and bade the two men to take her kebabs.

At first Kim and Van looked suspiciously at Grandmother Pan's monkey kebabs. But as the old woman kept grunting softly, bidding the two men to take them and eat, they decided to trust in her. Being famished had something to do with it too. They reached thru the bars and took all of Grandmother Pan's kebabs.

Grandmother Pan nodded her head as they reached out and took. That's it, boys, she seemed to say, that's the good boys. She smiled once more, happy to see they had taken all, and then she softly shuffled away, carrying her empty mat.

Kim and Van sniffed the meat, then gobbled it up as fast as they could. When they were done, they slumped back on the floor of the cage and took up their thinking where they had left off. Van took up thinking about his fear, only his fear, for his hunger was gone. Kim took up thinking about the fifteenth, about what was going to be.

* * *

Captain Yancy had been waiting for the darkness, for the buzzing to subside, for the juices to soak in. The villagers had been milling and buzzing since the procession. He waited for them to quiet down. He didn't want them snooping around. He waited for that and because he wanted the two Viet Cong to consider their fear—to marinate in their fear for awhile.

When it became good and dark, when the people had settled down, when the two Viet Cong had marinated, when Captain Yancy was satisfied, he called for the interrogation, started to, but then the whispering began. From here, from there, from everywhere.

Shhhh—Shhhh—Whissssspering—

"What are they whispering about? Why do they have to whisper like that?"

"The boars," said the interpreter. "They must whisper."

"The boars?" said Yancy.

"And other wild animals too."

"What about the boars?"

"The rice fields," said the interpreter. "They must whisper."

"The rice fields?" said Yancy.

"And other crops too. But mostly the rice."

*Shhhh—Shhhh—Whissssspering—*from all the houses of Buon Yun.

"But what are they whispering about? Why do they have to whisper like that?"

"Today was special sacrifice. For permission to plant the rice. Y Blo, he make the sacrifice."

"But why is everyone whispering?"

"Everyone tell everyone about sacrifice. Tell in small voice. Very *shhhh*."

"Why small voice? Why *shhhh*?"

"The boars. Other wild animals too. Mostly the boars."

"The boars?"

"So boars don't know. Don't hear, don't know."

"But what's wrong with boars? Why can't they know?"

"Then they kill the fields, eat the new rice. Good rice, too. Everything good. The spirits promised to Y Blo."

When it became even darker, when the whispering had stopped and the people settled down, when the juices had soaked deeper, when Captain Yancy was satisfied, he called for the interrogation.

Yancy, Lovelace, and the interpreter gathered in the far back room of the operations hut. The room was lit by a kerosene lamp, and the walls were bare but for shadows. Pale yellow powder, the munchings of termites, covered the floor. The room was empty except for the lamp, and the thick film of powder, and for several gourds of water. The room was soundless except for the *tic-tic* of termites gnawing, and the lamp hissing, and chickens clucking beneath the floor, chickens which Triple Threat was raising.

Captain Yancy called for Kim. He figured that Kim would have more information. Yancy wanted information, and to stifle Kim's pluckiness.

When they came for Kim, he gave them no help. They had to haul him to his feet, and drag him all the way to the hut and into the room. Van watched them take Kim away. He thought about how the soldiers had once dragged his father off. His chest felt hollow, his throat felt bone dry. He felt like his juices were eating him up. He was glad there was no one to see him cry.

Kim landed with a thud where they had flung him to the floor. A cloud of pale yellow powder rose and covered him, crept into his eyes and nose and mouth, and he coughed for a time. His coughing was the only sound—except for the *tic-tic* of the termites, and the hiss of the kerosene lamp, and the clucking of Triple Threat's chickens beneath the floor.

"Name and unit, ask the bastard his name and unit." Yancy made himself sound as harsh as he could, and much louder than was necessary.

"What is your name and unit, bastard? Better speak up."

Kim had stopped coughing, but he didn't speak up—or down or

anywhere at all. He sat squatting on the flats of his feet with his hands bound behind him. His hands had been bound when they had fetched him from the cage. Yancy, Lovelace, and the interpreter stood in a circle around squatting Kim. Perhaps he would have spat at them if his mouth hadn't been so dry. *Ptuu!* The powder was terrible!

"The others—ask the bastard how many others and where they are."

"How many others and where are they, bastard? Better speak up."

But Kim wasn't speaking up or down or anywhere. Instead, he considered the taste of the powder and stared down thru a crack in the floor, watching the chickens.

"Purple smoke hell! Names, unit, others hell!" It was Lovelace and he was heated burnt-orange again. Lovelace had heated up faster this time, much faster than he had in the chopper. Perhaps he had never really cooled down. Fritz, they got Fritz! And Goodbody, too. Here he was doing Fritz's job! Fritz would have done the interrogation. Goddammit to hell, Fritz, they got Fritz! So whether he had heated up faster, or whether he had never cooled down, Sergeant Lovelace reached for Kim and raised him by the hair. One-handed, he held up Kim by his hair—with Kim's feet barely brushing the floor—and with the other, pinched off Kim's nose.

"Take him, sir. Hold him for me. Keep his nose shut." Yancy took hold of Kim's hair with one hand, and then took hold of Kim's nose with the other. "Tighter, sir. Keep his nose shut." Sergeant Lovelace put on his gloves, good thick gloves, and reached for Kim's mouth. Kim, who had opened his mouth wide for air, quickly clamped his jaws together as Sergeant Lovelace came reaching for them. "Tighter, sir. Twist it a bit. Keep his nose shut as tight as you can." Captain Yancy twisted Kim's nose. "That's it, sir. That's the way." He shut Kim's nose as tight as he could.

They stood that way, with Kim dangling by his hair, with Yancy gripping onto Kim's nose, twisting it and pinching it tight, with Sergeant Lovelace waiting there and cooing encouragement to

Yancy. "That's it, sir. Nice and tight. Atta' way, sir." They stood that way until Kim turned purple, until his jaws parted and Kim gasped for breath. As soon as he did, Sergeant Lovelace made his move. He jammed his gloved hands into Kim's mouth and kept Kim's jaws pried apart. Then he shouted at the interpreter: "Get me a gourd! Goddammit, hurry, get me a gourd!"

Keeping one hand jammed in Kim's mouth, Sergeant Lovelace took the gourd and began pouring water down Kim's throat. Kim's body stiffened, then it spastically jerked about. Kim's eyes rolled wildly in his head and filled with tears. The water bubbled, gurgled down. Kim tried to gurgle some back up, spluttering, but it got mixed with the stream of water coming down, and all of it wound up gurgled down. Kim twitched and spluttered and swallowed it all, and in his desperate gasping for breath, some wound up down his windpipe too; which caused Kim to drivel up thru his nose, and all over Captain Yancy's hand.

With Kim jerking about like that, Lovelace was hard pressed to get all the water into Kim's mouth. Lovelace and Yancy were getting wet, and Lovelace was getting even hotter because he was getting wet, and Lovelace was pouring faster in his greater heat, and getting wet faster because of it. "Another one! Another gourd! Goddammit, get me another one!"

Lovelace poured the second gourd down Kim's throat, getting himself and Yancy soaked. He poured and poured, and Kim's belly swelled. He poured and poured, and Kim's belly blew up like a balloon. He poured until he sensed it was time, and then he yelled: "Time! Let's get him over there quick! Hurry, sir!"

Captain Yancy let go of Kim's nose. Lovelace freed his hand from Kim's mouth. Then he grabbed Kim by the scruff of his neck and rushed him to the only window—a low, square cutout in the back wall. He got Kim there just in time. He got him there just as Kim heaved-ho. It didn't take its time bubbling or gurgling, but gushed right out like a blown well. Poor Kim was at it awhile—with Lovelace holding his head thru the window—and when Kim seemed just about done, Lovelace walloped him in the belly and more came gushing up after all. The last of the two gourdsful of water and Grandmother Pan's monkey kebabs.

After Kim had emptied himself, Lovelace dragged him back to the center of the room and dropped him to the floor. Kim felt drained, weak, and wrung out. His head buzzed. His throat burned. His mouth was sore where Lovelace had jammed his thick-gloved hand, or it was numb, he wasn't sure. He lay on the floor, soaked thru, with his hands bound behind his back, with the pale yellow powder gathered in clumps on his wet black rags. He wanted very badly to spit in Lovelace's face. But Kim couldn't manage it. With all that water, he couldn't manage one little drop.

"Ask him again. Goddammit, ask the bastard again."

The interpreter asked.

But Kim wouldn't answer. He lay there drained and soaked and aching and not being able to manage one drop. He lay there staring thru the crack, looking at the chickens.

So they went thru it all over again. With Yancy holding Kim by the hair, and twisting and pinching tight his nose. With Lovelace's hand jammed in Kim's mouth, and Lovelace pouring down gourd after gourd. With Kim gagging and thrashing his legs, and swelling up big like a balloon, and retching it all up and out thru the window. They went at it a second time, and several more times after that, but Kim wouldn't speak. His body grew weaker, his throat more scratchy and more fired, his head spun faster with each purge. He felt he had drowned several times over. He expected to drown several times more, but he wouldn't speak. Kim about whom Mac had once wondered if he hadn't made a mistake.

Sergeant Lovelace left the room because he had always liked spicy food. It had given him an idea.

It was quiet in the room except for the *tic-tic* of the termites, and the hiss of the kerosene lamp, and the clucking of Triple Threat's chickens. Yancy brooded in the quiet. He wished that Lovelace would get it done. This was painful stuff, he thought, painful, yes, but necessary. It pained him to be a part of it. It pained him to be getting sopping wet.

Lovelace returned with a straight-backed chair, and with a long narrow three ounce bottle of good ol' *Louisiana Hot*. He sat Kim in the chair, then sat on top of Kim himself, face to face, heavily straddling Kim's thighs with his own. "Hold him good, sir. Pull his head back. All the way down, sir. Over the back. That's it, sir. Yank it back good."

So Yancy did. He yanked Kim's head over the back. Then Lovelace uncapped his long narrow bottle of good ol' *Louisiana Hot,* and poured a few drops down Kim's nose or up, whichever it was.

Kim's head slammed forward into Lovelace, and Yancy was left with a handful of hair. Kim roared with pain. He roared with being eaten alive. He roared from the fire consuming his nose. He roared and his eyes filled with tears. He sat there and roared, with Lovelace heavily straddling him, and beat his head against Lovelace's shoulder, till Yancy reyanked it over the back. Kim twitched and roared, and when he stopped roaring, he whimpered softly.

They asked him again about name and unit and all the rest, but Kim hung in there pluckily and refused to answer. So Lovelace added more seasoning: about a full ounce down Kim's nose or up, whichever it was, of good ol' *Louisiana Hot.* The burning, the roaring, the slamming forward, the beating against Lovelace's shoulder, it happened again; and several more times after that; but Kim wouldn't speak. Even after passing out, and being revived, and being seasoned more and more highly, plucky Kim wouldn't speak.

So Yancy and Lovelace gave up on Kim—at least temporarily. They decided to work out on Van instead, with Yancy giving Lovelace bad looks for not getting it done. Kim was dragged back to the bamboo cage. He was flung inside and landed almost on top of Van. He wished that he were dead.

Captain Yancy didn't send for Van right away. He wanted Van to examine Kim, to look him over carefully, to see what awaited him as well should he refuse to speak. He wanted Van to soak up what had happened to Kim, to marinate in that awhile.

* * *

Kim lay in an aching heap almost on top of Van. It pained him to shift his body, or move his head, or even to breathe. His nose smoldered, his head whirled. It felt very tender where he had beat it against Sergeant Lovelace. The breeze which struck up each night at Buon Yun gently whipped at his wet black rags. He fancied he had drowned for good, that he had washed up on some beach. He lay there at the end of his strength, and wondered why he wasn't dead.

"Will it be bad, Kim? Very bad?"

What's wrong with this boy? Can't he see?

"They're pigs, Kim. They're dogs and pigs and everything low and filthy and bad."

Sure they're pigs and all the rest. How I wish I could have spat.

"I'm scared, Kim, very scared. Will it be bad?"

Everyone's scared. I was scared too, plucky me! Will it be bad? What's wrong with you, boy? Can't you see?

"Listen, Kim, what should I do?"

What should you do? How do I know? At least you could untie me.

Van sat there and marinated and finally he untied Kim. It was the least he could have done.

"Will it be bad, Kim? Very bad?"

"Bad enough."

"Then what should I do?"

"Prepare yourself, Van. Then it will go better."

"But *how* do I prepare myself, Kim?"

"By a dry run, by going thru that."

"What's a dry run?"

"You've got to match conditions, Van."

"Conditions, Kim?"

"It's like this. Let's pretend that I'm the American, the mean orange-headed one, and that you're me. Then I'll do to you what he did to me. We'll do it realistically but, of course, not too realistically. That way you'll know what to expect, and then the real thing won't be so bad. What do you say? A dry run, Van? I wish I had gone thru one. Shall we give it a try?"

"Yes, Kim, let's give it a try. But let's hurry, too, before they come." Van was willing to try anything, tho he wasn't quite sure what Kim had in mind.

Kim pushed himself to his knees until he was eye to eye with

Van. The boy looked at Kim for sympathy and Kim looked right back, bloodshot-eyed and all, full of the truest sympathy.

"Turn around, Van."

Van turned around, and Kim bound his hands behind his back.

"That's the first thing. Now turn again."

Van turned again, his hands bound behind him, facing Kim.

"What's next, Kim? Will it be bad? Not too realistic, all right?"

"Just to give you a good idea— Ready, Van? Should I begin?"

Van nodded yes, and Kim's hands reached out for Van's neck. They took a firm hold, and began to squeeze, and Van began to understand exactly what a dry run was about.

It was good that they were trying it, that Kim was showing him what to expect. But Kim was squeezing a little too hard, wasn't he? Maybe just a little too hard. Come on, Van, don't be a baby. How else will you get used to it? But it hurts. Come on, Van, be a big boy. Kim knows what he's doing. He wouldn't do anything unnecessary. But it's hard to breathe. Aw, Van, stop being a baby. Stop whining and start getting used to it. But it hurts, and it's hard to breathe, and I'm all done getting used to it.

Van tried to tell Kim to stop, but he couldn't muster his voice. His face was red, his eyes full of tears. It was realistic, all right.

It was realistic, all right, because Kim had gathered the last of his strength and was squeezing for keeps. He looked right at Van with the deepest truest sympathy, but also with absolute resolve. Van looked back thru his cloud of tears, and saw the resolve, and if he didn't understand, he understood enough to panic. He wrenched his head, and twisted his body, and kicked out his legs, but Kim hung on. He tried to free his hands but he couldn't. Kim had bound them good and tight. The two of them flipped about in the cage, with Kim holding on as best he could. They flipped about, and Kim poured it all into one great surge, and finally strangled Van to death.

It had to be done. I had to do it. The Americans are dogs and pigs and everything low and filthy and bad. They would have forced the boy to speak. He would have told them everything. He would have told them about the fifteenth.

Kim rolled to one side of the cage, full of the deepest truest sorrow, and there within reach, there shining in the light of the newly risen moon, there discarded carelessly, was just what he needed. He stretched thru the bars and gathered it in. He examined it, thinking he knew what it was, but wondering how it had gotten there, and then he pricked open the veins of his wrists and lay down to die. He knew that he couldn't make it thru a second session, not without telling them name and unit and everything and about the fifteenth. So he opened his veins and lay down to die, Kim about whom Mac had once wondered if he hadn't made a mistake. Sergeant Moon hadn't made a mistake. It was one of those things. It was a number five stainless steel needle, the kind with which you pique for Hsieh, the kind for depressing the energy.

△ SQUARING OFF
☆ _____
△ _____
_____

Y M'dhur lay awake, smelling the mustiness of the blankets and getting his eyes used to the dark. His wife slept fitfully, tossing and turning, burrowing mole-like into the blankets. Eghh, what a wife! thought Y M'dhur. He would have preferred someone younger and firmer who didn't smell musty like the blankets. There was a cough every now and then. It was the only sound in the longhouse. Eghh, thought M'dhur, that's a bad cough. It's a bad life all around.

When his eyes had gotten used to the dark, Y M'dhur slowly slipped from the blankets, shivering. His wife stirred, but didn't wake, just tossed and turned more fitfully, burrowing deeper into the blankets. Eghh, what a wife! thought Y M'dhur. He would have preferred someone who didn't toss and turn, and didn't burrow, and had a few specialties of her own, like Grandmother Pan's monkey kebabs. She wasn't even good for pleasure. Eghh, what a wife! groaned Y M'dhur.

Yet there was a time he had cared for her, if mostly out of gratitude for having accepted his proposal in spite of the fact he was amber-skinned. But why should he have been so grateful? She should have been the grateful one, for wasn't he a hard-working fellow, and sensible, and owned the fattest buffaloes? That was some time ago, thought Y M'dhur, and their marriage had since grown slack like his wife, or, at least, his feelings for her. How he wished she wouldn't mother him so! And not only that, thought Y M'dhur of his woes, but now people looked at him somewhat askance, because he had dared to tell them the truth about the rope. Well, let them look! Let his wife grow slack and musty! Let them stare as if he were touched! *They* were touched! *Everyone* was! Couldn't they see that, rope or not, it was the same! And so were people everywhere! Always seeing amber or whatever color, when what was beneath the skin truly mattered. People everywhere were blind. If only they could be made to see! If only they could be perfected! Oh, what a wife! Eghh, what a life!

Y M'dhur rose from the mat, as slowly, as softly as he could, trying not to rouse his wife, but all for naught. Her scraggly head peeked out from the blankets. "What are you about, Y M'dhur? Why do you rise?" she asked.

"Agh, foolish woman, to get to my feet."

"Yes, Y M'dhur, but where do you go?"

"I go where I have to go, that's where."

"It's cold, Y M'dhur, and very dark."

"Maybe so, but it can't wait. My bowels grumble and make lots of wind."

"I haven't heard nor have I smelt."

"Agh, foolish woman, go back to sleep."

"Don't forget to put on your boots."

Y M'dhur carried his boots in his hand. They were fine canvas boots with thick rubber soles, issued to all the Strike Force. Y M'dhur's eyes were used to the dark, still it was good he knew where to step, so as not to step on the others. He reached the front ledge, climbed to the ground, and put on his boots. His wife had already dropped back to sleep.

Y M'dhur heard a barking deer off in the distance. He stood and listened to hear it again, but the barking deer must have wandered off. There was no moon, only the starlight, but Y M'dhur could have made his way blind. He had known Buon Yun for most of his life—ever since he had left Phu Dinh where being a half 'n half had its faults. He knew Buon Yun like the palm of his hand. The cracks of his skin were sealed with its dirt.

The trenches were off to the south of the village, and that's where Y M'dhur made his way, stealthily, considerately, careful not to wake a soul. Once, he thought he heard someone else, and he scurried under the nearest longhouse, hiding up against a pile. His shyness was strange, for there was no shame in eliminating, certainly not enough to cause someone to scurry and hide. In any case, there was no one else. He waited and listened and made sure of that. The people slept well, happily, all whispered out from that night and before, about their hopes for a bountiful year. Not even the spirits which hovered and lurked and rustled at night, not even they seemed to be abroad. So Y M'dhur continued on, southward toward the trenches.

When he got to the trenches, Y M'dhur looked around, shy as ever, and then he reached in. He felt around, but they must have sunk. So Y M'dhur reached in deeper. He turned his head, and closed his eyes, and puckered his nose, and reached to his armpit. Eghh, thought Y M'dhur, trying not to breathe, what a terrible way to do one's part! Then he, one by one, drew up the bamboo tubes, the ones he had smuggled inside his load of firewood on the day the people had jeered at him, on the day that Fritz had been fixed. He drew up the tubes, and then he carried them to the fence and set down to work. The tubes had been sealed off from the filth. They had been packed.

Gung Ho Dung snagged his pajamas on the fence. He lay still for a moment, flat on his belly, and drew a long breath. Dung wanted very badly to swear, but knew that to swear would not be wise. He lay there prone on the chill damp ground, scared and listening very intently. There was a time when Dung had been proud of his special assignments, looked forward to them; but these last two had been something else, what with the straining for all he was worth and now with being snagged on the wire.

Dung shuffled his body back, careful not to make a sound, but his pajamas refused to come free. He shuffled forward and shuffled back several times, trying to unpin himself, but he stayed hung. Eghh, thought Dung who was caught in the seat, what a terrible way to do one's part! Why me all the time? Why not someone else?

Peeved they hadn't picked someone else and scared that he might never get free, growing more scared with each hopeless shuffle forward and back, Dung decided on something more drastic. He turned on his side as far as he could, shutting his eyes, gritting his teeth against the pain, and wincing as the barbs bit in. Then Dung reached back and felt for the snag, scraping his arm on the barbs as he did. He searched about, he struggled back there, until he touched ass where his pants had once been. Well, Dung found the snag and finally disengaged himself. A flap had been torn from the seat of his pants, exposing his rear. It hung there like an open trap door.

Disengagement complete, Dung went back to snipping a passageway thru the fence. He snipped, and stopped to listen for sounds, and snipped again. He was glad that the airfield was guarded by ARVN and not by the Americans. It was just as Mac had said. Things were going according to plan. He considered his gladness, and why he was glad, and paused in confusion. Eghh, thought Dung, hadn't Mac also said that Americans were the unworthiest of enemies? How could it be? Dung asked himself. If the Americans were so unworthy, then why should he be glad it was ARVN? Since Dung was Vietnamese himself, he felt that he should stick up for ARVN; but since ARVN was a mockery, since ARVN was the enemy too, he didn't know which way to think. He wished Mac were there to tell him how. But Mac was lying splattered, of course, between the Brake of the Rattling Bamboo and the village of Buon Yun. So Dung resigned himself to his confusion, and concentrated on the snipping, on getting his special assignment done.

The guards were asleep, the ones Dung could see. He wondered how the others were doing, how far they had snipped thru the fence. There was only the starlight above, and a firefly dancing about his head, and he felt alone tho he knew there were others snipping, too. He took comfort from the weight of the plastique against his hip, and he reached for and snuffed out the firefly, for every bit of darkness helped. He felt quite alone and very scared as each snip he made caused a *thtic* of a sound which sounded louder to Dung than it was. He was scared that something might go wrong, that the guards might awake.

Y M'dhur had barely set down to work when he heard a sound which wasn't the scraping and stopped to listen. The sound came again, but it was only the barking deer which hadn't wandered off after all. So Y M'dhur went on with the work, with scraping the second length up to the first, with fitting the bamboo tubes together.

The fitting done, he pushed the tube thru a gap in the fence, just gap enough for the girth of the tube, and into the field of *punjis*. He pushed the tube slowly, taking his time, taking great care to push it exactly along a path where there were no mines. Y M'dhur knew where there were no mines, because he had worked with Sergeant Goodbody when they had been laid.

He pushed until he had pushed enough, and then he reached for a third bamboo tube, scraping it over the ground to him, and fit the second and third lengths together. That done, he pushed the tube deeper into the *punjis*. He pushed the tube slowly, taking his time, sliding it easily over the ground. He pushed the tube slowly, taking great care to push it exactly along the right path. He pushed but now the tube wouldn't budge. He pushed but the tube wouldn't slide farther forward. He had it up against a *punji*.

Eghh, thought M'dhur, first a wife who won't sleep, who's no good for pleasure anyway—then the terrible filth—and now this!

Y M'dhur didn't roll the tube off the *punji*. He didn't dare roll it to either side—not with the mines laying everywhere. Instead, he lowered himself, he leaned right into the end of the tube, into the smell. He pushed ahead giving it lots of shoulder, giving it all of his slow steady strength. He strained and strained, and had to sneeze, and sweat stung his eyes, but he couldn't suppress the sneeze with his hand or against his arm, and he couldn't wipe the sweat from his eyes, because both his hands and both his arms were covered with filth.

So he bore with the sneeze puckering there, and with the stinging, and with the smell. He bore with it and pushed ahead, scrunched there on the chill damp ground, trying hard to breathe minimally. He bore and bore, and finally the *punji* snapped, and the tube slid deeper into the alley between the fences, deeper toward the outer fence. The *punji* just went SNAP!

Y Bong snapped up straight. He had been drowsing, he had been slumping, but the snap—there had been a snap, hadn't there!?—had snapped him up straight. The ironsmith stood up straight and listened, and listened, and listened. Hadn't there!? He listened intently, turning his ear every whichway, but he didn't hear any more snapping. He started to wonder if there had been a snap after all. There had, hadn't there!?

He stood with his carbine raised to his shoulder and aimed it uncertainly into the darkness, straining to hear, to see thru the black. Perhaps there hadn't been a snap, but he was so sure. The only sound Y Bong now heard was a barking deer. It hadn't been that! The other sound, the snapping sound, it had come from the other direction, from somewhere back along the fence and not from the forest's edge. Hadn't it!?

But there was only the barking deer, so Y Bong dropped his carbine down to his side, and reslumped. His legs were tired. His lids were heavy in spite of the chill. He was bored. It was pretty dull stuff, standing guard by the gate, with the gate bolted shut and everything snug and nothing at all to worry about. It was no job for a hero, he thought. And he was something of a hero— ever since he had betaken himself and tried to smooth down the clump of grass and wound up down the tunnel instead. No job for a hero at all. They could have picked someone else!

But since they hadn't, Y Bong reslumped, and dropped his carbine down to his side, and dropped his lids, making the best of a bad situation. He drowsed and dreamt about his wife—how he wished he were back in the longhouse with her, laying snugly up against her, there beneath the blankets. Y Bong dreamt about being relieved, and about going back, and it seemed that time passed very slowly, and indeed, it had hardly passed at all, before he snapped up straight again.

Someone, something, was hurrying toward him in an urgent, breathless way. What could it be!? Who could it be!? wondered Y Bong. Whatever it was, whoever it was, it wasn't stopping or slowing down, but came on and on toward the ironsmith, so that he prepared to leap aside. But whatever it was, whoever it was, it screeched up short, it stopped just in time. It was Y Gar.

Before he spoke, Y Gar paused for breath, which only stoked the ironsmith's anxiousness all the more, his franticness to learn what was up. He started to grab Y Gar by the shoulders, to shake

the news out of him, but the hunter managed to grab him first, and
shook him and said breathlessly: "Y Bong! Y Bong! I must tell!"

"Y Gar, you—you startled me. I thought—just maybe—"

"Y Bong! Y Bong! I've seen it! I've seen it!"

"It's dark, you know, and scary too—"

"Y Bong! Y Bong! It's terrible!"

"And the sounds. I've been hearing these sounds—"

"Y Bong! Y Bong!"

"So I thought that—maybe—you were—"

"Y Bong! I've seen it! It's terrible!"

"What, Y Gar!? What!? What!?"

"The treachery! I've seen a great treachery."

"Treachery!? What treachery!?" Y Bong was still tight in the
hunter's grip. He tried to spin free, but that only made Y Gar
grip tighter and shake him the harder.

"The sound was muffled, a low thumping sound. Sometimes it
came and sometimes it went. And then, when it went, it was very
quiet. So, at first, I wasn't sure. Then it came again, the low
thumping sound, but this time it was a sharp quick sound, sudden
and loud, and I crept up close to see with my eyes. I'm a hunter, Y
Bong, and good eyes are very important for me. So I crept up to
see."

"The treachery! What about the treachery!?"

"My eyes had never failed me before and—"

"The treachery, Y Gar! What is the treachery!?" Y Bong was still
trying to spin himself free, and getting shook harder for his effort,
and wishing Y Gar would get to the point.

"I blinked my eyes—they're hunter's eyes—but, all the same,
I blinked them, Y Bong, just to make sure. I *saw* him, Y Bong! I
saw him there. He was wiggling, Y Bong! Like a snake in the grass.
And the pole, Y Bong! It was long and stout, and he was pushing it
deeper in, and—"

"Who, Y Gar!? Who did you see!? Who was pushing it deeper
in!?" Y Bong had finally spun himself free, and in his turn, in his
anxiousness, he gripped onto Y Gar and began shaking him. "Who!?
Who!? Tell me, Y Gar! What kind of treachery is this? What made
you hurry and scare me like that? Tell me! Tell me!"

"I *am* telling you. Don't shake me like that. I came as fast as I could, didn't I? I knew it was your night to guard the gate. So listen, Y Bong, while you stand guard, there's a breach being made. A breach, Y Bong!"

"A breach!? What breach!? Where, Y Gar!?" the ironsmith noisily, anxiously asked.

"These gates are secure, but others are not," answered the hunter sorrowfully.

"What others, Y Gar!? Quick, tell me what others!"

"Your wife's gates, that's what. Y —— is laying with your wife. Right now he is, at this very moment."

Y Bong snapped up straight. He stood there with his mouth wide open, but with nothing coming out.

"Hurry, Y Bong. See for yourself. I'll stand your guard until you get back. Hurry, now!"

Y Bong didn't even thank his friend. He thrust his carbine at Y Gar, and then hurried off to see for himself. He put his head down and raced ahead softly, taking care not to wake up the village. The very last thing he wanted was to alert them all to his shame.

Y Gar examined the carbine which the ironsmith had thrust at him. A crossbow was better, thought Y Gar. *All* the old ways. No one called to the birds anymore, except for him. And when they whispered about the planting, it wasn't as softly as before, just like Y Blo had said. And everyone wore these uniforms, when air and sun were all a man needed, and a breechcloth for decency' sake. Soon they'd be wearing teeth that clacked, just like Lovelace, and wouldn't that be a pretty sight, never mind the spirits' anger. Traditions were always best, thought Y Gar, and traditions had been going fast since the Americans had arrived. If only *they* would go instead! It's not a crossbow, thought Y Gar, as he felt the carbine carefully, running his hand along its stock. Then he drew back the bolt and opened the gate.

As for the ironsmith's naughty wife, it was the one night that she wasn't.

After the trouble with the snag, things had gone so smoothly for Dung that he had snipped thru. He came thru eager to place the charges and hurry back. He came thru scared and feeling alone. He came thru unscathed except for a slight scratch on his rear.

Dung came thru and looked around and gathered his wits. The guards were still sleeping, the planes were still waiting. He got to his feet and he plunged forward low to the ground. The seat of his pants flapped as he bounced and there was a nice, cool breeze on his bottom. He reached the planes undetected, a step or two behind the others.

Just as he did, a radio suddenly squealed from somewhere, he didn't know where and he didn't know it was a radio. But there was this squeal, shrill and setting his flesh to crawl, and he dropped to the ground. He lay there with his nose to the dirt, feeling more alone than ever, waiting to hear how it would turn out. It turned out to be the radio, and the squealing stopped when it was tuned to the right frequency, and then the volume dropped below hearing. So Dung got to his feet again and finally set about placing the charges.

The placing went fast, and when it was done, he couldn't believe that it had all gone so easily. The scratch, after all, was only a scratch, and the guards still slept, and the charges were placed. It was time to hurry back. So Dung plunged forward low to the ground, and the seat of his pants flapped as he bounced, and it felt nice and cool on his bottom, and Dung reached the fence still undetected, a step or two behind the others. Everything was going great.

He got back to the fence. And then the hole! *He couldn't find the hole!* The radio suddenly squealed again and the guards stirred and where was the hole!? Where!? Where!? There to the left? No, not to the left! Then where!? Where!? Here to the right? No, not to the right! Then where!? Where was it!? Where was the hole!? Dung looked and looked, and things looked grim, and they got worse; he was at his wit's end. It squealed, and the guards were on their feet, *and he couldn't find the hole!*

Dung, poor Dung, tore at the wire in search of his hole. The others were thru. All his life he had always been a step or two behind the others. Poor Dung gripped onto the wire and tried to tear the wire apart, never mind tearing in search of his hole. All his life he had been picked for the nasty work and not someone else. He rattled the fence in search of his hole, and tripped a flare, and the sector around him burst into light. The guards weren't so sleepy now. They ran up fast, spraying, ratta-tat-tatting everything inside the light, with Dung there rattling away on the fence.

When it was over, the guards moved away. They saluted themselves for their vigilance, for turning back the assault on the airfield, for snuffing it out before it began. They moved away, roundly slapping each other. They moved away to make their report, to tell what a fine job they had done.

They moved away while there on the fence, tangled hopelessly in the wire, there drilled thru his grinning ass, on his hands and knees bleeding to death, there still trying to find his hole was poor conscripted Dung.

* * *

"What a godawful war it's turned out to be." Culpepper said it and he yawned.

"That's what happens," said Jasperson. "They all turn out so." Jasperson was sleepy too, but he had to sit there and guard thru the night.

"I've been looking at bugs, Jasperson. I've been thinking of them."

"Yeah, what about them?" asked Jasperson, who was keen on hearing Culpepper out, tho not especially keen on bugs.

"We're just like them, Jasperson. Dung heap and all."

"Yeah, what about it?"

"Everything!" Culpepper shivered and tugged at his zipper. "You ever seen bugs just crawling all over a big heap a' dung? Just swarming all over? You've seen 'em, I know. Drawn to the dung and hooked on the smell and yet all the while bewildered too. Just marching up and marching down and back and forth and getting nowhere. You following?"

"Yeah, yeah, I'm following—but I ain't getting nowhere, too."

"That's it, Jasperson! That's just what I mean! You, too. You and me and all of us. We're just like them. Up and down and back and forth and getting nowhere. We're drawn and bewildered just like them—just like the bugs. We're crawling all over a dung heap like them."

Jasperson wasn't saying a word. He was nodding his head to keep Culpepper going, taking company from his voice. He was nodding but he wasn't convinced that he was crawling up and down and back and forth, over a dung heap or anything.

"You know, Jasperson, it frightens me bad. I get this quivery feeling at times—you know, one of those deep lurking feelings."

"Yeah, I know."

"I get this feeling everything's gonna get still more godawful—a lot more godawful, maybe soon—that we're about to be squashed down good. Ground so deep down into the dung that we'll never get out. Buried in it. What do you think?"

"That you sound demonized, that's what I think." Jasperson sighed and shook his head and clicked his tongue. "Maybe you better go squat with Y Blo, so as he can make 'em scat."

"Make what scat?"

"The demons, of course."

"Jasperson, you know better than that," said Culpepper sighing and shaking his head. "I'm a man of science, of medicine. I couldn't go squat with that sly old fake."

"Okay, you couldn't, but anyway—"

"Besides, he doesn't like me so much."

"Yeah, okay, but I'm not so sure he is a fake and, anyway, you got a point. He *has* been doing some bashing lately, Charlie has, what with Fritz and Goodbody too."

"No, not Charlie! Not Charlie at all!"

"Whaddaya mean, not Charlie at all? The squashing, Culpepper, you just said."

"It's not Charlie that's squashing us down. It's the situation, generally, and it's us—our big feet, our own damn weight—that's pushing us thru."

"The situation," said Jasperson sighing and shaking his head, "start with that."

"Well the situation, generally, is that it stinks, doesn't it? Nobody cares except Charlie and us and I don't know why us. Nobody really. Not the peasants, Jasperson. Not the ones in Saigon—except who's getting rich off the war or making a name or something. Nobody cares and especially ARVN, it doesn't care. Nobody wants to stand up and fight. Nobody sees anything worth standing up and fighting for. Nobody and especially ARVN and that's the general situation."

"Well, Culpepper, that's probably true but hell, what did you expect? That the gooks should stand up and fight for themselves? That's why we're here—to do it for them. Gooks just don't stand up and fight."

"Hey, Jasperson, have you forgot? They're gooks, too. The VC are gooks. And they're standing and fighting, huh—what with Fritz and Goodbody, too. So how does that grab you? Whatta you think?"

It was quiet in the hut. A barking deer sounded off in the distance.

"It's a matter of huffiness, Jas'."

"Yeah—sure—huffiness."

"We're in a huff. And Charlie too, he's in a huff. But ARVN, it's not in so big a huff about what the war is all about. Not all those lazy jokers, Jas'. Not the ones who get yanked from the paddies and stuck into uniforms 'stead of mud—"

Jasperson nodding.

"Maybe we been exaggerating, seeing doom where it's not. Because, regardless of what happens, Jas', their lives will stay about the same. All those lazy jokers, Jas'—"

Jasperson nodding.

"So what's there to get worked up about, maybe that's what they're saying, Jas'. Just because the Americans are big and clumsy and stupid enough to go out of their way and get themselves killed. Follow me?"

"Yeah—sure—huffiness."

"Listen, Jas', what are we doing here anyway?"

"We were asked."

"Yeah? By whom?"

"The people, of course."

"The Government, that's what you mean."

"Same thing, isn't it? It stands for the people."

"But what if it doesn't? What then? What if it stands for only who's fat, and wants to stay fat, and who maybe wants to get fatter still?"

"Yeah—sure—"

"What then?"

"Yeah—sure—but what about big feet and all that weight?"

"Huh, Jas'? What big feet? What's this weight?"

"You just said. How it's squashing us down."

"Yeah, Jas'—well, it's like this. The more weight, the more we step thru and sink in deep. Isn't that right? And with more of us coming every day and stepping down harder every day, huffy and all—"

"If it was really a big old cowpie, then maybe—just maybe—we'd step thru and sink. But it's land and people and not just a cowpie. Not really a cowpie."

"But it is, Jasperson, it really is. Land and people can be a big cowpie. It's just as easy to stomp right in and squush right down and get stuck in the muck. It's just as easy with land and people. It's gonna happen. It's happening now. We're gonna be squashed, I feel it bad."

The barking deer barked. Nothing further was said. Culpepper decided to hit the sack. He left Jasperson to guard thru the night and stepped outside.

Culpepper stood there in front of the ops hut and watched himself sizzle on the ground. He watched the steam rise, and followed its drift thru the crisp night air, and saw something slinking in the shadows and racing across the open ground. Whatever it was, whoever it was, Culpepper whirled to follow it and watered his leg. Culpepper swore, he hurried and finished and tucked himself in, then grabbed up his gun and took off in pursuit.

Whatever it was, whoever it was, it suddenly stopped at the foot of a longhouse, looking about and sniffing the air for things unseen. Then it started to climb up to the ledge, as softly, as sneakily as it could. Culpepper shouted and froze it a moment, but then it continued to climb. He shouted again but this time it didn't even stop. It started to dart into the house and Culpepper dropped it with one shot. It was, of course, the ironsmith.

* * *

Sergeant Moon sighed his relief. His sigh turned to mist in the chill musty air. He closed his lids, pressing them back against his eyes, trying to squeeze out some of the tension. Ban Me Thuot had just acknowledged his airstrike request and now he was waiting for confirmation, hunched there over the radio, with the earphones hugging his head. He was waiting to hear when the planes would be on their way to Buon Yun and how long it would take.

It was dank inside the commo bunker, clammy inside. The earthen walls had once been newly covered with burlap, but now the burlap hung rotted and peeling, sloughed by the walls. A naked bulb hung over Moon's head and the radio, glowing a feeble yellow. Moon flexed his fingers and his wrist to keep them limber for the key. He worked his right fist just like he was squeezing a hard rubber ball. Moon was bare-footed, his feet were cold, and he was feverish with excitement. No boots, no jacket, still no word from Ban Me Thuot. Moon was cold and he was hot. What's keeping them!? What!? What!? What the hell's keeping Ban Me Thuot!?

Moon strained to hear thru the earphones. He pressed them tight up against his head. But the sounds of the fighting came thru just the same—from outside the bunker and up on top—yelling, cracking, booming sounds. And, anyway, there was no Ban Me Thuot. Moon squirmed in his seat, and his feet were cold, and he felt wretchedly ignorant about what was happening up on top. He was dying to get up there himself. He was panting, he was practically foaming to finish down in the commo bunker and rush to the top to play his part. It's trickling! It's trickling! It's fast trickling down! He didn't want to miss out.

Confirm, goddammit! Confirm! Confirm! Moon stamped his feet because they were cold, and because he didn't know what else to do, and he blew on his hand to keep it limber. Confirm! Confirm! He knew it would be a matter of minutes, maybe seconds, before the VC realized their lapse, and then either tore the antenna down, or else came storming into the bunker after him, or even both. Come on, you guys, goddammit confirm! Moon's words tore thru his teeth. They begged to be heard. Oh, how he didn't want to miss out!

Moon's fear of missing out was something Rhadeo couldn't quite figure. He sat there in the bunker with Moon and wondered about Moon's anxiousness, how intense he could be. Since there was nothing to do but wait, he also wondered about all the strange and marvelous things that Moon had described. He wondered about the people who lived in houses of snow and chewed their boots; or who lived in the sand and veiled their women and prayed five times; of ships that traveled from star to star, and whether A'de minded that, or if Moon wasn't making it up; of gypsy wagons, and holy men who walked on coals, and that the world spun round like a top, as he had told the notables, and kangeroos with pouches. He also wondered about Sergeant Fritz being fixed to the ground, if now they would put him under glass, lay him out like his butterflies.

Next to Moon, he had liked Sergeant Fritz. He had liked going out on patrol with them, prowling the forest, because Moon let him pretend they were searching for the Nile, and Fritz let Moon. Rhadeo liked being part of the Strike Force, carrying the radio and talking to people you couldn't see. It was all a great game, these bodiless voices, and searching for the source of the Nile, and not being able to laugh if Y Bong stepped out of his boots or call to the monkeys, and there was the M-1 that stood as high and weighed about as much as he did.

Now Fritz was gone and Moon wasn't quite the same anymore. He had always been a quiet one, but always asking questions too: like didn't the ancestor spirits get cramped inside their dew drops, or what kind of grip A'de used on the rope. But Moon had become quieter still after Saigon. There was a hurt or a bitterness back of his smile, or the beginnings of cynicism; Rhadeo didn't know it for such, but he could sense the change. They still skipped stones across the river, and sat by Y Blo as he worked at his magic, and talked about girls, if not as much; but now there were times when Moon was there and yet he wasn't. Rhadeo sighed, and patted his harmonica, and wished he could have helped his friend.

"Help me, for Chrissake, Rhadeo! Get on the hand-crank!" shouted Moon. BMT had come back on the air; the power had all of a sudden gone dead. "Get on the hand-crank, Rhadeo!"

Little Rhadeo was confused. He wasn't sure what was expected of him.

"The hand-crank! The hand-crank!" shouted Moon. "The goddamn hand-crank! Get on the hand-crank!"

But Little Rhadeo still wasn't sure.

So Sergeant Moon got out of his seat, and picked up the boy, and sat him down hard on the seat of the hand-crank generator. It was the kind of generator that had to be turned manually, that had to be cranked, to power the radio, the transmitter. The faster the generator was cranked, the more it powered. So having seated Rhadeo, Moon leaped back onto his own, wild to answer Ban Me Thuot, while the boy began to crank.

"Faster! Faster!" shouted Moon. Not enough power was coming thru. "Faster! Faster! Faster!" he shouted, head down, barefooted, working the key. Trying to get thru himself. Trying to get the airstrike confirmed. "Faster! Faster!" shouted Moon, all hunched over, and stamping his feet, and desperate to finish and get to the top. "Faster! Faster! Faster!" he screamed, as BMT kept repeating its call, asking if Buon Yun was still there. "Faster! Faster! Goddammit, faster!"

Sergeant Moon whirled in his seat—Moon who had anguished over Phan and over Sergeant Goodbody too, and now that the boy was cranking so slow—Moon spun around to find out why and to get him to speed it up. He spun just in time to catch the boy's smile, and the harmonica there in his pocket, and the flash.

Moon pitched down, having seen these three things, and as he did, as he fell open-mouthed thru the chill dank air, Moon didn't see all his life flash by in one speeding frame after another. He didn't even think of Phan, about her making the shadows for him, or wanting to see the Kandy bear, or anything. Or that he was sorry he'd taken the time to teach Rhadeo the harmonica. That he wanted it back, his harmonica too. Or that he hadn't understood about there being another M'bu. All Moon thought about as he pitched down was that he didn't want to miss out, but that he was going to after all.

* * *

"So good to see you, Colonel Nutley."

"It's not so good at all, Colonel Quoc."

"Please you must sit. I send for tea."

"Listen, Quoc, it's about Buon Yun."

Quoc barked out something to an aide.

"Quoc, dammit, listen to me. Buon Yun is under heavy attack. We've got to do something. Something fast."

"Please you must sit. Better to sit."

"You've got to order up the troops. Maybe a Ranger company. Maybe two."

"Very dangerous to drive to Buon Yun. Very dark. There are enemies everywhere."

"We'll *fly* them, Quoc. We'll *fly* them there."

Colonel Quoc smiled. "The planes," he said, "they all boom-boom!"

"Not the choppers. They're not boom-boom."

"Much better first to sit and drink tea."

"I don't like tea. Listen, Quoc, they didn't touch the choppers, God knows. So let's haul ass, huh? Let's go!"

"First the tea," said Quoc as his aide hurried back.

"Didn't you hear? I don't like tea."

"Tea first, that is the custom."

"Dammit, Quoc, first things first! We don't have time."

"It is the custom," Quoc repeated, looking hurt.

"Listen, Quoc, Buon Yun needs troops. Troops first, you understand? Now are you gonna send them or not?"

"I can not do."

"Why not?"

"I do not have authority."

"Dammit, Quoc, you're in command!"

"Not quite, Colonel Nutley. There is the chart."

"The chart, Colonel Quoc?"

"The Astrological Ministry chart."

"What the—!?"

"The chart advises to stay at home."

"Listen, Quoc, what's a chart? Now are you gonna send them or not?"

"I do not have authority."

"Listen, Quoc, so maybe you don't. This is no time to play it cute. There's boys out there, American boys, and they'll be dead if we don't haul ass. So are you gonna send them or not? Dammit, Quoc, these are uncommon times!"

"Not so uncommon, Colonel Nutley. For eighteen year, we having war. Many boys dead, Vietnamese boys."

"Listen, Quoc, it's *this* year now. And those are American boys out there. So are you gonna call up the troops? They could all be killed, those American boys. The troops, Quoc, what do you say?"

Colonel Quoc sipped at his tea.

"Huh, Quoc? What do you say?"

"The troops must stay for Ban Me Thuot."

"Dammit, Quoc, you've got thousands of troops in Ban Me Thuot. No one's gonna hurt Ban Me Thuot. Just give us a few."

Quoc sipping. Nutley waiting.

"Come on, Quoc. A couple a' hundred."

Now just because Quoc insisted on customs, because he felt times were run-of-the-mill, didn't mean that he didn't have feelings. He had his share like everyone else. He appreciated Nutley's dilemma, Nutley's concern for the boys out there, and wanted to give him a bit of good cheer. So even if it meant loss of face, Colonel Quoc happily made his concession—almost too happily it seemed. "Yes, Colonel Nutley, thousands of troops. Lots of troops. But each troop not so brave and strong like American boy," Quoc conceded generously. "So I need all thousands here."

"Goddammit, Quoc, for the very last time, are you gonna call up the troops or not!? Call them up!"

Quoc got rather heated himself. "Call them up! Don't call up! You own the place, so you both think—!"

"Both?" asked Nutley.

"Crashing here! Sneaking there! And when he gets lost, find him, you say!"

"By the way, what did you find?"

"He just disappeared, who knows? Who needs you, so I ask!? Poking into everything! At least why don't you mind your own business? It's not polite. He's not polite, that Captain Yancy. So what if a man sells some rice here and there?"

"Rice?" asked Nutley.

"And with the *Moi!* Why do you love the *Moi* so much? They're dirty and stupid and they stink. Why not us!? *I* know why," he answered himself. "It's because you're very religious."

"Religious?" asked Nutley.

"Exactly!" said Quoc. "It's just like with the Communists."

"The troops, are you gonna send them or not?"

"You each have a certain vision," said Quoc, "how things should be. You like to take people and make them into something else."

"What's this religion?" asked Colonel Nutley. "There are no monks or priests or such."

"What do you think this Yancy is? Or this Casper who seems to have disappeared? Or Mac Dong Dong, the ugly-faced one?"

"The troops, Quoc—"

"Religion," said Quoc, "is a very bad thing, a hungry thing. It eats up everything in its path. All this crashing here and there, all the sneaking. You're making yourselves at home, Colonel Nutley, and not even stopping to wipe your feet."

"Who? Us?"

"Communists! You! It's all the same!"

"Why the *Moi?*"

"I was raised in a hut with dirt for a floor, but I know how to wipe my feet!"

"Why the *Moi?*" asked Nutley again. "Why do we want to eat them up?"

"Because they're so digestible."

"But you said they're tough and bitter and stinky."

"Yes, yes, of course they are! But simpler fare. Simpler than us."

"Than you?" asked Nutley.

"Than us!" said Quoc. "Isn't it clear!?"

Nutley mumbled that it wasn't.

"We're game, too. All of us! But *Moi* go down easier."

"Easier?"

"Do you take me for a fool?"

Nutley mumbled that he didn't.

"Colonel Nutley," Quoc confessed, "people may think I'm somewhat hard, and shifty too. Rooting out Communists, trampling them down. And with Americans, having a little joke on them. But it's to keep us from being eaten. It's for that." Then Quoc shook his head. "I'm really not so terrible. Sometimes when I pass a beggar, I don't spit, and maybe even give him a coin. And once when I sent a man away because he was a Communist, I let his family go along. And other things."

"By the way," said Colonel Nutley, who was embarrassed by Quoc's confession, "are you gonna send them or not?"

"I'm not so terrible at all."

"By the way," repeated Nutley, "what about the troops for Buon Yun?"

"I can not do."

"Yeah, sure, we've been thru that."

"According to the worthy chart—"

Nutley reached out and grabbed Quoc by the neck. It hadn't looked like much of a neck, and Nutley was surprised by its toughness. "Listen, Quoc, we're paying your way! Those boys out there are American boys, and we're paying your way!" Nutley was showing who was who, and squeezing Quoc's throat, when Quoc cried out hoarsely: "The black pajamas! The black pajama bottoms!" he cried.

Colonel Nutley stopped choking Quoc. He loosened his hand reluctantly. What did Quoc know of the black pajamas!? How could he know!?

What Quoc seemed to know was that Nutley had this secret stashed away in his room. He had been hoarding VC pajamas, the bottoms of them, taken from VC killed in Dar Lac, stitching them into one great roll of riddled black cloth. He knew that, one day, a VIP would arrive from the States. Sooner or later, all of them came. And when he did, he would meet the VIP at the airfield and roll out the long black carpet for him. And when the man wondered about the black cloth that stretched almost from the plane to the fence, Nutley would tell how the cloth was made from VC pajamas, from the bottoms, from all the VC killed in Dar Lac. And when the man wondered even more, Nutley would tell its significance: that the cloth was as great as their strides in the war, as black as their lousy enemy's heart, that every step he took down the cloth would be like a boot in the ass of Charlie. "Look how long it stretches, sir—almost from the plane to the fence. Many VC went into it, sir. Impressive, sir, isn't it?" Nutley had figured to feather his cap. He hadn't figured on Quoc finding out. He wanted it to be a surprise.

"Maybe you want it to be a surprise?" asked Colonel Quoc. "I keep secrets pretty good. I keep secrets very good if you drink tea, then leave me alone."

"But the men, Colonel Quoc, what about Buon Yun?"

"What about your surprise?"

"But those are American boys out there."

"Maybe it isn't American boys you care about? Maybe it's all those VC pajamas. Enough to stretch, for sure, to the fence."

"I don't know what you're talking about."

"Come now, Colonel, have some tea."

TALON AND CLAW

Youngfellow was yellow and on toward green. He tried closing his eyes, then pressing his head up against the cool glass, but neither helped. Youngfellow's color was on toward green because *Forever Samantha* rattled, shaking him up. She snorted and wheezed but mostly droned thru the clear night sky. She was arthritic, cantankerous, and she shook Youngfellow bad. But rattling or not, snorting and wheezing, *Forever Samantha* flew straight ahead, sped to the rescue. She seemed dead sure of the way.

Aside from getting on toward green, Youngfellow was cold and frightened of something, he didn't know what. As a war correspondent, he thought he had gotten control of his fears, the ones that had to do with battle, and so he had. But the fear he felt now was more a premonition than fear, and all the worse for being so vague. He wasn't sorry he'd come for the ride, but he wished that he were better prepared, don't ask him why. Why the war at all!? he thought, as they droned thru the clear night sky.

Youngfellow didn't hate the war the way some kids hated spinach, then grew up to live with it tolerably. Youngfellow's wasn't the kind of hate which slackened into tolerance, which one could learn to accommodate. It wasn't that kind of acceptable hate, not that kind at all. He hated the war intractably, grimly. He hated the war enough to risk the wrath of MACV.

Youngfellow was a dismal fellow; his grimness extended to all other things. He felt that to laugh was irrelevant—a luxury no one ought to enjoy in those troubled times, those imminently catastrophic times. Of course, he did laugh now and then in spite of his feelings on relevance. How could he help it? He was as human as anyone. But when he laughed, he laughed very grimly. To his credit, he wondered at times if he took himself too seriously. But there was nothing comic at all, *no sir,* about the war.

What was comic was how he had come to meet Smiley. Perhaps if his eyes had been off the ground, if he hadn't been so taken up with the briefing, with thinking back to the lemonade, cookies, and other confections, then Smiley wouldn't have run him down. But fed up with lies, however sweet, and chewing instead on bitter stuff, on his forebodings, he had almost been run down by Smiley. It happened as he had been walking south along the river, toward the floating restaurant there. It happened like this:

Smiley was pedaling as fast as he could, wild with joy, as Dong or Ding or whatever the hell came chasing him down Bach Dong Street, flailing his arms and squeaking at the top of his lungs. Smiley was pedaling ferociously, with his head down into the wind and his teeth bared, as Dong or Ding, or whatever the hell, came on gamely after him, head down too, gold teeth bared, shirttails straying out behind. The pedicab had given him trouble, and veered off course from time to time as Smiley's legs thrashed with the pedals. It was on one such lapse of control that he had almost run Youngfellow down. *Yahoo! Whoopee!* shouted Smiley. Rat-faced pig! squeaked Dong or Ding. When the pedicab man grew short of wind and heavy-legged, he began to lag and his shirttails to fold and the contest as well. So Smiley caromed to a stop against the curb, and waited for him. Pedaling flat out was not as much fun without Dong or Ding in hot pursuit. It was no challenge.

It wasn't till later, at the My Canh, that they introduced themselves. It was then that Smiley apologized, and the two became friends, and Smiley invited him up for a ride. "Hey, if you ever get to Nha Trang, I'll take you for a ride, okay?" Smiley had seemed a nice enough fellow, if somewhat possessed about the war, how it was his duty to strike Charlie down, whether it was fun or not.

"What's it like?" Youngfellow had asked, as they sat by a starboard window, listening to the wash of the river, and smelling the garbage, and watching the sampans. "What's it like, way up there, playing God with Charlie below?"

"Listen, Youngfellow," Smiley had answered, "it used to be something, really something. It used to be godawful great playing God. It used to be, but not anymore. The fun's all gone. I just go thru the motions now. And, anyway, it's not quite so."

"What's not so?"

"Charlie doesn't believe in God, and I don't either. Perched up there to strike down the godless and striking down more of the godly instead."

"I wouldn't have guessed you felt that way."

"Well, I do, I do feel that way. I feel pretty strongly about it— all this striking down left and right."

"So where was the fun, Smiley? *Why* the fun? About striking down Charlie or anyone."

"It had to be done, right? It has to be done. So why be so god-awful gloomy about it? Only I couldn't help getting gloomy, or more like bored. It was all the same. It is all the same."

"I don't get it, Smiley. First you come down on striking down. Then you say it has to be done, that it should be fun."

"Listen, Youngfellow, don't get me wrong. I'm down on striking down left and right. Not on striking down only left. The godless, see? It's gotta be done and I'm proud to do it, no matter if it's fun or not."

"No need to be proud."

"Why not? At least there're none of those goddamn mistakes. None of that striking down left and right."

It was then that Smiley excused himself, and left for his encounter with Phan.

* * *

It started as a far-off rumble, then became a louder one, then a chugging, then a clatter, then the light. It burst in a flash upon Buon Yun. It burst in a soft hissing explosion, but fell as a glare and silently. In the bottom rim of that explosion, the men on the ground were glued hard and fast, suspended for a fraction of time. Then they all unstuck themselves and dropped to the dirt as the light floated down. A solitary helicopter hovered above, come to drop flares, to light up Buon Yun.

What the sudden light had glued hard and fast was the 825th

banging together their sticks of bamboo, banging out clunky xylophone sounds, and firing away. What the light had also glued hard and fast was the village Strike Force, mostly bootless, ignoring the clunky xylophone sounds and firing back. The Americans too.

What the light didn't have to glue hard and fast, because they were already stuck, were all the lumps, all the dead. As it floated gracefully down, the flare revealed the butchery. It lit up what was in the pot.

Buon Yun was a pot, a great iron cauldron. Buon Yun was full of hell's worst brew and it was surrounded by warty-nosed witches giving the brew a hearty stir. Witches cackling *heh-heh-heh* and stirring well, then tasting with their icy lips and making wry faces and deciding—*heh-heh-heh*—that worsening was needed. Those witches were stirring and making lumps that stirring usually didn't.

Buon Yun was lumpy with men who had fallen, who had stuck; it was slick with their blood. And those who hadn't fallen and stuck were running around possessed by demons or standing their ground, trying to fell and stick each other, trying to cancel each other out.

Not only the men were demonized, but the chickens and pigs, especially pigs. They were running amok and squealing their terror and neatly bowling men off their feet. They were stopping for nothing except for one sow, big-teated and black, which paused long enough to tug at the innards of one of the dead, rooting in them. His belly was open and so were his eyes, the dead man's were, wide to the sky, as if looking for the sun to shine—just like Fritz had always said. It was Lovelace stuck there and wide-eyed. So was Culpepper, but his eyes were closed.

The VC were banging their sticks of bamboo because the favors hadn't come. They were banging their sticks, but they weren't pleased—not with the sounds, not with the results. It wasn't driving anyone *yeowww!* and setting them to clambering. It wasn't causing anyone to fling his gun and run away. Gongs and klangs and horns and toots and those screechy, ratchety things from New

Year's—that's what they needed. They needed the favors. Things weren't going as well as they should—the back-up plan wasn't—not without the party favors.

Things had begun to sour from the start. The VC had started to file quietly thru the rear gate—nodding hello to Y Gar the hunter, thumping him warmly on the back—when Culpepper's shot had roused the village. The VC had planned to sneak up to the houses and seal them off—also the American huts—and then to gun down everyone inside. But Culpepper's shot had upset that plan as well as upsetting the ironsmith.

The back-up plan had been to come charging thru the rear gate, making all sorts of klanging, tooting, ratchety sounds and driving the people up a wall, to flinging their guns and running away. But the favors hadn't come, and they had to substitute sticks of bamboo, and all they made was a clunky sound. That's why things weren't going as well. So what they were doing was banging on their sticks anyway, and running around or being knotted by the gate, and hoping for the best. Well at least the gate had been opened for them. At least they hadn't needed the tubes. Not before, anyway. But now, they could have used it now, knotted as they were!

When Y M'dhur had heard the firing break out sooner than expected, he had assumed that his mates were thru and into Buon Yun and already executing the plan. So he had gotten to his feet, leaving things lay, with the fence unbreached and all the people trapped inside. They had to be perfected, right? Y M'dhur had run to take part. But what with the VC being knotted and so many dead, he would have run back to breach the fence, but, of course, he was dead too.

So they banged their sticks, making xylophone sounds; and some were deep into Buon Yun; and others were driving hard on their way; and there was a sizable knot at the gate, just inside, clogging up the gateway so tight that a few were even backed outside, waiting their turn impatiently. They were like hotshots on carnival night lined up in front of the shooting stall.

The VC were knotted at the rear gate because the Strike Force was making a stand, not being impressed with the xylophone sounds. They were making a stand, and stubbing their bootless toes on the lumps, because they were brave, and because there was no place else to go, and because it was only a clunky sound. It wasn't an orderly stand they were making, but rather haphazard. It was a sort of every man running around and making his own private stand.

The women and children were down on the floor inside the houses; the matted bamboo walls didn't help. Or else they were flat down on the ground beneath the houses, which was better. Or running around like everyone else, which was worse than being inside.

Grizzled Y Bun was out there making his stand with the others, bootless and otherwise disrepaired and wearing his shiny silver medal. He was leading his people, and sorry that he had led them to this, and feeling the specters thrashing it out against his skull. Y Bun was fighting for his life, and out of pride, and because his people had given their trust. He was fighting fiercely, valorously, as he had fought years before; but this was worse, for now all the fighting was here in his home, and worst of all, because he wasn't so young anymore and already he was growing weary. The shiny silver medal helped.

One-eared Y Blo was out there too, with his head thrown back and his eyes shut tight and his arms shot high. He was raking the air with his scaly hands and jabbering. Taking on all the countless spirits that hovered and lurked. Maligning them. Jabbering that they had promised him it was going to be the most overwhelming season ever. Jabbering that they had danced for him. Asking what happened. Getting no answers. Clawing at them for letting him down. Jabbering, too, about the teeth. That Lovelace's teeth were surely to blame.

They were all running around, the VC and the villagers, except for the knot by the rear gate and except for who was keeping it there. Everyone was running around and bumping together and canceling each other out; it might have been two VC or two villagers, who could tell in the dark? No one could really tell too well until the flares began to burst.

Yancy, Plunket, and Jasperson were all who were left of A-123, what with Lovelace looking for sunshine, and with Culpepper stuck there too, and whatever happened to Moon. They were trying to organize the Strike Force, which took some doing in the dark, and also trying to stay together, which made it doubly hard. Captain Yancy's square, dimpled chin had never seemed more staunchly set, and his eyes never so clear.

These were the moments for Captain Yancy, the ones for which he had been trained, the ones he had always looked forward to, the ones about his fiber. But tho he had always looked forward to them, Yancy discovered that these moments weren't really the moments for him. They were different and they were exciting and they tested his fiber, all right, but he wasn't eating them up. Yancy wasn't eating them up, savoring them, because there was no time. It was enough to stay alive and stay together and to organize the men. And also he wasn't eating them up because, from the one or two bites he had taken, the moments were bitter after all. They were too different, and they were more hectic than exciting, and they were gritty. They were wearing his fiber thin.

Plunket was worn pretty thin himself, because of events. Plunket was trying to stay with the others, and trying to organize the men, but most of all, more than Yancy, he was trying to stay alive. He gave that more attention than Yancy, because he wasn't also thinking about the moments, about how disappointing they were. Plunket had never looked forward to them. He was thinking, instead, about how events had been building up. Like the time when he hadn't asked for a shave, how bad that had been. And then when he had jammed one last fistful down Goodbody's throat and they had lain side by side watching the fire and the VC guns had burped, how that had been worse. And then there was now, which was worst of all. Whatever had been building up, it was getting there fast, all right.

Jasperson being the steadiest was steadier still—because he had neither moments nor events to ponder. Jasperson just got on with the job, cool as ever, except for one ankle, hot and swelling where Plunket had kicked. Jasperson got on cool and fluid, seeing only what had to be done, not disappointments, not what had built up. Certainly not what Culpepper had meant. Not even what was begging attention. Jasperson didn't stop to look either.

So there in the light was the butchery. There in the pot were all the lumps, revealed and crying out for attention. Begging for it. Hey, you! And you! And you, too, mister! Hey, look at me! Please look at me! Look and see! But no one took the time to look, except maybe while hurdling one of the lumps. Each man had only time enough to look out for himself—to keep from falling and sticking too. Look at me! Please look at me! Look and see! But no one did.

The horror cried out begging attention, but no one attended, and so the butchery wasn't stopped or even reduced. It picked up instead. It took on order because of the flares. Now that the men could pick out who was who—at least where the eerie light floated down—now that they could *see* at last, the men didn't see what begged for attention, but only more men to cancel out.

The chopper danced high over Buon Yun, dropping flares left and right. It hopped and darted and skipped back and forth, trying to keep on top of the action and not getting hit and lighting up as much as it could. It skipped, dropping flares, and the flares sizzled, then burst into light, and the light was harsh as it first floated down, but as it dimmed it softened the night.

*　*　*

It was just as Smiley had said. The war was no longer fun for him. All the destruction, all the sameness day after day, made him feel brittle and stale and mouldy. The war numbed him thru and thru; it bored Smiley terribly, tho it hadn't always been so.

In the beginning, he had looked eagerly to each mission, excitedly. But later, in the heat of a strike, of a strafing run, all he felt was the longing to get it done. It wasn't, then, that he operated with any less efficiency. He was much too professional for that. And besides, he wanted to live, to return. It was that Smiley was no longer high. There was no more newness, no more excitement, not even fear, for enemy flak was not what it would later become.

There was only something thick and sluggish, something sedimentary, settled down inside him.

That's why he had gone to Saigon, that's why he had borrowed the cyclo and pedaled flat out: to celebrate life, to revel in it once again, to stir back up whatever had settled down inside, to get a good shake.

But Saigon was full of taxi drivers and street-corner boys whose sisters were number one cherry girls, and the mutilated and destitute, and other assorted casualties; it was the same, if perhaps not as bad, in all the cities of Vietnam. Smiley's eyes took it in. He was aware that things weren't right. But Smiley's seeing stopped with his eyes and not in his brain. He didn't bother to ask himself why things had gone wrong or how they should be. He wouldn't have known. All that Smiley knew for sure was that he needing a stirring up, but Saigon had only made things settle deeper.

And pedaling the cyclo had been a lark, but nothing more.

And as for the girl, she had this boyfriend who knows where, and anyway, he had gone and said it about the bear, that it wasn't really sugar-coated.

"It was bad what you said," she had said to him.

"Do you like animals?" he had then asked.

"I like animals very much. Soft little animals."

"What's your very favorite?"

"Muntjac is my favorite. I know story, sad old story. I should tell?"

"Please do," he said.

"One time, Kra and Bru have very same thought—"

"Who's that? Kra and Bru."

"Kra tiger. Bru eagle."

"Yeah, okay."

"They decide to give muntjac warm snug home—"

"The little deer, right?"

"Kra grab muntjac, and Bru too. 'Why you grab muntjac?' Bru ask. 'Why you grab muntjac?' Kra ask. They fight very mad. Poor muntjac, he right between. They fight to give him warm snug home. But they just want to eat him up. They fight and fight and pull him here and pull him there and pretty soon no muntjac left. Just big red spot. 'What happen to muntjac?' Kra ask. 'What happen to muntjac?' Bru ask—"

"Hey," he had asked, "when do you leave!?" To hell with these idiot animals!

"But the animals—?"

"Never mind them. When do you leave?"

"Pretty soon. It close at twelve."

"Do you live far?"

"Not so far."

"I'll come home with you, okay?"

But it hadn't been.

"I have boyfriend."

"Here in Saigon?"

"Not here. In Buon Yun."

"Look, if he's not here now—"

"You're very nice."

"I'll come home with you, okay—?"

"But it was bad what you said."

"How's that sound—?"

"About the bear."

"Yes? Okay?"

"No. I go home alone."

"But he's not here."

"No. He loves me very much."

"He'll never know."

"I love my boyfriend very much too."

"You're a lovely girl. Just to your door."

"I go alone. Better you sleep."

Captain Smiley was wide awake as *Forever Samantha* flew to the rescue. Everything would be different tonight. Saigon, the cyclo, the girl with the butterscotch smell, or vanilla, all these disappointments were past. Tonight he would get a good stirring for sure.

* * *

It was bound to happen and it did. It happened with a *Szzzzz-zzzz!* One of the flares landed on one of the thatched longhouse roofs and *Szzzzzzzz*ed on the roof and set it to fire. It was touch and go for a while, sputtering up and pooping down, then up again. It was during the rainy season and the straw was taking hard. So up and down the fire went, till it finally sputtered up for keeps and sizzled out to either side, then crackled even farther out, and soon it was running the length of the roof. The people inside were down on the floor, heads to the floor, covering their ears with their hands, and so they didn't hear at first. That and all the shooting outside and the heat going up. It wasn't until the flames came eating down the walls that the people understood.

Then it was women shrieking and clutching up their babies, and big children clutching up smaller ones, and everyone rushing out onto the ledge and pulling the old ones after them. Once on the ledge, it was down to the ground, and the fastest way down was to jump. So everyone did. The old ones were stiff-limbed and scared to jump, and bit their fists, and hung back until the press was too much, and when they jumped, they cracked their hips and cracked their legs and lay there flopping. The children jumped and landed better, except that for them the jump was longer, and so they banged themselves up too. The shrieking women jumped best of all and landed best, except for one who landed neatly upon her infant, crumpling its head, which set her to shrieking even more.

The longhouse was up in flames, and people were jumping left and right, breaking things, and the VC were firing into them. They aimed and fired impersonally, as if the people were so many rats, burned out from a heap of straw.

❋   ❋   ❋

"What's her name?"

"Can't recall."

"Where'd you say?"

"Forget that too."

"Too bad."

"Easy to find, tho."

"Then you'll go back?"

"Not a chance."

"How come?"

"Like I said."

"Her boyfriend, huh?"

"That's it."

"Maybe next time."

"Yeah—maybe."

"I'd go back."

"Yeah—you would."

The men were quiet after that, thinking their thoughts. Young-fellow thought about the strides. "Colonel Crocker," he had said, "these body count figures, how accurate are they? I know of several actions in which the true enemy body count was multiplied by a factor of three—"

"Mr. Youngfellow—"

"And several in which civilians were listed among the dead, the enemy dead. Add in all those dead civilians, multiply by a factor of three, and—"

"Mr. Youngfellow, you must realize that the enemy makes every effort to drag off its dead. I suppose, to compensate for this fact, some of our units may have reported more enemy dead than were actually counted. And as for civilians being included, I assure you it's not deliberately done. As you must also realize, it's often very difficult to tell a civilian from a VC, to tell the dead. It's very easy to make a mistake. We're all allowed a mistake now and then."

"If it's easy to make a mistake with the dead, then it's just as easy with the living. Isn't that so?"

"No, it's not."

"Our units are under instruction to produce statistics, favorable ones—to make a better showing regarding the enemy, the number killed—"

"There's no such instruction."

"Then under pressure. It's all the same."

"It's not the same. They've been instructed only to take more initiative in seeking out the enemy. That's why there's been more enemy dead. As for civilians," continued Crocker, "it's hard to tell just any old peasant from a VC. Our boys in the field are targets, sir. They can be shot just as easily, just as effectively, by some harmless-looking farmer as by a known VC. It makes the same hole, it certainly does. So, occasionally—but only very occasionally—an innocent farmer or two might get killed. But who's to judge? Maybe this farmer's arm was cocked suspiciously. What would your reaction be?"

"Look, Colonel Crocker, I'm not contending with any of that. I can appreciate those things. It's something else I have in mind. That maybe we're headed down the road toward something we haven't bargained for, something catastrophic. First, there's the zeal—"

"What zeal, Mr. Youngfellow?"

"The zeal in response to the instruction, the one to come up with better statistics—"

"Wrong! To take more initiative!"

"It's all the same."

"It's *not* the same."

"First there's the zeal. Then there's the fact that it's hard to tell just any old peasant from a VC. So the more zeal, the more civilians killed and included in the count—"

"Not so at all!"

"Zeal, then civilians mistakenly killed and included in the body count, then the multiplication by three—"

"Wrong again!"

"Then there's the trait."

"What trait!?"

"The national trait. The one that progress must go on, no matter where. So new instructions go out to the field—to come up with even better statistics—"

"No, not so! Initiative!"

"So then it starts all over again—the zeal, the mistakes, the civilians counted, the multiplication, the trait and around we go once more. Only now, since everything's more, there's also more civilians killed. Among other things, we're fighting this war with statistics, sir, with the most glowing we can produce. It's good psywar strategy, isn't it? Not so much on the Viet Cong, as on all the folks back home."

"Mr. Youngfellow—"

"This policy, Colonel—this stress on figures—doesn't it all contribute to killing far more civilians than we would believe—than is tolerable?"

"No, it doesn't!"

"Okay, let's say it doesn't. But couldn't it affect the men—to ask fewer questions—to take more for granted—to figure 'aw, what the hell a gook is a gook is a Viet Cong?' *Couldn't* it?"

"No, it couldn't!"

"Damn it, Colonel, these instructions, couldn't they be misinterpreted, overly so?"

"Mr. Youngfellow, just what the hell are you suggesting!?"

"That we're headed down the road toward something catastrophic—toward something we haven't bargained for."

"Mr. Youngfellow—Damn it, Youngfellow, hear me out! Gentlemen, it is the policy of this Command to be as considerate of civilians as we can. As for killing them, it's not allowed. These instructions—I never heard of such things. This implication that we send quotas out to the field—it's preposterous. This catastrophe—it's unthinkable, absolutely unthinkable."

While Youngfellow thought about the strides and how it wasn't unthinkable, Smiley was thinking about whats-her-name and what it was. There was still time—not much, but some—before he had to think of Buon Yun. He didn't like to think about things too far in advance. He felt loose and sharp as he flew *Samantha* to the rescue. His chin jut a perfect ninety degrees. His hands were unyielding at the controls and, in fact, were gripping them tighter. He usually flew *Forever Samantha* without regard for what lay ahead, and that's the way he was flying her then.

Smiley was growing rather excited. He hadn't been for a very long time—except for when he had pedaled head down into the wind, with Dong or Ding or whoever he was chasing behind, and that didn't count. Maybe it was Youngfellow back there, because he wanted to show Youngfellow a trick or two. Or maybe it was because of Saigon, because of the girl, because he hadn't resolved a thing. Smiley hated things unresolved. He liked things to be one way or the other. He liked them neatly tied off at the ends. He wanted something resolved that night.

Smiley sat checking his instruments and trying to recall whats-her-name. He had this trouble seeing Vietnamese as people, at least the way he saw Americans. That's why he couldn't keep their names straight, or even remember them at all. It gnawed at his mind: whats-her-name? It was Smiley's neatness again. Now that Youngfellow had brought up her name, Smiley wanted it resolved. Her name, goddammit, what was her name? They were getting very close.

✱ ✱ ✱

It was bound to happen and it did. First it threatened for a time, whooshing up, flicking out its many tongues and shaking off sparks, then falling back. But finally it whooshed high enough, two of its tongues flicked out far enough, and the fire leaped across to the houses on either side. *Snap!* went the houses. *Crackle! Pop!*

"I told you! I told you!" went Y Blo. "If only he had come with his dream!"

There was shrieking and scrambling and hips being cracked and the VC taking careful aim. Plunket saw what was happening and ran up to help. He ran up even tho, most of all, he was trying to stay alive. Yancy and Jasperson ran up too, to help the people down from the ledges and also because Plunket was there. They were trying to stay together.

It was hot and bullets were whizzing by, as the three reached up and swung down the children and the old ones, leaving them to their own on the ground. It was thirsty work and Plunket was wishing for a Coke. He was swinging one old man down from the ledge, the one who had been so discomposed by Lovelace's teeth, when suddenly he gave up his grip and clapped his hands over his face as if the glare from the flames was too bright. Plunket clapped halfway thru his swing, and the old man, of course, went sailing and landed *kerplunk!* on the ground. The old man rattled as he landed and muttered something which wasn't nice.

Plunket, himself, dropped to the ground, square on his knees, and scratched at his face. He thought he was blind but he wasn't sure. It was too wet to tell. Plunket didn't want to be sure. But he was sure enough to panic, *almost* panic. He didn't go over. He stayed at the edge, holding back. A bullet had skipped across his brow, shaving bone and filling his eyes with the spill from above—with the blood. But Plunket knew only that it was wet and that he couldn't see.

He stayed at the edge and didn't go over in spite of the heat and bullets whizzing and people rushing by every whichway, bumping him, and some landing almost on top of him and others flopping nearby on the ground. He stayed right there, down square on his knees, feeling his face. He kneeled there, at the foot of the longhouse, taking the bumps, and calmly screamed for Yancy or for Jasperson—if you can imagine such a thing.

When Yancy and Jasperson realized what happened, they also stopped swinging halfway thru, letting their old men land *kerplunk!*, and rushed to his aid. They grabbed Plunket up by either arm and started to haul him away from the action, which was going rather bad. They had just begun to haul him away, when suddenly out of the southeastern sky, *Forever Samantha* swooped down on Buon Yun. She screamed right over their heads.

The fighting didn't really pause. All the mad scrambling of women and children, all the swirling around of the men, it didn't stop. Not even for a fraction of time. But everyone flicked his head to the sky and wondered what the plane meant to him. They all flicked up together.

* * *

Ha-ha-ha! It was worse than he had expected, yet it wasn't all that bad. Ha-ha-ha! The VC must have hit the power. There were no perimeter lights. There was no directional arrow pointing toward the enemy's strength. There wasn't even radio contact. Not one single friggin' response. Ha-ha-ha! But there was the chopper. That and the flares. They almost made up for all the rest. Ha-ha-ha! He had to laugh.

Smiley concluded that it was worse but not all that bad as he pulled *Samantha* out of her dive. The comic bastards! Ha-ha-ha! Oh what a sight! Ho-ho-ho! He laughed tho he supposed he shouldn't. Ha-ha-ha! He laughed because they had looked so funny, the way he had taken them by surprise; the way everything had suddenly flickered, jerked all at once—*pppppppt—pppppppt* —like worn old film spit thru a projector.

He also had to laugh at the chopper, the way he had almost tickled its belly, swooshing in right under it. Ha-ha-ha! He must have scared the hell out of them! Oh-ho-ho! It tickled him pink that he had almost tickled the chopper.

Aside from everything jerking at once, and aside from almost tickling the chopper, two things stuck sharpest in Smiley's mind from *Samantha's* first dive. One was a big knot of Viet Cong around what seemed to be a gate. Smiley could tell that they were Cong because they were firing into the place and because, tho he couldn't hear xylophone sounds, he could see they were trying to bang out a tune and who would do a thing like that except for maybe some crazy VC!

The other thing which stuck in his mind was the Beckoning Virgin. The light from the flares relieved the contours of the ground. It heightened the swells and deepened the hollows when come on obliquely. It made all the ground shapes leap right up, those that bulged; and those that dipped, it made them dip deeper.

Seen from above in that uncanny light—with all her bulges leaping right up and all her hollows dipping deep down—the Beckoning Virgin came alive, looked amazingly real. She looked like some newly ripe young girl waiting to be taken gently.

The way she lay, with her legs apart and with one arm flung out, beckoning, was just the way Smiley pictured her—whats-her-name. That was how *she* would have looked. Strange thing, Smiley thought, how he couldn't recall her name.

Smiley planned to cut it close. He planned to aim the bomb for the gate on his second dive. What with the chopper dropping flares, the light was enough. Some were already deep into Buon Yun, and others were driving hard on their way, and then there was that knot at the gate. Smiley was after that big knot of Cong. The houses closest to the gate, well they seemed far enough away. Captain Smiley made his plans as he leveled *Forever Samantha* out, and also he thought about whats-her-name, trying to recall it.

* * *

Maybe it was *Forever Samantha*—the confidence she gave them. Or maybe it just happened that way, with the VC growing tired from fruitlessly banging their sticks and taking heavy losses too. Whatever it was, the Strike Force rallied, a large group of them, about as large as the knot at the gate. They mustered their grit and all their last strength to drive the VC out of Buon Yun. They had taken many dead, and three of their houses were up in flames, and there was nothing else to do. Dead and flames and pigs neatly bowling them off their feet, and women and children madly scrambling, and old ones scrambling but not as well, cracking their hips and flopping about. There was nothing else.

So the Strike Force rallied, a large group of them, and started driving on the VC. They were led by Y Bun who, all of a sudden and much too late, had recalled what that tale had been about, who finally glimpsed the simple truth. It had all come back when *Forever Samantha* dived on Buon Yun, blacking out the light of the flare, just as he had seen great wings blacking the sun. The Strike Force rallied near the ops hut and started driving toward the rear gate. It was all or nothing; one way or the other. Everything hung on their drive to the gate. They were scared, more than before, more than if it had been the *m'klaks*. Scared because there was no turning back. Because it was one way or the other, and they didn't want it to be the other. So they drove with Y Bun at their head, with his medal proudly pinned on. They were the last hope of Buon Yun—they and *Forever Samantha*, of course—and they were gaining!—*gaining!*—GAINING!

While all this was going on, men were still madly swirling around, busy waging their own private wars, colliding where there wasn't light and canceling each other out.

Amidst the collisions, there was Y Blo raking the air, maligning the spirits for breaking their promise; and screaming at *Samantha*, too, telling her to mind the rope. There was the big-teated black sow, back at Lovelace, tugging away, rooting some more in Lovelace's innards. There were lumps and there were flames, and people driven out of their homes, and men driving toward the rear gate, and others colliding in the dark, and up above, over it all, there was the chopper skipping lightly back and forth, dropping its flares.

And down below in the commo bunker, most frightened of all, was Triple Threat. He was squatting there in the dark, his head bruised and tucked between his knees, his arms round his head. He was back up against the wall, touching the wall and shivering, not only because of its clamminess, but also because of the terror above and the terror keeping him company. That's why Triple Threat's forehead was bruised. He had stumbled over Sergeant Moon on his way in, striking his head hard upon the ground. Triple Threat knew it was Sergeant Moon because of the harmonica. He had felt the harmonica as he struck. Rhadeo had given it back.

* * *

And then there was *Forever Samantha*, with Smiley strapped in, trying to recall whats-her-name, and growing ever more excited, and Youngfellow too. Excitement was sweeping into him and whisking out all the yellow and swelling Youngfellow rosy instead. The sweeping had started a while back, very lackadaisically; then during *Forever Samantha*'s first dive, the sweeping had come on with a rush, choking Youngfellow full of joy. He had been too taken up with the dive, and with pulling out, and with coming around again, to bother about being rattled yellow. He was taken up right then.

Hmmmmmmm—MMMMmmmm—MMMMmmmm—MMMM-mmmm—

He pressed his head up against the glass as they came around. He pressed it straining to see down below, and not to cool his head this time. He pressed it to see how it would go on the second dive. He was awed that the second would be for keeps, that men would be bombed. That he—Youngfellow—was witness to it. He was thrilled.

Hmmmmmmm—MMMMmmmm—MMMMmmmm—MMMM-mmmm—

Youngfellow's pulse throbbed with *Samantha,* one with it, and he pressed his hand up against the frame, feeling one with *Samantha*'s skin. He was feeling part of events, what was happening, what was going to—part of *Samantha* coming around. He felt free and loose and very tight too. It was Youngfellow humming along, in tune with *Samantha*.

Hmmmmmmmm—MMMMmmmm—MMMMmmmm—MMMMmmmm—

But what with these feelings, he was also feeling ashamed, appalled at himself for being so joyful, for being so eager to see the bombs dropped and men as well. Not that Youngfellow really wanted to see bombs away!, but if there were going to be any bombing, then, of course, he wanted to see. It was the prospect of witnessing, the fact he was there, that gave him joy. It was his privileged seat in the house. It wasn't the bombing, itself, so much. No, not that!

Hmmmmmmmm—MMMMmmmm—MMMMmmmm—MMMMmmmm—

Nonetheless he felt ashamed, because to know joy at such a time, whatever the reason, was cause for shame. But shame or not, the thrill was there and wouldn't quit. It's me, Youngfellow, yesiree! He pressed his hand tight, feeling *Forever Samantha*'s skin, grafting his own skin onto it. Aw, hell! What a story he'd write!

Youngfellow wanted to scream out his joy, to open his valves and release some excitement, else he would burst! He wanted to scream out the pain, the suspense clutching him. Hell—aw, hell! He wanted to cut loose a crazy, high-pitched *Aghhhhhhhhhh!* of a scream. To roar from deep down. Or laugh like a goddamn lunatic. The laugh was lurking just inside his throat. That's how demonized he felt. It's me, Youngfellow, way up here! It's me speeding ahead to the rescue! Me who'll be right there on the spot! Me who'll see it for himself! Oh, what a story I'll write!

He pressed his nose against the glass, squashing it up, trying to get Buon Yun in his sights. Then he raised back his head and laughed to himself. It came out easily, lurking right there. Then he roared from deep down. Then he closed his eyes and balled up his fists and screamed out his joy, his suspense. It was a crazy, high-pitched scream. AGHHHHHHHHHHHHHH! he screamed.

"Hey, was that you!?" Smiley screamed back.

No answer.

"Hey! Hey! Was that you on the squawker!?"

Still no answer.

"Hey! Hey! You still back there!? What the hell!?"

"Still here! Still back here!"

"Hey, was that you!?"

"Me what!?"

"Whatever it was! Whatever you said!"

"Not a word!"

"Okay, well don't! Not now! Hang on! Here we go!"

Forever Samantha wheeled out of the west, screaming and cold-eyed and with talons bared. She came swooping down on Buon Yun. Smiley coaxed her steeper and steeper, getting *Samantha* angled in right. He gave her thrust. He pointed her nose straight for the gate. He brought *Samantha* down gleefully, just like he was head down into the wind and cycling flat out and being chased. He brought her down tickled pink over the chopper and everything jerking all at once. He pointed her nose straight for the gate, anxious to show Youngfellow back there a trick or two, and to resolve something that night, and also to recall whats-her-name. He bore *Samantha* down hard on Buon Yun.

Hmmmmmm—MMMMmmmm—MMMMmmmm—

Youngfellow bore down hard on his molars, humming along. He was taken up with *Samantha*'s dive, and with trying to force his eyes open wide, and with pressing forward to see out the glass. He was taken up with the weight pushing heavily down on his lids, half-shutting them, and driving hard against his chest, containing him, pressing him back into his seat while he was pressing forward. He was busy with that and with keeping tune. He hummed along and his ears hummed too, from *Samantha*'s vibrations, and so did his groin. It tingled from a hundred plunging elevators all at once. Me!—me!—it's me, Youngfellow!—humming and tingling and diving straight down! It's me diving down to the rescue! He had never dove to a rescue before, especially one so exciting as this.

Hmmmmmmm—MMMMmmmm—MMMMMmmmm—

Buon Yun came up fast now—faster and faster—rushing to meet *Samantha* halfway. *Samantha* screamed down, reaching out for Buon Yun. Everyone flicked their heads to the sky—*pppppp-ppt—pppppppppt*—then dove to the ground. It's me! Me! Young-fellow cried. It's really true! The Beckoning Virgin leaped into view. Smiley counted off to himself—5—4—3—2— Phan! Phan! PHAN! That's who!

❋   ❋   ❋

Captain Yancy emptied his gun but, of course, it was late. Much too late. Far out of range. Whoooosh and away. He emptied his gun, and then the whole truth balled up its fist and bashed him square between the eyes.

Yancy couldn't even swear or curl his lip or shake his head. Neither could Sergeant Jasperson. They were too stunned. As for Plunket, he hadn't seen, but only heard. He thought they were being rescued.

They stood there stunned, not saying a word, then Captain Yancy started to blubber and Sergeant Jasperson started to swear. It was Plunket bewildered now. What was this!? Hey, what was this!? He asked Yancy why he was blubbering and Yancy told him and then Plunket started to blubber too. Of the three, only cool fluid Jasperson didn't blubber but swore instead.

Buon Yun—the chill, damp earth of her—didn't blubber and didn't swear. She was much too shocked herself. The great gouge torn by *Samantha*'s bomb was her gape of astonishment. That's how it looked. As if the chill damp earth, herself, was open-mouthed and wondering what had happened to her. Oh! Ooooooh! That's what she seemed to say.

Captain Yancy reloaded his gun, then he and Jasperson latched back onto Plunket's arms and hauled him away, themselves as well. They were trying to get the hell out of there, what with dead all over the place and three longhouses burned to the ground and the earth agape. There was nothing else, but to get the hell out. *Samantha*'s bomb had gouged out the earth beneath the feet of the Strike Force driving toward the rear gate, and of course, had gouged out the Strike Force too.

* * *

Youngfellow was stunned, oval-mouthed, just like the chill damp earth below. He couldn't move. He couldn't swear. He couldn't believe what he had seen. He could but he didn't want to believe. There was nothing good left to believe. He had seen, if Smiley had not.

He sat there slump-shouldered back in his seat, while, all the time, it was there inside him waiting to go—the guilt and the anger and wanting to act, to make amends. It was waiting for him to take up his hands.

Youngfellow didn't take up his hands, but he did close his mouth. There were many things he did not understand but, most of all, what Smiley had done.

Smiley, oh Smiley, what have you done—what kind of trick have you played?

What Smiley had done was that he had faltered for only an instant, tripped by his recollection of Phan. The time between that and resuming the count and releasing the bomb had been laughably thin and so light on its feet it could skip in and out of a winking eye. Just time enough for one good sneeze. Just time enough to recollect and to overshoot the rear gate. Smiley had goofed. He had made one of those *goddamn mistakes*.

God, oh God, wake up old man. You've been napping much too long. Why did he do it? Why them? Hey, old man, why anyone? Why was it done? That's it, old guy—just rub the grit out of your eyes. Dammit, why didn't you raise a hand? Where's your shame? Where the hell have you been?

As for Youngfellow, he was ashamed, filthy disgusted with himself. For going along. For just sitting tight. For his easy complicity. For passing it on to the grit-eyed old man, for trying to pin the blame on *him*. For that and for having exhilarated.

So he finally took up his hands and did the only thing left to do: he leaned far forward in his seat and he began to beat on the glass, the one separating him from Smiley there up front.

He closed his eyes and lowered his head and beat away. He didn't want to go along for the ride anymore.

Smiley, I'm gonna clip your wings. Smiley, I'm gonna bring you down.

* * *

Where, oh where did the piggie go? Oh where, oh where has he gone?

They were rooting by the fence, Captain Yancy and Jasperson were. They were poking here, prying there, feeling for something which probably wasn't. They were filled with lumbering fright, wild to escape, like pigs being chased for the butchering. To poke and pry was their only hope. The enemy was closing in fast, and from above.

Where, oh where has the piggie gone? Where, oh where did he go?

They were closing in fast as the fighting tapered. It had a sad one-sided sound. There weren't many defenders left. Time was growing very short. The butchering was catching up. The Viet Cong were hunting for them.

Here piggie, piggie. Nice little pig. Where, oh where did you go?

Yancy worked right, Jasperson left. They moved in a waddle along the fence, jamming their hands, raking them bloody. They waddled at first, then mostly they skidded along on their knees, raking up their knees as well. The light from the flares didn't reach the south fence, so they skidded along and groped in the dark, and the smell of their sweat was sour. And Yancy said it was Jasperson's fault, that Jasperson should have remembered where, that he didn't want to go to camp. It was Yancy right and Jasperson left, frantically feeling along the fence, like Plunket was feeling at his eyes, and all the while, the VC were closing, their butchering knives sharp and drawn, hunting for the three of them. *Where, oh where did that piggie go?*

It was Yancy asking where, softly singing to himself. They were searching for a hole, the hole thru which the piggie had strayed, ages back, and blown itself up. They knew they couldn't get out of Buon Yun and into the safety of the forest. The outer fence was solid thru, and even if it hadn't been, there were the mines and the *punjis*. They couldn't hope to cross thru that, not in the dark. They weren't so ambitious. They wanted only a place to hide, a piggie-sized hole to wiggle thru. They wanted only to squirm thru that hole, and to chance a few steps to either side, and to hide tight against the outer side of the inner fence. Maybe Charlie would leave before dawn. *Where, oh where is that goddamn hole?*

Lieutenant Plunket called softly to Yancy, and then he called softly to Jasperson, but neither answered and he didn't try again. He had thought that hearing a voice would help, if only his own. He was alone, there by the fence, trying to decide if he was blind or not. They had left him to poke and pry, telling him to stay where he was, saying that they would return for him as soon as they found where the piggie had gone.

Well, he heard his voice, but it hadn't helped; and he couldn't decide about his sight; and he began to feel deserted, to pity himself. But worse than feeling deserted and pity, he felt uninformed: about how the fighting was getting along and especially about the pighole, how close they were to finding it. They oughta be pretty close by now. If only he could see! Plunket tossed his fuzzy head from side to side, softly at first, then harder and harder. He tried to shake sight back into his eyes, but all they were was wet.

Plunket couldn't stay put anymore. He couldn't just stand there and wait. There were all sorts of sounds leaping around— scary unidentified sounds—and he felt they wouldn't sound quite so bad if he moved around too. He felt he would be less vulnerable. So he began to wander about, cautiously, not very far—in case the others should look for him. He wandered about with slow, mincing steps, testing the ground with the toe of his boot. He didn't even have a stick. Nothing had happened right that night! He held his arms forward, stuck straight out—for balance and not to walk smack into things, and because that was how he envisioned it from all those ghosty stories he'd read. He felt a little like a ghost. He wished he were one. At least ghosts could fit thru anything! They didn't need a piggie hole.

There was a keen bite to the air. Dammit, thought Plunket, the smell from the trenches was stronger than it should have been, powerfully close. Dammit, he thought, coming on top of everything! Why didn't he keep the trenches limed, the ding-a-ling!? Wait'll I catch hold of him, that Triple Threat!

Plunket stepped out faster and faster because of the sounds, because they were leaping around faster too. He moved to keep ahead of the sounds—that's how it looked—but mostly he circled. He moved more resolutely now, with his shoulders squared back and his arms stuck out forward. He moved to keep distance between himself and whatever it was that was hounding him, or else he was stepping to meet it halfway, to get it done. Whichever it was, he stepped out smartly as if something good might come from that. Nothing much good came from staying put.

The sounds came closer and Plunket stepped out, arms straight ahead, when all of a sudden the world spun out from under him. Plunket squeaked, his arms scrambled for a hold in the air—and down he went—down on his back—down to the chill, damp ground.

Yancy and Jasperson ran up fast. They found Plunket flopping on the ground like some broken baby bird. The smell of dung hung heavily. But it was just a bamboo tube. A lousy, stinking bamboo tube! As if we ain't got troubles enough!

* * *

Crash! Bang! Crash!

Smiley couldn't understand what all the racket was about. It didn't make sense. *Forever Samantha* had never rattled so fiercely before, so violently. She had never been so set upon. It was a banging, crashing commotion, that's all he knew, and that it seemed to come from behind. It was a protesting kind of sound.

Smiley had just brought *Samantha* around. He was *yahoo!* and *whoopee!* and hellbent on getting the rest of them on this, her third pass. He hadn't seen; he didn't know. He tried not to pay too much mind to the banging. It was the drop he was hyped-up about. As long as she wasn't coming apart, there was only the drop. Smiley wasn't satisfied. There was dropping left to do.

Bang! Crash! Bang!

Youngfellow's fists beat on the glass. They were battered and getting on toward pulpy but he beat on. The pain didn't matter, nothing mattered, except getting thru, thru to Smiley. Young-fellow put all his strength into it, whatever hadn't been shaken away or leaked out thru his sweaty skin or stunned to death by what Smiley had done. *Bang! Crash! Bang!* Youngfellow's head was forward and down, and his jaws were locked, and his cheeks were wet tho his eyes were shut tight, and the wings of his nose flared wide out just like he were snorting fire. Enough! Enough! Goddamn enough! Whatever comes next, I've sat on my hands long, long enough! *Bang! Crash! Bang!*

Forever Samantha streaked thru the sky, bearing implacably down on Buon Yun. With Smiley holding her tight as he could, closing his mind to the racket behind him, thinking only about the drop. And Youngfellow single-minded himself, fired and laying into the glass, trying to get thru to Smiley.

CRASH! At last! And everything flew, bits and chips. They filled the air, they sped sharp-pointed, slashing Yancy there up front. And then the hunks, like pummeling fists, slammed into his back. Hey, what the hell! He was taking a pounding.

So were Plunket and Jasperson. The three had been belly down to the ground, heads covered up, thinking for sure they were far enough back, when the tube bomb went off, ripping a gash thru the fences, and thru the mines and *punjis* between. They covered up tighter and took the big hunks; then even as bits and chips still settled down, Yancy and Jasperson leaped to their feet, yanking Plunket onto his own. Then they galloped off for the fence, knocking together, clopping like a three-horse team unevenly matched. With Yancy and Jasperson half-dragging Plunket in between, shouting him on, yelling at him to pump like hell. "Come on, Plunket!" "Hey, hey, hey!" "Hey, come on, you ding-a-ling!" It was a little easier, because a flare had been caught by the breeze and was drifting south, lighting the way a tiny bit, lighting it brighter and brighter.

Forever Samantha was diving again, screaming and cold-eyed and with talons bared. Smiley was feeling the start of a headache from back of his skull. Goddamn, not now! Just too friggin'

much! His lips were curled back. His blue eyes were gray. "Hey!
Hey!" he croaked to Youngfellow. "Hey, you hanging together
all right!?" There was no answer. "Hey, stay tight! Here we go!
We're at 'em again!"

The VC were swarming all over Buon Yun, groups of them
bolting this way and that, smelling out the situation, looking for
little piggies to stick. Smiley aimed to get himself one, to show
Youngfellow a trick or two. He had lots more tricks to show, lots
of groups to choose from. He wondered if what they were still
banging out, if it sounded as bad as the racket behind. He hoped
to hell not.

Samantha was diving faster and faster. Buon Yun was rushing
to meet them halfway, tho not so eagerly as before. There ahead
—off to the left—caught in the light. *Yahoo!*—there ahead—

Bang! Crash! Bang!

Goddamn, not now!

Smiley, oh Smiley, now and how! Smiley, I'm gonna fix you
good!

* * *

They tried to keep their six legs straight and not whipped together, but it was hard. It was hardest of all on Jasperson who
was limping badly and wincing everytime Plunket kicked. The
three of them were tender where they had taken the hunks, and
slashed as well, and they were anxious to get thru the fence and
into the forest beyond.

They galloped along, jostling each other, until they reached
the opening, then it was single file. The tube bomb had cleared
a strip of ground as wide across as a buffalo's rump; but, to
either side, the *punjis* stabbed up and most of the mines lay un-
detonated. Yancy went first, being the Captain, pulling Plunket
along after him. Sergeant Jasperson brought up the rear, gamely
hobbling as fast as he could, whipping Plunket on the butt. They
hurried in tandem down the strip, smelling their freedom, jubilat-
ing. They were getting thru!

It can't be right! thought Plunket, amazed. It just can't be! His
eyes had just begun to clear and, what he saw, he saw in a burning, shimmering way and so he couldn't be sure. But there it was

—close up ahead—so close he could almost reach out and touch. Close upon all that had gone before: the lumps and the fire and being blinded and what *Forever Samantha* had done. After all that, it had come to this. It can't be! It can't be! It can't be right! We're almost thru! Then Plunket cried out. It was a jagged, soul-torn cry. He had gotten his cry only halfway out when *Forever Samantha* pounced on them.

* * *

Youngfellow's fists crashed thru the glass as Smiley brought *Samantha* out. And everything flew, bits and chips, forward and down, all over Smiley. Then Youngfellow's fists landed too, a left and a right and another left, slamming into Smiley's back, bouncing off his head. "Hey, what the hell!?" Smiley cried. He tried to shield his head with one arm and, with the other, control *Samantha*.

"Smiley, oh Smiley, I'll fix you good."

"Hey what the hell are you trying to do!?"

"Smiley, I'm gonna do you in."

"You crazy bastard! You'll smash us up!"

"Up yours, Smiley. All the way up."

"Lemme go! Get the hell off! I've got bombs to drop!"

"Drop dead, Smiley."

Youngfellow had Smiley against the ropes and turned around. He pounded away. Smiley defended as best he could while *Forever Samantha* zigged and zagged and spun about.

"Hey! Hey! What's it all about!?"

"Time, Smiley. It's about time."

"Time for what!?"

"To do you in."

A right and a left and another right. Youngfellow working out two-fisted, looking good. Smiley crowded and looking bad, trying to communicate. *Forever Samantha* hard in a spin.

"Goddammit, Youngfellow! What's it about!?"

"It's about a bull. A fat maddened bull."

"Bull!? What bull!? Quit pounding on me!"

"A piqued bull. A near-sighted bull."

"*What* kinda' bull!?"

"A bull in a goddamn china shop."

"Hey, why there!? Goddammit, lay off!"

"A bull bred to fight."

"Hey! Hey!"

"To hold his turf."

"Hey! Hey!"

"To charge at the tiniest flicker of red."

"Hey, what the hell!?"

"A bull just charging himself to death."

"Why!? Why!? Hey, lemme go!"

"Mad to kill and getting killed."

"Goddammit, Youngfellow!"

"All for the sake of his big dumb pride."

"What bull is this!? Hey, lemme go!"

"A bull fit only for bologna."

"*What* bull? You're breaking my head!"

"You *still* don't know? Don't bullshit me!"

"No bullshit! No bullshit! Tell me, goddammit!"

"I've *been* telling you! Here, listen to this!" Youngfellow fetched his hardest blow yet. Smiley took it and spurted blood. Then he tried to twist around. "Sword! Sword!" Youngfellow cried. "Keep your head down!"

"Hey, I'm no bull! You got me wrong!"

"It's all the same! Sword, where's my sword!?"

Diving—diving—faster and faster. *Forever Samantha* was screaming down and Buon Yun was rushing halfway up, but hesitantly. Smiley had finally twisted around, intent on paying Youngfellow back with a left and a right and another left. To hell with *Samantha*, to hell with it all, but pounding two-fisted right back on Youngfellow—*yahoo! whoopee!*—pounding right back. And Youngfellow carrying on about bulls and eagles and tigers and barking deer. And, all the while, *Samantha* tumbling, looping down. That was it. Just snatches of sky and ground whirling by, quick upon each other.

△ AFTERMATH
☆
△

There were just enough blankets to go around. Some were gray and some were black and some had big bold stripes of each. There were fine new blankets; and slightly worn blankets with lots of use left; and blankets tattered, but still of a piece; and Swiss-cheese blankets; and even worse. There were barely enough blankets, altogether, bundling everyone snug as potatoes on that sunny-bright, puff-clouded day.

Potatoes, newly dug up potatoes, scattered over the muddy ground, that's how the bundles must have looked to whatever lived up in those puffy white clouds. Even up close, nose-wrinkling close, up in the thick disagreeable air, the bundles seemed unexciting enough, just knobby old things. Not a part of the landscape, of course. Enough out of place to make one wonder about all those blankets, what they were doing draped on the ground. Enough for an over-the-shoulder look. But no more extraordinary than that. Except when a pair of feet stuck out here, or a single limp arm lay flopped out there, or maybe just fingertips inching out.

If not for those extremities, then who would have guessed there had been a bash? That snugly tucked beneath all the blankets was last night's crowd, most of them? Tucked out of sight and sleeping it off. If not for the feet and arms and fingertips inching out; if not for the ashes of three longhouses and for the splinters of several more; if not for the mutilated ground, for the stink in the air—then who would have known? Who would have guessed that A-123 was all squashed down? That the rope had, indeed, been cut for Buon Yun?

If not for these things—and for the litter of bamboo sticks—and for *Samantha*, there in the Hump of the Beckoning Virgin, there stuck nose down in the torn ground and poking wrong end up in the air, there tightly stuck in the Virgin's groin. You could tell that it was the Beckoning Virgin because that was where she had always been, but other than that, she was too messed. *Forever Samantha* had come on too strongly, savaging her. You couldn't much tell *Samantha* either, who was pretty messed as well. Their coming together had proved to be more than either had bargained, what with the Virgin bled to death and *Samantha* stuck much too tight to pull out.

There were just enough blankets to go around, to snugly tuck in last night's crowd—and that didn't count the odds and ends, which Colonel Quoc's men had gathered together, then heaped in a pile. It didn't count all the bits and scraps and joints and sides of everyone butchered by Smiley's bomb. Jigsaw pieces piled high, bulging, sticking sharply out. Pieces from puzzles too hopelessly scrambled to ever be fitted together again.

So not counting the odds and ends—except where some careless attempt had been made to piece together a puzzle or two, to reconstruct someone who might have been. Like two bony arms of unequal length. Or a withered old leg with a supple young one. Or a shrunken, gray-haired, leathery head atop a child's body.

And not counting the Viet Cong either. Quoc's soldiers had found the VC bodies just within the edge of the forest. The victors had tried to drag off their dead, but the number of dead had proved too great and so the bodies had simply been dumped. Quoc's soldiers had kicked and butted the bodies and spat on them and pissed on them too. They had stuck out their tongues and pulled out their ears and thumbed their noses, taunting them. They had rumbled into Buon Yun by the truckload late that morning, not expecting to find Viet Cong—not live Viet Cong, anyway—and that's just how it had turned out to be. So Quoc's men had mugged, there by the forest, and then had returned to pile the pieces, and wonder about *Forever Samantha* and if their own world hung secure.

* * *

Grandmother Pan was badly upset. She had known, at once, the leg was Y Bun's. Somehow she could tell by the shape of the

foot, by the spread of the toes, by the swell of the calf, by the over-
all impression it made. But none of the other parts laying there
had anything to do with Y Bun. Grandmother Pan hunkered down
and picked up the leg and drew it across her withered cheek. She
sat there and felt it and smelt Y Bun. She would have forgiven
everything—*Forever Samantha*, the Viet Cong—if only the leg
were warm and reattached to Y Bun and he were standing upon it.
But it was so cool! And what was there to attach it to? And where
could a man stand, anyway, what with the ground all littered with
dead? Grandmother Pan sat there awhile, asking these questions,
then tottered up. Then she continued to scrape along, shuffling
tight-jawed from blanket to blanket, gripping tightly onto her prize,
searching for more.

Grandmother Pan searched here and there and everywhere. She
searched high and low. She searched quite dry-eyed and deter-
mined. She shuffled along, feeling hollow inside, except for the
acids etching her and to find more of her dear Y Bun. She wasn't
satisfied with a half-length of leg. She wanted to remember Y Bun
as something more than his knee to his toes. A half-length of leg
wasn't enough. It was no way to say good-bye.

That's why Grandmother Pan was searching: to accord a decent end. It wasn't like searching for the dew drop. It wasn't to
start someone off right.

Colonel Quoc called her to Nutley's attention. He pointed to
the scruffy old woman and to her remarkable burden. He didn't
laugh, for Quoc was no monster, but he was nonetheless nicely
amazed.

Grandmother Pan was just the first. The others straggled in
after her. The women straggled from out of the forest where the
VC had driven them. They straggled in slowly, tentatively, fear-
ing the soldiers from Ban Me Thuot almost as much as they feared
the VC.

They straggled in and shuffled tight-jawed from blanket to
blanket like Grandmother Pan. Their bare horny feet scraped over
the ground. They trooped right by Colonels Nutley and Quoc,
and right by Quoc's men who were grinning and pointing and
some who were sympathizing with them. They trooped past the

men from Ban Me Thuot, looking high and looking low. Their
tightly bunned hair lay bare all the pain scribbled onto their faces.
They pulled at the blankets and poked beneath, looking for their
men.

But they looked without a glimmer of hope. There was nothing
at all to be hopeful about. Each lumpy bundle which wasn't theirs;
each which belonged to someone else; each which they ticked off
as they stopped and poked around, then shuffled on; each bundle
less which lay ahead, it didn't increase the odds that their own
men were still alive. Each bundle less didn't mean that. It didn't
mean anything at all. Every last man was dead. Those who hadn't
been killed in the fighting, they had been lined up and shot afterwards. The women knew. They had seen. There were no happy
surprises in store. They were searching to say good-bye, just like
Grandmother Pan.

The women searched silently. They searched resigned. Yet their
grief was so full and bitter-tasting and pressed up tight against
their throats, that when they finally found their men, it rushed
up in a great sudden gush, and as it went rushing past their throats,
it twisted into a scream. Then they hunkered down by their men.
They jammed their bony fists into their mouths and rocked back
and forth on the flats of their feet. They wailed for their men and
they wailed for themselves. It was a terrible dreaded thing, their
loneliness.

Grandmother Pan went from blanket to blanket. She pulled at
the blankets and poked beneath, and when she had poked beneath the last one, all she had to show for her poking was that
half-length of Y Bun. So Grandmother Pan hitched up her skirt,
and off she shuffled to the pile. She huddled there in front of the
pile and studied the tangle of odds and ends. Her small eyes were
dry. Her thin lips pinched tight. Her crinkly face was shattered
to bits but holding together. Not friendly, not impish, not marvelous. Just cracked all to bits but holding on. Her knob-knuckled
hand was drawn up tight, hard and steady as a rock, the one which
wasn't gripping Y Bun. Grandmother Pan looked the pile over,

then carefully placed Y Bun's leg to the side and set right to.

To sorting the pieces one by one. She didn't know who or what to blame: the bad, bad VC or *Forever Samantha* or Sergeant Lovelace's teeth or what. She just sorted slowly, patiently, taking care to start at the top and work her way down, and not to yank from every whichway for fear that all the odds and ends would slither down and bury her. From the top and silently, that's how it went. Grandmother Pan stood cracked to bits, but holding together, and rummaged for the rest of Y Bun.

* * *

"It's done, and that's that," said Hoang with a shrug.

"That's that," agreed Mau.

"That's that," chirruped Xuan, "of course it is."

"That's that," echoed Chau, "but maybe not."

"It's not at all," protested Buc.

"What do you mean? We should celebrate."

"Celebrate what!? Nothing's changed."

"Nothing?" asked Hoang.

"It makes no difference," answered Buc, "whatever happened at Buon Yun or not. Each day is like the day before, and the day after, and so is the struggle. It has a momentum all its own. Buon Yun makes no difference."

"It makes a difference," said Mau, "yes it does. Otherwise why the directive at all?"

"It probably makes a difference," said Chau.

"Of course it makes a difference," said Xuan. "There's no more Buon Yun, is there Buc?"

"There's no more Buon Yun," said Hoang, "that's true. But perhaps Buc is talking of what comes next, if it was all worthwhile or not."

"It was worthwhile," said Mau, "yes it was. Now, I can prepare my lessons."

"It probably was worthwhile," said Chau. "And I've got some prescriptions to fill."

"Of course it was worthwhile," said Xuan. "And I've got some prospecting to do."

"It was neither worthwhile nor not," said Buc. "The struggle will go on, no matter what. Until the big day, and after that, and everyone getting his hair cut short."

"What does that mean?" they all asked Buc.

"It's just a joke," answered Hoang Bang.

"It's no joke at all," said Buc for himself. "And neither's Buon Yun. It's just a big nothing."

"But now the Americans are gone. That's something, Buc."

"That's something, all right," said Xuan and Mau.

"It is, it probably is," said Chau.

"So they're gone, so what!" said Buc. "They'll come and come until they've had enough Buon Yuns."

"One less Buon Yun is still one less. It all went well."

"What do you mean, it all went well!? Mac's dead, isn't he? And many others."

"But Mac, the others, they died for a cause."

"Yes," said Xuan, agreeing with Mau, "*someone* has to die for a cause. Otherwise, it's not worthwhile."

"A cause is a good thing to die for, Buc."

"It's a good thing, all right, but it wasn't ours."

"It wasn't *ours?*"

"Then whose was it, Buc?"

"It was General Ba's."

"But his cause is ours," protested Mau.

"It probably is," protested Chau.

"Of course it is," protested Xuan.

"Not always," said Buc, "and not with Buon Yun. There were more important objectives."

"Let's not get into that," said Hoang, remembering the dominoes.

"Yes, let's not," they all agreed. "Let's celebrate."

"How?" asked Mau.

"Fat Anna's, of course."

"Of course!" said Xuan. "But not with Betty. I understand she's with it again."

"Betty wasn't one of yours?"

"*Comrades,*" said Hoang Bang with a blush, "it's not our objective to talk about whores."

"That's right," said Buc. "There are more important objectives. There were at Buon Yun."

"Such as what?" asked Hoang with a sigh.

"Such as liberating the people. Isn't that what it's all about?"

"Of course, that's what."

"It's probably what."

"But what's your point?"

"That no one's left to liberate."

"That's because they got in the way."

"Yes, it's too bad."

"Much too bad."

"There were the Americans."

"But we *purposely* destroyed Buon Yun!"

"Only to liberate people elsewhere," said Hoang Bang. "It's the lesson that counts."

"People count too, those in Buon Yun."

"Yes, people count, but not as much."

There was nothing more to say.

"Comrades, can't we change the talk? What's done is done."

"There's no denying that," said Mau.

"Perhaps it's for the best," said Chau.

"It's for the best, of course," said Xuan.

"Life rolls on," exclaimed Hoang Bang.

"Have you fixed my bike?" asked Buc.

* * *

Triple Threat had never run a niftier broken-field pattern. He darted here. Cut back there. He stepped quickly over an arm reaching out to trip him up. He zigged and zagged and changed his pace. Not a hand was laid on him. He picked his way thru the field of men, taking great care not to tread on any, searching the village from end to end, looking for someone to comfort him. He wasn't sure which he should be: wonder-eyed or horrified. So his chimp-like face changed expression in turn, now curious, then full of fright. He grunted steadily, picking his way, but sometimes he mewed. He was annoyed and angry and scared at having been left so very alone.

All these feelings confused the poor fellow, and more so because, only two days before, there had been a joyful procession to lead, and his anxiousness for Lieutenant Plunket had been just that and not a dread, and life had been newly kind to him. What was he going to do? he asked. Who was going to care for him now? Why had everything turned so about? In his confusion, he turned on the chickens which crossed his path, the ones which the soldiers had not carried off. He kicked at the chickens. Spat at them. He flailed his arms and chased them squawking, perplexed as he was and because they didn't show any respect. It put him off to see the chickens scrabbling the ground between all the dead, scratching away as usual. He kicked so hard and always missed that, once or twice, he almost kicked himself to the ground. And all the while he picked his way and grunted and sometimes mewed.

Then Triple Threat stopped. He gathered his courage and stooped down to see. He trembled and gripped the edge of the blanket delicately, scared that it might singe his fingers or maybe rot them fast away. He pulled the blanket up and back and peeked beneath. It was Y Blo. Stubborn Y Blo. The sorcerer's face was uncommonly smooth as if he had finally come to terms with all the spirits which hovered and lurked, but the sorcerer's hand was crabbed and twisted, showing its claws. It was reaching stiff up, right at the mute, who dropped the blanket and hurried away. He zigged and zagged and searched Buon Yun and didn't dare another peek.

Triple Threat didn't stop again until he came upon Grandmother Pan. She was squatting in front of the great big pile, only it wasn't so great any more, but sorted into smaller ones, risen around her, with Grandmother Pan there in the center, keening over that half-length of leg. It was all she had to show.

Triple Threat came up from behind, thru two of the piles. He bent down over the old woman's shoulder, practically nuzzling her in the ear. He bent down low for a better look, grunting his sympathy as he did. He poked his cold nose in her ear, poking for someone to comfort him, grunting their common misery, and the old woman screamed. She whirled around and up to her feet and flailed her arms and shooed him away. She wasn't about to be pestered then.

He darted here and cut back there. He zigged and zagged, puzzled, hurt more than ever. Chased each time he stopped to offer condolences. Each time he poked someone to comfort him. Shooed away by all the women keening over all their dead. He wished that *he* had someone dead, someone *he* could keen over too. It was for sure he had no one alive.

When Triple Threat reached the south end of Buon Yun, the first thing he saw was the breach in the fence. He looked it over appraisingly, cocking his head, sniffing the air with his short broad nose, swiveling his head from side to side, jerkily, just like the chickens. Triple Threat studied the breach from all angles, then started thru. He managed to step in a fairly straight line, which for him, was no mean thing. He shook his fist and grunted fiercely at the *punjis* lining his path. He stepped right thru. Maybe there was someone at the other end to comfort him.

There was no one to comfort him. There was only the forest close up ahead, and the grass in between, and Buon Yun at his back. There was nothing. Triple Threat didn't know what to do next, and started to turn back not knowing what, when there ahead in the torn-up grass—there glinting brightly in the sun, was something he had to investigate.

Triple Threat didn't bound up and down like a chimpanzee. He didn't hop madly about in circles. He didn't flail his arms and grunt. He didn't do the usual things. Instead, Triple Threat got down on his knees. He got down on three points, his forehead and knees, like someone at prayer, and started to whimper. He clawed at the ground with one scrabbled hand, while with the other, he beat himself on the crown of his head with the side of Lieutenant Plunket's face. And as he did, the blood-smeared eye, which had glinted in the sun, which, last of all, had seen *Forever Samantha* zoom down, the blood-smeared eye popped to the grass. It landed close to where the dew drop had been found.

As Buon Yun cooled in the late afternoon, Triple Threat remained in the grass, whimpering and beating away, understanding nothing at all, except that he was quite alone. Whimpering and beating his head, trying to beat out the things he had seen. Beating, and wishing they hadn't been, that he could get up and return

as he came, and cook up a pot of chili for Plunket, and sit down at
the table by him, and dream of more processions to lead. Beating,
and moaning as much for himself as for his dear friend. Angry with
Plunket for leaving him. Thru the late afternoon and into the night
tho he should have been petrified of the dark. There was nothing
to do but beat away. He had been orphaned again.

* * *

Matters weren't standing well with Brigadier General Lyman.
That's why he had summoned Crocker for a chat. The map on
the wall told the whole story. It was full of little red flags that
stuck up wherever some nosy reporter had nosed about. General
Lyman hated reporters as much as he hated the Viet Cong. He
hated them individually, and he hated them as a group. But all the
press corps in Saigon hadn't really earned his hate. For, while it
was true that there were little red flags sticking up all over the map,
most of the flags pinpointed the nosing of only a few. Mostly the
nosing of one, in fact. General Lyman itched to grab up all the
flags and snap them in two. He itched to hear them go CRUNCH!
in his paw. But General Lyman wisely knew that matters would
not be made better by that. And, besides, to grab up all the flags
and snap them in two was no way to act. Not in the presence of
President Johnson who gazed benignly from the wall in back of
General Lyman's desk. President Johnson hung crookedly, but
General Lyman did not seem concerned. His concern was about
all those little red flags. General Lyman rubbed his side as he
studied the map. The flags, all the nosy reporters, they were like
thorns which had to be plucked.

The General's office was brown and plain, and that was the way
he wanted it, for he was a monochromal fellow. He neither gen-
erated excitement nor ever became excited himself. He went about
his making war as if it were some boring task. The world could
jerk to a sudden halt, and General Lyman would pick himself up
and dust himself off and get on with what he was doing. His face
had only one expression and that was no expression at all. When he
spoke, his voice was flat, even when he tried to be genial. Maybe
it was that his sap had run dry. It was an overcast day in Saigon.

"The money, Colonel—"

"What money, sir?"

"The money, Colonel. How much do you think we spend on ARVN, trying to shape that ARVN up? A whole lot, Colonel, a damn lot of money. So what we need is an emphasis."

"Emphasis, sir? Just what sort?"

"On the strides, Colonel, on the strides."

"Yes, sir, the strides."

"Look, Colonel, I understand that some Congressmen will be at the briefing. They'll want to know if that money they voted—which wasn't so much, after all—if it's being well spent. So perhaps you might want to point up the strides—"

"I have been, sir."

"You have been, huh? Well, even more. About how we've been training ARVN to stand up and fight. How ARVN's been taking over more."

"But, sir, it's not exactly so. Our own units, sir, they've been reinforced. They've stepped up their activities, sir. As a matter of fact, the orders were sent out from *your* office, sir."

"A temporary state of affairs, that's what it is. Until we can make some strides, Colonel Crocker, in getting ARVN to stand up and fight. So handle that part of your talk accordingly. Know what I mean?"

"I know what you mean, sir," said Colonel Crocker, "but still it's not exactly so."

General Lyman raised his eyebrows just a notch. Now what kind of thing was that to say when, of course, it wasn't exactly so? What kind of public relations man was this Crocker, anyway?

"It's exact enough, Colonel Crocker. Exact enough to suit this Command, know what I mean?"

"Yes, sir, I do, but isn't my duty—?"

"Your duty is to say exactly what suits this Command, even if it's not quite so." The General's eyebrows rose a notch higher. "Colonel, you don't relate very well."

"I have a duty to myself, General Lyman. To the facts."

"To hell with yourself, Colonel Crocker. Your highest duty is not to yourself, not to the facts, but to this Command. Your duty is to relate the truth so as no one gets upset. Why make it hard on someone else? Why fill others with concern? No need to do that, is there, Colonel?"

Colonel Crocker felt very distressed. In his distress, the Colonel looked up at President Johnson, hanging askew. Somehow it comforted Colonel Crocker just to see the President's face.

"No need to do that, is there, Colonel?"

Colonel Crocker wanted badly to do himself right. That's why he had spoken up. It was a pretty brave thing to have done, and Colonel Crocker was pleased with himself. But tho Colonel Crocker wanted badly to do himself right, there was only so far he could go. To do himself right was good, very good, but if he continued on like this, he would end up wronging himself.

"IS there, Colonel?"

"No, sir, no need to do that."

"Good for you." General Lyman lowered his eyebrows just a notch. "Another thing, Colonel. See all those little red flags on the map?"

"Yes, sir, I do."

"Know what all those flags are about?"

"Yes, sir, I do. You told me before."

"Listen, Colonel, perhaps you don't know, but the press has been throwing some dirt at us, some pretty dirty charges they have—"

"Not any more, sir, they won't be."

"How some of our units conduct themselves—"

"Yes, sir, but not any more."

"So maybe it's time to set an example. To choose just one and —not any more?"

"Youngfellow, sir."

"Oh yes, of course."

"Youngfellow was a good man, sir. At least he meant well."

"Really, Colonel!? Well, that's not enough. What the man did was treasonable."

The Colonel looked up at President Johnson, on the wall. He looked up, hoping for some sign, for strength, for consolation. But this second time, President Johnson had nothing to say, no comfort to offer.

"What I meant, sir, was that he wasn't out to subvert a thing. Just to get all the facts and put them so."

"What in hell do you think is subversion!? You know what this Youngfellow went around saying?"

"Yes, sir, I do."

"Perhaps you don't know, but this Youngfellow claimed that we, this Command, were responsible for killing people."

"Isn't that our duty, sir?"

"Of course, it's our duty, Colonel Crocker. But only the right ones, know what I mean?"

"Yes, sir, I do."

"Bad, Colonel, bad, forgetting your basics."

"No, sir, I haven't."

"It's just this. This Youngfellow fellow went around claiming we killed a lot of the wrong people, too."

"The briefing, sir—"

"Yes, what about it?"

"What should I say?"

"About Youngfellow?"

"About Buon Yun."

"Give them the counterinsurgency bit, that in spite of its apparent fall, Buon Yun represents the high-water mark of our CI effort. Tell them about the kill ratio, how unparalleled the ratio was. Only three American bodies against ninety-seven enemy dead. How about that!? Remarkable, huh? A handsome statistic, wouldn't you say?"

"But what about the friendly dead? Didn't they help?"

"Help?" said Lyman. "There's reason to think that some of them weren't so friendly at all, that they infiltrated the Strike Force, is what. Which means, of course, they didn't help. In fact, one could say—and easily so—that we accounted for more than just ninety-seven VC."

"Yes, sir, one could."

"You bet, one could."

"But, sir," asked Crocker, "our Strike Force program, doesn't that speak badly of it?"

"Certainly not!" answered General Lyman. "These incidents have to be expected now and then. As you well know, in this kind of war, the truth can be an elusive thing. Slippery, Colonel, slippery. You wanna know what the real truth is?"

"Yes, sir, I do."

"That it's often hard to tell your friend from your enemy. Remember that."

"I suppose we'll send in another team, sir?"

"Didn't you say there's no people left?"

"To the area, sir."

"Oh yes, of course. We'll have to do that. We can't be having more Buon Yuns."

"No, sir, we can't."

"There must be two or three villages more."

"Two, I think."

But neither knew about Buon Sop, that the heads were still up there on the stakes, if mostly skull and a few scraps of gristle. Or Buon Yak, where the women hauled water atop their heads, as they labored up from the stream down below, careful not to spill a drop. Or, for that matter, about Y A'dham who, of course, had died in the hospital and was cold and adrift somewhere in limbo, having no spirits to show him the way.

"And make sure the lemonade is cold."

"The lemonade, sir?"

"For the briefing, of course."

"Oh, by the way," said Colonel Crocker, "Nutley sent in a strange request. He says he's got this little surprise, that it's ready now, so how about sending a VIP?"

"Never mind Nutley. It's Buon Yun I'm thinking of. Not *one* of us left?"

"No, sir, everyone's dead."

"If there were just one—we could make him a hero."

Colonel Crocker thought on that. "There *was one* survivor," he finally said, "at least in a way."

"There was?" asked Lyman.

"Not really, sir. More like he missed out."

"And who would that be?"

"This Fritz who was medevaced earlier."

"Which one is Fritz?"

"The one, sir, who always says how the sun is going to shine."

"Of course, it will."

"Things look pretty gray now, sir."

"Whaddaya mean?"

"What with Buon Yun."

"Colonel Crocker, get this straight. Sunshine is a wonderful thing."

"But Buon Yun, sir."

"A wonderful thing."

"Yes, sir, it is, but where is it now?"

"It's around. Don't you fear."

"Excuse me, sir, but how do you know?"

"There's rainy days and there are sunny, aren't there?"

BOOKS ABOUT VIETNAM
FROM AVON

DISPATCHES
Michael Herr   52639-5/$2.50

A NATIONAL HARDCOVER
AND PAPERBACK BESTSELLER

"I believe it may be the best personal journal about war, any war, that any writer has ever accomplished." Robert Stone (author of DOG SOLDIERS), *Chicago Tribune*

"Quite simply, it is the best book to have been written about the Vietnam war." C.D.B. Bryan (author of FRIENDLY FIRE), *The New York Times Book Review*

"Michael Herr has elevated reporting to a level of art reached by no other modern war correspondent—no, not even Hemingway." Perry Deane Young, *Newsday*

COOKS AND BAKERS
Robert A. Anderson   79590-6/$2.50

"An authentic account of the Vietnam War . . . The confusion, the camaraderie, the terror as seen through a marine lieutenant's eyes and written by someone who's been there." Al Santóli, *Everything We Had*

"This compelling novel is about one man's struggle to cope with the futility of war." *Publishers Weekly*

"The author's lean and simple style gives the story power and pace." *Philadelphia Inquirer*

"*COOKS AND BAKERS* is no left-wing indictment, but a tough-minded, unblinking report from hell." *Penthouse*